"A captivating story on the bonds between mothers and daughters and a powerful meditation on secrets, gentrification, family legacy, and more. A must-read."

—*Hey Alma*

"Rich. . . . Jerkins effectively blends folk legend with contemporary details. . . . It's vividly conceived, and the strong plot will carry readers to the end."

—*Publishers Weekly*

PRAISE FOR
Wandering in Strange Lands

"*Wandering in Strange Lands* intertwines segments of past and present travel as a reminder that the past is present in the US."

—*O, the Oprah Magazine*

"Jerkins weaves a vivid and painful backstory of Black people forced into enslavement in the American South. . . . The book is filled with poignant examples from across multiple centuries, including those retold in classrooms and those relegated to forgotten parts of our country's consciousness. . . . It's when Jerkins sews her familial threads with those poignant historical facts from deep in the archives of America that the book is most impactful. Equally heartbreaking and reaffirming are the trials and tribulations too many Black people in the United States have faced and somehow conquered, coming out more resilient on the other side." —*USA Today*

"Traveling throughout the country, [Jerkins] explores the path her family took as well as her cultural identity as a Black woman. Her desire to understand both her personal and cultural origins will inspire you to do the same."

—*Elle*

"A thrilling, emotional, and engaging ride that almost commands the reader to turn the page, *Wandering in Strange Lands* is required reading, accurately widening the lens of American history." —*Booklist* (starred review)

"[A] forthright and informative account. . . . Jerkins's careful research and revelatory conversations with historians, activists, and genealogists result in a disturbing yet ultimately empowering chronicle of the African American experience. Readers will be moved by this brave and inquisitive book."

—*Publishers Weekly*

"Driven by a need to understand her own identity, cultural critic Jerkins mounted an investigation into her family's tangled history, recounting in this candid memoir the surprising discoveries that emerged from her emotional journey. . . . A revelatory exploration of the meaning of Blackness."

—*Kirkus Reviews*

PRAISE FOR
This Will Be My Undoing

"Without turning linguistic or lyrical cartwheels, Jerkins lucidly articulates social dynamics that have dictated the realities of American Black women for centuries. . . . Indeed, [*This Will Be My Undoing*] is a book I wish everyone in this country would read." —*New York Times Book Review*

"In Morgan Jerkins's remarkable debut essay collection, *This Will Be My Undoing*, she is a deft cartographer of Black girlhood and womanhood. From one essay to the next, Jerkins weaves the personal with the public and political in compelling, challenging ways. Her prodigious intellect and curiosity are on full display throughout this outstanding collection. The last line of the book reads, 'You should've known I was coming,' and indeed, in this, too, Jerkins is prescient. With this collection, she shows us that she is unforgettably here, a writer to be reckoned with." —Roxane Gay

"Jerkins's forthright examination of her own experiences leads to a triumphant reclaiming of Blackness in all its power." —*Booklist*

"Jerkins is one of the smartest young writers of her generation, and this is an insightful, revelatory collection of personal essays about a variety of today's important issues. So fantastic." —*Book Riot*

"The truth about a writer being anointed a Voice of the Generation is that it's also a curse . . . [but Morgan Jerkins's] exhilarating new essay collection *This Will Be My Undoing* makes her a leading contender for the title—and the writer most likely to rewrite the rules for it, too. . . . If this collection is any indication, [Jerkins's] blueprint for a lifelong intellectual and creative enterprise will continue to challenge, thrill, and delight her readers throughout a long career." —*Salon*

OR

Caul Baby

"The child's power drives the tension of Morgan Jerkins's first novel, *Caul Baby*. . . . Profound. . . . The women Jerkins creates do not need men or any other outsiders to rescue them; they rescue themselves."
— *New York Times Book Review*

"A debut novel that blends family drama with magic." — *Time* magazine

"This magical novel brings together the weight of tradition and the power of family."
— *NBC News*

"*Caul Baby* gave me chills almost every time I turned the page. . . . The book traces a legacy of Black female pain through the somewhat softening lens of magical realism. It's an unsparing take on the ramifications of trauma on Black American women, and Jerkins manages it as a spellbinding story, the furthest possible thing from a lecture."
— *Glamour*

"A fascinating, of-the-moment story about the intersection of motherhood, power, and community."
— *Real Simple*

"The astounding talent behind nonfiction must-reads *This Will Be My Undoing* and *Wandering in Strange Lands* turns to fiction with *Caul Baby*. . . . An exhilarating tale of family, belonging, and bodies, this promises to be one of the most exciting releases of the year."
— *Elle*

"Jerkins, a bestselling nonfiction writer, applies her scrupulous prose and storytelling prowess to the realm of fiction in her beguiling debut novel."
— *O, The Oprah Magazine*

"This engrossing story is rich with mystery, page-turning tension, and the powerful ways family can hold us even in toxic circumstances."
— *Good Housekeeping*

"Morgan Jerkins's fantastic, expansive novel of mothers and daughters and Harlem, *Caul Baby*, is a meditation on the limits of inheritance and legacy. It's also a love letter to a rapidly changing neighborhood."
— Kaitlyn Greenidge, author of *Libertie* and *We Love You, Charlie Freeman*

"*Caul Baby* is a deeply inventive meditation on survival and inheritance. Morgan writes about the intricacies of Black motherhood in a way that is tender and at times magic."

—Raven Leilani, *New York Times* bestselling author of *Luster*

"Excellent. . . . An audacious debut novel, telling a powerful family tale that does not shy away from the dark reaches of capitalism, greed, gentrification, tradition, and ownership. It is a moving piece of fiction that showcases the very best of what the author has learned from her previous work in nonfiction and expounds on that foundation in a way that only someone as skilled and multifaceted as Jerkins could pull off."   —Shondaland

"Jerkins's incisive social commentary shines through in her fiction debut, *Caul Baby*. . . . Laced with generational pain and sprinkled with magic, *Caul Baby* is a sweeping family drama with no shortage of action. During a pandemic that has laid bare a nation's inequities, Jerkins's work feels more relevant than ever . . . a blazingly original debut." —*Chicago Review of Books*

"A multilayered reflection of contemporary dilemmas with a touch of magic realism. . . . Readers are taken through a spectrum of emotions with a satisfying payoff. On the heels of her excellent memoir *Wandering in Strange Lands*, Jerkins solidifies herself as one of our guiding literary lights."

—*Booklist* (starred review)

"Ambitious and unique. . . . *Caul Baby* is like nothing I've read before. It has historical references but is overwhelmingly a book of our time. It delivers a story that weaves the nuance of Black womanhood with intergenerational struggles and triumphs and the heartache of contemporary racial injustice."

—*New York Journal of Books*

"An expansive, folklorish tale of two families—both headed by Black matriarchs—that intertwine for over twenty years. . . . *Caul Baby* hones in on the power of a healing legend in a community systematically ignored and harmed by the medical establishment. . . . Jerkins's debut novel asks what it means to be a mother and emphasizes that a community's care for its own can be the most radical form of love."   —*Bust*

"A decades-long exploration of the gentrification of Harlem, the ethics of nontraditional family-making, the enduring power of tradition, and more."

—*PureWow*

CAUL BABY

A NOVEL

MORGAN JERKINS

HARPER PERENNIAL

NEW YORK • LONDON • TORONTO • SYDNEY • NEW DELHI • AUCKLAND

HARPER ● PERENNIAL

This is a work of fiction. Names, characters, places, and incidents are
products of the author's imagination or are used fictitiously and are
not to be construed as real. Any resemblance to actual events, locales,
organizations, or persons, living or dead, is entirely coincidental.

A hardcover edition of this book was published
in 2021 by HarperCollins Publishers.

FIRST HARPER PERENNIAL EDITION PUBLISHED 2022.

Designed by Nancy Singer

Library of Congress Cataloging-in-Publication Data has been applied for.

ISBN 978-0-06-287318-7

22 23 24 25 26   LSC   10 9 8 7 6 5 4 3 2 1

To Black Mothers (Past, Present, and Future)

"I was born with a caul, which was advertised for sale . . . Whether sea-faring people were short of money about that time, or were short of faith and preferred cork jackets, I don't know; all I know is, that there was but one solitary bidding . . . The caul was won, I recollect, by an old lady with a hand-basket . . . It is a fact which will be long remembered as remarkable down there, that she was never drowned, but died triumphantly in bed, at ninety-two."

—*David Copperfield*, Charles Dickens

"When I was handling this caul of hers downstairs I could feel some mighty power in it. Shoot, Lena may be able to . . . do all kinds of things."

—*Baby of the Family*, Tina McElroy Ansa

PART I

I

Something was bound to happen to Laila's baby, and everyone from the pews of Abyssinian Baptist down to the northern shore of Central Park knew it. One of the last vestiges of the Black elite in Strivers' Row, she was the only one whose brownstone was not punctuated with the sounds of pitter-pattering feet or wails in the dead of night. The first few times Laila became pregnant, she couldn't wait to tell everyone who crossed her path. Then, weeks later, some of those same people would casually ask for an update and she'd reply, her face crestfallen, her posture slouched. As the first failed pregnancies turned into several, people stopped asking though she never stopped announcing, hopeful that collective faith would carry her flailing belief in the power of her body, and in God's will. Eventually, she lost count of how many children abandoned her after the first heartbeat, or how many times she'd wake up with blood soaking her backside. Her body was desolate land, each crack in her earth a forewarning from the last child to future ones that this place was no home. Some of the fetuses grew, saw the dents of their past siblings in her womb, and joined them in the ether. After they disappeared, they left a hollow hole as a reminder of what could have been.

Seven months after her latest loss, Laila found out that she was pregnant yet again. She stared for a long while at the two pink lines that formed on the pregnancy test she'd purchased from the nearby Duane Reade. In her earlier years, she would've squealed; she would've danced, knocking over Q-tips and tweezers and extra rolls of toilet paper. But this time, she turned toward the mirror, holding the test with one hand and with the other pinching the side of her belly, saying, "Don't fuck with me this time. Please."

Laila figured she'd keep this pregnancy a secret. Any woman with a smidgen of common sense should know that this child—like the others—would not live past the first trimester. She continued on with her life: attending social events around the neighborhood, busying herself with redecorating her home and taking on the occasional interior design gig, a skill she pursued out of love rather than necessity. Her husband, Ralph, an architect, was usually out of town at least two weeks a month due to a long-standing assignment in Boston, and so he barely noticed the extra snacks lying around when he returned home or her frequent dashes to the bathroom. Neither he nor anyone else suspected anything. That is, until one night, Ralph returned home a day early and found a copy of *What to Expect When You're Expecting* lying half-open on the arm of their love seat. When Laila emerged from the bathroom wiping her mouth, a few water droplets dotted her slip so that the satin clung to her belly, emphasizing its roundness. He shook his head while holding the book with both hands and smiled as he approached her. She stood like a deer caught in headlights in front of Ralph and weakly said, "I'm sorry." He then swooped her into his arms before they released a glorious laugh. That night, he went out and bought a fudge crunch ice cream cake from Baskin-Robbins and they ate it in bed, his hand caressing Laila's stomach the entire time.

Neither of them could remember the last time their home had

been filled with such happiness. He offered to relinquish his responsibilities for his Boston-based project in order to wait on Laila hand and foot, but she refused. He thought it might be best to care for Laila more carefully this time around, but she would hear nothing of it. The money that he would receive for the completed job would be helpful since they planned to spoil their miracle baby rotten. To make up for his absence, Ralph began to send flowers or small gifts like boxes of chocolate or handwritten love letters. He'd call morning, afternoon, and night for brief check-ins and hired a twice-a-week housekeeper so that Laila would not overwork herself and jeopardize her health.

This child was different because it was growing and changing her from the inside out, persevering from the first trimester and moving past the middle of the second. Laila's brown skin became dewy, a sunset behind a hill. Her hair, once fine and short, sprouted thick and unbridled. Her neighbors craned their necks when she passed them on the sidewalks. Her walk was different. Instead of her usual erect posture, she hunched slightly, her legs waddling. "Missus Reserve got a baby in 'er," bystanders whispered on their front stoops behind their potted amaryllis bulbs and hibiscuses. A pair of meddling women could not restrain their curiosity and approached a five-months-pregnant Laila as she walked by their brownstone's front stoop one sunny afternoon.

"Oh, hi, ladies." Laila smiled and placed a hand on her belly.

"Good afternoon, Laila," they replied one after the other.

The women—Sydney and Constance—could smell the sweat and sweet, doughy aroma stemming from her groin. They squinted with intrigue when they could not find that caul, that special cork skin-like membrane dangling from her neck. What else would explain why she was still pregnant if not for the extra assistance that no gynecologist could provide? When these meddling women did not say anything else after their initial greeting, Laila followed their intense eyes to her bare neck and nervously rubbed her throat.

"What are you staring at?" Laila asked.

"Sorry, it's just—I mean, it's a miracle that you're still pregnant," Constance said. She received a sharp elbow to the side of her left breast by Sydney.

"What she means is that it's a blessing, and we're happy for you."

"Thank you, but that still doesn't answer the question. What were you looking at?"

Sydney and Constance looked at each other with uneasy, tense faces.

"What? Spit it out!" Laila laughed, but inside she found nothing funny about the moment.

"Well—" Sydney answered. "We thought that you might have gotten help from those Melancon women."

"Oh no. Nope." Laila wagged her right pointer finger in the air and shook her head. "I don't want to get involved with that mess. You're not saying you actually believe in that, do you?"

"I admit that I've been curious from time to time," Constance said. "I mean, have you ever seen one of them up close? They must have something extra on their skin because it doesn't look like ours. It's like . . . another layer, like a shield, it's hard to describe. What if it's true what they say, that it can protect or heal you?"

Laila stared at the ground and made small circles with her right foot. Her belly was extending her shadow, and she imagined the day when her shadow would part into two: she standing, her small child leaning against her side. "I don't know," Laila said. "I don't know. It just seems weird."

"Well, we've all heard the stories," Sydney said. She sighed. "You have to wonder why some gossip like that would float around all these years if there wasn't a lick of truth to it. And since you got money, it's—" Constance elbowed Sydney again. "All right, jeez! Hey, listen, if you don't believe, go to their bodega up on 142nd and Adam Clayton Powell. The daughter, Josephine? She may be in there."

"Good luck with your pregnancy, Laila." Constance gently pulled Sydney away so that they could walk in the opposite direction of Laila. They argued all the way to the end of the block over whether or not it was appropriate to bring up the Melancons until they became too distant for Laila to hear anything else that they were saying.

It didn't matter. The seed was planted. Laila rubbed her throat and sternum as she reconsidered their questioning of her pregnancy. In fact, Laila forgot which errand had made her leave her brownstone in the first place. Who was she kidding? Laila thought. For all the kicks and hunger pangs, she was haunted by the fear of another miscarriage. No matter how many times her doctor assured her that the baby was safely growing with a steady, fast heartbeat, she could not be too certain. What if there was some truth to what they said about the Melancon women? She'd never actually seen one up close. Her curiosity got the best of her. She decided to see if they appeared just as Sydney said.

The bodega was on the end of a block full of similar real estate, as was the way with many a Harlem street corner: another deli, another Crown Fried Chicken, and a Laundromat. When Laila entered the store, there was a young, curly haired woman filing her nails at the cash register and a man placing hamburger patties on the griddle. But Laila was the only customer. The entrance door chimed, and Laila turned her neck to see a sophisticated woman strutting into the bodega wearing black patent leather pumps and a cream-colored tweed suit dress. She had mahogany skin and amber eyes that alternated between rolling around and cutting into two fine slits as she reprimanded the cashier for her repeated tardiness. She had to be one of the Melancon women. She was indeed a sight to behold! Laila strolled down the aisles and saw the usual brands of Oreos, Cheez-Its, multipurpose house cleaners, and canned goods. These items were cheaper by forty or so cents than those sold at the bodega closest to her home. How was it that this woman could afford such expensive attire from managing a run-of-the-mill bodega? Did she think she was too good to wear T-shirts and jeans like everyone else who worked behind those counters? From there, Laila created an entire narrative in her head about this woman: she had to be stuck-up, and her attire was a way to prove that she was better than everyone else. Most stuck-up people tended to be bitchy and rude. That's probably why people always gossiped about the Melancons but no one ever knew them. They didn't let people get too close because they were bougie, and though the moniker applied to her too, Laila knew that bougie Black folk were the most insufferable kind of Black folk.

Laila looked over the top shelf of the aisle where she stood and saw that Melancon woman watching her.

"Good afternoon," she said, and flashed an ebullient smile. Her voice was like fresh silk, with a slight rasp at the end.

Laila's throat dried up. She cleared it and said, "Good afternoon."

"Let me know if you need any help, okay? We've moved some things around in here."

"Huh. Oh. Sure. Thank you."

Laila lowered her head and grabbed two boxes of Chips Ahoy! for when she would be hungry later. When she approached the register, the Melancon woman was watching the television mounted on the back wall beside all the over-the-counter drugs and travel-sized toiletries. The local news was reporting that the International

Monetary Fund was expanding its anti-money-laundering units across the United States. What put Laila at ease was how much this Melancon woman fidgeted during the announcement. The action softened her intimidating appearance. As she leaned closer to the screen, the sleeve of her jacket inched higher and Laila's eyes bulged at the sight of a glossy film on her wrist that dazzled in the light.

"Is this all?" the woman asked.

Laila jumped. "Oh. Maybe— Can I get a copy of *New York* magazine?" Laila pointed to it. The Melancon woman moved too quickly along the edges and hissed as one of the pages sliced her fingers. A paper cut was painful, but Laila didn't think that her response of hurriedly turning her back, hunching over, and covering her entire hand was necessary. There were a box of Band-Aids and a bottle of hydrogen peroxide right on the back shelf if she needed it. After a few seconds, Josephine turned around and said, "Sorry, how embarrassing."

"That's okay. Don't worry about it."

As the woman reached for the *New York* magazine with the same hand as before, Laila saw that there wasn't so much as a nick on any of her fingers.

The woman looked down at one of the titles of the inside stories, detailing a new labor trafficking act being debated in New York, and smirked. "That's some pretty heavy reading for a pregnant woman."

Laila chuckled. "It's always good to be aware of what's going on."

"Indeed." She slowly rang up the newspaper and took a beat with the two boxes of Chips Ahoy!. "If I can ask, how far along are you?"

"Excuse me?"

The woman repeated herself and blinked her eyes twice with anticipation.

"Oh." Laila took a beat and peered deeper into the woman's eyes but could find nothing beyond pure curiosity. "Five months." The woman directed the cashier to go to the back to check inventory. The male cook was in the middle of grilling the hamburger meat, and the grease popping from the griddle was loud enough to drown out their conversation.

"First kid?" she whispered as she leaned over the counter.

"I— Well, not quite." Laila winced. "You see—I-I don't want to unload on you, it's just—"

"It's okay. I get it. I've been there too."

"You have?"

The woman nodded. "Many times."

Laila sighed with relief and dropped her shoulders. "I'm scared. I've been feeling so lonely throughout this. How did you get through it?"

"I'm Josephine."

"Laila. Laila Reserve." Laila extended her hand, and Josephine shook it.

Josephine surveyed the large emerald-cut diamond on Laila's left ring finger and said, "Are you getting all the proper care you need?"

"I think so. But you can never be too careful, you know?"

"Indeed. Six thirty-nine."

"Huh?" Laila saw her bagged items and blurted out, "Oh. Sorry. Thanks."

"You're welcome and good luck with the baby."

When Laila left the bodega, she thought that perhaps she had made a new friend in the most unexpected of places. As much as she wanted to find any characteristic of Josephine's to hate, she couldn't, and then Laila felt bad for assuming the worst about her before their conversation. Josephine wasn't bougie-acting, rude, bitchy, or stuck-up. She was beautiful and kind, and they were two women experiencing the same problem with their wombs. No matter how special that extra layer of skin was, it could not prevent the plague of infertility, and this misfortune made Josephine more human than any gossip had led her to believe. Laila sat on her love seat with both packages of Chips Ahoy! Each time she took a bite out of a cookie, she was reminded of Josephine's scent, replete with notes of vanilla and sandalwood. In between the chewing and swallowing, Laila could hear Josephine's comforting voice inside of her head and soothed her protruding belly. As for Josephine, her thoughts toward Laila were much more pointed and grand.

The following Sunday, Laila attended St. Philip's Church, where she and her entire family were members. Laila always sat toward the end of the pew with her eyes closed, her shaking hands holding a rosary. This was her tradition whenever she was with child. No one bothered her, for they would not have disturbed anyone deep in prayer. But when they saw her hard, bloated belly, the congregation agreed that Laila needed more divine communication and angel encampment than anyone else at service. The vestry came to her when it was time for Communion, but before they did, at the altar, they shared knowing glances: *Do not ask Missus Reserve nothing. Keep your eyes on her. Nod and smile. Do not say anything.* They were afraid to ask about her pregnancy in the house of the Lord, worried that their words could send tremors to her body and endanger her child. Every congregant of St. Philip's knew there was life and death in the tongue.

Laila was aware that she was being watched. Folks needed to touch her. Whether it was a female elder in the church gently caressing her knuckles while they prayed as a congregation or an auntie double tapping her shoulder as they walked by her pew, Laila felt like a child being delicately handled. The more she thought about it, the more offended she became, until her anger broke, and a calmness settled upon her spirit. What faith could do for a soul, if only for a moment.

She needed to be delicately handled. She looked down at her body and saw that her hands were tightly clasped together on her lap and her shoulders were up to her ears. She shook, almost uncontrollably. As quickly as it had left, fear had taken hold once more. The service was halfway through; she figured that everyone had already sensed her fear so there was no need to try to straighten up now. But she was uneasy still because Landon Thomas, a longtime family friend and godfather to Laila's niece, could not stop looking over his wife's shoulder to stare at her. Any time there was a pause in the service, whether for clapping, hymn singing, or tithe giving, the man looked hurriedly, as if checking to make sure she didn't leave.

As he walked back from Communion, he shook Laila's hand. When Laila retracted her hand, she found a small note wedged in between her pointer and middle fingers. But by the time she could question if it was a mistake, Landon had already taken his seat alongside his wife, Valerie. She quietly opened the note: *Stay after service lets out.*

Laila waited until the rest of the congregation filed out, then the rector, then the organist. She waited with uneven breath, unsure if the note was a gentle wish or a threat. As the voices in the vestibule of the church dwindled, she gripped her rosary tighter but couldn't steady her hands or thighs from shaking. Then Landon returned to the sanctuary and sat beside her. They both stared at the altar before she finally spoke.

"You know, you didn't have to stare at me like I'm some zoo exhibit."

"Sorry, Lay. I'm just happy for you—congrats."

"Yeah, yeah, yeah," Laila facetiously said. "What's up?"

Landon took a deep breath and replied, "It seems you made quite the impression on Josephine."

"Excuse me?"

"Josephine. Josephine Melancon."

Laila blinked. "How do you know that?"

"Because she told me. We're business partners."

"Business partners? I thought you worked in the Financial District. Either I have pregnant brain or you're just not making sense right now."

Ignoring her question, Landon said, "There are two different kinds of people in Harlem—those who believe in the caul and those who don't. Which kind are you?"

"It doesn't matter which side I'm on. I'm not sure I want any part of that." Landon was right in that the Harlem community was divided over the mystery of the Melancon women: one side believed the family's power and owed their longevity—and greater income—to the caul. The other side banished the thought as pure nonsense, a fabrication brewed by old time Harlemites who could never trust institutions with their health and therefore needed another practice to get them by for the time being. Whatever root work that the old folks did could not be found in Harlem's labyrinthine streets but in the South, where it belonged and flourished, the soil having absorbed blood and sweat from the enslaved.

Laila was readying herself to stand to her feet before Landon gently placed a hand on her wrist to lower her back down in the pew.

"I think you do want to be a part of it. She told me how much you were staring at her in the bodega. I know she's striking, but she got the impression that you were holding back, like you wanted to ask her something."

"Why is this any of your business?"

"She offered to give a piece of her caul to you in order to protect your unborn child, and I can make this transaction happen."

Laila winced at the double-edged sword of a promise. Normally, superstition and folklore never appealed to her. She believed that the solution to most of her problems could be found in either a medical doctor, the book of Psalms, or anointed oil from a Pentecostal elder. Then again, that oil could be considered as superstitious as a caulbearer, or one who was born with the caul. And if she could place her Christian faith in an oil, why not place some secular faith in the caul? Even the saints of the Gospels stumbled in their faith from time to time—even while God was in their midst. And those saints were not women who bore children. Those saints may have seen many gone on to Glory, but none of them understood the grief of someone dying inside of their body several times. None of those saints knew death as neighborly and parasitically as she did. And besides, if this proposition was being presented to her now, within this sanctuary, what if God ordained it? What if what everyone suspected about those caulbearing women was true? She had to explore any and all possibilities for the sake of her child or the regret would splinter every last one of her nerves.

When they left St. Philip's that afternoon, Laila asked for more time to think about it, but Landon was confident that delay did not mean denial. He told her that they would reconvene next Sunday after church.

That evening, Laila phoned Ralph while he was away and filled him in.

"Oh, Laila, come on," he joked. "You never believed in this caul nonsense. You laughed it off before when friends brought it up at parties."

"I know, I know. Believe me, I know it sounds crazy, but what if it's true?" Laila asked.

"And what if it's not?"

Ralph sighed. She pictured him extending his legs as far as they would go underneath the seat in front of him. His cool breath only seconds away from being coated with a shot of bourbon.

"Don't you think you still being pregnant this long is proof that you don't need it? Why don't you just believe in yourself?"

"Because I can't be too sure, Ralph. Even though the doctors say I'm fine, and I feel fine, I just don't know. I'm scared."

Ralph held the phone closer to his lips and said, "I'm scared too. I told you I can come home."

"No, no, it's okay. I just need to acknowledge my feelings and maybe be okay with it being this way till the baby comes."

"But you don't need that stress, Lay."

"Then how about we just explore this option? If it fails, it fails, but at least we tried."

"But you want help from someone you don't even know. Don't let that desperation lead you to another breakdown."

Her heart stopped from that pointed statement. She wasn't sure to which breakdown he was referring: the episode in college that led to a brief stint in Bellevue or the one in front of the relentlessly interrogative adoption caseworker that ultimately led to the rejection of their application. The specifics didn't matter, for she quietly wept all the same.

"Lay, I'm sorry—I-I'm sorry. That was an awful thing to say. I didn't mean to bring that up."

Laila breathed heavily into the phone and said nothing.

"Look. If it'll put you at ease, if you will stop stressing, then I will support you one hundred percent. I don't like it and I don't want you to be hurt, but we don't need to be fighting right now. So if you need someone to rally behind you, then I'll do just that."

They exchanged multiple *I love you*s until Laila hung up the

phone, but she was still left unsatisfied. Ralph was unsure of himself, and she could hear the wavering all in his voice. For days she
reflected on their conversation and turned angry at his unenthusias-
tic response until she finally confided in her sister, Denise, and her
niece, Amara, about what was going on over dinner. Denise sucked
her tongue. "They're the bougiest motherfuckers from Sugar Hill to
Central Park."

"Oh, here you go," Amara interjected, and smiled.

"What?" Denise said. As the younger and more dramatic sibling,
she felt overly protective of Laila. "It's true! Now I don't believe in
all that hocusy-pocusy stuff but if I did, I know that Melancon family ain't help nan one Black person since the crack era. Maybe even
earlier. You know, pre-pre-pre-gentrification. But it's almost the
new millennium, baby. White folks are starting to move in, can pay
more for that caul, and they lap it up like pigs in shit. All skinfolk
ain't kinfolk, Lay. You might as well forget about it. I can give you
some omega-3 pills, and we can read devotionals every day. Amara
can bring books from that store in Morningside Heights near the
school for you to read to the baby. But don't get involved with those
people. Us women selling parts of our bodies is just unnatural. Slav-
ery is over! They just ain't get the memo!" Denise cackled.

"Aunt Lay, what does Uncle Ralph think about you getting help
from them?"

"Uncle Ralph grew up in Providence and didn't even know he
was Black until he listened to Outkast for the first time! What does
he know about anything that concerns Black women?"

"Oh, come on now." Denise dropped her silverware on her plate
and held both of her hands in the air, palms facing in front of her.
"By the end of you and Ralph's first big date, he was already opening
another set of legs other than those damn famous lobsters they got
up there in Rhode Isle. Knock it off."

"Denise—" Laila could hardly control the giggles struggling to break through her tight lips. "Do not talk like that in front of the baby."

"The baby is twenty years old and a Columbia student." She massaged Amara's right shoulder and nudged her. A glimmer shone in her eyes. "My baby. She's going to be a lawyer someday, y'know. A fine one."

"Oh yeah? What kind of lawyer do you want to be?"

"I haven't decided yet."

"Well, just make sure you become one for a good reason, and not just because you want bragging rights. Seems like everyone always wants to be a doctor or a lawyer these days. Whatever happened to the arts?"

Amara nodded in between shoveling macaroni and cheese into her mouth. "I will have a reason. I want to declare political science as my major but with some anthro and women's and gender studies courses to fill my plate. Yale Law is the goal. I'll settle for Harvard, though."

Laila scoffed and tucked her top lip into her mouth. "Wow. You're on a roll."

"A butter roll. Amara, baby. Slow down with the food. They ain't feeding you over there at Columbia?"

"I've just been hungry, that's all. Cafeteria food is terrible. And besides, I got stress from papers and exams and Model UN, you know?"

Denise nodded then reached her hand across the table. She first sought to caress Laila's baby, but when Laila flinched, Denise laid her fingers on Laila's place mat instead. "Laila, your baby is going to be fine. Think about your last babies. Were you as far along as you are now?"

"No."

"All right, then. Hell, in a minute, it'll be time to plan a baby shower."

"No baby shower. I don't want anything to jinx this baby. Not until it gets here. Not a moment sooner."

"Okay. Whatever you want. But don't get hooked up with those Melancon women. Who made you have a change of heart about them, anyway?"

Laila darted eyes at Amara, who was still fitting as much food as she could in between her cheeks. Amara was Landon's goddaughter, and she could have implicated him even though they met in secret. She finally said, "No one in particular. I just heard the word from around town."

"Well, let that word keep traveling around town and you don't get in its way."

Laila did as she was instructed and waited in the pews the following Sunday. After the elderly hobbled out of the church, Landon returned to the sanctuary and took his place next to Laila. Their eyes remained fixed on the high altar, where the organist acrobatically played a mash-up of Vivaldi and Mozart under the assumption that he had no audience.

"Sorry I'm late. I was looking for your niece. She hasn't been coming to services lately, and I'm concerned."

"Really? Well, I saw her on Friday and she said she's been busy with classes."

"Hmph. I guess that's the Ivy League."

"Maybe."

"So, are you interested?"

Laila looked over her shoulder then nodded.

"Good. Come with me."

"Wait, where are we going?"

"Uptown. You'll see."

No sooner than they walked into the vestibule of the church, Amara came dashing through the door, panting, with fried chicken crumbs on both sides of her mouth. Laila sniffed Amara's scent and caught a whiff of her own likeness. A suspicion sparked but fizzled just as immediately as it began.

"I'm sorry," Amara managed to get out in between her uneven breaths.

"Relax. Take a breather." Landon placed a hand on her shoulder. "Where were you?"

"I'm sorry I'm late. I've just been busy."

"But you weren't too busy to get fried chicken from Crown Fried or Popeye's, were you?" He turned her chin from left to right.

"I've just been hungry, that's all. Stress from papers and exams and Model UN, you know?" Laila remembered that response verbatim, almost as if Amara had rehearsed it. Amara paused and shot a glance at Laila, whose hands were now on her hips.

"I understand you're in college, but you have responsibilities here too, Amara. You're my goddaughter. Think about how this reflects on me."

"I'm sorry. I'll do better."

"Okay."

"Do I have enough time to eat my biscuit? I bought one for you." Amara raised her Popeye's bag, and all three of them laughed.

"You know what, stay here. I have to make a run right quick. I'll be back. Don't you move," Landon said.

"I won't."

When Amara saw that Landon and Laila were leaving together, she stared inquisitively and mouthed a question to Laila as to what was going on when their eyes caught each other. Laila smiled and shook her head, indicating that it was nothing important, and Amara nodded.

Landon checked to see if there were any parishioners hanging around the block as soon as they exited the church. When the coast was clear, they walked to the corner of 134th and Adam Clayton Powell Jr. Boulevard, where he hailed a cab. They made their way to West 145th and Frederick Douglass Boulevard, and Laila took a deep breath. A large wreath of gooseberries in green, burgundy, and cream foliage adorned the front door of a brownstone on a quiet, picturesque block. A sienna-colored rug with the calligraphic letter *M* bold and centered lay on the porch. Fleur-de-lis spearheaded the wrought-iron gate that made the entrance inaccessible, the only brownstone of the entire row that bore this feature. Since Landon was on the side nearest to the sidewalk, he exited first but closed the door in Laila's face before she could leave the car. She didn't know whether or not to move, so she watched the meter run. She heard Landon's voice and that of another woman conversing with each other. Moments later, Landon returned from the brownstone with a few bills in his hand and opened the door for Laila.

Standing in a pin-striped dress with pumps and a set of pearl earrings, Josephine was at the threshold of the entrance with that same lovely smile adding even more luster to her appearance. As soon as Laila reached the top step, Josephine gave her a large hug that caught both her and Landon off guard. She pressed a hand on Laila's shoulder to guide her inside, and the two women turned their backs on Landon, who was not permitted within the intimate space and bond that they shared with each other. This separation was made quite clear when he followed them both into the living room and Josephine eyed him down until he backed out into the hallway.

There was a ceramic pot of tea along with two cups placed in the middle of the coffee table. Josephine sat on an upholstered chair and Laila on the living room sofa. As Josephine fetched some sugar, honey, and milk from the kitchen, Laila admired a large painting of three women—including Josephine and what looked like her mother and sister—and a child hanging above the fireplace. The living room was aesthetically pleasing, with its warm-colored design, books, and furniture, but there was something off that Laila could not quite place. The floor-to-ceiling window curtains rustled slightly, but the air was so stale that her eyes watered. There were small holes in random spots on the walls, but they weren't large enough for any rodent to crawl through.

When Josephine returned, Laila sat upright even more and smiled.

As Josephine poured the tea into Laila's cup, she said, "This is rooibos. It's great for pregnancy."

"Thank you." Laila sipped her tea and placed her cup on a coaster. "Josephine, I have to be honest, I'm a skeptic about all this, and we don't know each other."

"I know. I just . . . wanted to help, that's all. It's not often that we help people from the community and—sorry—" Josephine waved her hands in front of her. "I'm saying too much, pardon me."

"It's okay. Does it work? Does it really work? Please don't lie to me." Laila half frowned and leaned back in her seat to prepare herself for what she expected to be a disappointment.

"Of course it does," Josephine said. "I've been doing this for years, trust me. It's for protection and healing. If you have an illness, you'll be cured. You got a wound, it'll get better. You have a baby in utero and—"

"I get it. I get it. And so I—I guess you . . . cut yourself? I mean you literally"—Laila held out her arm and made a diagonal motion across her skin—"cut yourself and give me a piece of you? Just like that?"

"Just like that."

"You cut yourself each and every time? Why can't you just cut pieces off it ahead of time to save the trouble for yourself?"

"The caul needs to be kept close to the body. So when we cut, it needs to be transferred to another's skin as soon as possible or it'll lose its potency."

"Oh. And I . . . wear it like a necklace?"

"You can. We've heard from previous clients that it's the easiest place since you always know where it is."

"Do I take it off in the shower?"

"I wouldn't. We encourage people to keep it close to their bodies at all times."

"And it can only be used for me, or can I take it off and give it to someone else?"

"Why would you want to take it off? Wouldn't that defeat the purpose of why you bought it in the first place?"

"True."

"But to answer your question, the caul and its properties bind to the first person it's given to. It could theoretically work on someone else, but it may be less effective."

"And what happens to you?"

Josephine was in the middle of sipping her tea when she inadvertently burned her bottom lip at the question. "What do you mean?" She massaged her lip.

"After you cut yourself, does it hurt? Do you hurt?"

Josephine's stomach churned at the question. She soothed her chest and dropped her eyes to the ground.

"I'm sorry," Laila said. "I didn't mean to—"

"No, no. It's just . . . no one has ever asked that question."

"Well, if I offended you, I—"

"Oh, come off it!" a hoarse voice from outside the room called out. Josephine closed her eyes and groaned. Laila opened her mouth to speak, but before she could get a word out, a tall, elderly woman staggered barefoot into the living room. She wore a long red dress and turban, and her piercing glare was heightened by the yellow where the whites of her eyes should have been. Laila did a double take at the painting and other features became apparent: the stoic face of this elderly woman juxtaposed with everyone else's smiles, her hands folded while the others' were open.

The elderly woman stood with her hands on her hips and said, "What is up with all this jibber jabber?"

"It's called being polite, though I wouldn't expect you to know that," Josephine retorted.

"It's called beating around the bush. And don't you talk to me like I'm your child. You don't have one, remember?"

Laila leaned forward but stopped herself short of defending Josephine, who shrank in size by curling her back and hunching her shoulders. Before Laila could recollect herself from the shock of the cold remark, she was startled by Josephine's mother's smirk. Silently, Laila hoped Josephine would say something else, but she receded, the color draining from her face.

"The rate for the caul is fifteen thousand dollars. Will that be an issue?" the mother asked.

"Fifteen—fifteen thousand?" Laila sputtered.

"Yes," the woman said curtly. "Will that be a problem?"

"No, it won't, Miss—"

"Melancon. Marceline Melancon."

"Miss Melancon, it won't be an issue. Josephine and I were just—"

"Discussing, I know, I know. But you see, Josephine isn't good with securing a deal. She's not as stern of a businesswoman as I've been teaching her to be." She gripped her daughter's left shoulder, and Josephine shifted uncomfortably in her chair.

"Fifteen thousand should be fine. Are there returns?"

Marceline scoffed. "Returns?"

"Maman—" Josephine interjected.

"Quiet!" Maman snapped. "We don't have the patience for your offensive questioning. I've had white folks with more savvy and money than you be out the door in the amount of time it took you to walk through it."

"I apologize. That amount is fine."

"Good. Then Josephine will see you out. Good day."

As Laila was being guided out of their home, she halted on the hallway carpet when another woman glared at her from the top of the staircase leading to the basement. Her silvery hair was dripping water all over a satin slip that all but exposed her naked body. Laila gasped at the sight. It took her a moment to recognize that this person was the third woman in the painting. Landon, who had been standing in the hallway the entire time, shielded his eyes while Josephine ran to place a large coat over her sister Iris's body. She tried to lead Iris back downstairs, but Iris gripped the carpet with her feet and locked her knees in place.

"H-Hello," Laila reluctantly said.

Iris sniffed and shot her eyes directly above Laila's head to yet another hole, this one in the ceiling. Her eyeballs ricocheted from the corner with chipped wallpaper to the other with the same wear and tear, and Josephine groaned again at the behavior. Then, Iris's eyes rolled into the back of her head and she made a choking noise.

"Is she all right?" Laila asked.

"She's fine. She's—oh." Josephine soothed her temples. "Who or what are you seeing now, Iris?" she asked in a deadpan tone.

Her eyes rolled back and immediately connected with Laila's. Her heart seized.

"They wanted me to tell you that they miss you and that they're sorry. They're really sorry."

"Okay, that's enough—" Josephine attempted to nudge Iris down the steps, but she was unmovable.

"It's not your fault, they wanted to say—what?" She looked to the hole in the ceiling again and said, "You're waiting? Waiting for what? Waiting for who?"

"Stop, Iris," Josephine said.

Suddenly, Iris hugged Laila and whispered in her ear. "I know what Constance and Sydney said to you. You were meant to meet us. But bottom line is you still a mother, Miss Lay. You still a mother."

Josephine pulled Iris away from Laila before Iris had a chance to say anything else. Laila stood there in awe. Iris's words convinced Laila that beyond a shadow of doubt this baby was gonna live and these women were going to help her.

"I'll take her." Landon grabbed Laila's hand and proceeded to promptly get her out of the brownstone.

On their way to Laila's home, Landon told Laila that he would follow up the next day with details on how and when they would exchange the money and caul. She beamed with expectation and kept her hand on her stomach all throughout the day and evening with the comfort of now being able to get lost in her dreams. She made never-ending lists of potential names for the baby, delighted herself with how she and Ralph's characteristics would show up in the child's personality or mannerisms, and researched Mommy & Me classes all throughout the city. But the next day passed and Laila heard nothing. She wasn't too worried, however. There were far too many things to preoccupy her time with: baby clothes, day care and preschools, and maybe even foreign language tutors. But after three days passed by without any contact, Laila took it upon herself to call Landon, and the call went immediately to his voicemail.

Now she wasn't sleeping so well. She abruptly stopped planning for the baby's arrival, and the days felt longer as she obsessed over when her phone would ring. Whenever Ralph would check in, she wouldn't respond immediately because she was frustrated that her husband and seemingly everyone else in her circle were contacting her and not the one person she needed to hear from to calm her nerves. At least, Laila thought, Sunday was approaching, and she could find solace in God's grace. But then Landon didn't show up there either, which was not like him at all. Convinced that Landon was avoiding her, Laila decided to bypass his role as the intermediary between her and the Melancon women, and returned to the bodega to speak with Josephine herself.

There was a police car parked outside the bodega, and an officer was in the midst of casual conversation with Josephine. When she saw Laila from the corner of her eye, she became tense and hurriedly rang up the officer's items and wished him a good day before the imminent confrontation. After Laila heard the door chimes of that officer leaving, she stomped to the cash register and yelled, "We had a deal!"

"Shh!"

"What do you mean, 'Shh!'?"

Josephine came from around the register, grabbed Laila by the arm, and walked her to the storage room.

"I'm sorry."

"What do you mean you're sorry? I have the money. I have it, I promise!"

"It's not you—it's—"

"It's what? What?"

"We just can't get involved. Something happened with Iris after you left. She said some more things and we—I just can't. I tried. I can't."

"What do you mean? Iris said I was meant to meet your family."

"She did, but—"

"But what?"

"I can't."

"That's all you can say is that you can't? Do you know how much pain I've gone through? Do you?"

"Believe me, I do. I know more than you think."

"No, you don't. You can't understand. I thought you wanted to help me. I thought . . . you maybe wanted to be my friend." Laila started tearing up, and Josephine along with her.

"I wanted to be your friend more than anything in the world. I think we do understand each other."

"You don't understand me. I shouldn't have believed you'd help me anyway. I thought I could because I saw how you didn't have a scratch on you when you cut yourself with that magazine, but it doesn't matter. I hope you live a sad, miserable life, you bitch." She waddled out of the storage room, but Josephine stayed behind to cry between the Lysol and dog chow. If only Laila knew, Josephine thought, how sad and miserable she was already.

For the next few weeks, Laila put herself on bed rest, afraid to move lest she shake her baby loose from her body too soon. Now that she did not have the caul to protect her, she suspended her normal comings and goings until her child was safe in her arms. But as she brushed her teeth one morning, she realized that she had not felt the baby move. Fretful, she tried to piece together when last her baby responded to her touch or the surroundings, until her over-worked mind created images and scenes of previous days that she wasn't sure had actually happened. The baby hadn't moved since the week that the Melancon family officially rejected her. She paced all around the second floor of her home, and when she went down-stairs, she heard the rainfall begin.

She looked around and felt ashamed at all the time, money, and effort spent on niceties in her home, objects that brought her no lasting joy: the corridor decorated with African art, the stacks of books in the living room, the empty upholstered chairs. Every step she made produced an echo that grated her ears. She was alone. Ralph was scheduled to come back later that night, but she did not care to see him. Nothing and no one interested her except her un-born baby. Whenever she moved to sit down, she felt a sharp pain ricochet from one side of her body to the other. She tried ginger tea to quiet her stomach, but the drink geysered from her mouth as soon as she swallowed. Her skin turned ashen, and that ringing re-surfaced in her eardrums. As soon as she leaned on an adjacent wall, liquid splattered out from underneath her dress. "Oh no." Her voice cracked. By the time she was able to phone Denise with a tearful and breathless plea, the bottom of that dress was steeped in blood.

She unlocked the door for Denise before staggering around the first floor. Denise ran down the five blocks from her home to Laila's. Bloody handprints smeared the walls, and all the outerwear from the fallen coatrack was scattered around Laila's body. Denise turned Laila over onto her back and said, "Lay, we gotta get you to the hos-pital. I'll call the ambulance right now."

"I'm not going to make it." Laila struggled through her labored breathing.

Denise nodded and sat Laila upright. "Yes, you are. Yes, you are! We gotta get there."

Laila shook her head and scooted to the nearest corner, where she pressed her back up against the wall. She winced as she parted her legs and gritted her teeth.

"No, Lay. No, no. Just wait!" Denise jumped to her feet and started for the phone but slipped and fell on the trail of blood, her arms screeching across the floor when she attempted to stop herself. When she was able to get to her feet, Laila's breaths intensified. Denise called 911 and yelled the address to the dispatcher. She gave Laila's name and address over and over again. She held the phone in the direction of where Laila was laboring and yelled the address again before slamming the phone on the receiver, the cord left dangling over the kitchen granite countertop. She opened all the cabinets until she found dish gloves and towels, then rolled up her sleeves. For a brief moment, Laila's increasingly loud moans paralyzed Denise. She stood over the stove boiling water in the biggest pot she could find to ease Laila's muscles and clean up the blood. Then Denise simply stopped. Her eyes followed the bubbles swirling around and around. She didn't know what she was doing. Her own child was birthed with an epidural and she was too dazed to remember any instructions besides "push." The baby wasn't supposed to be born for another four, five weeks. Denise did not want to go back in there. She didn't want to be involved in Laila's revolving misery and cursed herself for answering her sister's call and loving her too much to not jump all at once.

Laila's breaths were becoming shorter and faster. Something switched off in Denise's mind. Whatever anxieties she had disappeared the moment Laila cried out her name. Denise ran on the sides of the corridors where there were no tracks of blood and peeked underneath Laila's dress. She could not see anything but blood.

"The baby's coming. She's coming." Laila laughed through her cries and grabbed ahold of Denise's hand. "Just hold my hand. Don't let go."

"I won't, Lay. Hold on. She'll be here soon."

The doorbell rang, then a loud rap-rap-rapping on the knocker. Denise let go of Laila's hand, and Laila screamed again.

Two police officers, one white and the other Black, were at the door, but before they could get a word out, Denise saw a small crowd forming on the opposite side of the street. Every single one of the bystanders was silent, their pity-filled faces contorting and flinching at what was happening with Missus Laila Reserve's baby in there.

"Yes, yes, come in. My sister is in labor. Where's the ambulance?" Denise looked past their ears for any flashing red sirens.

"Where is your sister?"

"What? Can't you hear her? She's right here." She reached out to pull them in, but they shrank, turning their lips up at her blood-covered arms.

The police officers entered the foyer and saw Laila bearing down without so much as looking up to acknowledge their presence.

"How long has she been like this?" Both took out their pads and pens from their back pockets.

"I—I don't know."

"How far along is she?"

"Seven months. Seven and a half months."

"Somebody do something!" Laila growled. Spit flew out of her mouth in all different directions. She sputtered like an engine before biting down hard on the fabric of the top of her blouse. The officers encouraged her to continue breathing while they called for backup. Laila unleashed a long scream, then a gasp. Everything collapsed to an unholy silence.

"Do you hear anything? Did you hear anything?" Laila asked.

Denise cradled the baby in both palms but did not inch out from underneath Laila's dress with her.

"Denise? Denise!"

Denise lowered her head between her shoulders. She closed her eyes, and the tears stung from the heat between Laila's thighs. She quickly searched the baby's bloody body for any sign of movement. But the baby, whose eyes were also closed, just lay peacefully in her palms.

"Give her to me."

"Close your eyes first, Lay." Denise softened her tone and continued, "Let me wrap her first? We'll count together and then open our eyes on three."

Laila leaned forward over her knees and kicked her legs on the ground before thrashing. Memories of her time at Bellevue and the adoption caseworker who bombarded her with questions about her mental health, daily routine, and sex life overwhelmed her already exhausted mind until it caved and collapsed again. She flashed her teeth at the ceiling and snarled, clawing at her breasts till milk squirted from her nipples and her whole face was covered in it. She cried and licked the milk around her mouth and cried some more, sniffling and drooling and snotting. She touched one of the baby's legs and used that blood to mark up her face, drawing 1, 5, and 0 over and over again—the digits in the figure Maman told her that she had to pay for the caul: fifteen thousand dollars. The police officers radioed for the ambulance.

"Lay?" Denise covered the baby in a towel. "Laila? Laila." She nudged Laila's knees.

"Bring me to my feet."

"Lay, sweetheart, I think you should stay where you are until the ambulance comes. You've just given birth."

"No, I didn't. Giving birth would mean my child was breathing."

She scowled at the officers and held her arms out in front of her. "Are you going to make yourselves useful or stand there and be a part of my home decor?"

The officers helped Laila to her feet, but she did not retract her arms after she found her balance. She turned toward Denise and said in an unrecognizably deeper tone, "Denise, give her to me." She scrutinized the shakiness of Laila's arms and how her bottom lip could not stop quivering as though she were uttering words only intelligible to herself. Or worse—believing that she were speaking and no words were coming out. She held the baby, now wrapped in a towel, closer to her chest and grimaced. "Lay—"

"Give me my goddamn baby, Denise! I'm not going to tell you again." Denise shrank from the demand and passed the baby over to Laila. But when Laila finally got her wish, she couldn't look down at the child's face. She covered it with the towel in hopes that the grief would be less unbearable. Still, she pulled the baby closer and fingered around the chest for any last hope that it would rise. Maybe she'd never been pregnant to begin with. The weight she held in her arms felt like a pair of pomegranates. Sweet things. Sweet, sweet things. She smiled and rocked from side to side, imagining the red juice staining her hands. Yes, that's right. Red juice staining her hands and fingers from all the pomegranate picking. A gentle hand touched her shoulder. A female's warm voice diffused the air, but her tone became more urgent and assertive. The acidity of that woman's voice broke Laila's trance and made her jerk.

"Missus Reserve. I'm an EMT officer. Let me escort you into the ambulance." The officer tried to guide Laila with her arms, but Laila elbowed her in the love handle.

"Ambulance. For what? What?" She inadvertently peered down at her hands and found no pomegranates but a reddish infant whose body was shriveling as her grief began to spread like fog across a barren field. The baby almost fell from her arms, but she crouched down before anyone else could take it away from her.

Once the EMT and police officers opened the door and Laila saw the large crowd taking up both sides of the street and cursing any driver who had an issue with the traffic, her determination sharpened. There was her loss, in her hands, for the world to see. Loss knew her body better than her husband. If loss could not be expelled from her body, then it would be her coconspirator. "You gon' be awright, Miss Lay!" "You still a mother, Miss Lay!" Women from imperceptible spots in the crowd called out to her as Laila made her way down her stoop. She smiled and nodded. She was still a mother. A lossed mother but a mother. The double ambulance door opened and one of the EMT officers gently told her to watch her step. She took one last look at the crowd and saw Valerie hugging all three of her children to her stomach.

"Give me one second, please?" Laila asked. "Just a moment. I need some air before I go in that truck."

"Sure." The officers radioed the hospital dispatchers from the side of the vehicle, which gave Laila the perfect opportunity to stagger away. The EMT officers attempted to grab Laila, but the crowd intercepted and formed a train behind her. Cars honked as they passed by. More onlookers hanging outside of bodegas, delis, and barbershops stepped outside to witness the pandemonium and fuse themselves into the crowd.

After Laila turned the corner, limping but pressing forward, an uncle outside of a deli took his cane and stood up from his wheelchair. "Here you go, Miss Lay. Go on and get in." She sat her blooded self in his wheelchair, and once she got situated, Denise was able to break through the crowd to push Laila herself. With each block they passed, more people added to the crowd.

"You okay, Lay?" Denise asked.

"Just keep pushing until I tell you to stop."

No one knew where she was going, but they knew from the anger stewing in her brow that she was going somewhere, and they didn't want to miss it. Aunties abruptly broke out into song and others joined in to contrive some revelry, but the growing number of police cars and ambulances patrolling the streets—yet unable to infiltrate—was the gas that made the dough rise. The people kept multiplying, and whoever had an issue with the inconvenience was quickly cursed back into reticence.

Once they arrived at West 145th and Frederick Douglass Boulevard, Laila told Denise to inch a little bit farther down the block until she saw the letter *M* outside a particular brownstone. Once she did, Denise helped her out of the wheelchair. The crowd quieted and swirled around her. Reluctance dented her momentum, but standing with countless people behind her should have been enough to get someone to step outside. After a few moments of inactivity, murmurs rippled throughout the crowd. Josephine peeked out one of the front windows and down at Laila with her baby. The hand that was gripping the side of the curtain was covered with a black glove.

Come outside, you bitch, Laila mouthed. She repeated herself using all the strength in her throat. Josephine closed the curtain and Laila strengthened her posture. One minute passed. Then another. She wasn't coming. Laila screamed, "If you would've given me the caul, my baby could've had a chance! My baby could've had a chance! But my money wasn't good enough? And for what? For what? Step outside!" Laila spat and laid the baby down at the foot of the gate. She stomped each foot, ready to charge. The crowd was fluctuating between drawing near to Laila and backing up, hesitant to step into her wrath. She grabbed onto the fleur-de-lis spearheads and screeched, pressing her palms into the points till blood streamed down her wrists. While repeating her demands, Laila disrobed and beat her chest. The first mention of a caul from her lips divided the crowd. Many dispersed, seeing the childbirth as causing a fissure not only in her body but also her sanity. Those who stayed parted ways for the police to arrest her and the ambulance to take the child.

As Laila sat handcuffed in the back of the police car, Amara was watching from the sidelines with the last remaining bystanders. One of her neighbors had run to fetch her just as the crowd was beginning to grow, and she was able to get a good view once people were dispersing. She soured at the sight of her aunt with spittle still glistening from the side of her mouth, hair matted and lopsided, head too heavy to sit upright on her neck, and eyes unable to focus. The car pulled away, and Amara remained standing on the sidewalk. She looked back at the brownstone with the wrought-iron gate and saw the curtains fluttering. Josephine's face floated behind them. The two women did not remove their gaze from each other. Amara felt a rough flitting in her stomach and touched above her belly button. Josephine squinted at her, then disappeared again.

"Why her, God?" Amara looked up at the sky with tears in her eyes. "Why didn't you take my child instead?"

2

The pot of boiling water that Denise used for Laila's labor had been left unattended for hours. As she waited in the psychiatric ward of Mount Sinai Hospital for any updates on her sister, a set of police officers found her in the waiting room to tell her that the pot had caught on fire, as had the rest of the kitchen. It wasn't safe for anyone to live in that brownstone until repairmen could gut the interiors and reconstruct what was incinerated. All the while, the nurses working the front desk of Mount Sinai had been trying to get ahold of Ralph, leaving a voicemail every hour on the hour about his wife per Denise's badgering requests. The stress of Laila's stillbirth compounded with the news of Ralph and Laila's marital home propelled Denise to snatch the phone from the nurse's hands and dial Ralph's number again. As soon as she heard the sound of the voicemail beep, she spoke into the phone, her hands shaking, and said, "Pick up, you motherfucker. Your wife just lost your baby, and your place caught on fire. Where are you?" She broke down into tears. "You have to be here. You have to."

When Ralph heard about the loss of the baby, Laila's breakdown, and the brownstone catching on fire, the tightness he held in his chest unclenched. At least, Ralph thought, he didn't have to go home. Not being able to go home was a relief. The fire had released whatever he and Laila had built within those four walls, and if the repairmen could not reverse the damage, even better. He waited a few days, mindlessly wandering around the Charles River during his lunch breaks and waking up to see miniature bottles of Maker's Mark on his nightstand.

The doorbell at last rang at Denise's home, and she had it in her to sock Ralph dead in his face for abandoning his wife. But when she opened the door and took note of his swollen eyes and damp, reddened cheeks, she released her fist and dropped her shoulders with the realization that grief had already beaten her to the punch. The porch light shone on a few scraggly gray hairs in the middle of his head that she had never seen before and mild crust on his eyelashes. He refused to look her in the eye and handed her two suitcases. She unzipped one in front of him and saw women's clothes with the tags still on them.

"Ralph—"

"These are for her. Since we can't go back there. I can't do it anymore, D. I can't." He sniffled. "This is too much for me."

Denise looked over his shoulder and saw two passersby staring back at her. She placed an arm around Ralph and pulled him into her home to preserve his dignity. Over a kettle of honey lavender tea, they sat across from each other at the dining room table in silence. The light bulb overhead was somehow much stronger in this steeped darkness. Its brightness was painful to both of their eyes because they could not hide themselves and the weight of all that had happened with Laila and the baby.

"How is she doing?" Ralph asked.

"They want to evaluate her for a few more days. Doctors didn't feel comfortable releasing her just yet. I tried to tell 'em that she's mourning. Any mother who lost a child would be just as crazy."

"How bad was she?"

Denise took a sip of her tea, placed her cup down on the coaster, and said, "Bad, Ralph. Really bad. She was acting like an animal. I guess all the pain and frustration finally broke her. It's only so long you can keep it together."

"Can I admit something to you in confidence?"

"Mm-hmm."

"When I got the call, I knew deep down that it wasn't good. I just knew. Don't ask me why, but I felt it in my gut and I felt sick. I didn't think about immediately getting the next ticket back home. I didn't think about what was happening to my wife. All I could think was, *Not again. Not this again.* And I wanted to run away. I even checked train times to see if I could get on the next one back to Providence or Montreal. I had my card out with the ticket agent and everything until I saw that the woman was pregnant herself. She kept caressing her stomach while asking me if I wanted a coach or business seat. Just that fast, I came back home. But not to see if Laila was okay. To start saying my goodbyes, D."

"So that's why you came over?" Denise leaned forward in her seat.

"Yes. I can't be the man Laila needs."

"But—"

"Just . . ." Ralph held a hand up and took a deep breath. "Let me finish. I love Laila. I knew from our first date that she was going to be in my life for a long time. We were young and successful. We got married, socialized with others, and had great sex. But when you keep going through miscarriage after miscarriage, it does something to you. For the woman, it's her body. And it fucks with her head. It fucks with a man's head too. It's my pride. I feel useless. I'm afraid that every time I touch her, she'll be thinking about, *Will this be it this time?* And if it is it and she loses it again, I'll feel responsible for that pain. That's no way to live, D. I just feel like as much as I love her, our parts don't fit! And the more we try, the more disaster happens. First it's her, then it's our home. What if she dies next time? I can't be near her, D. Because every time I see her, when I close my eyes, all I see is death. Not my Laila, not anymore."

"In sickness and in health, Ralph. In sickness and in health. She needs you. And she's your responsibility! You're just gonna up and leave?"

"Denise, if I don't leave now, then you're gonna have two extra people to take care of. I'm going back to Providence. I'm going to stay at my parents' until I close on an apartment. In the meantime, I'll get some therapy. Hopefully. I can't stay here. People can't stop giving me their condolences when I walk down the gahdamn street. I'll suffocate."

Denise nodded. "And divorce?"

"One step at a time."

Denise shrank back in her seat and harrumphed, crossing her arms over her chest. "A wise woman once said, don't let a man tell you more than once that he don't want you. Guess the same rule applies for when he wants to walk out the door. But don't think you can just leave that easy. I work two jobs, and taking care of one extra person is enough."

"Good that you mention it."

"Excuse me?" Denise blinked as Ralph reached into his pocket and pulled out three wads of cash.

"Here are a few bills for Laila. I'll be sending money every month for her until . . . we figure our stuff out. And if there's any left over, use it for you and Amara."

Denise looked at Ralph, whose bottom lip was set to tremble with his pleading, and concluded that she must not hurt his already wounded pride. She placed a hand on the money and nodded at him before he saw himself out. Once he turned his back on her, she lifted her hand and began to count each bill. There was enough cash to cover the rent for at least six months, groceries, and incidentals. This was 1998, and everything was changing. White people were trickling in, unlike in the eighties, when they wouldn't venture beyond Ninety-Sixth and Broadway. She suspected that this was just the beginning and that rent was going to skyrocket. She'd already heard about other people whose rents had been raised twenty-five or fifty dollars a month—not enough to panic but enough to brace oneself. So far, Denise and her landlord had been chummy since they were classmates at St. Hilda's & St. Hugh's day school. He could charge more, especially if some Columbia or NYU students began to inquire, but he promised Denise that he wouldn't get rid of her for anything in the world. To him, Harlemites needed to remain in Harlem. Nevertheless, Denise recognized that money was still green, and everyone and everything could be bought in a matter of time.

Before Ralph left, he shot a glance at the staircase and saw Amara standing at the top. He did not speak because he sensed that Amara did not want a conversation, and neither did he. Maybe she'd heard all that he confessed to Denise. He tipped his head at her and turned his back at the same time she scurried back into her room. Amara planted her face in her pillows but faced toward the door and hoped that her mother would knock and tell her what was going on. But that talk never happened.

The apartment remained uncomfortably still for the rest of the night, until the next morning, when Denise picked Laila up from the hospital and set her up in the room next to Amara's. By that afternoon, Laila's sniffling and weeping seeped through Amara's bedroom walls and ruined her ability to focus on anything. Whenever Laila wasn't crying, Amara could hear her talking to herself in random broken sentences. Amara decided not to stay at her Columbia dorm because she would feel guilty leaving her mother all alone with Laila. But if she stayed, she couldn't concentrate on her work—and it wasn't like she could help. Amara fretted over the day and the hour that both her mother and aunt would find out about her secret. After all, she was already four months along when Laila settled into their home.

She had not planned for it to happen. During the first few weeks of spring semester sophomore year, she found herself already behind in her reading for her Law & Ethics course. The only way to focus was to shut off her phone and check in with her accountability partner, Elijah. Elijah had an on-and-off-again relationship with his high school sweetheart, who anxiously awaited a proposal as soon as he graduated. He was someone with whom she'd struck up a rapport during admitted students' week, and they worked alongside each other in her dorm. One night while studying, she kept her cell phone on silent, and the alarm to remind her to take her birth control pill, which she'd been prescribed for acne, was neglected. As the night progressed, their concentration loosened and they started to crack jokes. Elijah pulled out two joints from his back pocket and asked if she would like a smoke. She agreed, and before dawn, they were naked beside each other in her soiled sheets. They never spoke of the night ever again. Amara never pried. When she first felt her stomach contort into knots in Butler Library, she thought it was indigestion from another greasy quesadilla, but the pain persisted for a week. Her period hadn't arrived in months, but even with the pill, her cycle had always been erratic. Yet her sense of smell was so acute that the soap on someone's body could make her gag, and she blew her monthly allowance on food in a week and a half. She bought three pregnancy tests down in Kips Bay, where no one would recognize her, and took each one in a Murray Hill theater bathroom stall. All came out positive. A doctor at a Washington Heights birth clinic where she booked an appointment under a pseudonym confirmed the pregnancy at eight weeks exactly. This wasn't supposed to happen to her. But she didn't want to get an abortion, for who would go with her, a friend? And could that friend keep a secret for the rest of their lives?

From the time of that doctor visit to days after Laila's arrival, Amara tried all kinds of abortifacients. She took a bath with boiling-hot water and removed herself from the tub with nothing but peeled, reddish skin to show for it. Not even three cups of St. John's wort tea did the trick. The consumption incapacitated her, leaving her dizzy and sensitive to any light. Then the flutters in her belly came—sometimes while she brushed her teeth, sometimes when she touched a side of her stomach, and most times when she lay down at night. Once the flutters came, she stopped trying. The movement in her belly meant that there was actually something there, and once she was mindful of a potential person growing inside her body, she didn't want to get an abortion. But there was no way that she could be a mother. Especially not now. She knew how each of her family members would react: Laila would kill her. Her mother wouldn't speak to her. Her child was the cruelest of ironies. Amara wished that she could swap bodies with her aunt to give her what could have been a blessing in different circumstances.

There wasn't much time. At five-foot-eight and 135 pounds, she would show soon, and it was dangerous to confide in anyone at school about her pregnancy. Her mom was too preoccupied with Laila and her healing to take on any other stressors. Landon was the only option. They arranged a time to meet in the basement of St. Philip's Church, where the acoustics were shabby and neither of their voices could travel. Ironically, her privacy was ruined almost immediately after Amara entered the church because she missed a step on the stairs, fell down the rest, and landed on her stomach. A searing pain rippled throughout her body, but it also occurred to her that an accident would do away with the problem. She groaned as she stood to her feet and patted her backside to feel any wetness there or between her thighs, but there was nothing. That was a hard fall, and the smack echoed from one wall to the other. Her legs and arms hurt. Her head definitely hurt. But in her abdomen she only felt a slight burn from the friction of the carpet at the bottom—not from the fall itself. Confounded, Amara stood up straight with her jaw hanging while Landon came running over to her.

"What happened?"

"I fell, but I'm okay. Really I am."

"You sure? You got a knot forming on your forehead. Let me get you an ice pack."

Amara leaned on Landon to walk to the kitchen in the basement and her protruding belly brushed against him. He halted, grabbed both of her arms, and scrutinized her. He placed a hand over her belly, and his eyes bulged.

"Don't say it. Just don't."

"How far?"

"Four."

"Four? We have to take you to a doctor."

"No!" Amara lowered her voice. "No. No doctors. I can't. Nobody can know."

"Let me see your stomach."

Amara lifted her shirt to reveal her round, brown belly. She'd fallen hard on her stomach, and there were no scars, no nicks, and not even a hint of redness. Throughout the course of their conversation, Landon looked at her belly, and the skin remained unscathed. The only bruises were on her forehead and elbows. The fact that she could stand to her feet without bleeding or cramping was an oddity alone.

"Go home and keep yourself covered with layers. I will call you within the next two days."

"Are you going to help me?"

"Yes. This conversation never happened. Agreed?"

"Agreed."

Later that night, Landon tucked his three children into bed and kissed his wife, Valerie, on the lips. She had known about his five-years-long affair with Josephine Melancon and regretted the day when her absence provided the opening for another woman to insert herself into his life. At the time, Landon was dissatisfied with his work as a trader on Wall Street. Since he'd survived the recession a few years before, he thought he might be up for a promotion and more perks. The Thomases weren't hurting for cash. In fact, they intended on buying a nice home, and they had their eyes set on the Melancons', even though it wasn't for sale. He knew from his days down in the Financial District that anyone could be convinced for the right price. Valerie was on her way back from visiting her folks in New Haven, but there were massive delays on the Metro North and she told Landon to visit the home without her and they'd talk about what he thought later.

When he first laid eyes on Josephine, he forgot the goal of his visit or all the events of the day that preceded this meeting. Her beauty disrupted time, and her presence marked an instant epoch. There were only two periods: before and after Josephine, and he refused to think about a life beyond that moment that did not include her. She entertained him in the dining room, and when Maman joined them, she immediately saw the attraction that they harbored toward each other. She extracted whatever information she could about him: his family life, his profession, and his earnings. He left the Melancon brownstone with a rejection of his offer on the home, but he returned home with an even greater prize: the potential love of Josephine and a return offer to be a part of their caulbearing business as an intermediary (since he already had the connections via Wall Street and he wasn't funny-acting around big money). They'd never employed a point person before, and his inclusion in the business would outsource the work of recruiting clients and help with their physical safety. So Landon decided to work for the Melancon women on the side while continuing his Wall Street career.

At first, Valerie hated the affair and how much light Landon carried in his eyes for another woman, but the money funneling through the Melancon enterprise to their joint bank accounts was of an abundance so sweet that silence was the best option. Besides, she had been a housewife for most of their marriage and she didn't want to enter the workforce again. But she would not allow him to kiss her after he returned, out of basic respect. He would need to cleanse his body with scalding-hot water while reciting a medley of verses from Song of Songs and First Corinthians and spend the remainder of the night sleeping downstairs before the children woke up as a mutually agreed-upon purification process, a commitment to which he was always faithful.

The night following his and Amara's meeting in the St. Philip's basement, Landon was uncharacteristically jolly. Valerie watched him from her side of the bed, dressed in off-color flannel pants, with a copy of a novel called *Baby of the Family* tucked underneath her right armpit. She lowered her reading glasses and monitored the spiritedness of him fastening his tie, the subtle smiles in between fastening his belt bucket and securing his cuff links. Once he began humming a little ditty, she placed her book on the nightstand and crossed her arms over her chest.

"I know where you're going, and the least you can do is not act excited in front of my face."

"Huh?" Landon looked at Valerie through their freestanding mirror.

"'Huh?'" Valerie mimicked him.

"I'm not happy about her or that."

"Oh? Is there another woman I need to know about? Only novelty can make a man that excited."

Landon sat on the edge of the bed and placed her feet on his lap. "There may be a new revenue stream coming through here in a matter of months."

"From where?"

"You just have to trust me. I'm on my way to Josephine's. I don't intend on being long."

"Sure," she said sarcastically. "Seems like y'all have a lot to talk about, especially since Laila tried to confront her. You check up on her?"

"Denise is not allowing anyone to see her. I can send flowers from the church, and when the time comes, I'll pray over her."

Valerie sighed. "I was there in the crowd when she lost her mind outside the Melancons'. I couldn't stop replaying the image of her crying and snotting and bleeding. Came home that night and got my period early. You have to make sure that she doesn't keep talking about the Melancon family, what they do, and what we do. It could hurt the business."

"She won't. I don't think Laila's going to be leaving Denise's apartment any time soon. Everybody knows her husband left her and her own place is all burned up. She's got nothing but her grief."

"She better not say anything."

Landon leaned over and kissed Valerie on the lips. Her breath always smelled slightly acidic, like citrus wine with a hint of dairy.

Valerie's scent was purposeful; she knew that when Landon would later go to kiss Josephine, she'd detect the smell and be reminded of which woman came first.

His routine was simple yet highly refined over time. He never wore his shoes while walking down the steps to avoid making noise and waking the children. He wore a Knicks hat, tattered sneakers, and a long trench coat. A driver was scheduled to be at the corner of the block where the Thomases lived at eight forty-five p.m. sharp. He would be dropped off at the corner of Frederick Douglass Boulevard, and on the nights when Josephine was expecting him, the porch light would be kept off.

The brownstone always smelled of rose and mandarin when Landon came. Maman abhorred the aroma, a conspicuous seduction tactic that led to sex, though Landon and Josephine's sex never led to children. She abhorred magazines and television just as much, but these were the tools God had given her to distract herself. She rolled her eyes and made herself comfortable.

This time, though, Josephine didn't greet him at the door or hold his hand as they tiptoed up the stairs like they had always done in the past. He went up the steps to her bedroom and knocked on the door. There was a long pause before Josephine opened the door in a slip and pulled him inside her room. Within a matter of minutes, there was a blur of naked, sweaty bodies, dangling rosary beads that swayed on the nightstand every time the headboard moved, and six dove pendants placed in no particular design on the ceiling. When it was done, Josephine did what she always did: she cried while sitting at her vanity mirror and wiping in between her thighs with a rag. In the midst of her sadness, Landon admired her beauty, the way her coily hair fell lopsided to one side of her head, the discoloration on the back of her neck, her almond-shaped eyes. The candles that would burn in her bedroom softened her. The incandescence made him feel like he was eavesdropping on some ritual that any other man would be forbidden to see and he felt not only lucky but also chosen. There was scut-scut-scuttling on the windowpane that an unseasoned New Yorker might take to be mice in the walls. But it was only the initial outbreak of drizzle.

What spoiled this scene were the shadows on the opposite wall. There were three: his, Josephine's, and some amorphous figure hanging over Josephine's body. He checked to his side and behind him, but there was nothing there. He jumped at the prickling sensation of something touching the nape of his neck, but again, nothing was there. And then he noted the holes in the ceiling that seemed bigger from the last time he visited and the chipped cream wallpaper that decayed into a fecal brown.

"You don't have to do that, you know."

"What?"

"That."

She scoffed. "I'm allowed to mourn, aren't I?"

Landon sighed. "Look, Josephine, we can keep trying if—"

"No, no. I mean. It's less about me this time. It's—"

"Laila again?"

Josephine sighed. "I'm sorry. I thought I'd be over it by now, but I'm not. I feel for her because I know what it's like. We know what it's like." Josephine placed a hand on her table and dropped her head. "Can I admit something to you?"

"Sure."

"I tried as best I could to convince Maman to go through with the deal. We all know Iris is a little touched. That don't mean what she says doesn't come true. When you left with Laila, she just kept saying, 'The brownstone will cave in from that woman. The brownstone will cave in from that woman.' And you know the police been watching the bodega ever since . . . the incident. I can hardly speak or think about it; it's too traumatizing. We can't be too certain, even if I know in my heart she wasn't some kind of mole and it wasn't a setup 'cause of you. It's like . . . we wanted that baby to die because we thought that if we gave her that caul and the baby lived, it would only mean trouble for us. It doesn't even make sense, but Maman refused to hear anything different. Besides, you and I keep having miscarriage after miscarriage. My child was supposed to be the successor in this family, since I'm firstborn. And I failed. I disappointed Maman and myself."

"Jo—"

"No. We're of no use to each other. That's why I sit by this here vanity mirror and cry after we make love. It's the least I can do." Josephine patted at the sides of her eyes with an embroidered handkerchief. "Don't try to console me. I won't have any of it."

"I wasn't going to."

"You know the part that hurts me even more? Is that you never cried for any of the losses I had."

"I wanted to be strong for you."

"And the way that Laila was crying. I almost jumped outside of myself. I wanted to console her and bring her inside. I wanted to say I was sorry, but I couldn't. She's not the first woman, you know. She's not the first woman to leave a baby by the doorstep. We've denied others before. Only difference this time is that she had a crowd with her. I've seen so many losses both inside and outside of this door that I see them in my sleep. I almost feel like Iris, and I can see them in the mirror when I'm brushing my teeth every morning or they're floating at the end of the staircase, and I have to hold on to the bannister so that I don't fall down and break my neck. Sometimes"—Josephine grabbed her throat with her right hand—"I feel like I'm suffocating in here. You got your wife and your children. What do I have? Besides the life I observe passing to and from the doors when I check in on the bodega, making sure everything runs smoothly, I have nothing. At least if I have a child, I got someone to love, someone to call my own, and I can ease Maman's fears that her legacy won't be for nothing." She paused. "I'd be able to take a good breath every once in a while."

"You may be able to soon."

"What?"

"I know a girl. She's pregnant and she has too much of a life to look forward to to have a baby right now. It'll all be under wraps to protect her future. She's not giving birth in the hospital, so there will be no record there."

"We've been over this, Landon. My child needs to have a caul."

"The caul protects people from harm, yes? Those who have it are impervious to it, yes?" He moved to the other side of the bed closest to her. "The girl fell down the steps, on her stomach, and nothing was wrong with her. No bruises, no redness, no scars, nothing. She walked out of there like she hadn't fallen at all. Even after she left, she told me there was no bleeding. I gave her money to go to a clinic under a pseudonym. The technician did an ultrasound and the baby was all clear. Heartbeat strong and all. I've never seen anything like it. If that baby was unharmed, then there's a chance that it's a caul that's protecting it."

"Hmph. Stranger things have happened."

"Have you heard of any pregnant woman falling on her stomach and neither her nor the baby being injured in some kind of way?"

Josephine paused then sighed. "No. No, I haven't. Is her mother a caulbearer?"

"No."

"Hmm," Josephine said.

"What is it?"

"She has to be a carrier if that child is born with a caul. Maybe someone in her family, generations ago, was a carrier or a caulbearer too. It can happen, so I've heard. But that's if—and I mean if—this baby she's carrying has it."

"Do not say anything to Maman. She'll worry you even more."

"There's nothing to say to her. If Maman can't see it, then she doesn't believe it."

"She'll believe it. She will."

Amara felt stuck. Her aunt Laila's cries were bleeding through the walls every night. Her mother, Denise, was either weeping or playing cabaret songs as loudly as she could, trying to dissociate herself from the tragedy that had draped over her entire home. Amara sat huddled in a corner in the dark with both hands over her stomach. She used to be afraid to sleep without a night-light, but the pitch black now granted her the peace of disappearing. However, she was not prepared to be this deeply plunged into her most sinister thoughts. A pillow could do, she thought. A gloved hand, a pillow held over Laila's face, her convulsing body slowly falling limp. Or she could stab her—put her out of her misery—but she did not trust herself to thrust hard enough into an artery or major organ, not while watching the light shrink from her aunt's eyes. She didn't hate her aunt Laila. She hated what her aunt Laila was enduring. The miscarriages were one thing, her stillborn baby—who could've been a bundle of joy had the Melancon women helped—wholly another.

Amara had heard of the power of the caul but thought it was a superstition that became real to some people when they were struggling with an illness or needed protection of some other kind. Now, it didn't matter if she believed the caul was real or not. She wanted this belief to be extinguished as quickly as possible and questioned why no authorities had ever infiltrated and shut the Melancons down. No, they weren't prostituting, technically, but they were selling their bodies. Someone had to do something about it. Being a lawyer was her dream, but maybe she needed to be more specific. She wanted them to be punished to the fullest extent of the law. Her murky cloud of a dream suddenly transformed into the sharp, narrowed end of a lightning bolt. But first, she had to deal with her little problem down below, and the more hours that passed, the more she grew antsy, until by the next morning she thought Landon had forgotten all about her.

He phoned her the day after she visited him in the church by saying hello and quickly rattling off instructions: "You're going to pack your clothes and you're going to move in with me until you give birth. You're going to tell your mother that the stress of being at her spot is too much for you. After class, you come straight to my place. After any extracurricular activity, you immediately come home. Do you understand?"

"Yes," Amara said.

The process happened almost too easily. Amara told Denise that she would be going back and forth between campus and Landon's home because Laila was distracting her from concentrating on her studies. Denise didn't put up a fight. Amara called the housing and residential life office to make plans to officially move out of the dorms for the remainder of the year and packed her belongings throughout the afternoon. That evening, a luxury sedan parked outside of her home was waiting for her.

In the weeks that followed, Amara found that Landon was doing more for her than what was initially agreed upon. Both Valerie and Landon were entirely too clingy, barely allowing her to cook over the stove or run errands. If they were in the midst of a conversation and Amara entered the room, they immediately stopped and bombarded her with questions: How was she feeling? Did she need anything? Had she taken her prenatal vitamins? She never remembered them being this doting even when she was a child, as they would pick her up every other week to do some kind of museum or ice cream outing.

As the months progressed, Amara found simple tasks, such as walking down the stairs and reaching for teacups in high cabinets, extremely difficult. Her feet had swollen to the thickness of gourds, and she could not see them unless they were propped up on a pillow or on the arms of a sofa chair. Her body seemed ill-fit to carry the child much longer. Her long stretch marks bore the strain of her skin overextending itself to cover a baby. If she ran her fingers along one of them, she could feel the heat and the depth of its jagged lengths, an indication of how hard her body was working for her. Fortunately, she had no morning sickness, light-headedness, or mood swings. She wasn't particularly large either. A shirt or dress twice her size could hide her belly. All the classes she picked for the fall semester—which coincidentally fell during her third trimester—were lectures where she could sit far in the back where no one could see her. Amara and Denise would call each other every week and she would bite down on her bottom lip to refrain from telling her everything. Denise would often tell Amara how much she missed her but thought it was best to give her daughter her space and wait till Amara said she wanted her around without asking the question of when.

All Saints' Day was approaching, and she could not be a part of St. Philip's altar guild this year to help arrange the flowers in the sanctuary to commemorate the souls of those who had transitioned. When she asked if it was okay to stay home, Landon nodded and asked if she would like any Earl Grey tea. The end to all of this could not have come soon enough.

It was Halloween and there would be an All Hallows' Eve service for all parishioners. Amara woke up that morning feeling as if she had just lain down after spinning around and around on a grassy knoll. This was a service to remember the dead, and many people would be wearing black and their eyes would be closed in contemplative silence; she would sneak in through the back because she never missed this holiday. But she could not move from the bed. On the day of service, she pulled back the covers and the entire lower half of her body was wet. Any time she made a movement, there was an accompanying squishing sound. She didn't remember when last she peed the bed and was repulsed that she had that much liquid stored inside of her and didn't feel any of it expelling. Putting two and two together, Amara yelled for Landon, who hurtled into the bedroom, both hands curled into fists. As soon as he saw the huge wet circle in the center of the bedsheets, he called for the doula, a legally blind Afro-Cuban woman by the name of Melinda, who delivered every baby to come out of the Thomas family home. She could see only twenty feet in front of her, but that was all she needed to do her job.

Melinda stood at five feet, but the strength of her voice and the distance it traveled could rival that of a man twice her size. When Melinda's body moved to the left, her behind swayed in the opposite direction. Her reddish-brown skin was a testament to her Taino heritage, her thick hair and nose from her Yoruba bloodline. She wore an *eleke* of alternating crystal and royal-blue beads and a muumuu to match. To assuage Landon, she placed a Bible on the nightstand and kept it open to the book of Matthew. "Both Jesus and Yemoja are here." She cackled and patted Landon on the back before using that same hand to nudge him out the door.

"How many months are you?" Melinda asked.

"Eight and a half," Amara answered.

Without warning or narration, Melinda pulled up a stool in front of Amara, parted her knees, and stuck three fingers in her until she felt a soft, wet rind and grinned.

"You're already dilating. Good. How are you feeling?"

Sweat glistened on Amara's forehead and slicked the hairs to the sides of her face. She gritted her teeth and bit down on her lip, focusing on what, she could not say. The instinct to pull herself together and keep firm as her body was dividing exacerbated the pain.

"Hey!" Melinda clapped her hands simultaneously. "I need you to focus, okay? But I don't need you to be scared. Your body is going to do exactly what needs to be done. Do you understand?"

Amara nodded.

"How old are you? You seem young."

"Old enough."

"Hmph. You're very young, then. I'm impressed you chose to go outside of the hospitals for this. A lot of them are death traps anyway." She massaged Amara's thighs and continued, "But don't let me scare you. You're doing great. Are you stressed at all?"

"How can I not be?"

"Give me your hands." Amara placed her hands in Melinda's palms, and Melinda cupped them and gently tugged forward until both hands were underneath her breasts. "Remember, your body is going to do exactly what it needs to do." No sooner did Melinda continue to reach her hand deep into her sex than Amara felt another contraction coming on and clenched.

"No, no, no, don't do that! Don't grit your teeth. Let it out."

"I can't do that."

"Why?"

Amara looked out the windows. The sun was beginning to set. More people would be out in the streets as they returned home from work.

"I just can't, okay?" Amara snapped.

"Then I need for you to focus on your breathing. Don't hold it in. Keep pushing it out. Try with me." Melinda poked out her chest as she inhaled then made an oval shape with her arms to accentuate the exhale. "Again. Again." This was a birth like no other for Melinda. In her experience, the laboring processes were always filled with laughter and light and music, not dimness, silence, and solemnity. Melinda looked underneath the sheet draped over Amara's legs. The gaping sight made her immediately roll back her sleeves and tuck any flyaway strands of hair behind her ears.

Amara got on all fours and started to grunt. The pain created comets and balls of fire out of the darkness. The bedroom walls were closing in on her, and Melinda's body ballooned. Amara felt so small and vulnerable, but her body was reacting at a speed quicker than her mind could process. Every part of her was on the verge of exploding, and she began to panic.

A gasp. A large splash. As Melinda was pulling the baby out from between Amara's thighs, Amara closed her eyes so as not to form a bond. With soft weeping and a cracked voice, Melinda congratulated Amara and extended her arms toward the child. Her fingers grazed over the baby, and her smile flattened. A transparent, plastic-like sac veiled the baby's body, which was still curled into a ball. Its face was pressed against one side of the sac. A surreal portrait, the baby was peaceful within that sac, calmly opening and closing its eyes. Melinda called for Landon to come quickly. He opened the door and his prediction was confirmed. The baby was indeed born of the caul. The flicker in Landon's eyes and his deep-set grin unsettled Melinda, and she nestled the baby closer to her breasts.

"Let me hold her," Landon said.

"The new mother should hold her baby before you," Melinda quipped, and turned her nose up at him.

"I don't want to hold it."

Melinda's jaw dropped. "Don't you want to at least—"

"Do not pressure her, Melinda. Now give it here."

Melinda pulled away and walked closer to Amara's side. "Sweetie, do you want to at least give her a name?"

"Her?"

"Yes." Melinda inched closer with the baby and leaned in toward her. "A girl. Give her a strong name. A difficult name. Not one that's too easy on the tongue. This baby's special."

Amara took a beat, heard the sounds of chattering trick-or-treaters outside, and said, "Hallow. Call her Hallow."

Hallow. Hal-low. The high and the low. All Hallows' Eve. A night for sainted souls. A night for a new birth. Halloween. Hallowed be thy name. Make her holy. Make her sanctified. Make her loved.

"Hallow," Melinda repeated. She made the sign of the cross over the child's body. "Maferefun Yemoja." She glared at Landon, who was delirious with glee over the baby, and then at Amara, who was still on all fours, her sweaty hair over her face, shuddering. Melinda wasn't sure what she had gotten herself into on this night. None of the other births were like this. She couldn't quite place why, but the translucent beads of her *eleke* became clouded, and that was enough for her to gather her things. "I should be going now." She took one last look at Amara and placed a hand over her chest before leaving.

"I'll have Valerie clean you. You don't worry about a thing. You're going to get well. You're going to do well in school and you're going to be what you always dreamed of. Everything is still going according to plan."

"Is she alive?"

"What?"

"Is she alive? I haven't heard her cry."

"Yes, she's alive."

"Then why didn't she cry?"

Landon thumbed Hallow's caul and said, "Because she knows exactly where she is. She's at peace." He covered Hallow with his trench coat and called Josephine. She had been waiting since the early morning for any updates and tried her best to extract any information out of him. He would not budge. He only told her to bring everyone down into the dining room, and that he would be over soon.

3

Maman had been crunching numbers in the crook of her office all day long. Her eyes were not what they'd once been, and there were always miscalculations somewhere, even with the help of her bifocals and megawatt overhead light bulbs. Long passages of notes were strewn across her cherrywood desk. Crumpled pieces of paper overflowed the waste bin near her feet. The B.B. King that crooned from her vinyl record player, usually a balm to her anxieties, made her back tense up and her knuckles flare. Maybe, she thought, in hindsight, she should have ignored Iris's premonition and taken Laila's money. Three thousand would've fixed the living room fireplace. Five thousand would've covered Josephine's wardrobe expenses. There just wasn't enough to maintain their lifestyle and clean the money they received from selling their caul by mixing it with the profits from the bodega. Maybe Maman should have pitied Laila, like the olden days, when the Melancon family migrated to Harlem from Cloutierville.

A small town situated near Bayou Camitte and Cane River, Cloutierville is said to have the biggest and foremost community of caulbearers in the country. The story passed down between families is that French sailors would buy pieces of caul from lovers or street vendors and wear them around their necks before embarking on the long journey to the West African coastlines and then to the Atlantic Ocean en route to the Americas. Unbeknownst to these sailors, some of the enslaved persons chained in the belly of those ships possessed spiritual and magical talents. When they landed in New Orleans, their relations with one another and with the Choctaw Indians produced caulbearing Creole families, who married and mated within their own separate communities. Once Louisiana became a part of the United States and people who lived within the colonies infiltrated these communities, some caulbearers married these newcomers until the former group became a minority—albeit powerful, and therefore threatening. Only women could be caulbearers. Though most stayed alive well past their centennial year to watch their descendants grow, their deaths were voluntary. Caulbearers were immortal under one condition: they could not be stripped entirely of their caul. Most stayed alive well into their hundreds, so stories began to circulate that caulbearers were found stark naked in the bodies of Lake Pontchartrain and Cane River, or buried in some unmarked lot in Isle Brevelle. Days after their disappearance, people would be walking around with cauls adorning their necks.

It was Maman's great-great-grandmother who thought it was best that they sell themselves before anybody killed them for what they had. She noticed that as children progressed through puberty, they would grow taller and the caul would grow with them, covering their bodies, leading her to believe that it would regenerate on its own until they turned twenty-one. At that time, the caul would get harder to sever, like cutting through the head of a cabbage. Maman's great-great-grandmother went back to the bodies of the caulbearing women who were slain and saw that not only had their bodies been stripped of their cauls, but their skin had harsh cuts and bruises. She ruminated for days over what it meant until she witnessed a caulbearing child who shrieked in pain in an open field after a dog bit into her and ran away with a bit of the caul caught in its mouth. The girl's caul never regenerated, and that's when Maman's great-great-grandmother knew two things: if a caulbearer was entirely stripped, she'd die, and if her caul was torn in a violent way, she would not be able to heal herself and the regenerative power would be gone.

She proposed that this network of caulbearers sell small bits of their cauls to anyone who wanted it as a means of survival. By the time that their communities had been infiltrated, there were families full of siblings who were both caulbearing and ordinary. Those who had the caul would be cut, and those who were ordinary would handle more administrative functions: selling and procuring deals. In a few decades, they needed that business to migrate out of Louisiana elsewhere, to untapped markets.

"Maman!" Josephine burst through the door, panting and wiping her forehead.

Maman lowered her bifocals and twisted her body around to face Josephine. "Don't you know that it's inappropriate to enter a room without knocking?"

Josephine abruptly stopped her panting and held on to the doorknob to steady herself.

"Do you hear me when I'm talking to you? I'm asking you a question."

"Yes, Maman."

"Then why did you do it?" Before Josephine could get a word in, Maman scoffed. "Forty-two years old and I still have to correct you like you're Helena's age. Well, now that you've interrupted me, what?" Maman dropped her pen and crossed her arms over her chest.

"She's here."

"Be specific, Josephine." She made a circular motion with her right hand midair to encourage her daughter to hurry it up.

"Your new granddaughter."

Maman patted the sides of her burgundy turban and stood up. Maman's rise to her feet never failed to spur Josephine to take a step backward and avert her eyes. The floor always creaked, and whichever room they were in always got a bit darker, for Maman's shadow would eclipse Josephine's body.

"Are you going to stop blocking the door or are you going to move out of the way and let me perform my duties as the mistress of this abode?"

"Oh. Right. Sorry." Josephine stepped aside with her head down. As Maman walked past Josephine, she scoffed and shook her head before venturing into the corridor.

Landon was holding a sleeping Hallow in his arms in the dining room. Five-year-old Helena, who was covered in bandages on her arms and legs, screamed whenever Iris drew near to her and limped over to Josephine for safety. But Helena sensed something different in her aunt's gaze, an excitement that she had never drawn out of Josephine. When Maman entered the room, she grinned at the sight of Landon holding the child, the translucence of her caul sparkling in the light.

"Boil some water and bring me my utility knife." Maman spoke with her chin hovering over her right shoulder. Whenever a caul-bearer is born, part of the caul must be steeped in tea, which the child must consume, or else she will be assailed with visions of both past and future along with the persistent voices of ghosts, which is what happened to Iris.

Josephine hurried into the kitchen and Maman approached

Hallow, pulling the cover back from her body. "Did anyone see you?" Maman asked as she stroked Hallow's head and arms.

"No one."

"You sure?"

"Yes."

"The mother. Is she a caulbearer too?"

"No."

"What about her immediate family—the grandmother, aunt?"

"None are."

She did a double take at Landon. "Interesting. It's rare to have only one caulbearer in an immediate family. Very rare indeed. Must be somewhere down the line but very, very rare."

Josephine returned from the kitchen with the knife, and Maman snatched it from her hands, causing Josephine to retreat to a back corner to watch.

Maman spread the cover on the dining room table and placed Hallow on top of it. She scrutinized the newborn's entire body, turning her over, to the side, peeking underneath her arms, and in between her small legs. Hallow began to fuss. Maman moved quickly, raising the utility knife in the air and inspecting it to confirm that its point would shine. That shine could sting the eyes when it was directly placed under the light. Landon focused to remain stoic. The vast wrinkles like river streams webbed from Maman's eyes, multiplied throughout her neck, and coursed through her arms and hands. The caul was a thin layer above the epidermis. One incorrect movement, one misstep in coordination, could affect future measurements of strips that could later be sold. Maman placed the tip of the knife in the middle of Hallow's forehead and then carved around the nostrils. The sound of the incision was akin to slicing through a gelatin dessert. Next, Maman had to delicately cut the part in her lips, ears, the hair, the spaces in between her fingers and toes, legs, vulva. Maman cupped some boiling water into her hands, and Josephine and Landon immediately averted their eyes from what was to come. She splattered the boiling water onto Hallow's body and the baby wailed as Maman pressed the caul firmly into the skin so that it would remain attached.

The caul from Hallow's face was then steeped into the remaining boiling water in which lavender, half a banana, and milk were the additives.

"Have you named her?" Maman spiritedly asked.

"Hallow is her name."

"Hallowed be thy name," Maman said reverently. She stroked Hallow's chin and clicked her tongue at her. "Yes, we'll keep that name."

The caul tea cooled in a small bottle, and Maman motioned for Josephine to give it to Hallow.

"Me?" Josephine asked, pointing at herself.

"She's yours to raise, and when she gets older, you'll homeschool her just like you do Helena. Treat her as if she were your own daughter."

Josephine and Landon locked eyes and inched toward Hallow. Josephine outstretched her arms and cradled Hallow, who shifted in her sleep to find the most comfortable position. She held the bottle to Hallow's lips and exhaled when the child began to suck. "Hallow," Josephine repeated. She quickly wiped the tears from her eyes so that nothing could obstruct the view of what she always wanted.

Josephine cradled and rocked Hallow from side to side, and everyone filed out of the dining room except Helena, whose own world as she once knew it was subverted. Helena used to be the miracle child. Before she was born, Iris used to harness her intuitive

gifts by practicing as a medium, setting up a shop near their bodega to keep her occupied. Until one day she turned up pregnant
like a stray dog. Didn't say nothing about the father. Joked about
the spirits impregnating her, since they hadn't left her side since she
was born. When Maman was in labor with Iris, there was a hurri-
cane, and its warpath wiped out the gas and electric. It wasn't until
days later, as Maman remained in a hallucinogenic-daze from birth,
that she realized she had forgotten to boil some of Iris's caul for her
daughter to drink in order to keep the spirits away, causing her to be
touched for the rest of her life.

The stress that Maman endured over whether or not Helena
would be a caulbearer was so intense that she lost all her hair. It
grew back in short stubs, and only after Helena was born, forcing
Maman—a woman unaccustomed to ever feeling forced to do
anything—to wear turbans for the rest of her days. When Helena
was born with that veil over her body, she was spoiled and deified—
though confined to the brownstone—until the accident happened.

Unlike Maman, Iris didn't want Helena to be a caulbearer. She
wanted her child to be free, even if she had to put the wheels in motion herself. Maman used to take afternoon naps around the same
time that she concluded her lunch: one thirty p.m. One day around
quarter to two, Iris lured Helena outside and took her to the Bronx
Zoo. The crowds and the abundance of animals distracted Helena
at every turn. So much in fact that when she looked up to ask her
mother if it was okay to feed the penguins, Iris was already en route
back to Harlem, and she continued to smack her face so that she
would not cry. Hopefully, Iris thought, another family would see
Helena by herself and take her with them. Any alternative would
be better than the environment she'd grown up in. And at the very
least, Iris had a photo of Helena to immortalize their last moment
together. She had captured the image with a Polaroid camera while

Helena was busy learning about the different species of birds, and it would now be the last snapshot she had of her.

When Iris arrived home, Maman shook her into a concussion over where she'd gone and what had happened to Helena. "I lost her," Iris said, and then she was slapped onto the floor. Josephine tried and failed to break up the fight between Maman and Iris, and soon all three women were wrestling on the ground until they got tired.

The phone rang. A nurse from Bronx-Lebanon Hospital urged the Melancon women to come immediately. Helena had been found wounded. After Iris disappeared, Helena searched high and low, and in her searching, she stumbled into an enclosed gorilla pit. She was dragged across the dirt, the gorilla biting her and whipping her tiny body around like a rag doll until keepers were able to tranquilize it. Helena suffered lacerations all over her body that required stitches. Her time as a viable—and sellable—caulbearer was all but over. According to the doctors, any lesser child would have died from the sustained injuries. The Bronx Zoo's board of directors and the Melancon women did not want this accident to get out to the press because both parties wanted to maintain privacy. To settle the score, Maman negotiated a seven-figure deal (compensation for what Helena could've acquired from caul selling) in exchange for not pressing charges. As Helena healed from home in the bandages and gauze pads that Josephine changed on the hour every hour, Maman barely acknowledged her, often walking past and harrumphing, seldom showing any affection. Helena was now in a unique position, both familiar and unusual—a member of the family and a pariah just like her mother, who conversely became more affectionate than ever before.

On the night that Hallow arrived, this new young girl whose name began with the same letter as hers, Helena felt another layer of abandonment that inflated into anger. It was a kind of anger she had not the faintest idea how to restrain. For the days and weeks that followed, her tantrums were long and distressing. She cried until her voice gave out and her face remained red and inflamed for hours. If someone shook her, she spasmodically blinked and swiveled her head around the room as if a force had relinquished its hold over her. Then she cried some more when she saw how angry Josephine got with her petulance. On late nights, Iris and Josephine would talk about Helena; they believed that all of this was due to envy of Hallow and, eventually, Helena would grow out of it. But the anger grew to be too much fun. This was not a phase but the essence of her personality itself, swallowing every other good trait about her and strengthening the rage. And once Hallow became old enough and Helena got out of her bandages, Helena had plans for her new cousin.

4

After Hallow's birth, Amara's room was deafeningly quiet. Valerie cleaned her up and ushered her back into bed without saying a word. The Thomas children were shushed if they so much as walked too loudly in the second-floor hallway. She lay there on her back in the dark, where only a sliver of moonlight permeated through window blinds, and she wished that someone—anyone—would disrupt the stillness to ask her if she was okay. She was sore everywhere from the waist down. She was exhausted but could not sleep. Every time Amara twisted and turned in her bed, she had to remind herself of what just happened, because the sequence of events passed so quickly: her water breaking, Melinda coming in, the pain, the screaming, the shooting stars, the birth. She thought she would have labored for several hours at the very least, but everything was done in under two. Maybe, Amara thought, it was a mistake not to look her child in the face, because now all she was left with was a primal feeling in the gorging of her breasts, the bleeding in her thick compression underwear, and the bloated belly.

The feeling overpowered every groove in her body and strained every nerve in her head.

The mornings were the worst. If she had the strength to make it down the stairs, she would have breakfast with the family, where everyone would engage in conversation about school, housework, and the front page of the daily paper while she sat there, food in hand, without so much as being spoken to beyond a "Good morning" and a "Can you scoot over?" Then everyone would go their separate ways once they walked through the front door, and she would take her time finishing her breakfast because the trek back upstairs would be long and excruciating.

Other times, she would sit in the living room (where Landon would regularly create a makeshift bed, much to Amara's confusion) and watch a little television, but loneliness met her there. If Amara so much as heard a sound effect of a crying baby on a sitcom or saw a baby in a commercial, she leaked milk. If she saw Valerie show any pronounced affection to her children or husband, like a lingering hug, doting eyes, or sweet compliments, she leaked milk. She leaked and leaked until she was always wet in the chest and sour in scent. The moments when she wasn't leaking were painful, and her breasts swelled and swelled with no baby to relieve her of the burden. In the shower, she would gently press down on her breasts to squirt some milk, which would then spiral down the drain. She wondered if Hallow was overworking her small mouth trying to suckle with not a breast in sight, all the while her milk was going to waste. But the plan had gone off without a hitch. She could return to the life she had before her pregnancy and carry on as if nothing had happened.

When her belly had finally shrunk back to its original state, about a month and a half later, Amara went to her mother's one Saturday afternoon unannounced, with all of her clothes stuffed in duffel bags. She left without telling either Landon or Valerie anything (and had no intention of talking to them for quite some time). She found the opportune moment to leave when the family decided to visit the Met. When Denise opened the door, her eyes grew wide and spit got caught in her throat, removing her ability to speak. They'd hardly spoken once Amara left; their conversations never extended further than a greeting, a "How are you?," then a one-sentence answer before Amara had to go. Denise quickly pulled Amara into her chest and kissed all around her forehead. Amara prayed that she would not leak through the three layers of shirts and two bras that she wore. They went inside the apartment, and Amara jumped at the sound of things dropping onto the hardwood floor upstairs. Concerned, she looked over at Denise, who said, "Come into the kitchen, and I'll explain everything."

There, as Denise pulled out bread, turkey, cheese, and bacon for both of them, she said, "Laila likes to throw things from time to time, and I let her, as long as it ain't sharp. Most of it is plastic, but she's got the arm power of an Olympic javelin thrower."

"How long she been throwing stuff?"

"Since . . . hell. Since she came back from the hospital. Didn't take them long to diagnose her with postpartum depression and bipolar disorder. But I'll never forget what she told me after she calmed down: She was gonna give those Melancon women fifteen grand to help her. Fifteen grand. And they told her no. Something about a curse or something happening to their family. I couldn't make it out because she was crying, but I don't get it, Mar. Why wasn't her money good enough? And if they aren't helping people from their own community, then who are they giving their cauls away to?"

Amara stayed silent.

"I can't help but wonder what would've happened if they would've said yes. Would it have changed anything? And at the same damn time, I wish they didn't exist at all. That this whole caul thing wasn't even a factor. Or—or that they could be stopped."

"Have you thought about talking to someone about that?"

"I'm only one person, baby. Those women got a ton of money. I'd drown in legal fees, and even then, what would be the charges? Folk magic?" She laughed. "I don't know the law like that. Look at me just rattling off problem after problem when you just got here."

"If there was a way, legally, for you to go after them, would you do it?"

"In a heartbeat."

"Then I'll find a way."

"Honey, I don't want you to start worrying about us like that. We'll be fine."

"But I'm already studying law. I can do this. I promise I can. Maybe not now. But someday."

"Someday," Denise repeated, and sniffled. "It's so good seeing you here. It's been a long time."

"Sure seems that way, doesn't it?"

"Yeah," Denise said weakly as she slathered mayonnaise on the slices of bread. Amara noticed how her mother's hands trembled while lifting pieces of turkey and provolone onto the bread, and how the sweat beads proliferated around her widow's peak over what should have been a simple task. As Denise walked over to the table with a plate of sandwiches in one hand and a bag of chips in the other, Amara held her breath with the worry that her mother would collapse at any moment.

"You want something to drink? Water?"

Amara nodded.

Denise went to the refrigerator, opened the door, and stared at the interior, her left hand flexing then gripping the door handle. She looked over her shoulder and assured Amara with a smile then brought the pitcher over to the table as well.

"I'll get the cups," Amara said.

"Thank you."

They took bites of their individual sandwiches while stealing glances at each other.

"So," Denise said. "How are you? What's new?"

"Nothing much. Same ol', same ol'. Model UN has been kicking my butt."

"What are you arguing?"

"What?"

"In Model UN. What are you arguing? What are you debating?"

"Well . . ." Amara leaned back in her seat. "It's complicated. It's—deciding whether or not a case was a crime of passion or pre-meditated."

"I see. And how are your classes?"

"Fine. Stress from the papers and exams."

"You said that last time."

"What?"

"I said you said that last time. It's a whole new school year, sweetheart."

"Well, yeah, but—" Amara stammered. "I'm an upperclassman now. It only gets worse before it gets better." Amara shrugged.

"Hmm," Denise replied. She cupped her glass with her shoulders arched then lifted her head to continue. "I know you're not telling me the whole truth, Amara. I know you aren't. And while I won't nag you to death over it, I thought we were closer than that."

"Mom—" Amara's voice cracked because she was fighting back tears.

"Nope." Denise held up her trembling hand. "I'm sorry. The last thing I want to do is guilt-trip. You will come to me when you're ready, and I won't allow it to be a moment sooner. I just had to speak my piece to you as your mother, that's all. I'm just glad you're back. Been lonely without you here."

"I did miss you, Mom. And I shouldn't have left you here with Laila all by yourself."

"Now you're guilt-tripping yourself. You have other things to worry about than being someone's caretaker. That's not what I want for you."

"But what about yourself?"

"What about me? I work and then I come home."

"But, Mom, look at—"

"Look at what? Me? I knew that was coming. I felt your eyes on me when I was making those sandwiches. And since you brought it up, there's no use in me hiding." Denise went to the refrigerator and brought a bottle of wine to the table. Amara watched as Denise downed her glass of water in one continuous gulp before filling that same glass with wine. She took one sip and the tremors in her hand began to subside.

"Do you drink? I may be your mother, but I know you're still a college student."

Amara finished the last bit of water in her glass and pushed it over to her. Taken aback, Denise alternated between pouring and looking up at Amara, whose face could not have been any more pitiful. When her glass was returned to her, Amara started guzzling, and Denise said, "Whoa, slow down. You don't want to down it like that."

"Sorry." Amara wiped her mouth with her sleeve and leaned back in her seat. From over the rim of her glass, Amara saw how Denise's hands were shaking whenever she stopped taking sips of her wine.

Just as Amara was about to ask if her mother was all right, there was a loud thud upstairs and Denise flailed her hands in the air. "I gotta go check on Laila."

She caressed Amara's shoulder as she walked past her to the corridor then pivoted on her heel. "You know, Amara, sometimes you just have to let it out. You've always been a reserved kind of person, but if you don't let out whatever it is you're keeping closed, it will eat you from the inside out and drive you crazy." Another loud thud from upstairs. Denise lifted her head to the ceiling then back down to Amara. "You and I . . . we aren't too far removed from madness."

That last comment motivated Amara to schedule an intake appointment with the university's therapist and thoroughly read and reread the lines that granted her confidentiality. Still, she told her assigned therapist that she had lost her baby through a miscarriage and was relieved that the counselor didn't press any further than that. It became apparent toward the end of her initial fifty-minute appointment that her feeling had a more specific name that would visit her without warning and make itself cozy wherever and however it pleased: grief, or worse—postpartum depression. She left the therapist's office at Alfred Lerner Hall with a suggestion to allow herself time and space to sit with her grief, but whenever the feeling overwhelmed her, she either distracted herself with wine, studying, or both simultaneously. During follow-up appointments, Amara asked for help to maintain the pace at which she thought she needed to be going as she considered what her future would be once she left the gates at 116th and Broadway for good as a new graduate. Then the doctor suggested that she channel her grief into something productive, advice that she knew before the session concluded would be the last she'd hear, because she had no intention of coming back. The doctor wasn't listening to her. Her grades could not have been better, and she'd acquired leadership positions in two of her five extracurricular activities—both law- and politics-related. At the same time, she was aware that she hadn't been entirely forthcoming with the therapist from the beginning.

Once she stepped out of Alfred Lerner Hall after her last session,

Amara descended into the uptown 1 station at 116th and Broadway to refill her MetroCard and head back home. At the machine there was a lady with a sour smell that made Amara's nose itch, shuffling about to find enough change for the machine. The other two machines were out of service, and there was no employee behind the glass to help her complete her purchase. Impatient, Amara shifted her weight from one side to the other and heard an approaching train. The lady with the sour smell looked over her shoulder then stepped aside. Amara saw that she had a newborn strapped to her chest.

"Sorry," the woman said.

"Oh, um, it's okay," Amara said.

"You have a good night." Then she pressed her child closer to her chest and walked the stairs to the street. By the time Amara looked back at the screen, the automatic doors to the train at the platform were closing, and then it pulled away once her now fully loaded MetroCard ejected from the slot. Amara couldn't see another train approaching down the tunnel so she figured she had enough time to buy a quick meal from the convenience store across the street. When she walked through its front doors, she saw the sour lady with the baby from the train station, who seemed to be in the middle of an argument with the cashier.

"I just need some kind of formula, but this is all I have." She dropped two bills and started to count the lint-covered pennies and nickels on the counter when the cashier annoyingly held his hand up and shook his head.

"Why don't you just breastfeed?" he asked flippantly.

"I can't breastfeed. Not every woman can breastfeed." The sour lady's voice kept rising, and the baby was beginning to fuss.

Amara started to leak again. She was hungry, and she only had enough cash to buy herself something and catch the train back uptown. It had been at least two days since she'd had a glass of wine, so the alcohol couldn't ruin her milk, because it was already out of her system. *Perfect*, Amara thought. The pain from her engorged breasts motivated her to barge right into the conversation to ask for a plastic cup and lid and then directions to the nearest bathroom, but he said there wasn't one. She moved to the nearest vacant aisle, walked all the way to the back, stuck the cup underneath her shirt, and pressed as firmly as she could on each side of her breast until her hand got warm from the milk filling up the container. She hurriedly closed the lid over the cup and saw that the sour lady wasn't at the counter anymore.

"Where did she go?" she asked the cashier.

"She just walked out," he replied without so much as lifting his head from an issue of *Maxim*.

Luckily, when Amara exited, she saw the sour lady rocking from side to side to get her baby to relax. She stretched out her hand with the cup and said, "Take it. It might not last till tomorrow, but hopefully it will for tonight."

The woman hesitated. She lifted the lid, sniffed the milk, and looked back up at Amara with tears that glistened underneath the streetlight.

"But don't you need it?"

Amara shook her head. "No."

"Thank you. Thank you. Not easy being a Black mom, you know? But I wouldn't trade it for anything in the world."

Not easy being a Black mom. Amara silently repeated the words. *Not easy being a Black mom.*

Amara returned to the 1 subway station and took the train downtown to Ninety-Sixth, where she switched to the uptown 3 train, getting off at 145th and Malcolm X Boulevard. From there she walked two avenues west to Frederick Douglass Boulevard and stopped at the corner, when her body suddenly seized at the memory. She was reminded of the roars and jeers of the crowd that day, her aunt Laila's mournful cry, the blood. Amara straightened her posture, took a deep breath, and persisted down the quiet block. She was unsure of what her intention was for drawing near to the Melancon home, but their name was the first thing that catapulted to the front of her mind, after that new mother's words.

A child was screaming from inside the brownstone, but her voice was quickly muffled. Amara saw the curtains rustling from the front-facing windows and lifted her head in an attempt to get a closer look, to no avail. She heard the lock being disengaged and ran off to the side, far enough not to look suspicious but still close enough to see who would be coming out of that brownstone. A white couple held hands while descending the porch steps. They giggled excessively like coquettish schoolchildren. The man was holding a small gift box that the woman could not take her eyes off of, and she pressed her fists to his chest, saying, "Oh, please, please. I can't wait. I just cannot. I must have it now."

Amara leaned forward with sweaty palms and armpits. She held her breath and waited.

"All right, all right, darling," the man said, to which his wife joyously clapped her hands together.

When the man faced his wife, Amara could not see what was happening. But in less than a minute, he turned to face the street again and Amara could see a cork-like membrane around her neck. She couldn't parse out all its details, but whatever it was looked thin and light. She released her breath in one sharp gasp once she came to the realization of what it was. "Aunt Lay was right. Aunt Lay was right. Fuck!" Amara said to herself. Now all she could hear were the voices of the new mother from the convenience store and her beloved aunt Laila. It was not easy being a Black mother, and Black mothers were not the Melancon women's clientele. They were too busy serving white people who, by the looks of that man's crisp suit and his wife's wool trench coat and diamond brooch, were well off. She wasn't sure if she was more mad at the bias or the fact that this practice was allowed at all, but nevertheless, she marched straight over to the 32nd Precinct, where every officer was occupied with answering phone calls about some petty crime in one corner of Harlem or a violent crime in another. Papers were flying everywhere, some officers were grumbling under their breath, and the atmosphere carried a heavy scent of ash and powdered donuts.

One burly Black woman with a swagger in her walk and a broad grin was slowly making her way over to her desk with the lightest stack of papers in her hand.

"Hey, excuse me." Amara made a beeline for her and breathed a sigh of relief when the woman stopped. "I have a complaint."

The lady, whose tag said ROBINSON, scoffed. "Chile, everyone has a complaint. But come on, pull up a chair." They sat over at her corner desk, and Amara felt guilty when she saw several other stacks on its surface. Officer Robinson placed her folded hands on one of said stacks and leaned forward. "What's up, sweetheart?"

"Lemme ask you something: You're not allowed to just sell products out of your home, right?"

"There's nothing illegal about being an entrepreneur. People start their own businesses from their kitchens, for God's sake."

"No, no, no, not like that. Not that type of product."

"Drugs?"

"No, I mean . . . people's bodies."

"Prostitution? So it's a brothel."

"No. Well—I—" Amara stopped and took a deep breath. "Can I ask how long you have been working in Harlem?"

"Born and raised. I grew up right around the corner from here."

"So do you know about the Melancon women?"

"Oh boy," Officer Robinson said in a singsong voice then leaned back in her seat.

"What?"

"My advice is to leave it alone. You're in over your head."

"What do you mean?"

"We've been getting complaints from the community for as long as I've been here, and even longer than that. Sometimes you have officers like me who try to help, but it feels like a fool's errand."

"Complaints? So there's more than one?"

"Plenty more. A whole lotta Black women been getting sick, losing babies, and everything—and they blame it all on those Melancons. I don't believe in correlation actually implying causation. But it does make you wonder who they are giving the caul to if not the women of this neighborhood. We tried to pour some resources into an investigation after one particular case, though. There was one woman not too long ago who was screaming and ripping at her clothes, accusing them of not helping her or something and her child dying. Very woo-woo if you don't believe in that stuff. And woo-woo is hard to translate into an indictable offense." Officer Robinson wanted to continue speaking until she saw tears pooling in Amara's eyes. "You okay, sweet?"

Amara sniffled and hurriedly wiped her eyes. "Yeah, I'm fine. Um—" She cleared her throat. "How can you translate that into an indictable offense, as you say?"

"The state legislative process, for one, or you need a prosecutor."

Amara's heart fluttered. "A prosecutor."

"Mm-hmm. But you need a real tight-ass. No one flimsy. Believe me. They're tough cookies. You need someone high-level. Hell, maybe even the district attorney."

"I see." Amara's voice tapered off, and her eyes wandered around the room. Then she smiled. She laid her hands flat on Officer Robinson's desk and said, "Thank you."

Amara left the precinct office with a new resolve and a spring in her step. She drew the cold evening air into her body, and her chest expanded with a revived ambition. Perhaps the therapist was right and she could channel her grief into something useful. If she could not stop grief from visiting, then it could be a partner alongside her political science studies, and she could work to help Black mothers like the sour lady and Aunt Laila. But that still didn't handle the Melancon problem. Judging from what Amara had seen on this night, their clientele was white people. She assumed they had no interest in helping Black women of the community, those like her aunt Laila. And who's to say the sour lady never petitioned for the Melancons' help, much less heard of them? Officer Robinson sure had, so clearly their reputation was not the most savory. From there, her path flowed right into prosecuting the Melancons, who'd taken advantage of Laila and God knows who else. If only Amara could acquire the power and the potential charges to carry out her plan.

5

Hallow was beautiful, and she was all Josephine's. When her first cutting was over and Josephine was able to get a good look at her, she counted all her fingers and toes. She traced the shape of her baby's nose, lips, and ears, and she cradled Hallow in her arms. "I can't believe you're here," she said.

A week after Hallow appeared in the Melancons' lives, Maman threw Josephine a post-birth party where she roasted Cornish hens, cooked wild rice and beans, and baked a large vanilla bean cake with chocolate ganache. The pink, round nested gift boxes full of onesies, bibs, and toys were stacked to the living room ceiling. Sade played on vinyl near the fireplace. With each gift that Josephine opened, Maman and Landon oohed and aahed in unison, while Iris scoffed and shook her head. For a brief moment, as Josephine looked around the room, sadness crept in when she remembered that there weren't any friends to help her celebrate this momentous occasion. Ironic that even as the baby brought everyone together and fulfilled a long-held desire of Josephine's, there was always something or someone else missing.

It had been decades since Maman last had a newborn and

Josephine could've used the communion with younger women who shared her same anxieties. But she wasn't going to propose the idea of Mommy & Me classes to Maman because this had been the longest stretch of time that Maman hadn't insulted her infertility and therefore deemed her useless. And besides, there was now someone to whom she could endow all the love she had to give.

Josephine was so enamored by the perfection that was Hallow that nothing else mattered. For weeks everyone left her alone so she could bond with the child as much as possible. She was shocked at how well Hallow slept at night. So much, in fact, that she would take a small compact mirror and hover it under Hallow's nose to make sure that she was breathing and woke herself up to repeat this task several times until sunrise. The only time she would allow anyone to hold the baby was if she was showering or using the bathroom. Otherwise, anything she did, from cleaning to eating, would be done with Hallow strapped to her chest or held with one arm. When Landon would visit at night, she wouldn't allow him to slip his hand underneath her nightgown lest Hallow catch a glimpse of something that was too mature for her years.

But one day, Landon visited the Melancon brownstone and did not immediately go upstairs to Josephine's bedroom. Instead, he and Maman sat at the table, where she adjusted her glasses to look at spreadsheets upon spreadsheets of expenditures, credit card statements, and other miscellaneous bills. Landon had his scientific calculator sprawled amongst an assortment of pens as they exchanged notes on the money that was coming in and the money that was going out. Josephine only realized that Landon was downstairs when she had to go to the kitchen to fetch another bottle for Hallow.

"Oh," Josephine said. "What are you two doing?"

"What does it look like, Josephine?" Maman took off her glasses and faced her. Feeling secondhand embarrassment for what was to come, Landon lowered and rubbed his forehead.

"If what you're doing is going over expense reports, then why wasn't I included?"

"I didn't think it was possible since you have that girl attached to your hip at all times."

"She's a baby, Maman."

"Well, since you have a moment by yourself, sit on down." Maman pulled out a chair beside her and tapped the seat.

"No, Hallow needs me."

"Jo, sit down," Landon gently chimed in.

Josephine took a seat next to her mother and crossed her arms over her chest. "What's going on?"

Maman took a beat and rolled her eyes. "Anyway. Landon was able to find us some potential new clients. A friend of a friend from Deutsche Bank."

"Eric and Amelia Weber are their names. He's a geneticist. She's an accountant."

"Right," Maman said. "Eric got into a car accident on his way back from Sagaponack. Traumatic brain injury. I'll let you tell it, Landon."

"Yeah, so, like Maman said, it's a traumatic brain injury. Doctors have to perform a craniectomy, where they remove parts of the skull."

"And?"

"It's a surgery with one of the lowest success rates. They want to buy, and—"

"And I told them there wouldn't be a problem because we have a new addition to the family."

Josephine alternated between looking at Maman then Landon before raising her palms out in front of her. "No."

Landon said, "Jo—"

"No! Wh-wh-wh—" Josephine stuttered. "She's too young!"

"She's not too young, Josephine, come on now," Maman said. "You and Iris were first cut when you were around four months old, and so was Helena. We gave you two extra months of wiggle room, but now she's got to earn her keep!"

"What about the bodega? Isn't there some money that we could take that would give us a little more time?" Josephine asked.

"Ha!" Maman said. "Come on, now, you've seen the books. You know more than anyone else that the bodega isn't bustling. Most fronts in this part of town never are. And after what happened with that woman, the profits have been dipping. Guess word really got around."

"She has a name, Ma."

"And the business may be on a downward slope for who knows how long," Landon chimed in.

"You—" Josephine leaned her chest over the table toward Landon. "As her father, you're not going to say anything?"

"He's not family!" Maman yelled before Landon could open his mouth.

"He's the stand-in father for your grandchild," Josephine retorted.

"Blood is thicker than water," Maman hissed.

Josephine buried her face in her hands and cried. Maman took off her glasses to clean the lenses before situating them back on the arch of her nose and loudly sighed with impatience. Landon placed his hands on the table to rise, intending to walk over to Josephine, but Maman said, "You stay right where you are. Now, Josephine, stop it, just stop it!" When Josephine continued to cry, Maman gripped the back of her daughter's neck and Landon jumped in his seat at the sudden aggression. "Now you listen to me, you know the deal: Landon brings in the clients and we give them what they want. They leave and survive. Now, you got two hours. Get yourself together, and get that baby together too."

Josephine's cries quieted. "Two hours?"

"Yes. They are coming tonight. Surgery is scheduled for tomorrow morning. Landon, take her upstairs and make sure she fixes herself up."

No sooner did Josephine make it to the top of the stairs than she flipped around to strike Landon in the face. But he grabbed her wrist midflight and inched her back into the bedroom so that he could close the door behind them for privacy. Josephine paced around the room as she kept an eye on Hallow, who was transfixed with a stuffed teddy bear in her bedside crib. Landon went through Josephine's closet to pick out a dress and pair of shoes and laid them across the bed. When he was about to head to Hallow's dresser, Josephine stood in front of it and said, "Don't you dare."

"Jo, please. Stop this."

"No, Landon!" Josephine stomped her feet, and Hallow started to fuss. "Landon, she's too young."

"You heard what Maman said. This isn't new."

"And you just sit there and not even defend me?"

"What would've been the alternative? She fires me. I lose part of my income, and I don't get to see you or Hallow again?"

"Who else is she going to get to help with all of this, Landon? We're cooped up in here!"

"She has the records full of the names and contacts of all clients, you know that. She could easily call someone else up to do her bidding, and then what?"

Josephine plopped down on her bed and turned her back to Landon.

He sat down beside her and reached to touch her shoulder, but retracted his hand when she flinched. He continued, "They're willing to pay two hundred thousand dollars, Josephine. Two hundred thousand. But they want to see it done in front of them. I get my twenty percent as usual. And then it's done."

Josephine looked back over her shoulder at him. "They practically foam at the mouth." She put her head in her hands.

"Who?" Landon asked.

She looked at him again, disgust curling her lips. "White people. When they watch us slice up our bodies for them. I won't have it for Hallow."

"It'll grow back, Josephine."

"Wow. That's probably the most heartless thing that you've ever said to me. It's almost like Maman's spirit possessed your body."

"Come on, Josephine. You know this is a part of your family's way. You know this."

"Well, sometimes I don't wanna be a part of it."

Eric and Amelia Weber rang the doorbell at exactly seven p.m. sharp. They immediately rang again after the sound of the first ring tapered off. As soon as Landon opened the door, Amelia took ahold of Eric's right arm and guided him into the foyer. Eric had an uneven gait and a large wound on the side of his temple. Amelia took off her wool hat to shake out her dirty blond hair then helped to remove her husband's coat. She said, "Thank you so much for letting us in. We didn't want to stand out there too long."

"Too cold?" Landon asked as he took both of their jackets to hang on the coatrack.

"Too dangerous," Eric answered, after which his wife cleared her throat and smoothed his forehead. "Sorry. I get these terrible migraines since the accident, so if I don't talk as much as my wife, it's because I'm collecting myself."

"Not a problem," Landon said.

"So, where is the baby?" Amelia asked.

"They'll be down in a minute. Please let me escort you to the dining room. We've prepared some light refreshments for you both."

"We can't stay too long," Amelia said as they walked down the corridor. "I want him to get a proper rest before the operation, and he's not allowed to eat anything." Moments later, after they sat down at the dining room table, she took a cracker with some cheese and crunched down hard on them. "Doctor's orders. He's gonna be put under."

"I understand," Landon said.

Maman was mixing lemonade with mint leaves in a tall glass pitcher. There was a charcuterie board along with a bowl of mixed berries. To its right, a utility knife—Dexter-Russell. Maman wore her emerald earrings, a tradition for whenever a new client arrived, and her best heels. The Webers looked Maman up and down several times as she took her place at the head of the table and smiled whenever she caught their stares.

"So how long have you been living here?" Amelia asked.

"Many years."

"You ever thought about selling?" Amelia asked again.

"Heavens, no. We intend on staying right here."

Amelia shrugged and looked around. "You could probably get a lot of bang for your buck. Though it might be better to wait too. If you hold out longer, I can see you getting at least three million for this."

"Thank you for your suggestion," Maman coolly replied.

Someone cleared their throat from the corner of the room, and everyone turned around to see who it was. Josephine stood in a dress and shoes that Landon did not pick out for her, Hallow in the onesie that she had been in all day.

"Oh, she's adorable!" Amelia gushed. She walked over to Hallow with outstretched hands and said to Josephine, "Can I hold her?"

"No," Josephine said, and moved farther away from Amelia.

"Jo—" Maman said sternly then smiled at the Webers. "Forgive her. She's a new mother, and like all new mothers, she's territorial."

"We understand," Amelia said. "We have three of our own, which is why"—Amelia turned to Josephine with a haughty expression and continued—"you can understand why this is important to us."

"Certainly." Maman stood to her feet and grabbed the utility knife.

"Wait," Eric said. "How do we know it works? This is a lot of cash we're handing over."

"You're right. You don't know. So let's do a demonstration." Maman sliced her left wrist. Eric yelped and Amelia flinched, only for them to watch as her gaping wound closed back up again before their very eyes. "Josephine—" Maman snapped her fingers, and Josephine held out her right arm.

"What are you doing?"

"My caul is just as good as anyone else's. Look, there's a piece left right near the crook of my elbow. Go ahead."

"No, no, no," Amelia said. "We wanted the baby. After all, she's newer. That's premium value."

Landon touched the right side of Josephine's waist and whispered in her ear, "I got you. It's okay."

With tears in her eyes, Josephine reluctantly handed the baby over to Maman, and Landon wrapped both his arms around her, pulling her into the corner.

"You don't have to watch."

"I do," Josephine said.

The process was completed in under a minute: a round incision on Hallow's chubby left thigh as she cried and stared at Josephine, whose own tears would not stop streaming down her face. Amelia plopped the cash on the dining room table, thanked the Melancons, and snatched the caul as soon as Maman held it out in her hands. The Webers could hardly contain themselves as they gathered their coats and left. With Hallow back in her arms, Josephine trailed behind the couple and watched as a driver opened their car door, started the engine, and drove away. She lingered by the window, watching the rustling of the leaves and the laughter of passersby, wondering if this was as good of a time as any to open the door and just leave herself. She repeatedly kissed Hallow on her forehead and said, "I'm sorry. I'm sorry."

"I'm proud of you," Maman said. "You know that, right?"

"That's bullshit and you know it," Josephine snapped back while keeping her eyes toward the front-facing window. "You're only proud of me for doing what you ask. You don't give a damn about my feelings, and you never have, so don't patronize me."

"We do what we do, not because we enjoy the process. It is a means to an end. Your first cut wasn't exactly perfect for me either. My first cut wasn't good for my mother. But we get on with it because we have to."

"Get on with it?" Josephine shook her head. "This isn't washing the dishes, Maman! Is everything so cut-and-dried with you? You don't ever stop to think that not everyone is like you or Grand-mère? These aren't just babies we have no connection to. These are our children."

"Exactly. And we must ensure that our children can survive, yes?"

"There are more things to life than just money."

"Ha!" Maman slapped her right knee. "The only people who

believe that cockamamie foolishness are the people who've always had it. But if you wanna try your luck . . ."

Maman opened the door, and the cold breeze enveloped all three of their bodies. "Go."

"What?"

"Go. You don't wanna be a part of this? You wanna go out there like a vagabond and see what it's like with no money, then go."

"Stop playing, Maman. You know everything would crumble if I took Hallow with me."

"Ah." Maman snapped her fingers and pointed in Josephine's face. "But not before you crumble first. You wouldn't make it farther than Marcus Garvey Park and you know it. Once you walk out that door, you have no money of your own that's not connected to me, no education besides the homeschooling I taught you, and you got no one outside of here but Landon, who already has a ready-made family of his own, and no space for you." She smiled, sure of her victory. "Nothing. But you go ahead and try." She paused. "Go on, now."

Josephine looked down at Hallow then out the gate and could not take one step out the front door. Maman laughed, then slammed the door. Hallow started to cry and Landon interjected and took her from Josephine's arms. The two women were now face-to-face, staring into each other without saying a word.

Then Maman slapped Josephine with the back of her hand, causing her to fall to the ground, and said, "Didn't think so." She straightened her posture and retired to her bedroom with her nose high to the ceiling as she walked by an incredulous Landon and a fussy Hallow.

There on the ground, the distance to the front door stretched longer and longer. She wasn't sure if she was imagining the length because of the impact of the slap or that was truly her mind's estimation of how difficult it would be for her to leave. Nevertheless, she averted her gaze from the lacquered brass of the doorknob, stood to her feet and straightened her posture like Maman, and soothed her red cheek before holding out her arms so that they could be full of her baby again.

6

There were cracks on all four corners of Maman's bedroom, and they were hungry. Black, jagged, and deep, they resembled outstretched hands whose claws leaned toward the center, anticipating when they could devour her whole. They were Maman's biggest nuisance. Over the years, she'd squandered thousands to get them painted over, but there was no polymer in the world that could overpower a vengeful spirit. She knew their brownstone was askew ever since Iris had been born. Cups stained in the cupboard minutes after they had been washed. Subtle sounds like fingernails scraping against windows or sharp winds on the inside persisted. But ever since Iris's premonition about that woman Laila, the outside presences became more apparent: the holes in the ceiling grew larger, the wallpaper chipped and crusted no matter how many times it was patched over, and the aroma in certain rooms was stale and dead even if perfumed oil in glass decanters was used to diffuse the smell.

She didn't want to believe it. The brownstone had been lived in for decades. Wear and tear was natural. But Maman was getting older. She'd had to move from her master bedroom down to the office on the first floor because her legs were no match for the stairs in her old age. Though the caul protected her body, it did not protect the mind in the same way. She had always been perceptive—paranoid even—which is why she took Iris's words to heart. But now she wondered if heeding the premonition about Laila's unborn child wasn't enough.

The Melancon family were accustomed to precarious living situations. Before migrating, they lived along the Cane River in Natchitoches, Louisiana. Each family owned a home on heirs' property from the river to the back swamp. The ranch in which Maman resided was on land between the river and an artificial levee, the living room itself right along the central waterway, a risk whenever there were high tides and hurricanes. *Cochon de lait* characterized many weekends—nightlong carrying on and feasting on roast suckling pig—before Sunday Mass at St. Augustine. When caulbearers lived peacefully, they distilled oil from their camphor trees and sold them as medicine and perfume as a side hustle to everyone from the neighbors to the priests. Ever since Hallow was born, Maman had been reminiscing about simpler days spent raising chickens and hogs, or watching the sun touch the valley's horizon through the sand hills. She felt secure; her family was secure, their legacy intact. Hallow regenerated caul more quickly than anyone Maman had ever seen. She was the future, the successor! For the first years of Hallow's life, Maman fantasized without worry. She would sink deep into her mattress and recall the smell of the sycamore or azalea—how, as a child, unlike her relatives, she was endowed with a sixth sense and felt a change that was sure to come to her congenial space where the land and water met..

Moving to Harlem had brought its challenges. The camellia red beans, White Lily flour, Creole seasoning, and Louisiana hot sauce did not cook so richly here. In the summertime, the scent of fried chicken wafted through the air. Then in the colder months, the air smelled of nothing but rain. They substituted their gardens for flow-erpots, lawns for stoops, camphor oil for their bodies. But at least they owned their brownstone outright. She and her husband, Alex-andre, had pooled their resources together—what she made selling her caul and what he made as a blacksmith—to move up north and start anew.

Of course, the city lights had been too much temptation for him. "Just like a man," Maman often told herself when she caught her-self missing him. He had no interest in being a blacksmith anymore or hearing about how Maman was progressing with the caulbear-ing business. Whatever earnings they cultivated, he squandered on drinking and gambling, until finally Maman caught him laid up with a cabaret singer. She kicked him and his belongings out on Freder-ick Douglass Boulevard, and he left without so much as a request for reconciliation, let alone an apology. The only thing she had to remember him by was a small, wrinkled photo of him that she kept on her desk and had never thought to remove after all these years. Since Alexandre left her with two small children, Maman poured everything she could back into their home, devoting painstak-ing effort to making sure every corner was dusted and every sur-face polished. The home, like her business and her children, was her world. And she was hell-bent on preserving her world, bound within these four walls.

A crack here or there wasn't going to change that. At least that was what she told herself. But the cracks, alongside the creaking floorboards and the shoddy lighting, had made her feel like a visitor in her own home for years. Maman stared at the cracks and won-dered if or when they would part this place in half. Her fear was now mitigated by the fact that Hallow was here. She was growing wonderfully year after year. A successor was now in place; Maman could pass on if she wanted. She was already in her late seventies and she had seen and heard enough. But she still didn't feel as confident as she wanted to in Josephine.

Maman should've known from birth that Josephine would never leave her side—sometimes to a fault. In the womb, Josephine relentlessly kicked Maman in the ribs whenever she ran errands, as if Maman could pull away from her. When Josephine was a toddler, after she had been weaned, Maman would fall asleep often and find that Josephine had unbuttoned her blouse and was sucking from her breast. What startled Maman most was that Josephine did not cry or unlatch when she knew that she was being watched. She sucked more vigorously until Maman pulled her away, massaging her red, chafed nipple and then banishing Josephine to her own room. But Josephine never gave her any other trouble besides not being able to produce a caulbearing child. She was always eager to please—sycophantically and annoyingly so. But as Josephine got older, Maman noticed a strength inside of her too. Maman would never admit it to her daughter, but she was worried and damn near convinced that Josephine was going to walk out that front door years ago. When Hallow was born and Josephine became a mother, there was a ferocity to her disposition that Maman had never seen before, and she liked it. In her innermost private thoughts, Maman wondered when and how Josephine would test her again.

Maman ran her finger along her own bare skin. Most of her caul had already been carved and sold. Fantasies of what it would be like to just rip those last few parts off—and, inevitably, welcome death—became more frequent and disruptive, appearing in and out of the back of her mind during the most trivial of activities. She was just tired, in every sense of the word. But that still wouldn't relieve her of the problem of what to do with these cracks.

When the sun came up in the morning, there was another thing to be fixed. The damn moisture in the air spoiled the stone on the exterior. There were the costs to clean, patch, and replace the stone, upkeep the stoop, repair a ceiling leak after Helena forgot to stop a bathtub from overflowing. The cast-iron work needed updating—another several thousand dollars. The constant hemorrhaging of money concerned the repairmen. They asked why Maman kept repairing when all the money going into it could be used for another home. With the rising property taxes, where else could she go in Harlem? She refused to be displaced to Inwood, much less Washington Heights. But Maman and the rotating repairmen knew that it was only a matter of time before the roof would cave in. The foundation was rotten, the cracks too wide, the decaying roots too deep.

The pitter-patter of feet running up and down the steps reminded Maman that it was a Saturday morning. Helena, now a thirteen-year-old, would barricade herself in her room, as most teenagers did, and eight-year-old Hallow would be whining for her to come out and play. Saturdays were the only days Helena promised to grace Hallow with her presence for more than thirty minutes at a time. But not today. No. These two were going to have a purpose. Hallow would accompany Maman to a block association meeting. Since Laila's stillbirth some eight years ago, Maman had been consistent in demonstrating her commitment to the Harlem community through these meetings, even though she still sensed that no one could trust her.

If they were lucky, Maman thought, perhaps there'd be another person there who had money to burn, though she hadn't sold to a Harlemite, much less a Black Harlemite, in years.

Her six-foot-two-inch frame was more gangly than awe-inspiring, due to her sagging skin and gradual weight loss. Maman groaned as she hoisted herself to stand. But she would be damned if she had to use a crutch to move around from place to place. A metallic peg was unseemly, and a wheelchair was out of the question. She would continue to do what she had always done: drape herself with layers upon layers of embroidered wool so that no one could see just how many times her legs wobbled to support her. She stood in front of her long, oval freestanding mirror and pressed her fingers into her cheeks, stunned by how easily they sunk into her skin like putty. She pulled out a blunt and lighter from her desk drawer and pulled as hard as she could until a tingly feeling danced underneath her skin. In her brief daze, she could envision that red river clay was still embedded in the wrinkles around her eyes and hands. Her now bare skin allowed her to see her beauty for real. She liked it. Though she would never admit that to anyone.

Her self-indulgence did not pull her too far from the present to realize that she heard neither the pitter-patter nor chatter from outside her door. She walked out of her bedroom and over to the staircase to see Helena and Hallow both at the top. Helena was clasping Hallow's arms, and Hallow was standing with her back to the staircase. Helena was rocking her back and forth, and Hallow's fingers were fidgeting at her sides. When Helena's eyes shot up to see Maman watching from down below, she pushed Hallow. In mid-flight, Hallow started screaming. The first part of her body to make an impact on a step was her elbow, and once that was turned inward, she rolled down the rest of the steps, banging both sides of her head and landing facedown right on her nose. When Hallow landed on the Persian rug, her limbs burned from the friction and her body turned limp. Instead of giving Helena the satisfaction of berating her, Maman pulled out some blankets from her bedroom and placed Hallow's body on top of them. Then she sat in a chair and waited. Hallow wasn't so shocked that she stopped breathing. Blood pooled around her widow's peak and small drops dribbled from her nose.

"Lord have mercy!" Josephine dashed out of her bedroom and gasped when she saw Hallow lying on the ground in a contorted position. She slapped Helena on the behind and ran down the steps.

When Maman saw Josephine about to crouch down, she held up her hand. "Don't touch her!"

"But—"

"I said, don't touch her. Leave her alone so she can learn."

Dejected, Josephine clasped a hand over her mouth and closed her eyes.

"She always does that. Always running after Hallow pretending she's ordinary like me." Helena crossed her arms over her chest and tapped her foot at the top of the staircase.

"It'll be over before you know it, Hallow. Just watch," Maman said.

In a matter of minutes, Hallow's elbow straightened and the blood drawn from her face receded back from whence it came. The knots and bruises mounting on the sides of her face flattened, and her breathing became more even. She opened her eyes and blinked a few times. There was a tingling sensation throughout her whole body, and suddenly, the pain vanished. Hallow stood to her feet and cracked her neck by leaning it from left to right as far as she could.

"See? You always get better. The time it takes just depends on how severe the injury, but it always happens. Now, are you two done?" Maman asked.

"We were just playing a game, Maman," Helena called out from the top of the staircase.

"A game? What kind of game?"

"It was a game of—"

"I'm asking Hallow." Maman leaned in toward her and blew smoke toward her side profile. "Hallow. I'm speaking to you."

Hallow sniffled and regarded Maman. The fire from Maman's

blunt almost fizzled out, for she was taken aback by how much Hallow resembled Josephine in both eyes and character. For a brief moment, she saw her daughter, and that unnerved her more than anything else, since Josephine was not Hallow's birth mother.

"Yes, Maman. It was just a game."

"It's not just some game. It's sick. And I'm sick and tired of Helena doing this," Josephine said.

Ignoring her, Maman continued talking to Hallow. "Well, you two can finish playing when we get back from our block meeting. I need you to be washed and dressed in forty minutes."

"I get to go outside?" Hallow beamed.

"Yes, dear."

"Do I have to?" Helena dropped her shoulders and whined.

"I was talking to Hallow and Hallow only."

"Well, why does Hallow get to go and I don't?"

"Because I said so. Now you get her out of your hair for two hours and you can do whatever it is you do up there undisturbed. See? Everybody's happy. Now you, make haste." Maman nudged Hallow toward the staircase. "I don't want to be late."

Hallow ran up the steps, and Helena purposefully brushed shoulders with her before Hallow went into her room. Once the door closed, Helena ceremoniously walked down the stairs, taking a brief pause at every step. When both feet were on the bottom, she placed one arm on the bannister and began tapping her feet.

Maman inhaled her smoke then blew it out of her nostrils. "You have something that you'd like to say to me?"

Helena rolled her tongue around in her mouth and mumbled, "Unh-unh."

"If you have the nerve to step to me like a woman, then address me like one. Lord knows that you're never at a loss for words with anyone else."

"Nothing. Seriously. Nothing. I mean, she is going to be the one who runs this place when you die, so it's only right you bring her up under you."

"Don't be jealous, Helena. It's unbecoming. But it does have purpose."

Helena narrowed her eyes and cocked her head to the side.

"Keep playing your little games with her. She has to learn to be tougher. She can't be a pushover like Josephine. Understand?"

Helena grinned and nodded. "I hope you two have fun."

"And Helena?"

Helena, who was starting up the stairs, looked over her shoulder.

"You haven't told her about . . ." Maman's voice tapered off.

Helena overacted a gasp and pressed a hand to her heart. "Of course not! I wouldn't dare. That would ruin everything, wouldn't it?" She laughed all the way back to her room. Helena was definitely her mother's child.

Hallow returned to the foyer dressed in a red-checked dress, black leggings, and small boots. Her coily hair was wrapped in a bun with a matching ribbon tied around it, and a golden star pendant necklace adorned her neck.

"Well," Maman said, visibly impressed. For all Hallow knew, Maman could have been taking her to the bodega or Laundromat, but she dressed as though she was going somewhere important. There were strict rules in place for whenever Hallow was allowed to go outside. The first one was that she would never be able to do so unaccompanied, even if she was just playing on the front porch. Every part of her body besides her head needed to be covered, no matter the season. If someone said hello to her, she was only to smile and nod. If someone asked her how she was doing, her response was supposed to be short and to the point. Any further probing and Hallow would have to go into the house and get the nearest adult family member that she could find. In either case, she would have to go back inside after the interaction was over. If someone so much as brushed up against her while she accompanied Josephine on a rare excursion, every part of her body would have to be searched once she got home to make sure her caul hadn't been tampered with. Long stretches of time would pass until she would be able to go out again. But she had never went out with Maman.

The texture of Maman's grainy palm pressing onto Hallow's left hand excited her. Once the front door was open, the fresh light stung her eyes. The air was uncharacteristically clean, the outside a Saturday-morning kind of quiet. They walked alongside each other down the block to the basement of a small old Presbyterian church.

"What other games do you play with Helena, Hallow?"

"Many games. Sometimes she pushes me down the steps, but she always says it's an accident. We'll play a game of putting our hands on top of each other's to see who will flinch first. I always flinch, so she gets to slap my hand as hard as she wants because I lost. Sometimes Josephine catches us and tells us to stop. But most times she does it when Mom isn't even looking."

"What is the purpose of this game?"

"She says she wants to see if I can do any of it without screaming or crying since I won't hurt for long anyway."

"And do you ever win?"

Hallow averted her eyes to the ground and shook her head.

Maman lifted Hallow's chin and said, "And what do you do back to her?"

"Nothing. She said I'm not allowed to touch her. That me and her aren't the same."

"Well, that's true. You wanna know why she said that, don't you?"

Hallow didn't blink.

"Because she almost died years ago. She doesn't have as much caul as you. You've seen her arms and legs, you know. So if you hurt her, she won't get better like you. You're the more important one. We don't want anyone trying to strip you. You're the future. Our legacy. Understand?" Maman winked.

Hallow, who was the youngest person in the room by far, flashed a smile and nodded.

The majority of people there had a crop of gray in their hair. A long communal table was placed in the center of the room and a small round table was pushed into the far corner. One woman was setting out scones, muffins, cinnamon rolls, biscuits, and fruits when Maman and Hallow entered. She took a breath and said, "Mornin'," her bottom lip tucked into her mouth. Maman reciprocated the greeting and ushered Hallow to seats on the side of the table farthest away from the woman. Each person who came in the door was immediately drawn to Maman and Hallow but dropped their eyes to the ground as soon as Maman looked back at them. Some flocked over to the food and beverage volunteer and engaged in merry conversations; others broke off into smaller exchanges at the table, their bodies turned away from Maman and huddled together.

"Okay, everyone." Patricia, a pint-sized middle-aged woman who'd served as the uncontested president of the block association six years running, emerged from the kitchen with several sheets of paper in her hand. "Take one, pass it down." She plopped the stack in front of Maman, who was taken aback by the impudence of the move. Nevertheless, she did as she was told and took out a pen, pressing the head onto the agenda sheet.

Patricia took her place at the head of the table and adjusted her pearly frames. She cleared her throat, smearing a bit of her fire-engine-red lipstick on the side of her pointer finger, then folded her hands on the surface. "We need to talk about the prostitution on this block."

The murmurs and scoffs began.

"Forgive me, Marceline." Patricia motioned to Maman. "Had I known you were bringing one of your grandchildren, I would've—"

Maman shook her head. "She's precocious for an eight-year-old, trust me. She's fine."

"Very well. Prostitution. Now, I don't have a problem with what grown people do in the off-hours, but it's getting to be too much. They're loud. Sister Evans's niece just had a baby, and there are other children on this block. Parents are starting to complain."

"What if we just call the cops on them? Simple as that," one white woman, Abigail, suggested. She attended every meeting, and when she ran to be a part of the board, other members voted her in for her diligence and because she'd been living in the neighborhood for over a decade.

"They'll take them down to the precinct, where they'll be for seventy-two hours tops, then be back to their old stomping grounds but smarter the next time," Patricia said.

"Besides, do we really need the police coming up and down the block? I mean, yes, technically they are breaking the law, but they're just loud. They aren't shooting or robbing and stealing. Surely, there's another way besides getting the police involved." Sister Evans extended her hands across the table and looked around for supporters, to which she found plenty who nodded.

"We shouldn't get involved—just let the police handle it," Abigail insisted. "Look how old we all are. Those girls are young, but they've been on the streets long enough to know how to fight or carry a weapon to protect themselves. It only takes one second for them to think we're getting too smart, then boom. Next thing you know, they break our noses and our hips need replacement."

The group laughed.

"I'm not that old," Sister Evans said meekly.

The group awkwardly quieted down.

"Well, you know what I mean—"

"I don't."

"But anyways!" Patricia interjected. "Should the first go-to solution really be the police?"

"What other solution is there?" Abigail asked.

The group scoffed. Abigail looked around the room at how everyone was exchanging discreet glances with one another.

"All right." Abigail leaned back in her seat and crossed her arms over her chest. "Well, let's hear it. Speak up."

"Well—" Sister McCleary, who sat beside Sister Evans, cleared her throat. "It's just . . . easy for you to say, Abi." She checked to her left and right. "That's all."

"Easy for me to say? Every one of us has a phone. We can dial three digits— Oh. Oh." Abigail stretched out her moment of comprehension with a resounding, singsongy sound. "I see what this is about."

"What I'm tryin' to say is that—" Sister McCleary half smiled. "We don't usually—historically do that around here. That's the most . . . extreme . . . approach. There are—"

"What she's trying to say is that you white people always want to run to the police for every little thing. What they call it, minor infraction?" Claudia, who had become more frank since her husband passed away, said.

"You call prostitution a 'minor infraction'? It's not like someone is littering or playing music too loudly."

"But y'all call the police on that too! I got a cousin living in Bed-Stuy, and she and her people can't even play music past nine because a new white couple have had enough."

"Well, was it on a weeknight?" Abigail asked.

The group scoffed again.

"That's not the point. It's tradition. The police don't need to be called."

"Look. All I'm saying is that if you have any other de-escalation method, then put it on the table. Otherwise, let's just ask them to keep it down."

"Marceline, what do you think?" Patricia attempted to refocus the conversation. "You've been mighty quiet, and you've been on this block longer than any of us."

"Give them what they want: money," Maman said.

"Money?" Abigail asked.

"Yes. If the girls are coming around here often, then this may be where they make a good portion of their money. Give them enough to keep them away."

"But what if they just come right back?"

"Give them enough so they won't come back for a while. Make a deal with them."

"And how do you expect us to pool together our resources for that? Is this charity? Can I use this as a tax write-off?" Claudia asked.

"You won't have to. I'll pay them. Let's decide on a figure and do away with this problem."

"With what? That caul you got?" someone murmured under her breath.

"I'm sorry?" Maman asked.

The room fell silent, and everyone stared blankly at Maman.

"What?" Maman asked.

"Marceline, I think I speak for everyone when I say that we shouldn't just throw money at the problem. We have to deal with it at the root," Patricia said.

"Isn't the root of why they're coming here money?"

"Yes, but—"

"What she's saying is that the purpose of a block association meeting is that it's for the block," Claudia said as if it were the last word. "We make decisions together. We pool our resources together. That's what community is. We don't just fling money at things, especially when so many of us have to fling money elsewhere, like saving our families from being priced out to Inwood or Canarsie or Jersey City. But I guess you wouldn't know about that since you and your ilk walk around here like the sun don't rise till you say so."

"You don't think I have to toss money down the drain too? Every time I turn around something else needs fixing. All of you have been here at least, what, ten years? You know."

"Yeah, but your kitchen drawers aren't full of outstanding bills," Claudia said. "You don't get people knocking on your door asking if you'd like to sell all the time. Oh no! The Melancon family has an iron-clad gate—all fancy. And what is it y'all do anyway? Has to be more than that bodega, yeah? How you livin'? How you not getting pushed out when the rest of us are clinging for dear life over here?"

"Ladies, ladies. Let's focus here, okay. Let's quell the animosity and get through with our agenda. We'll table this and move onto our upcoming elections," Patricia said.

Once the meeting was adjourned, Sister Evans walked over to Maman's side and whispered to gain her attention. "Please stick around. I have something I want to ask you." Maman nodded and motioned for her and Hallow to sit back down. By this time, Hallow was getting antsy, kicking her feet and drawing imaginary circles on the table. She was only interested in the debate because of how passionately everyone was speaking—not because of the topic itself. Now that everyone was filing out and kissing each other goodbye on the cheek, she wondered when Maman would grab her hand to lead her out the door along with the rest of the crowd.

"Maman, why don't people like us very much?"

"The simple answer is envy. It's petty gossip. Do you ever see them drop by?"

Hallow shook her head.

"So would you consider them friends?"

Hallow shook her head.

"If they aren't friends, then they don't know us. And if they don't know us, then whether or not they like us isn't really our concern, is it?"

Hallow nodded. "But Maman, no one comes over."

Sister Evans placed a hand on Maman's shoulder and took a seat beside her. "Thank you for waiting."

Maman twisted her body toward Sister Evans and raised her voice an octave. "Not a problem! What's going on?"

Although they were the only people left in the basement, Sister Evans leaned in and whispered, "Is it true what they say?"

"Is what true?"

Sister Evans scrutinized Hallow's clothes and how tightly the material encased her body. "That you all were born special. That you can heal. Is it true?"

"Depending on what you believe."

"Oh, I want to believe. I want to believe. But I need something to hold on to. Even Jesus performed miracles for his followers."

Maman grabbed Hallow's left wrist with one hand and removed her glove with the other. She pulled out a lighter from her purse and ignited it. Hallow's eyes bulged, and her chest quickly rose and fell. Maman nonchalantly held the flame to Hallow's fingers and Hallow screamed. Sister Evans yelled for Maman to stop, and it was the immensity of that plea that made Maman close the top of the lighter. Hallow trembled and cried at the sight of her finger, which now looked like a burned sausage link. Sister Evans's eyes alternated between Hallow and Maman, completely beside herself at what just happened, until Hallow's charred skin reverted to its original state.

"God almighty," Sister Evans gushed. She grabbed ahold of Hallow's fingers, pushing them from side to side, looking on top and underneath them. "Well—there's nothing there. Not even a nick or scab." Maman had been so used to this carousal of emotions—from the first pain to the shock to the wonder— that she was desensitized. As a matter of fact, Maman was bored. There was a time she gasped and screamed when her mother and her mother's mother had put her on display like this, and their stoicism was indelibly printed in her memory. This performance was all she knew.

Hallow whimpered and snatched her hand away from Sister Evans before running to the nearest corner, where she huddled into the fetal position. Maman was gobsmacked. With her face turned away from Sister Evans, Maman mouthed words to Hallow, but Hallow closed her eyes and shook her head. "I wanna go home," she said repeatedly until she heard the women stand to their feet. Maman apologized for Hallow's tantrum and held her wrist so tightly on the way back home that her handprint made a deep red mark on her wrist. Once they entered the foyer of their home, Maman walked into the dining room without so much as regarding Hallow and the morning they'd shared together. What Hallow needed at that moment was an adult who could make sense of all the different feelings she had. She wanted to tell Josephine, but Josephine always deferred to Maman.

There was only one other adult left in the brownstone, who Hallow would not have considered had she not been desperate. For as long as she could remember, she'd hated walking past the stairs that led to the basement. The air emanating from down there was frigid and stale. The darkness stung her eyes if she lingered too long. Sometimes she heard whispers creeping in and around that darkness. But if she could not be hurt and this was in fact her home too, she thought it would be okay to at least say hello. She turned on the light leading to the basement and lowered herself onto one step and looked over her shoulder. One step became two, two became five, until she finally reached the bottom of the stairs.

"Who's that?" Iris called out from behind her closed bedroom door.

"It's me," Hallow stuttered.

"Me? Who's me? You know who you are. I do not."

"Hallow."

"Come closer to the door."

Hallow took one step toward the bedroom door.

"Closer."

She took another.

Iris opened the door and smiled. "I knew it was you all along."

Dumbfounded, Hallow curved her eyebrows inward and squinted. "I . . ."

Iris laughed and placed a hand on Hallow's back. Her touch zapped Hallow as if an electric current sent a shock wave from the top of her hair to the soles of her feet. Iris guided Hallow into her bedroom, which seemed upon first glance to be too crowded to fit two people. Various books of faded colors and tattered spines were stacked high by her bedside. Heaps of clothes were stuffed underneath her desk. Vinyl records without their sleeves were scattered across the floor, and the Impressionist paintings that adorned her walls were all hung lopsided or upside down. Each of the drawers of her dresser was left open, but the middle one stuck out farther than the rest. Hallow was drawn to the rose-gold wrapping paper in that middle drawer. Something had to be inside, because it was folded over and closed with a red wax seal. She moved her upper body toward the middle drawer, and Iris immediately slammed it shut.

Iris sat down on the chair near her desk and crossed one leg over the other. Her blue veins were thick and covered the entire lower half of her body. Her hazel-gray eyes were piercing. The wrinkles in her neck resembled a spider's web, and she had a dent in the space between her eyebrows.

"Something's vexing you. I can see all over that young face of yours. Children aren't old enough to construct masks."

"When you were a kid, were you ever played with?"

"Played with? Sure I was. I wrestled and horseplayed, pulled hair and made messes unafraid. I played until I got tired. I played as long as I desired."

"No, I mean . . ." Hallow scooted closer to Iris. "Did Maman ever try to show you to other people? That you couldn't get hurt?"

"No. But I wasn't like you, little Hallowed. You're different from everyone else. You're Maman's favorite."

"But what if I don't want to be anyone's favorite?" Hallow sank her head into her hands.

"Being a favorite is out of your control. But fickleness and favorites are two halves that share the same body."

"Huh?"

"Never you mind. I am touched, you see. You shouldn't be down here consorting with me."

"Touched?"

"I see things, little Hallowed. When I close my eyes at night, my cohorts greet me on the other side. When I do whatever I need to do during the day, there they are, like shadows or mice scurrying in the corners. So whenever I speak, my words tend to go above people's heads because I do not walk on the same plane they do. I am between worlds, as the old folks would say."

"Between worlds?"

"Sometimes I get into my moods. I go into a fit. But I am left alone most of the time until I am called upstairs to give." She ran her fingers along a piece of caul on the nape of her neck. "You know, I like being left alone with my things here." She made a circle with her arms. "They keep me occupied. They're always here, you know. You may not be able to see them like I do, but they make themselves known through every crack and crevice."

Hallow remained silent in wonder at Iris's impassioned words.

"Anyway, you like my art? Art encompasses many different worlds too. And the past and present are one and the same. Do you like it?"

Hallow looked around. "It is a lot. But it's pretty."

"And it's mine. All mine. I wouldn't dare live up there." She pointed to the ceiling. "Say, why you still have your coat and gloves on?"

Hallow peered down at her chest. "Oh. Sorry."

"Would you like me to relieve you?" Iris reached out, and Hallow shrank back.

"No! No. I don't want to be touched. Please."

"Okay, little Hallowed."

"I'm gonna go." Hallow got down from the chair and started toward the door. She glanced over her shoulder and asked, "All yours?"

"All mine." Iris grinned.

On the way back up the stairs, Hallow wondered what could be called hers in this spacious brownstone. She climbed into her own bed with her coat and gloves still on and rested her eyes. Once she heard Helena calling out for her in a voice dipped in mischief, she clutched her chest with both hands and cried into one of the flaps of her coat, repeating, "Mine. Mine, mine, mine, mine, mine."

7

Josephine couldn't figure out what seemed to be vexing Hallow. After her conversation with Iris, Hallow ran upstairs to her bedroom, where she buried her head in a mountain of pillows that she soon saturated with her tears. Josephine was occupying herself with fixing her vanity and jumped when she heard Hallow slam her bedroom door, which she had never done before. "Hallow?" Josephine asked as she treaded lightly into the bedroom. "Hallow, sweetheart? Baby, what's wrong?" Hallow didn't respond. When Josephine went to touch her back, Hallow smacked her mother's hand away. Josephine soothed her stinging right hand and gazed at Hallow with bewilderment. "Is something wrong?" she asked. "Did someone hurt you?"

Hallow's cries gradually ceased. She raised her puffy, wet face and rested her chin on a pillow. Josephine repeated her question, and Hallow shook her head.

"No?"

Hallow nodded.

"Yes?"

Hallow shrugged her shoulders.

"Which one is it? I'm trying to understand, baby. You got to speak to me."

"Maman. She—she—" Hallow choked back some more tears and struggled to catch her breath.

"Breathe. Take a deep breath. I'm not going anywhere."

Helena peeked her head into the bedroom, and Hallow immediately buried her face again.

"What's going on?"

"Helena, please get out. I'm trying to see what's going on with your cousin."

Helena entered the bedroom, shut the door behind her, and stood in the corner.

"You are so hardheaded," Josephine said.

"I wanna know what's going on."

"She's been hurt, that's what. And I'm trying to see what's going on."

"Been hurt? Been hurt? What about me? I'm the one who's been more hurt than anyone else up in here, and y'all treat me like some throwaway kid."

"Is there some competition for hurt that I don't know about? Is that why you play those cruel games with Hallow, so someone can hurt just like you do? You know, Helena, just because someone heals doesn't mean that they don't feel pain. We all carry something."

For the first time that Helena could recall, she could not get the last word, because Josephine was right. Helena felt a rush every time she slapped and pushed Hallow. Redness, scratches, bruises delighted Helena whenever she saw them emerge on Hallow's skin before they disappeared all over again. But now, in this moment, when Josephine exposed her deepest motivations for why she did what she did, she was filled with remorse.

"I'm sorry, Hallow," Helena said. "I'm sorry." She opened the door and backed out of the room, and it wasn't until the door shut again that Hallow sat upright.

"Now back to where we were," Josephine said. "Maman did something. What did she do? Show you off? Burn you?"

Hallow's pupils dilated.

"Yeah, did you know she was gonna do that?"

"Sooner or later."

"But why?"

Josephine shrugged her shoulders. "Because it's the family way. She . . . is trying to appeal to other people, I guess."

"But I don't like it."

Josephine replied, "I don't like it either."

Over the next few weeks, a transformation had overtaken the Melancon home. Helena became withdrawn but made more of an effort to be kinder to Hallow by allowing her to play in her hair or regale her with stories underneath their blankets with a flashlight at night. Then, without warning, Helena would withdraw again, apologizing hours or days later for her moods. She was still trying to find her own way like any teenager would, and, as such, her temperament and behavior were often unpredictable. But since that talk with Josephine, Helena worked to be gentler with Hallow and swore never to play games with her again. In spite of Helena's fickleness, that promise was the only constant she honored.

Josephine was overjoyed while Maman was annoyed, because she did not want the two girls to become too close to each other. Hallow was the successor, and Helena was not. As such, Maman would allow Helena to roam outside unaccompanied while forbidding Hallow to trail after her older cousin. But whenever Helena would return, she would always be carrying some book, pamphlet, or magazine to entertain both her and Hallow. It was during this time that in her private moments, Helena collected mental notes not only of Hallow's improved mood but her own as well. For those few weeks, everything felt all right, even as the cracks in the walls continued to grow and the holes in the ceiling became more cavernous. Helena felt so good that she wondered if that goodness could extend to other people and places and be of use in ways that possibly transcended what she could do with her caul. Sometimes she ran her fingers along the deep, permanent scars and fragments of the caul left in a few spots on her skin and did not cry with the memory of the accident. She began to interpret them all as a topography of a body that was truly hers. So now what was she going to do with this new body, this new life?

Ever since Landon set up a computer in the corridor adjacent to the dining room, Helena had spent hours researching and cataloguing fall clothes and different kinds of school supplies at night and came upon an institution in an ad on some teenager-geared website: the Spence School, an all-girls' private school based in the Upper East Side. When Helena brought up Spence as a potential place to be schooled, its prestige and location appealed to Maman. She assumed the students were more disciplined and better behaved than those at public schools. Although Helena was of no use to the family caul business, Maman didn't want there to be any chance of her being fully stripped. Whatever caul she had left could be easily covered with regular clothes, either for classes or PE. Besides, being at an all-girls' school like Spence removed the worry of curious boys. Whatever slight Helena felt from being seen as damaged disappeared when she was granted permission to attend.

Throughout the summer, Helena watched movies focusing on high school, organized her journals, and created color codes and legends according to her classes. The more summer progressed, the more time she focused on actual school, and the less time she had for Hallow. Hallow was doing everything she could to get her attention. She tried to make conversation with Josephine and Maman, but the exchanges never lasted for long. She arrived at a heartbreaking conclusion one evening at dinner as the first weeks of Helena's school were underway: Hallow had nothing worthwhile to say. As Helena enthusiastically spoke of all the courses she was taking and the extracurricular activities that she'd participate in, Hallow shrank, unable to do anything but nod, smile, and say, "Tell me more." Hallow's homeschooling didn't compare to Helena's real schooling, with other kids, events, teachers, and the outside. When Landon came to visit one evening in late September, Hallow realized just how much was changing.

He tiptoed up the stairs and knocked three times on the door. Josephine was wearing a sheer pink slip and sauntered across the room with a perfume bottle in hand to spray both her neck and the bedroom. Josephine hummed a melody to her daughter, who collapsed in her arms every night when the loneliness got too much for her to handle. Josephine paused before letting Landon enter the room, a hesitation that annoyed Hallow for its insincerity. She knew that they would soon indulge in licking in and around each other's faces. They constructed their own world with each embrace and kiss, and Hallow would watch. When they finished, Josephine flattened the ends of her slip and Landon wiped the rouge from his lips.

"Good evening, Hallie."

"Hi, Dad," Hallow said dryly.

"Are you having trouble sleeping?"

"I'm not tired."

"What about some warm milk and cookies?"

"Not hungry."

Landon sat beside Hallow and said, "All right. What is it that you want?"

Hallow stared at Landon inquisitively, leaned in, and sniffed his breath. "Ugh. You smell like . . ." She sniffed again. "Oranges or . . . grapefruit and rotten milk. Why would you kiss Mommy with that breath? Where have you been?"

"Hallow Melancon," Josephine said. "I happen to like that breath, so never you mind that."

"But where have you been, Dad? And can you stay longer tonight?"

"Hal—" Landon said.

"Well, why can't you? Where do you have to go?"

"Hallow—" Josephine said more sternly.

"Why can't you just stay with us? It can be so lonely here. For me and Mom."

"Hallow, goddammit!" Josephine stamped her foot then turned her back. Shoulders raised to her ears and her hands now open by her waist, she started to cry, and Landon wrapped his arms around her from behind.

"You've upset your mother now. Tell her you're sorry."

Hallow remained silent.

"Hallow." Landon raised his voice. "Tell your mother you're sorry."

Hallow got up from the bed and wrapped her arms around Josephine's waist. "I'm sorry, Mommy," she reluctantly expressed, only to pacify Landon and to get him to stop addressing her with his rancid breath.

"I just don't know why you can't stay if you love us."

Landon patted Hallow's head and said, "I got you a gift."

Landon stepped out of the bedroom and returned with a blue

wool duffle coat. It was Hallow's favorite color. "You want to try it on?" He held the coat out closer to Hallow's eyes. As soon as Hallow stood up, Landon removed the coat from the hanger and placed it on her shoulders. "Go ahead and button it up. You'll never know how a coat fits if you don't button it up." Hallow's breathing started to become difficult from the moment her fingertips grazed the lowest button. Each button she fastened brought about a different kind of airiness in her head. Once she finished, Landon said, "You look beautiful. Spin around for us." Hallow spun around and around until she got dizzy and fell on the floor.

Hallow looked down at her wool coat and conjured images of all the places she could go, places that she had only ever seen in Helena's magazines. She imagined that Helena would be going to those places and she would remain here forever.

"I want to go to school like Helena."

"Oh, that's what this is about."

Hallow sat upright and pressed her back up against one of the legs of the bed. "Why can't I go to school?"

"Because it's not safe, Hallow. That's why."

"But I can be really, really careful. I won't get in trouble."

Landon said, "What your mother is saying, Hallie, is that she's not so much worried about you but other people."

"But I want to be around other kids. I want to look at clothes in magazines and get ready for the day." Hallow flung herself across Josephine's bed and pulled at the window ledge. "I wanna get out! I hate it here!" Josephine patted Hallow on the back and brought her into her bosom. Her eyes floated to the top of the ceiling, where the paint chipped at the corners and the crushed but repaired wood would forever bear the marks of termite damage. She could not remember her bedroom ever being pristine, only the first markings of age with photographic precision. The further Josephine pressed into her mind, the tighter she held Hallow to her chest, because there was no getting around the truth: Hallow was right, and she wanted to get out too. Josephine looked over at Landon, who shut his eyes and shook his head, and that was the extent of their silent conversation with each other.

"I still remember the night that you were born, Hallie. Have I ever told you that story?"

"No," Hallow replied through a muffle.

"It was unexpected." He kept his eyes on Josephine, waiting to see her response to his storytelling. "Your mother had been bedridden. You know what that means?"

Hallow shook her head.

"She had to stay in bed so that she could rest and you could grow and be strong. Then you were about to come on All Hallows' Eve. That's how you got your name. It's a very important holiday in the Episcopal church. We're Episcopalians, you know. I called upon a midwife and you came soon after. You barely cried, like you were ready to make your arrival into the world." His eyes moved to somewhere off-center, and they began to fill with tears. "I'd never seen anything like it. That's how I knew—we knew—you were special. I knew you were special before you were even born. We had waited for you for so long. Right, Josephine?"

Josephine then realized he was crafting the story as if Josephine had been the one to give birth, and the fact that he was smiling made her think that he hoped both she and Hallow would feel better. She looked up at the six dove pendants on the ceiling and mouthed, *God help me. Lord, help me*, and wrapped her arms around Hallow's chest.

"Ma, I can't breathe."

Josephine squeezed, and Hallow screamed.

"Jo, let go. Let go!" Landon yelled.

Josephine started sobbing and Landon jumped to his feet. He pulled Hallow away from Josephine and they glared at her, awaiting an answer. She flicked her hands at them and ran out of the room down the stairs and did not return to her bedroom for the rest of the evening.

When Josephine went to check in with Maman, she discovered that her mother was still awake.

Josephine placed one hand on Maman's bedroom door and heard the scraping sound of a pen dragging across a sheet of paper on her cherrywood desk. She knocked with the other hand and heard Maman sigh. The springs on her bed creaked. The TV was playing at a low volume. Josephine knocked twice.

"Yes?" Maman called out.

"Can I come in?"

"Must you?"

Josephine twisted the doorknob and let herself in. Maman moved closer to the edge of the bed and grabbed onto the sides of the mattress. When Maman did not rise to her feet, Josephine proceeded to lock the door and start toward Maman's desk chair. Her mother's eyes, unblinking and glaring, followed her to where she sat. They sat across from each other with their hands wedged between their thighs. Maman squinted. "I didn't think you had any of that in you."

"Had what?"

"Never mind. What's going on? You're disturbing me."

"I couldn't be up in that room tonight." Josephine looked off to the side, beyond Maman's left ear, and shook her head repeatedly. "Not tonight."

"Isn't Landon here? I know I heard his footsteps going up the stairs."

"He's there with Hallow. I left them alone. Both of them were getting on my nerves."

"Both of them, huh?"

"Both of them!"

"Both of them, huh?"

"Yes, Maman, I already answered your question."

"I just wanted to be sure." Maman pulled out the top drawer of her nightstand, where a blunt lay beside a copy of the Book of Common Prayer and a miniature bottle of absinthe. She placed the blunt in her mouth and produced a lighter while giggling to herself. She laughed and ignited the end of her blunt. Her fingers curled as the blunt lowered from her mouth so she could blow the smoke toward the ceiling. She closed her eyes and grinned, then tipped her head down to acknowledge Josephine. "Welcome to mother-hood." Maman handed Josephine the blunt, and Josephine took a long pull.

"There you go. You still got it."

"You know I don't like to smoke."

"It's probably because you got it all out of your system. You stole a lot of mine when you were a teenager, but the body always re-members, you see. The body always remembers."

Josephine tapped the blunt onto the ashtray on the desk near Maman's papers and said, "The body remembers, yes."

Josephine lowered her head and passed the blunt back to her mother. She placed her face in her hands, and her shoulders bounced up and down in sync with her soft weeping. Maman sighed and took multiple hits of the blunt. She usually waited for whatever Josephine needed to release from what happened in her bedroom before she said or did anything. But this night was different, and Maman was feeling good. Once her head felt less compact and more airy and her upper back tingled like her muscles were readying to detonate, she leaned over and caressed Josephine's abdomen. The touch froze Josephine into surprise.

"What are you doing?" Josephine hoarsely asked.

"I'm mothering you. You came down here for that, or did you just want to spill your frustrations?"

"I thought that was the same thing."

"Are you looking for affection? That's not the mother I ever was, Josephine. Still, you keep this fortysomething-year-old hope that I'll be better to you in the way that you like it—sweet, saccharine, doting, devoted."

"I wouldn't say that."

"Then how would you say it?" Maman passed her the blunt and leaned forward. Even while sitting down, Maman was a massive figure. Her legs were parted underneath her muumuu, and they extended like branches. She stretched her long neck and moved her hand down her frame.

"I would say—" Josephine inhaled. "You and I are just different, that's all."

"Different? Heh. Josephine, you came from me. I knew you before you knew yourself."

"You knew me as a child but not as a woman."

Maman raised her eyebrows. "Well. Pass me my blunt, then. I'm listening."

The cannabis hadn't cleared the trees in Josephine's mind yet. The more she inhaled, the more detached she was from anything that she was saying. "You don't know me as a woman, Maman. You see me walking around here and helping you with the numbers from time to time or helping with Helena and Hallow, but you don't know me. You don't know what this body remembers."

Maman leaned forward and caressed Josephine's abdomen again. "Grief never goes away, you know. It comes through many forms. Maybe . . . Hallow is that new form. Unfortunately."

"She might be. I didn't think she was at first, but tonight, I'm not so sure. She had on this pretty little coat that Landon bought her, and I started to hate her. I hated her because as she spun around, I kept asking myself, 'Whose pretty little child is this?' But no, no, she's mine. That's my child, but I didn't birth her. Yes, I take care of her, but she didn't come from me. We are close, but there's a deeper bond that we'll never have. And you know we don't do adoption. Our family has never done it. We never had to until now. And why would we? Whatever we needed we always found in one another, in our own blood. We never had to look outside of us."

Maman sighed. "How long are you going to beat yourself up for that, though, Jo?"

"You mean for raising somebody else's child?"

"She's not someone else's child. Shit. If I knew you were going to have this much guilt, we would've remained Catholics." Maman scoffed.

Josephine half smiled and said, "I'm serious."

"So am I. Here." Maman reignited the end of the blunt and took a swig of her absinthe. "I would've made us both a glass of Sazerac like the old days. Every time a woman has a problem that a man just can't fix, Sazerac helps—for the night, at least. But I don't feel like getting up."

"I know, I know. But I don't want it."

"You know, Jo, I will never know that kind of hurt. I will never know what it's like to lose in that way. But then again, I gave birth to two caulbearing daughters."

"What do you mean?"

"What do I mean?" Maman took the blunt from between Josephine's fingers and pulled. "If any of your children were supposed to live, then there was always a probability that they wouldn't have been born with a caul. But all your children died, and so we know that they weren't. Even if they had lived and weren't born with cauls, what kind of life were they going to have in here anyway? They would not be useful here. I've seen these dynamics play out back in Louisiana; the non-caulbearing ones always feel left out. Look at how Helena was lashing out at everyone when Hallow first moved in here. Now imagine what would have happened to your children. The body remembers, yes. But your body did you a favor." Maman raised the blunt toward Josephine as if she were toasting in her honor and took another hit.

Josephine's bottom lip dropped. She leaned back in her seat and replied, "My God. Is that what you think—that all children are good for is to be useful?"

"For our home, yes. Actually . . ." Maman's chest expanded as the smoke filled her insides. "For anyone's home. Children have to be useful. They weren't born just to be born but to continue a lineage. We have been given a gift, Josephine. Can't you see? The reason we've been able to stay here is not because there's ample opportunity for Black women to get ahead in traditional jobs, nor is it because of some benevolent landlord, but because of this . . ." Maman ran her fingers along the caul on Josephine's leg.

"I wouldn't say good as new but since we're on the subject of children, I actually have something that I've been sitting on for a while."

Maman placed her hands on her knees and leaned forward. "Go on."

"I would never do what you've done to Hallow, what you've done to me."

"What are you talkin' about?"

"You showed her off like a pet monkey. When you took her out a while back, you had to show her off by hurting her. You did the same thing to me when I was a kid and—"

"And what?"

"And it's fucked up."

Maman grinned. "Ah, now she has some bite. Keep it coming."

"It's bad enough that even to this day I have to look away when you cut her, and she just takes it like a good child. Doesn't nearly cry like I used to. But whatever you did to her when you took her to that block association meeting, Maman . . . it wasn't good."

"She'll get over it." Maman flicked the ash from her blunt into a silver tray.

"You have no idea what you're talking about. Nobody just 'gets over it.'"

"Sure they do. With time."

"I never got over my miscarriages."

"Because you like to be stuck in the past and wallow in your own misery."

"And you never got over Dad leaving you. His picture is still on your desk."

"Wow." Maman cackled then started to clap. "Brava. Someone's talkin' spicy now."

"Don't mock me."

"I keep your father's photo on my desk because he still gave me you and Iris. In my life I found that men are only useful for two things: money and children—both important to keep a family strong. Love is just a by-product."

"For you. I'm not like you. I love and then I love again. I love Landon and I love Hallow, and as her mother, I'm telling you, don't do that to her again. You only take her out if I say so, and I want a rundown of what happened when you two come back. Nothing happens off my watch, do you understand?"

"Hmm. Very well. Understood."

Josephine sat a little bit taller in her seat, grateful to finally have the respect that she had sought for a long time. In her proud posture, she could see the cracks on the wall behind Maman. They did indeed look like claws, and she was not sure if it was the cannabis or the flickering of the glowing light, but those claws flexed and retracted as though they were readying to snatch Maman up.

"How do you sleep at night with that? They look bigger from the last time I saw them."

Maman looked over her shoulder. "Oh, you mean Scuff? Aww, Scuff ain't so bad."

"You have a name for it?" Josephine asked, disgusted.

"Once you're so familiar with it like I am, you might as well give it a name since it's been around so long." Maman shrugged. "What are you gonna do? It's an old brownstone."

"Yeah, but—"

"Listen." She ignited her lighter while holding the blunt in her mouth. "This is my home. I worked my ass off to the white meat to maintain it. I'm gon' live in it and I'm gon' die in it and that's that on that. Do you understand me?"

Josephine nodded.

"Anyways, I'm getting tired." Maman placed the lighter on the nightstand, where the end of one of her pillows was hanging over it.

"You're never nervous about that?"

"About what?"

"That." Josephine pointed to the cloth of the pillow beside her lighter.

Maman shrugged her shoulders. "No, I'm not. I'm tired, Jo. Go back to Landon and give him what he came for and what you certainly dressed for."

"I'm not in the mood," Josephine said with her eyes still fixated on the lighter.

"You want him to go back to Valerie?"

"He can do whatever he wants. Valerie and I aren't in competition with each other. I like this freedom right now anyway."

"Spoken like an other woman."

"I'm not the other woman. I'm just someone he visits from time to time. Got no children between us so there's no one keeping him here."

"You forgot to count yourself."

"That's probably the nicest thing you said all night."

"And you do share a child together. Hallow is your child. You're the only mother she's ever known."

"Make that the nicest thing." Josephine yawned. "Maybe I will go back upstairs." She rose to her feet, and Maman grabbed her wrist.

"Do you feel ready to go back there? You had better make sure you've fully composed yourself before you go back up there with your man and child."

"You never told me why you even tolerated Landon, or me with him for that matter. He doesn't remind you of Daddy?"

"That he reminds me of your father is exactly why I tolerate him. I recognize the behavior. I knew from the first time he saw you that he would do anything for you, and that's why I brought him in. The money didn't hurt either. The devil you know is better than the devil you don't."

Josephine imagined herself twisting the doorknob, grabbing the bannister in front of her, and walking the path that led to the dark corridor upstairs. She slowly sat back down.

Suddenly, Maman stood up and walked over to a chest, where

she pulled out a rag, some micellar water, bobby pins, and a thick hair cream. She pulled Josephine and the chair closer to the side of the bed before dabbing the rag with some of the micellar water. "You remember when I used to do this?"

Josephine smiled. "Years and years ago. Back in the day."

"Mm-hmm. You know, Josephine—" Maman swiped the rag over Josephine's forehead, and the material turned brown with small streaks of a sheer highlighter. "When you take off your makeup at night, you can take off more than one mask. I know that you beautify yourself because you feel like you have to, don't you? You have to be on your p's and q's even when Valerie isn't. But you have more control than you think you do, and you have a family now." Maman stood up and parted Josephine's hair into four sections: one horizontal line across her scalp and the other going straight down from the top of her head to the nape of her neck. She took one side and slathered the hair with cream before twisting and pinning it to her head, then did the same to the other side. "I am impressed that you can juggle a man and a child. That wasn't my story, and maybe that's one way you and I are different. But you have to be assertive even when you don't feel like it. Even if you're wrong. I've been preparing you for this all your life: to be a mother and to pass on what I teach you to your child." Maman wrapped Josephine's hair in a turban similar to her own. She then handed Josephine an oval-shaped mirror and placed her hands on her shoulders. "Don't you see?"

As Maman rested her face on Josephine's right shoulder and smiled, Josephine sensed a quiet rage in her chest. How could she be assertive when all her life she was trained to serve no other interest but her mother's and that of the family as a collective? Josephine surveyed both their faces: their half-moon eyes, their widow's peaks, their high cheekbones, prominent lower lips, and hilly noses.

She had never noticed how much they resembled each other until tonight. Josephine couldn't remember the last time they'd truly seen each other eye to eye. Since Josephine was a child, any time they were speaking to each other, Maman made sure that in spite of her height, she would tip her chin anyhow. But now they were equal, and maybe it was time for Josephine to carve space for what she and only she wanted.

"I see, Maman." She shot a glance over at the lighter then back at their reflections, and broadened her smile.

8

Scuff was the first thing that Josephine saw when she woke up. Maman's breathing burned the nape of Josephine's neck, and her snoring tickled Josephine's ears. The sensation caused her muscles to tighten from the neck down, and she extended her arm toward the nearest claw. Its length was much deeper than when she last touched it. The inside of the crack was full of jagged chips, and she blocked the light piercing through with her slow touches. Its growth excited her. The more it grew, the better the chances of the claws all connecting in the middle and splitting the brownstone in half. Or maybe the claws would hit wires in the walls, strip them of their covering, ignite a spark, and incinerate everything. The concrete and the fire would fall onto their bodies, and once the rubble was cleared away, they would reemerge and begin their lives someplace else.

Josephine retracted her hand at the height of this fantasy, for she was disturbing herself with how much destruction aroused her. A creaking from upstairs caused another vein to emerge in the crack. She thought it was growing right in front of her. She hadn't yet wiped the crust from her eyes, but she blinked and that vein was still there. She didn't want to move just yet. The last time she had been lying in bed with Maman was when her father left for good.

"Who's making breakfast?"

Josephine looked over her right shoulder, and Maman was already at her desk cleaning her bifocals. The smell of bacon grease and buttered croissants overwhelmed her nostrils as soon as she faced the bedroom door.

"How would I know? I just woke up."

"No, you didn't." Maman chuckled. "I don't have to see your eyes to tell when you're sleeping or not." She uncapped one of her pens and shook her head with a smile. "What was on your mind?"

Josephine swung her legs over the edge of the bed and sat upright. "I suppose there's no point in lying because you'll know when I am doing that too, huh?"

"Yes, because you just told me that you were about to tell a lie. At least be more discreet about it."

"I'll try harder next time," Josephine sarcastically replied.

"You better. Hallow won't be small forever, and you have to invent more ways to elude her the older she gets."

"Especially with the biggest lie of them all."

Maman's bifocals slid down her nose when she leaned toward Josephine. She caressed Josephine's abdomen and said, "There's no lie. Do you know who her mother is?"

Josephine shook her head.

"Then how can you lie about what you don't know?"

"But I didn't birth—"

"Ugh." Maman slapped her thighs. "Josephine, I won't hear any more of this. You're going to have a very difficult life if you don't get over this. Think about what kind of life she would've had otherwise. Her birth mother didn't want her. There you go again with wallowing in your misery." Maman returned her attention to her study and began sifting through a stack of papers on her desk.

Josephine stood up and started toward the door.

"Wait."

Josephine turned around, her mouth slightly ajar and her eyes full of supplication.

"You don't want to fix your hair before you walk out the door?"

Josephine touched the top of her head and felt the satin of a large, pillowy bonnet. Underneath that bonnet was crimped hair in twists that Maman had pinned to her head last night. But she was hungry, and she didn't want to spend time getting her hair together in order to look presentable for her man. She couldn't remember the last time Landon had seen her without makeup. There was never a justifiable excuse to get up from the postcoital bed and remove her mask. At the very least, she would have some rouge and apply some bronzer. After climaxing, she would go to her vanity, have her moment to cry or get lost in her mourning for all the children she couldn't carry to full term, and retouch. She looked down at her right hand loosely hanging on to the doorknob and gave it a sharp twist.

The grease was popping loudly in the kitchen. Her mouth watered, and she licked her lips. When she turned into the dining room, there was a basket of fluffy yellow biscuits in the center of the table. Josephine could hear Hallow smacking her lips before she could see her small body behind the biscuit basket. Her mouth was smeared with grape jam and butter. Hallow looked up from her biscuit, and her eyes sparked. She did not say a word; she merely continued munching and smacking. Josephine held a finger up to her lips and tiptoed to the kitchen, where Landon was moving from the stove to the oven and back again. The grease from the bacon soaked the paper towels laid over a plate. The eggs were scrambling in one skillet, and the sausages were charring in another.

Josephine leaned on the wall with her arms crossed and said, "You've never done that before."

Landon whipped around.

"Good morning." Josephine smiled.

Landon beheld the dark circles around her eyes and the pockets of blemishes on her nose and chin. Her eyebrows weren't as full as they'd been many nights prior, and neither were her lips. He shuddered, then became embarrassed that he could not restrain his surprise that he was looking at his lover for the very first time. She saw him watching her and curled a small nap at the base of her head. Its length was not enough to justify her spinning her finger around and around. Her right hand rubbed along her shoulders, and the stretching emphasized the long, arachnid veins circumscribing her throat. Her left hand crossed over her abdomen to brace herself for an insult about her looks. "Good morning," Landon said. "You've never done that before either."

"You've never seen me look this plain before, I know."

"You could never look ordinary to me, Jo. Never in a million years."

Josephine's smile faltered, but Landon immediately changed the subject. "Please have a seat. I'll make you a plate. What do you want on it? Everything?"

Josephine nodded and took a seat on the opposite side of Hallow. "Where's Helena?"

"I tried to get her, but she told me she'll be down in a minute."

"Hm. More for us."

Hallow loudly gulped and wiped her mouth with the back of her wrist. "Mommy?"

"Yes, dear?" Josephine asked while pouring a glass of orange juice from the large glass pitcher beside the biscuit basket.

"Where were you last night?"

"With Maman."

"Is everything okay?"

"Everything is fine, sweetheart. Sometimes mothers need their own mothers."

Hallow chewed on the end of one of her pieces of bacon and asked, "Mommy?"

"Yes, baby?"

"Dad said that when I was born, you were on your knees like a dog and an old lady helped you and she was praying and whispering to me and you were dressed in blue and there were seashells and you were so tired from trying to have me. Is that true?"

Josephine's eyes locked with Landon's as soon as he entered the dining room with her plate. He halted at the head of the table and breathed heavily. Hallow's eyes bounced between both parents.

What? Josephine mouthed to him.

She asked, Landon mouthed back. This was what Josephine was afraid of: the lies having to beget more lies, especially for a child as curious as Hallow.

"Yes." Josephine cleared her throat. "Yes, it's true. But I blocked so much of it out, Hallow. I was in a lot of pain, baby. I forgot all about it once you were born."

"Are you going to have any more kids?"

"No." Josephine shook her head. "No, Hal."

"Why not?"

"Eat your food, sweetheart." Josephine nearly swallowed her biscuit whole and quickly guzzled her orange juice so that neither Landon nor Hallow would say anything else to her until she was physically capable of responding.

Helena finally came downstairs with her nose buried in a book. She plopped down at the closest available chair and turned the page.

"Hello," Landon said. "Don't you think you can put the book down and have a conversation with us?"

"Sorry." Helena put the book down. "It's just really an interesting read. We were allowed to pick any book we wanted to write a report on, and I chose this."

Hallow grabbed the red paperback book and read the title. "*Push*."

"Mm-hmm. It's about a girl who grew up right here in Harlem. She's having a lot of trouble as a teen mom. And her mom abuses her too—"

"Don't you think this is a bit of a heavy conversation in the morning?" Josephine asked. "Food is in the kitchen. Help yourself."

"Not really. I mean there are parallels."

"Between the book and what?" Landon asked.

"Here."

Landon, Josephine, and Hallow stared at Helena.

"Child abuse?" Hallow asked.

"Helena, go get something to eat," Josephine said.

"I mean, yeah," Helena said, and turned toward Hallow. "You don't think what y'all do here is normal, do you? We're dysfunctional."

"What does that mean?" Hallow asked.

"Helena—" Josephine interjected.

"Out of whack. Broken. Don't worry, I didn't tell anyone about our family. I wouldn't. But I can't wait to turn eighteen. The social workers here in this book help Precious—that's the girl's name. Maybe I can be like them. It ain't caul selling, but it's something."

"Child abuse." Hallow dropped her fork on her plate and stared at the napkin on her lap.

"God, Helena. Do you ever just shut up?" Josephine slammed her fist on the table, and everyone jumped. "I'm sorry. I—I don't know what's gotten into me this morning."

"Take it easy." Landon rubbed her back.

Hallow's head lifted when Iris stood at the threshold between the corridor and the dining room. The ends of Iris's teal nightgown billowed with the air that she sucked out of the room with her unforeseen arrival. She wore oversized, amber-colored lenses that softened the wrinkles around her eyes. The top half of her hair was twisted and bobby pinned; and the lower half, cluttered with many split ends, seemed to elongate in front of Hallow's eyes whenever she raked her fingers through the strands.

"Good morning, everyone," Iris said. Helena, whose back was facing the entrance, slowly sat upright and tightened her grip around her fork. "Breakfast seems delicious. Would've been nice if someone would've alerted me earlier, since y'all seem almost done with your food." Iris walked to the kitchen and continued, "Either you wanted me to see for myself or you didn't want me to join you at the table."

Iris walked over to the side of the table where Hallow sat and winked at her as she lowered herself into her seat. Hallow beamed. Iris gave a drawn-out sigh and started pouring herself a glass of orange juice. "I don't really give a shit if you treat me like I can't hear the things you say, but I refuse to be a beggar in my own home." She flicked a bit of cumin that she held between her fingers into her glass of orange juice and drank it.

"You sounded busy down there," Landon replied.

"I'm always busy, Landon. I take it you were the one who cooked, right?"

"That's right."

"Hm." She kept her eyes on him while she chewed a piece of bacon with her mouth open. "It's good. I don't mind my bacon with a lot of fat on it. Makes me think the swine lived a full life before the slaughter. But you should've cooked it longer. Bacon's best a little burned, don't you think?" She took another bite and chewed loudly, her mouth slightly open. "Then again, you gotta be careful with the smoke, especially in a place like this. Too much smoke and not enough attention and . . ." She blew a sharp gust of air with her mouth that made everyone jump.

"Iris, can I ask you a question?" Helena asked.

"Hmm?" Iris took another bite of her bacon.

"When I had that accident at the zoo years ago and I couldn't find you, where were you?"

Josephine and Landon dropped their utensils on their porcelain plates and looked up.

"I—"

"We shouldn't be having such a discussion first thing in the morning," Josephine interrupted Iris.

"So when would be a good time? It's been years already," Helena said.

"Helena, drop it for now, hmm?" Landon said.

"I'm sorry. I just . . . I just feel like it was my fault, but I was just a kid and I can't make sense of it and—"

"It wasn't your fault," Iris said. "It was never your fault."

"Iris," Josephine sternly said.

Suddenly, Iris dropped her silverware and her head slumped over her shoulders.

"Oh no," Josephine whispered.

"Iris?" Hallow asked and gently tugged at the end of her night-gown. "You okay?"

"Stop touching her, Hallow," Landon sternly said.

"Yeah, Hallow. Leave her alone."

There was a buzzing sound followed by whining, but Iris's jaw wasn't moving. The sounds got louder, as if there were mosquitoes filling her mouth, and when she finally lifted her head, she did not look toward anyone else in the room. The ceiling was her focus. Her eyes remained fixed on the upper right corner of the room. After a moment, the sound stopped. Her lips began to move, and the words delayed.

She looked down at her plate and up at the corner of the room. "No. No, you can't have some of my food. Why? Because you're too little, kids. You don't even have teeth. Your mouths aren't even all the way there. When will they get there? They won't, darlings. They won't, I'm sorry. No, no, I can't do anything about it. You left on your own, remember? You left on your own. We wanted you here. But you left. Well, I'm not the one you should be speaking to. No, no, I will not drag her into this. Because she can't see you. She'll never be able to see you. She's not like me."

"Iris, stop it."

"You can see her. She's beautiful, isn't she? No, no, babies, she can't see you. She can't see dead people."

"Stop it, Iris," Josephine repeated herself.

"Oh no." Iris began to tear up. She walked toward the corner of the room and said, "Don't cry. It's better this way. Look how beautiful you are. Aw." Iris cocked her head to the side and pressed her palms together in a praying stance. "I see her in all of you."

Josephine hurriedly poured herself the last bit of orange juice in the pitcher and kept her hand on the handle.

"Why—you have her nose. And you—you—oh. That mouth. That's our mouth. And look at that big belly—"

Josephine swung the pitcher at the back of Iris's head, and Hallow screamed. Landon ran over to shield Hallow, but she pushed him away, screaming and crying until he had no choice but to put her over his shoulder. She beat her fists on his back, begging for him to let her go, as Helena casually carried her plate into the kitchen to rinse and place in the dishwasher.

Josephine stood over Iris's body, breathing heavily and shaking as Iris's gray hair gradually became a sea of red and the glass shards embedded in parts of her head glimmered in the light. Moments later, Maman dashed into the room and saw an unconscious Iris on the ground and Josephine shuddering in the corner.

"Now I see who you really are without all that makeup." Maman smirked. Impressed, she placed a hand on her hip, tucked her upper lip into her mouth, and nodded. "Drag her into the corridor and bring me my utility knife."

9

Hallow was inconsolable and would not stop screaming. She planted her face in the mound of Josephine's bedsheets and would not turn to face Landon, no matter how much he nudged and pulled at her shoulders. She would lift her head to catch her breath and stick her head back down to scream into the sheets. Landon looked toward the bedroom door, where Josephine was leaning against the hinges, her sister's dried blood crusting underneath her fingernails.

"Josephine!" Maman called from downstairs. "Bring her downstairs! I'm ready to start." A one-two sharpening sound of some metal succeeded her last words.

"Jo—" Landon said.

"Just give me a minute, okay?" Josephine shut the door and pressed her back up against it. "I just . . . I'm trying to catch my breath, and Hallow is scared."

"But you don't want to piss Maman off."

"You know something? Sometimes I wonder if you have less of a backbone than I do."

Josephine walked toward her bed and knelt down close to the side where Hallow was curled into the fetal position.

"Hallow, baby. It's Mommy. Hallow, baby, can you hear me? I

need you to come downstairs with me. Maman wants us. Hallow, baby?" She extended her arms toward Hallow and retracted them as soon as she saw the hills and valleys of blood. She wiped them on her blouse and held Hallow up to face her. Hallow's face was red and her eyes swollen from all of the crying. Josephine waited for Hallow's cries to simmer down to whimpers and picked her up. "Just hold on to me," Josephine whispered in Hallow's ear as her face rested on her chest. "It'll all be over soon." Landon followed behind with his hand on the small of Josephine's back, and offered Hallow a small smile whenever she looked up at him as they made their way down to the foyer.

"Iris, wake up now," Josephine said. "Iris, this isn't funny. I know you're fine. Get up."

Iris wouldn't move.

"Forget about it. It's better if she doesn't move anyway. Let her stay there."

"Maman . . ." Josephine leaned forward toward her and said more quietly, "I thought we had an understanding."

"We did. Nothing happens off your watch, and it's not."

"But I told you not to do that to her again."

"You told me not to put her on display, and I'm not. I am, however, teaching her how to cut since she'll need to do it when she's older. Besides, I'm sparing Hallow from being cut for the next time we have a client and having Iris go this time since she's already lying flat."

"But don't you see Hallow's scared? Enough, Maman, okay? Enough!"

"Her fear was not some prerequisite that we agreed upon. Don't forget who makes executive decisions around here. Now move." She brushed past Josephine's shoulder, which sent her daughter's balance off-kilter.

"Dexter-Russell," Maman said as she waved an eight-inch butcher knife in the air. "The polypropylene handle makes it easy for anyone to use, dexterous or not. Pull up a chair. The both of you."

"No, I'll stand," Landon replied. Josephine tightly closed her eyes and pursed her lips but did not give him the satisfaction of showing him how annoyed she was with a cutting glance.

"Fine. Jo, take my seat, and Hallow, you take this seat."

"Maman, she wants to stick by me. She's scared." Josephine pressed a hand to the side of Hallow's face and pulled her in closer to her chest.

"Both of you are being extremely difficult when it was not I who soiled my Persian rug. But fine. Whatever." Maman stood over Iris, who was now lying on many plastic sheets, and held her knife up to the light. "Like I was saying, the grip of this Dexter-Russell knife is important. This is how you make the most precise cuts. The pointed steel blade. The straight edge. Are you listening to me?"

"Maman, I know what you're talking about already," Josephine said.

"I'm not talking to you, you idiot. I'm talking to Hallow."

Hallow lifted her head and wiped her eyes. She looked down at Iris, who was seemingly still unconscious, with small shards sticking from the sides of her head, and asked, "When will she wake up?"

"She's up. She's just jerking your chain, being extra as usual. Think about what happened when I burned your finger and when Helena pushed you down the stairs and you broke your bones. You got better, didn't you?"

Hallow nodded.

"Same goes for Iris."

"But—"

"But nothing. I could jam this knife in your chest right now, and before you know it, that gash would seal itself and you wouldn't even see a faint hint of a line down your sternum. But if I did the same to ol' lover boy over here . . ." She made a stabbing motion in his direction, causing him to flinch. "Heh. He'd die of shock before the ambulance even got here. Look at her chest, Hallow. You see it rising and falling? She's not dead."

Hallow leaned over to get a closer look at Iris, and when she saw that her chest rose and fell, she removed herself from her mother's lap and sat in her own chair.

"Very good. Now, what did I just say to you? Do you remember what I said about this blade?"

Hallow repeated what she'd said word for word.

"Perfect. Now, we don't need much. Only as much as a thumb or a pointer finger length's worth of caul. One piece of it should be enough to pay to get that rug cleaned or replaced."

"That's it?"

"That's it. We help people, Hallow. Never forget that. Everything here was maintained by us, by our bodies, so that we don't have to answer to anyone or anything. You may not understand how powerful that is now because you're still young, but one day you will because all of this is going to be your responsibility. Understand?"

Hallow nodded.

"I cannot hear you."

"Yes, Maman. I understand."

Maman placed the knife in front of Hallow and said, "Here. I want you to hold it."

"Maman—" Josephine interjected.

"Shh! Go ahead, Hallow. Just grab the handle." Hallow turned her head slightly, and Maman commanded, "Don't look at your mother, look at me."

Hallow reluctantly held the knife with a slack wrist, slowly turning it from side to side to assess its range.

"How does it feel in your hands?"

"Cold. Smooth. I don't know."

"Well, you better know soon enough. You're going to have to learn how to use it."

"Maman, that won't be for years," Josephine chimed in.

"No. It's going to be today. Hold my hand here, sweetie."

Landon walked over to Josephine and gripped her shoulder with increasing pressure with each step that Maman and Hallow took toward Iris's body.

The doorbell rang followed by three loud raps.

"Were you expecting someone?" Maman whispered to Josephine.

Josephine mouthed *No*.

"Police!" a voice yelled from behind the door.

Maman straightened her posture and started toward the door. "Out of all the years I've been in this place, not once have the police come." She cut her eyes at Josephine and Landon. "Neither of you better be lying to me."

She opened the door, and two portly officers stood on her porch. One of them took off his hat in deference, and the other squinted and sized her up from head to toe.

"We've gotten some complaints about some suspicious activity that's been going on here, and we've come to inquire." The interrogating officer, whose badge said EVANS, pulled up his trousers, which could not be supported by his thin belt. His gut pillowed over the buckle, and one button on his uniform shirt was hanging on by a single thread. Maman relaxed her shoulders and leaned toward him, as she surpassed him in height by several inches.

"Do you have a warrant?"

"No, we do not, ma'am." The younger-looking officer removed his hat and smiled. "We just want to check to see if everything is all right."

"But we'll come back with one if need be," Officer Evans added.

"In that case, I'll await your return. Good day to you both." As Maman stepped back to close the door, Officer Evans looked beyond Maman's left shoulder and saw Hallow holding the knife that Maman had given to her without the support of a strong wrist. The handle was bigger than the girl's hand, and her elbow pointed at the side of her rib like she did not know what to do with the knife.

The officer placed his foot in between the door and the frame and said, "Just a moment." He pointed. "What's that child doing with that knife?"

Maman half turned around and opened the door wide enough to reveal Iris's body on the rug. The two officers entered through the space she inadvertently opened up by pivoting. Now that the police were in, Maman could not kick them out without force. She surveyed the block for witnesses, but there was no one else but a white couple walking their baby on the other side of the street, and she gently closed the door.

For a moment, no one spoke. All the adults' eyes jumped from person to person. Their bodies circled Hallow and Iris.

"Somebody better start talking soon, or I am taking you all down to the precinct."

"Hover your hand over Iris's nose. She's fine."

Officer Evans did what Maman said to do and felt hot breath in his palm.

Maman caught a glimpse of the officer's badge. "You wouldn't happen to be the husband of Sister Evans, would you?"

The officer faced Maman. "Yes."

"The one who attends the block association meetings at that Presbyterian church down at the corner?"

"Yes, that's right."

"She's sick, is she not? Poor woman. I saw it in her walk. You could set a glass on her back. And those hands. She has more stems than a tree, and her face looks like a mold falling from the cast. For someone still fairly young, she's not well. She came to me and asked what I could do for her."

The younger officer turned to Officer Evans, whose eyes had now welled up with tears and whose Adam's apple bobbed up and down in his throat with the words he could not say. "Mike, I think you ought to go back to the precinct," Officer Evans said through clenched teeth.

"And leave you here by yourself?" He leaned into Officer Evans's ear and whispered, "I'm supposed to be your backup for things like this."

"I don't need backup," Officer Evans replied at regular volume. "Go on. I'll fill you in later."

"You sure?"

"Boy, I said go on."

His backup took one last look at everyone in the room and left.

Once Officer Evans heard the door close, he walked up to Maman and tipped his chin to meet her face.

"What all did she tell you?"

Josephine and Landon leaned forward and waited.

"Many things. Things women only tell to other women. Things a man cannot know because what he cannot fix would drive him crazy. But I have something for her."

"No, no. I've heard about you lot, and I was there."

"There for what?"

"There for what you did to Laila Reserve."

"Who's Laila Reserve?" Hallow asked.

There was a brief pause. Josephine, Landon, and Maman alternated looks at one another.

"Quite frankly, I don't give a damn what you believe. Your wife does. It's already started." Maman swiveled to Hallow and said, "Sweetheart, it's time for you to practice. Come kneel down right here with me."

Hallow did not move until Maman placed her arm around the right side of her body and pulled her toward Iris's legs. They knelt beside each other, and Josephine balanced Hallow's grip on the butcher knife. Softly, she said, "Remember what I told you. Can you see how the light shines on the caul? You see it?"

Hallow nodded.

"I cannot hear you."

"Yes."

Hallow did a double take at Josephine, who nodded. "Go on." She watched Josephine and Landon, whose faces were just as stricken with apprehension as her own; Officer Evans, whose bottom lip protruded and eyebrows caved into the glabella; and finally, Iris, who remained dormant in spite of everything that went on. Hallow tapped the caul right above Iris's left ankle and flashed a glance at Iris's face. Then she thumbed the caul in and around its ridges and noticed that its texture felt different than her own. The caul was much harder and crystalline, unlike hers, which was softer and luminescent. Hers was dew and Iris's was armor. Because of Iris's age, the distinction between Iris's caul and epidermis was more defined than what it would be on a child. Maman wasn't close to finishing the next part of her instruction before Hallow cut a piece of Iris's caul in the shape of a boot and became overwhelmed with surprise at the crunch from the incision. She held the severed part of the caul, which had now shrunk in her hand, up toward the chandelier so that she could get a better look at it. Maman coaxed the caul from Hallow's fingers and patted her on the back. With the caul now dried and browned in both hands, Maman laid her palms out in front of Officer Evans and said, "Take it." Hallow noticed from the periphery that Iris's eyeballs seemed to be moving while her lids remained closed and wondered how much time had passed from Josephine striking Iris to her being moved out into the foyer. She should've been awake by now if Maman's estimation was correct. The layer of skin now bare from the incision was smooth and glossy like a newborn's. Hallow wanted to reach out and touch it, but she refrained. She was not aware of all that she had done, and yet she felt vital to whatever plan Maman was concocting. She was precocious, but her wits had their limits.

"I don't want it," Officer Evans replied. His bottom lip dropped lower, toward his chin, giving him the look of a petulant child, and he took one step back with his right foot.

"Come on. This is a gift, and we won't ever have to speak of this day again. You write me up for disturbing the peace or whatever and we go on about our business. I'll even wrap it in our signature matte paper with a wax seal."

Officer Evans took one look at Iris and could not fix his jaw to hold back the floodgates of his emotion for his ailing wife. He snatched the caul and stuffed it in his pocket. "I'm taking this in for our files. I don't believe in any of this shit."

"I believe that you do," Maman said. She escorted Officer Evans to the front door and made sure that it clipped the backs of his feet as he exited. She kept her hand on the door panel and grinned with clenched teeth. "Now that he's implicated . . ." Maman pivoted and returned to the foyer. "We can all disperse. I, frankly, need a nap."

"We're just going to leave her here?" Hallow asked.

"She'll be fine."

"But she hasn't woken up yet."

Maman rested her right elbow on her left arm and said, "This is true. Strange but true. But she will. Run along now. You're not needed any longer. Jo—take her."

"Come on, sweetie." Josephine pulled Hallow to her feet and gradually inched her toward the staircase with Landon following behind them.

Hallow staggered her steps to keep an eye on Iris through the spaces of the balusters and saw how she rose, shook some shards out of her hair, and walked toward the stairs leading to the basement. The brownstone fell silent as everyone dispersed to different corners. When Hallow returned to her room, she sat on her bed in a stupor over what had just transpired. Josephine and Maman were right: Iris was conscious or had to have been conscious the entire time the police were questioning them and when Hallow was cutting her. But why didn't she just open her eyes? What game was she playing? Hallow could hear her heartbeat in one ear and an incessant ringing in the other. Hallow never felt more like an interloper than when she witnessed the way everyone continued on with their days almost completely and utterly detached from what they were doing to one another.

Maybe Helena was right: this family was broken.

10

The spirits became more charged and needy since that day of the police visit. For the next five years, they appeared more frequently to Iris after Josephine struck her with that glass pitcher, dislodging her mind's processing of who said what and when. The accident made Iris seem even more untethered from this world. Her gait was uneven, and her bones cracked as if her ligaments needed oil to keep the machinery of her body from rusting. If one were to look close enough around her hairline, they could see small dents where the shards were once wedged in her head.

Eye contact became a challenge. When in conversation with another relative, she had gone from looking beyond the person's face to toward the ceiling, as though she was searching for something above her head. Iris's conversations with the spirits, once relegated to the basement, now happened anywhere and everywhere. Since that day when the NYPD came to the brownstone, Josephine never trusted herself whenever a glass pitcher was in reach, and Hallow wasn't sure if she forgave herself for cutting Iris, even if it was tradition. She was now thirteen and deep in the throes of puberty. The more she grew, the more she distrusted Josephine's authority. Meanwhile, Helena could not be bothered with her. She was in her senior year, and homework and parties and college applications commanded most of her attention.

Ever since that encounter with Officer Evans, Maman had become much more paranoid and banned anyone from working at the bodega so that she could keep an eye on everyone at all times, though she still attended block association meetings. Maman wanted to know who'd called the police and why. Because she couldn't find a culprit, she was suspicious of everyone besides Sister Evans. Sister Evans was enfeebled, and everyone knew what they would not say aloud. For the majority of several meetings, Maman scrutinized Sister Evans's body for the caul and could not find it anywhere. Maybe, she thought, Sister Evans maintained modesty and placed it somewhere only her husband could see. But if that was the case, then why was she still hunched over? Why had her hands lost the strength needed to hold a mere teacup? Then one morning Maman got the call from Patricia. Sister Evans had finally been called home. Her husband found her in bed after she didn't come down for breakfast despite his repeatedly calling out to her. Word was that when he found her body and realized that he'd kissed her after she had already passed away that morning, he had just enough in him to call the cops before having a stroke that paralyzed the left side of his face.

Maman contemplated sending her condolences through flowers and money, but that would have given the rest of Harlem all the affirmation they needed that she thought a homegoing service for one of the elders was beneath her, the lasting proof that she could not show compassion for another's mortality. Besides, she needed to find out why Officer Evans never gave his beloved wife that caul. The man's stubbornness had sent his own wife to the grave. Throughout the days leading up to the funeral, Maman roamed around the first floor absentmindedly. On the day of the funeral, Maman was shocked to find her entire household standing in the foyer, dressed in black. Her daughters had black veils over their faces, and the granddaughters wore black gloves. She wasn't expecting for them to come, but she didn't disinvite them either. They fetched a cab to Abyssinian Baptist Church—where Sister Evans was a member—and arrived in the middle of "His Eye Is on the Sparrow." Because of her Catholic upbringing, Maman was not one for the loud and ecstatic services that characterized most Black Baptist churches and motioned for everyone to make a beeline for the pews farthest in the back of the sanctuary. The members of the block association saw Maman and made a come-hither movement with their hands so that the Melancon family could sit near them.

They sat in the second row directly behind Officer Evans and his children. Everyone eyed down the Melancon family as they got situated in their seats. No one had ever seen the family together at once. Even the organist quieted down as the Melancon women made their way through the congregation. Josephine shielded her face with large, black sunglasses to avoid revealing her nervousness, and Iris wore the same to avoid making eye contact with anyone whose life she could see in a flash of images.

Hallow fidgeted, and Helena busied herself with her phone that she hid inside her wristlet. Whenever the pastor called for the congregation to stand, Hallow could feel the hot breath of a parishioner sitting directly behind her burning the nape of her neck and the spittle sprinkling her earlobes from every "Praise him!" and "Jesus!"

The hands of the clock on the wall behind the pulpit did not move. Or maybe they did but not fast enough, according to Hallow. She could feel everyone staring at them, and every point on her body began to throb with pain. When Hallow observed her family and how they were able to pretend that their presence did not unnerve every last parishioner in the sanctuary, she wondered for the first time in her life if she was truly related to any one of them. Not sure if her discomfort was due to teenage hormones or something deeper, Hallow immersed herself in her thoughts throughout the service, looked toward her mother for some assurance, and found her to be a stranger. She never noticed how different her mother looked in the open and wondered now if this were the reason why Josephine seldom let Hallow outside.

From Hallow's vantage point, she could see Iris slowly removing her right foot from her black heel and turning her knee inward, revealing her bare ankle. The boot shape was much more prominent in the fluorescent lights overhead, and when Hallow looked up at her aunt, she soon realized that she was being watched the whole time. Iris grinned at her then dropped her head. She jerked. Her neck cracked with each movement. Once the sermon and singing solo were over, the time had come for the congregation to form a long line in order to view the body. The transition provided Maman with the opportunity to inconspicuously twist Iris's arm and spit in her left ear, "Not now." Josephine reached into her blouse and pulled out a long strand of rosary beads. She cupped them in her hands and began to pray to God for restraint to not hurt her sister again. "Not now," she uttered. "Not this time. Or if it will be this time, let it be from someone else. Don't let my anger have anything to do with it."

Officer Evans was rocking back and forth in his seat while the choir roared a rendition of "Total Praise." With each octave they reached, his wavering body needed another person to lay hands on his arms to steady him. He buried his face in his hands and unleashed a cry that cut deep beneath the chorus and repeat of the bridge. When he lifted his head, he looked behind him out of embarrassment and choked back another cry upon seeing the Melancon women taking their place behind him. If he were not a man of

God and the law, he could have strangled every last one of them. He briefly wondered if he could at least slap the breath out of Maman and still bargain his way into heaven.

"How dare you," he said. The evangelists and deacons tried to restrain Officer Evans as he lunged forward at the Melancon women. "You have the audacity to take the pew behind me like you're family? Like you're friends?" He raised his voice and his circle of supporters gently shushed him and pulled back his shoulders to thwart his advancing lunge.

"We came to give our respects," Josephine answered.

"What respect? To the dead? You can't respect what you do not know. And y'all don't know nothing 'bout no death. You're—you're a bunch of witches! Witchcraft—that's what you do!"

"We're not witches, Officer Evans. We loved Sister Evans, and we as members of the community wanted to do right by her."

"You aren't members of this here community. Y'all are all for yourselves, and you lie to me to my face in God's house, of all places. You no good and you ain't honest."

"Your wife's all right now." Iris lifted her face and removed her sunglasses to regard Officer Evans the only way she knew how. "She's all right now. But she's unhappy with you."

"Now—now—now you cut that out." One of the deacons wagged a trembling finger at her. "Cut that out right now. That ain't of God."

"She won't leave me alone, Officer. No, no, no. Yes. No. Well, I can't ask him that. Not here. He's not ready, Sister Evans."

"What's she saying?" the same deacon asked but shrank when Officer Evans and the other deacons glared at her.

"She knows about the caul. She found it in your office drawer, and she wanted me to"—Iris cracked her neck and cleared her throat—"she wanted me to tell you that she had been waiting for years—five years—for you to give it to her. Though the caul wasn't going to work. You took too long and rendered it ineffective any-way. But she didn't know that. She just wanted to know why. She wasn't going to steal from you, but you never gave it to her. She gave up fighting, Officer. She was only forty-four. You were only forty-five. You both had many years left together. She wants to know, 'Why did you let me go?'"

Officer Evans leaned over the pew and slapped Iris in the face. He wrapped his hands around her neck and shook her like a chicken. The deacons tried to pull him off, but their strength was no match for the weight of grief and his physical rotundness. Iris's eyes rolled into the back of her head then toward the ceiling, where she could see Sister Evans take flight around the sanctuary. She no longer had a hump in her back or uneasiness in her gait. Iris allowed him to get all his frustration out and fell on the ground. To avoid drawing attention to what was happening, the evangelist threw a long white cloth on her and yelled a couple of *Yes, God*s for Iris appearing to be slain in the spirit. But then Iris crawled onto her hands and knees and used the edges of the pew to support her getting to her feet. When she finally stood up, people could see that the marks from Officer Evans's hands around her throat had disappeared.

The funeral attendees left saying they saw the marks vanish with their own eyes. Others would say the lighting was bad in certain parts of the church and they couldn't see a thing. Many would not speak of what they had and had not seen. But what filled everyone's spirit when the benediction was given was an entrenched contempt for the Melancon family—and this spite extinguished the incense of Christian worship and Christlike friendliness well beyond the walls of the church.

This contempt was subtle at first, as most grudges tend to be. Passersby on their block would slow their pace as they approached their gate and cease all conversation. They would extend their necks in hopes that the brownstone interiors would be accessible by eavesdropping. Some would be vocal in their belief that the Melancon women were possessed by some demonic spirit. Eggs were thrown at the street-facing windows, and dead birds were left on their stoop. There were two additional expenses that Maman had to account for: a vestibule, in case someone was strong enough to break down the doors, and more advanced home security.

On an otherwise uneventful afternoon, Josephine placed several layers over her body, adorned her head with a hat, and put on large sunglasses to prepare for a walk around the corner to visit their bodega. As soon as she exchanged greetings with the cashier and deli counter employees, the workers trailed Josephine with their eyes as she made her way down the aisles. She grabbed ahold of a bag of oatmeal cookies, blinked, and found that she'd misread the label. They were macadamia. When she raised her eyes to the row of processed snacks, the corners of her vision became blurry, and multicolored circles were floating everywhere. She was stressed and anxious; her skin constricted and her breathing became shallow. Unbeknownst to everyone else, from the moment Josephine hit Iris, she didn't trust herself, and though she hadn't had an outburst since, this visit was what she thought she needed to get out of her own head.

"Well, look who it is." A voice addressed her.

Josephine spun around to see a Black woman with long dreadlocks and skin the color of drenched red clay before her. The stranger leaned forward with a grip on her mobility scooter, and the other hand balled into a fist on her left hip.

"Excuse me?" Josephine asked.

"You're that bitch who took my sister's child away from her before she ever been born."

"Excuse me. I haven't any idea who you are."

"Take off those cotdamn glasses and maybe you'll see me better."

Josephine removed her sunglasses and immediately knew. She recognized the lines in the woman's face, which gave way to the rage that her sister displayed that Sunday afternoon. Her jaw dropped. "You're related to Laila."

"I am, and I haven't forgotten you. I can tell you ain't never had no children. Your hips the size of my ironing board. You walk around here all high and mighty. You ain't nothing but a doll. A pretty doll in a big ol' dollhouse." She spat on Josephine's pump. "You'll reap what you sow. You hear me? You done turned my sister crazy. Can't even walk outside, husband left her. This ain't the last you seen of our family. You hear me? I may not be able to beat your ass, but one day we will get you back for what you've done."

Josephine pushed her sunglasses up the arch of her nose and feigned a smile. "Good day," she said, and left.

Later that evening, Landon visited her bedroom and Hallow, who was old enough to know what they would do, left the room. When he mounted her, his foot accidentally hit a hard object underneath the bed and made a knocking sound. He hissed and leaned backward to see what had caused the pain, but Josephine pulled the ends of his shirt to bring him closer to her chest.

"What was that?"

"It's nothing." She smothered him with kisses before he grabbed both of her hands from his neck.

He got a good look at her face, looked underneath the bed, and pulled out an antique cherry trunk. He unlatched the locks to find several blouses and skirts stuffed on the inside and a wad of cash.

"Going somewhere?"

Josephine sighed. "Maybe."

"Where?"

"Someplace better. Come on, you shouldn't be surprised. I've wanted it for so long. And now that Hallow is older, I . . ." She dropped her hand on her thigh and leaned toward the window.

"You just want to leave her?"

"I—"

"Jo, no. No." She kept shaking her head. She closed her eyes and the tears streaked her cheeks. Landon crouched down and grabbed ahold of both of her arms. "Jo, listen to me. Listen to me."

"No. I want you to cut off most of our cauls and we'll sell them to our women in need in this neighborhood. I don't care about the price. We don't need much to leave, and we can move to White Plains or Pleasantville or, I don't know, the Berkshires."

"We? I can't leave, Josephine; you know that."

Josephine sniffed his mouth and said, "Your breath doesn't taste like a foul mix of citrus and dairy. She's given up caring. So why do you stay?"

Landon released his grasp and sat on the bed beside Josephine. He clasped his hands between his legs, and she recounted the confrontation she'd had at the deli.

"Damn," Landon said.

"Yeah."

"Did she say anything else? Are you really sure it was Denise?"

"Yes, it was. Why wouldn't it be?"

"I mean, your guilt has been eating you up all these years. Just wanted to make sure you saw what you really saw."

"I know what I saw. I ain't crazy. But, God . . ." She shook her head and started to cry. Landon touched her back, and she popped her shoulder to reject the touch. "Don't you see?" She turned toward him, and the glow of the nearby candles kept one side of her face in the shadows. "We're a cursed people. Always have been, always will be. And I can't stay here any longer. I'm dying. Don't you see? That's why I couldn't bring forth life. Don't you see? You're not looking at anything but a doll. A doll in a big ol' dollhouse."

Landon was familiar with Josephine's sadness. But this time, it was meted out through flickers and not large explosions. He didn't know what to do, so he did nothing. They sat in silence long enough for the glow of the candle to dim. In the darkness, he could see traces of Josephine's figure bending down and pulling the trunk to the middle of the floor before plopping into bed, which stunned him into immobility. How many nights had he touched her arms and not taken heed to his fingers sinking deeper and deeper into her skin? How many nights had he entered her body and she whispered to him to plunge deeper, to where he thought she intentionally wanted him to hurt her? How many nights had she asked for him to drag his fingers along the remaining pieces of her caul and pull? Before sliding underneath the covers alongside Josephine, Landon silently drew breath in his open hands and smelled traces of peppermint. Valerie did not give a damn about anything. The children were getting older. One needed money for college applications; another needed money for basketball. As the children grew and learned about autonomy, the distance between him and his wife stretched into a ravine. He and Josephine had Hallow, yes. But she was getting older, and she was becoming more independent even while sequestered in this dilapidating brownstone. The further Hallow pulled away from them both, the more he and Josephine pulled away from each other.

At least when she was a child, he and Josephine could try to imagine themselves in her small, chubby face, where the fixed mold of who she was destined to be had remained to be seen. But now her cheekbones sat high where his and Josephine's slumped. Her strands of hair roamed throughout her scalp, each one of different curl and texture, which alluded to her muddled origins. When she was little, she mimicked Josephine, but once she got her period, her mannerisms—from her stride to her manner of speaking—echoed Amara's.

Whenever Hallow would ask for him to pass the butter at mealtime or straighten her back and speak with the air of a diplomat about the minutiae or highlights of her day, he would have to do a double take, beam at her with pride, then find a quiet moment alone where he would seek a soothing word from the Book of Common Prayer. He thanked God that Josephine never asked questions about whatever became of Amara Danville and Laila Reserve, but that might soon change. He wouldn't know what to say, where to start. After the birth, he hadn't heard from his goddaughter Amara. She hadn't been to St. Philip's since she fell down those steps. He would call intermittently throughout the years, but whenever they would speak—always over the phone—her voice was erratic and rushed as soon as he said hello. She never gave details about her life and kept the conversation short and superficial.

But Pleasantville did seem nice, and the suburb was just outside of the city. He had been there twice for its hiking and cycling routes. He imagined a two-level colonial custom home with French doors, a sweeping staircase, and a dazzling chandelier that the neighbors could see on their evening walks with their partners or dogs. They could go to 125th and Park and take the Metro-North train and be there in less than an hour. Under any other circumstance, twenty-six miles is not enough distance to escape, but he was certain that neither her mother nor his wife would follow them. In fact, they both might be relieved in their absence. Valerie had her nice home and packed social calendar, and Maman had Hallow. The ease with which they could pull this off scared him. But that glimmer of excitement burned into ash once he also realized that the ease with which they could pull this off was due in part to his thinking his child was disposable. That's how he knew that he was not and never would be her father.

He readied himself for bed alongside a sleeping Josephine. He thought to pull the sheets off her body or unfurl her onto the floor. He looked at himself, looked at her, looked at them both, and experienced one of those subtle yet beautiful epiphanies that together, they'd gotten what they deserved. He could move with her to Pleasantville, file for divorce, and make her happy until they re-created this home and brought whatever they were running away from with them. Didn't he see now what he could not see before? They were in an amorous entrapment, sentenced to comb through the same problems in different seasons over and over again. Yes, her soul was withering away, and he along with her, to furnish a love that never produced anything, grew anything, or moved anywhere. The only thing that flowed between the two was money, and perhaps that was the most useful part of their relationship. He didn't know what Josephine liked. He didn't know what kind of woman she was outside of these four walls. Maybe, he thought, it was better if they parted ways, though he loved her tremendously. But he wasn't sure if that love could override his exhaustion. He didn't know what he would do in the meantime. He hadn't thought that far ahead.

When he opened the bedroom door, he decided to creep down the stairs to get one last look at Hallow before leaving, but the air felt tampered with. There were footprints on the cotton rug covering the staircase, but not on every step. The last three steps were clean, like whomever was there had jumped over them. He closed the door and walked toward Josephine's trunk. There, he got on his knees and started to fold her clothes piece by piece.

II

Hallow did not hear every word exchanged between Josephine and Landon, but she heard enough from her bedroom, where she eavesdropped. Usually, she couldn't care less what Josephine and Landon did. In her eyes, she didn't know what they were doing together. They weren't considerably affectionate, and any conversations they had were stale and repetitive. Their joint effort of putting up a guise of a nuclear family in Maman's brownstone was laughable. No one had to say anything. Hallow knew that he had other obligations that rivaled those at West 145th and Frederick Douglass Boulevard. She imagined him to be a criminal, but she knew he couldn't lie through his teeth to pull off a misdemeanor. She thought he could be an in-demand businessman, but he never made mention of any meetings or coworkers. Nevertheless, she felt that if he was her father, and the three of them were a family, why couldn't he be here all the time?

There was nothing on television that was compelling enough to overshadow the gravity of Josephine's confessions. Hallow chuckled at the thought of Josephine making her way down the staircase, much less leaving out the front door. If Josephine wanted to, Hallow assumed, then she would've already done it. Besides, neither

Josephine nor Landon was a match for Maman. They were flowers that leaned toward Maman's blazing energy. Every time Maman entered a room where they were already present, they turned to acknowledge her arrival. Every time she spoke, they maintained strong eye contact with her out of respect and fear. In short, they weren't going to do shit, and they were fooling themselves playing make-believe like children.

But Hallow could leave. For a few hours. She could grab her coat and walk around the corner with no destination in mind and smell that sweet, sweet air again. She was tired of regular cutting, the sound of the caul being severed from her skin, the parts held between Maman's fingers and packaged away in wax paper and cute bows for some buyer whom she did not know. There was no proof of how much had been taken away from her body, and if she was not careful, she could easily fool herself into believing that these procedures never happened. They all transpired like fever dreams anyway: dim lighting, Maman and Josephine and maybe Landon around her, her lying down on some cool sheet, maybe new age music playing softly in the background. Maybe none of this was real. But something about them had to be real, or else the rest of Harlem would not have hated them so much.

Why hadn't she refused to cut Iris? Why couldn't she have just told Maman no and gone upstairs? She soon realized that she was just as afraid of Maman as Josephine was and that they were two peas in a pod—pathetic. But she was not like Josephine. If she were a mother, she would not speak of abandoning her family that nonchalantly. Either Hallow never fully existed in Josephine's private thoughts or there was a much deeper reason for their metastasizing unfamiliarity with each other.

The legs of a bed dragging across the floor produced a screeching sound from the ceiling. Hallow supposed that their heartfelt conversation had been the foreplay for this moment. She crossed her arms over her chest and rolled her tongue around the inside of her mouth before standing up. Her frustration had to be released in some kind of way, and there was no remedy where she sat. As she was growing up and becoming more aware of consequences, there was hesitation to rebel and strike out. But there was no one else who might have a smidgen of an understanding of what she was going through besides Iris. The pariah is always the one who can give the best details of what's going on, because it's from a distance that everything becomes clear.

She crept down the staircase to the basement and heard how busy Iris was through her animated talking and the constant shuffling of items.

"Yes, yes, yes, what do you want? What do you want?" Iris asked in response to a knock on the door.

"Aunt Iris? It's Hallow. Are you busy?"

"Obviously. What do you want?"

Hallow pushed back the door and saw Iris walking around in circles and waving a blunt over her head. The lingering smoke added an element of theatricality to Iris's mutterings, and it was through the clouds and the eventual shapes they made in the air that Hallow deduced Iris had never been talking to her in the first place.

"I-I-Is it okay if I s-s-stay with you for a little b-b-bit?" Hallow stammered.

Iris twirled around and jerked her neck backward. "It's late— leave me alone."

"But you said—"

"Not you, child. I'm just—go ahead. Just give me a moment." Iris took a deep breath and said, "Okay. I think they've quieted. What's going on?"

"I can't sleep. Landon's here."

"Oh." Iris scoffed and sat down at her desk. "Say no more. I don't want a visual of that. Move those books and crap if you want to sit down."

Hallow quickly pushed them off onto the floor and sat down opposite her.

"You know . . ." Iris cracked her neck and cleared her throat. "Stop it. Stop it. I'm speaking to my niece. I know you been here. Well, you're just gonna have to wait. There's a long queue. Now . . ." Iris took another pull on the blunt, spread her knees apart, and leaned forward. "You know you're not supposed to be down here, little girl. Unless you're looking for trouble."

"I don't know what I'm looking for, Aunt Iris."

Iris could see the tears welling up in Hallow's eyes and sighed. "Aw, shit, girl." She moved her right hand with the blunt between her fingers toward Hallow's chest. "You want some?"

"I thought I'm not supposed to have any of this."

"You're not supposed to be down here either. Seems like you stopped asking for permission a long time ago."

Hallow hesitated to feign offense at Iris's response. That break signaled to both that Iris had her. Because of this, Hallow relaxed her shoulders and took the blunt in between her fingers, surveying its length, and felt as though she were a young child witnessing a pencil for the first time.

"Take it all in your mouth, okay? Hold the smoke in there so that it gets deep in your lungs. Don't just blow it out. That's my last one, and I don't take kindly to amateurs."

Hallow did as she was told, and the passageway from her throat to chest electrified with a rough, peppery sensation. Her cheeks stretched to hold the smoke, and when Hallow finally let go, she violently coughed and hid in a corner, hunched over and afraid that she would regurgitate bile or a piece of some organ. Those peppers migrated to the middle of her skull and dispersed throughout every angle of her head. Tears streamed down her face, and her nose became congested.

Iris cackled. "It got into your lungs, all right. Come on back over here. You'll be fine."

Hallow kept her right hand over her throat and once again took a seat opposite Iris. The roof of her mouth dried, and the tops of her shoulders and feet tingled. She watched Iris take another hit, and then she took another herself. The next hit did not sting or burn nearly as much as the first, so she took another and another until the skin on her face felt like it was slowly sagging lower and lower toward the earth. Her eyes were open and focused, but she was asleep on the inside, helplessly smiling at Iris as she mumbled off to the side and spoke half words.

"Since you're here . . ." Iris twitched. "I have a confession to make to you."

"Hmm?" Hallow sat upright then slumped in her seat.

"After Jo hit me with the glass pitcher, I was only out until I was pulled into the hallway. I was awake the whole time when you were cutting me. Felt every incision from top, bottom, and around the sides."

"Why didn't you say anything?"

"Because I wanted to see if you would do it: to get in line and do whatever you're told. And unfortunately, I was right all along. Pity. Thought you might be different." Iris raised the blunt to her lips, and Hallow grabbed her wrist.

"What do you mean by that?"

Iris shook her wrist free. "Exactly what I said. Don't matter, though. You're supposed to be what you're supposed to be."

Hallow took the blunt from her hands and pulled long until Iris had to stomp on her feet for her to stop. Hallow blew a long chain from her mouth without coughing into Iris's face.

"I have a question for you."

"What?"

"You talk to spirits, don't you?"

"You ask as if it's voluntary."

"Do you see my mother?"

Iris squinted and asked, "What are you talking about, girl? You high. You are really, really high."

"Is Josephine really my mother, Iris?"

"No. Are you happy? No. But she's as much a mother as you're going to get, so what's your problem?"

"Where is my mother? Can you summon her? Is she in here? Have you ever seen her?"

"No."

"No to what?"

"No to all."

"Why not?"

"You're a smart girl. Guess."

Hallow stared into Iris's eyes and watched her become more foreign than they ever had. She looked around the room, hyper-ventilating, and the walls were caving in on them both. Unsure if this was paranoia or an epiphany, Hallow crawled to the floor in the fetal position and placed a hand over each ear. This brownstone became far too small now that there was something else of her beyond those four walls. There was someone existing somewhere out there. Here. On earth right now. There was someone who Hallow could rightfully call her own. When the truth sank in and she realized that for years she had been stuck here, needed and unwanted simultaneously, the desire to be full was a pain now too familiar to hurt.

PART II

12

It had been two decades since Laila's public breakdown when another birthing story rocked Harlem. There weren't large crowds of Harlemites surrounding a woman to confront the Melancons this time, however. Instead, the crowds were protestors decrying the terrible fate that had befallen a child. The condemnations—at Duke Ellington Circle near Central Park on West 110th and Fifth, at St. Nicholas and Jackie Robinson Parks, and within the pews of several churches—were so loud and overwhelming that the Melancon brownstone was affected just like everyone else's home. With Hallow as the succcessor, she saw to it that the family was made more aware of what was happening in the neighborhood, but her family's interest could not be aroused. They were reluctant to get involved because they were relieved that their family name was not at the center of the drama. So Hallow tried another route.

Nearly twenty years old, Hallow was fixated on this particular story, as well as the voices of young Black women across the nation. She read every op-ed and watched all of the televised interviews, hanging on every word spoken by a Black woman about Black girls and their vulnerability, and the treacherous road for many to motherhood. She read them day and night, and when she couldn't contain her earnestness any longer, she invited other caulbearing women from other major cities—Oakland, Chicago, Houston, and Detroit—to convene at the Melancon brownstone to see what could be done, a rare move that no one else had tried in decades. Most caulbearing families had migrated out of Louisiana; most caulbearing families stayed apart from one another. They knew "safety in numbers" wasn't a universal truth. But this, Hallow argued, was urgent. She arranged their flights and hotel rooms, and lured them with the attraction of the Apollo, Broadway, Central Park, and the Empire State Building—sites that most of them had never seen before.

After kisses and hugs were exchanged, Hallow moved them all into the living room, where she plopped the latest issue of the *New York Times* on the coffee table. One woman, Maha, leaned forward to see the front-page news story, where a young Black girl's large mug shot was centered right underneath the headline, sucked her teeth, and said, "Chile."

Two weeks prior, on a Friday evening smack-dab in the middle of September 2018, sixteen-year-old Asali Givens staggered into the Dunkin' Donuts and Baskin-Robbins store near the corner of West 116th and Lenox Avenue. Abandoning protocol that restrooms are for customers only, a sympathetic cashier gave Asali the four-digit PIN to unlock the bathroom after she begged and pleaded that she could not wait any longer. Teens often hung out in that store, and three of them formed a line outside the bathroom. The first person in line repeatedly knocked on the door and cursed for whoever was in there to hurry the hell up. He was about to kick the door until his friend, second in line, tapped on his shoulder and pointed a finger at the blood pooling around his Air Jordans. The boys ran over to the cashier, who opened the door with a crowbar from the storage room and found Asali trying her best to wipe the lower half of her body. The cashier yelled for the manager, who shrieked at the sight of Asali's blood-soaked jeans. She called an ambulance, but Asali refused and left a trail of blood as she exited the store. The manager followed that blood all the way back to the bathroom, where she noticed a red line that split between the toilet and the garbage can. There were bloody paper towels crumpled up and folded over the surface. The manager urged the cashier to stay back. She grabbed a pair of latex gloves from that same storage room, crept over to the trash can, and pulled a few of the paper towels from the top, revealing a dead newborn.

In a matter of hours, the police were able to locate Asali by the tracks of blood on the ground and the white transplants, who were more willing than Black natives to point them in the right direction. No one in the neighborhood would have predicted that the story would gain traction beyond *Amsterdam News*, but then the local CBS station reported on it, then *New York* magazine and *Ebony*, and finally the *New York Times* added its own layer of drama to the story. Asali's defense team argued that the child had died almost immediately after birth, though Asali admitted that her child did open her eyes. But nevertheless, the story divided people across the city over whether or not Asali's abandonment constituted murder and if she deserved to be charged as an adult.

"Chile, what?" Hallow asked. "This is serious."

"It's a shame. A pity." Houston-born Maha popped her shoulders up and down. "But that's none of our concern. Ain't nobody tell her to put that baby in the trash can. She didn't want that baby, and she could've gone on birth control to keep her from having a baby in the first place. You know how many people would love a child?"

"That's not the point." Hallow grabbed the front page and read from it, "'In an unprecedented move from the Manhattan District Attorney's Office, Assistant DA Amara Danville will charge Givens as an adult.'"

"As she should! It's not like this girl simply jaywalked or toilet-papered a home—this is murder. She should be punished to the full extent of the law. I'm not understanding how any of this is relevant." Judith, a middle-aged woman from Oakland, rubbed her temples. "What does this have to do with us? What's done is done. And can we make this quick? I have *Hamilton* tickets for tonight, and I know traffic is gonna be a mess."

"This girl was from Harlem. She was born and raised right around here. The papers say that she was from a broken family and that she had behavioral issues. What if that child could've lived? What if we could've helped her?"

Josephine, who was sitting to the right of Hallow, lowered her head and sniffled. Hallow, along with the rest of the women, directed their attention toward her.

"Sinuses," Josephine said. "The air in here can be tough to work with, you know?"

"That's assuming the girl wanted the child, and even if she did, it's not like she would've been able to afford us," Maman chimed in. She was seated near the fireplace, and a cane rested against the arm of her chair. Above her head was an updated painting of the Melancon family, one in which Hallow was included. A stern-faced Maman and a disarmingly smiling Hallow sat side by side in the front row, and the rest of the women—Josephine, Iris, and Helena—stood behind them.

"Exactly," Hallow said. "She can't afford us. When's the last time we helped to serve anyone from our community—just anyone? We've had so many white people coming in and out of here, you would think it was a slave auction."

"Hallow—" Josephine said.

"No, Mom. White folks in here. White folks out there. This whole entire block is almost white now. What are we even doing?"

"We're having the same problem over in Oakland," Judith said. "I can't even tell you how much my rent has jumped these past few years, but if I wanna stay there, I gotta sell to these tech bros out in Silicon Valley, not the Black bohemians out in the west part of town. And let's just put this out there: most Black people ain't putting up the cash like white folks can. That's just a fact. So are we gonna be so altruistic that we sacrifice ourselves?"

"All I'm saying is that there has to be some kind of balance," Hallow answered.

"What balance?" Nevaeh, whose tone was as cold as the Windy City from whence she came, asked. She was only in her early forties, but her synthetic wig made her look a decade older. "We have to be more versatile nowadays. It's not like before, where you could just have a middle person find people to help seal the deal. Now we gotta use more technology and go online and find other routes like message boards and what's that name? Red—red . . ." Nevaeh was snapping her fingers.

"Reddit?" Hallow asked.

Nevaeh snapped her fingers once more. "There it is. And you know they are talking about us there, right? Mm-hmm, honey. Keep going down the rabbit hole of the World Wide Web. We ain't as much of a secret as we once were. We gotta be careful."

"A reporter was sniffing around here just last week," Josephine said.

"A group tour was taking pictures the week before that," Maman added. "I can't hear any more of this. Excuse me." Maman grabbed her cane and stumped across the living room to return to her bedroom.

"Is she always like that?" Jamellia from Detroit leaned toward Hallow and whispered to the group.

"Not always. But she has been for quite some time. I'll check up on her later," Hallow replied. "But anyway, ladies, let's refocus. What are we going to do to help the Black women in our communities? There has to be more that we can do."

"We can't save 'em all," Judith retorted. "You're not even twenty-one yet, so your caul still grows. The rest of us are in our thirties and forties. There's only so much of our cauls that we got left to give, and we can't risk our bodies and our livelihood for situations like this. For all we know, this girl may've never wanted the child in the first place and smothered her with paper towels in the bathroom. You said yourself that she didn't have a good home life. What kind of life would that child have anyway? It would've wound up in the projects and on government assistance."

"You sound like Republicans who think young Black mothers are welfare queens," Hallow said.

"I am socially liberal but fiscally conservative," Judith proclaimed with a straightened posture and a high chin. "You have to be realistic, Hallow. You're still very young. Listen to us."

"I am listening, but from what I read, Asali wanted this child. At least that's the sense I got."

"You're hearing, but you're not listening," Nevaeh said. "Even if what you say is true, if, hypothetically speaking, you would've given Asali the caul to what end? The caul couldn't make Asali rich, so she couldn't properly take care of that baby. She could've placed the caul on the child, and it could've lived, but then what? She put the baby in a Dunkin' Donuts bathroom trash can, for God's sake, Hallow. Does that sound like love to you?"

Hallow remained quiet.

Nevaeh leaned across the coffee table and touched Hallow's right hand, which was lying on top of the *New York Times*. "Sweetheart, that child was not wanted. There's not much hope for abandoned children, we all know that."

Hallow stared at the headline of Asali Givens's story and lost herself within the words. The child was abandoned, and maybe someone could have taken the child if it had lived. She was reminded of Iris's claim that Josephine wasn't her biological mother, a memory she had not dwelled upon since that night to avoid pain. But she had more questions now: If Josephine was not her real mother, then who was? If her mother was still alive, then hadn't Hallow been abandoned too?

"My apologies, I . . ." She pressed a fingertip to the corner of her right eye and said, "Will you all excuse me for just one moment? I seem to have gotten a bit ahead of myself."

Hallow walked to the hallway bathroom, twisted the doorknob, and tripped into the interior before locking the door behind her. Feeling constricted, she loosened a few buttons of her satin blouse before waving her hands in front of her face. The tears streamed down quicker than she could dry them. Once Hallow was able to steady her breathing, she straightened her back and leaned over the sink to inspect her face for any resemblance to Josephine or Landon. Where Josephine's nose was aquiline, Hallow's was wide. Hallow's eyes were round, and her parents' almond-shaped. No matter which angle she turned her head, the light could not contour her enough to fool her into believing that their face shapes were in any way similar. She wanted to believe that Iris was lying, to not allow the pain to settle in, but she saw no resemblance to either Josephine or Landon.

Now she was beginning to recall more of what happened the night Iris alleged that Josephine wasn't her mother. The morning after Hallow visited Iris, she woke up on the living room sofa feeling as though her body and mind were torn apart from each other. When Josephine had asked what happened, Hallow told her nothing and did not change her story, no matter how much coaxing and brib-ery were presented to her. Hallow never brought up the issue with Iris again, and Josephine could not be in the same room with her sister unless they were at opposite ends. These loose threads were forming a spindle that was pulling Hallow more toward paranoia than measured inquiry. What if everyone else in that brownstone knew that Josephine wasn't her mother? What if their persistent eyes were filled with pity and their smiles with pleasure at the im-postor sitting before them with such counterfeit confidence?

Someone knocked three times on the door, interrupting Hal-low's thoughts. The diminishing force behind each rap was enough for her to know it was Josephine. When Hallow opened the door, Josephine peeked her head in and flashed an unimposing smile that made Hallow step back and allow her into the bathroom.

Josephine gently closed and locked the door behind her. "You okay?"

"Yeah, I just needed a moment, that's all. I'm fine."

"Okay."

Hallow raised her shoulders and opened her palms simultane-ously. "Was there anything else you wanted to say?"

"Not really. I just wanted to make sure you were okay. They were pretty intense back there, weren't they?"

"Yeah, but I can take 'em. I just wish Maman hadn't left like that. I'm still getting used to having more responsibilities around here, and it seems like she always dips out too soon because she's tired or upset or something. It's like she wants to be detached from everything nowadays."

"Maman is close to one hundred, Hallow. You have to be mind-ful of this. She has seen a lot."

Hallow sighed. "I know." She placed her arm on the wall and rested her forehead upon it, slowly rubbing from side to side.

"Hal, you seem stressed."

Hallow lifted her head and blinked at Josephine. "What do you think about this story, the one of the sixteen-year-old girl?"

"Nothing of it."

Hallow scrutinized how tightly the ends of Josephine's mouth were pulled back and said, "I don't believe you."

"I'm serious. I may not be as old as Maman, but I've seen things too. I know of too many women who wanted children and couldn't have them or had them, but they didn't last long."

"How do you know of any women? You don't have any friends. You barely go out."

Josephine folded her hands and swallowed. "I had a life before you, Hallow, and I've seen things."

"What things?"

Josephine said nothing. Instead, she kissed Hallow on the forehead, gripped her shoulders, then left the bathroom.

A few moments later, there was another knock at the bathroom door. Hallow flung the door open, assuming it was Josephine again.

Iris rested her elbow in the crook of her left arm and propped her chin on her knuckles.

"Oh, Iris." Hallow rolled her eyes and placed her hands on her hips. "What is it?"

She asked, "We never painted over the spearheads, did we?"

"We did."

"Did the painters use a primer before painting?"

"Why would they have needed to use a primer?"

"I see. Probably best to return to the party, don't you think? You don't want to keep our guests waiting." She placed a hand on Hallow's back and led her out into the corridor. The ladies were engaged in some kind of lively conversation in the meantime, which made Hallow think they weren't all that concerned about her interlude.

Out at the front gate, Hallow examined the spearheads with their fresh paint job and ran her fingers along their smooth surfaces. She rubbed once or twice and could smell the chemicals. She dug her sharpest fingernail into a spearhead, and a side of the paint cracked off and fell onto the pavement. There was a deep red mark that rusted the wrought iron. She chipped away at another spearhead to find another red mark, more jagged and less symmetrical. Every last spearhead she chipped and there were more red marks that stained the fleur-de-lis design—some were long vertical lines dragging down, others looked like fingers, as though someone had grabbed the gate and held on for dear life. Whatever it was elicited chills throughout Hallow's body as frightening possibilities of what kind of story lay underneath the paint sprang up in her mind.

She looked up at the brownstone and cocked her head to the side. From a certain angle, it looked as if it were sinking, but when Hallow blinked again, the structure stood upright. Then, a few moments later, at the left corner of the first floor, the curtains rippled and a person emerged. There was Iris standing and watching her. Then she vanished.

13

Amara had done everything she was supposed to do to get ahead. She worked tirelessly day and night at the Lillian Goldman Law Library while she was studying at Yale Law. She completed the most prestigious internships and clerkships, mingled and hobnobbed with Connecticut blue bloods, and sublimated her vengeance toward the Melancon family to extreme discipline that put her on the fast track to becoming one of the biggest rising stars in the Manhattan District Attorney's Office. She blew through all the low-level crimes, such as disorderly conduct and marijuana possession, as an assistant: a fine here, a month spent in Rikers there, 720 hours of community service, so on and so forth. The goal was not to release but to confine those who dared to test the law. Finally, as she gained seniority, she moved over to the Major Crimes Unit, where she worked on Class A and B felonies: insurance and health care fraud, money laundering, criminal sale of a controlled substance, predatory sexual assault, murder. She prosecuted more people in her first year in the Major Crimes Unit than any other of her cohorts. She reveled in this accomplishment. But it was the Asali Givens case that she thought would make her a shoo-in for the next Manhattan district attorney. The current DA, Virgil Clarence Jr., was planning on shifting his career to academia, and speculation as to who would replace him was already buzzing.

Virgil was the one who gave her an overview of the case before dropping a large stack of papers on the desk in her corner office in a Chinatown building. Later that evening, as Amara pored over the documents detailing where Asali lived and went to school, her parents, her dead child, and even the interior of the Dunkin' Donuts and Baskin-Robbins, her chest burned with the knowledge of what she was going to do. The Raise the Age law, which stipulated that no child under the age of eighteen would be prosecuted as an adult, was put into effect a few weeks after the alleged murder of Asali's newborn happened. Since the law had no retroactive clause, Amara could either charge Asali as an adult and garner fanfare from law enforcement, or charge her as a child and maintain the support of Black women everywhere—especially in Harlem.

When the *New York Times* story came out, the police union gifted Amara with a bouquet of roses thanking her for upholding the law. But no sooner than they did, days later, she received a barrage of letters and emails from Black women who either pleaded for her to reverse the decision or mocked her as an "Uncle Tom" and a "bed wench." This was the first time that she received nationwide attention for a case, and she wasn't sure if she could handle the pressure. She had been in the local news plenty of times, but this new level of exposure was overwhelming.

Though Asali's story was devastating, she was just one girl, Amara thought. But there, in a bathroom, where Amara huddled over the toilet to parse her logic, she felt ashamed. Asali wasn't just one girl, just like none of the people Amara had sent to jail were just one person wandering aimlessly through the world. Each had a family. Each was loved. She stuck her head in the toilet bowl and dry heaved, but nothing from her stomach would come up. And then she realized that she hadn't eaten all day. She patted the sides of her sweating face with crumpled pieces of toilet paper and breathed slowly until her nausea subsided.

When Amara opened the bathroom stall, one of her colleagues, Amanda, a brunette who always wore her hair in a sideswept bun, beamed at her and said, "Well, well, well, if it isn't the famous Amara Danville. Congratulations, champ."

"Congratulations?" Amara asked while washing her hands.

"Yeah." Amanda rubbed her upper back. "You did good. We all knew you could do it."

"Thanks," Amara said dryly.

Amanda leaned in closer and added, "It's okay to own it, you know. You lowball yourself when you're that self-deprecating, and you better get used to the big leagues."

As soon as Amara exited the bathroom and walked down the hallway, she was ambushed with the clapping and congratulatory remarks of other coworkers until all their voices clashed together and the cacophony worsened her mood. Not a single person even called Asali by name. She was "that girl" or "the case," whereas Amara was the "exemplar" and "titan" of the District Attorney's Office. By the time she made it back to her office, she looked at the stacks of paper and notes that took up real estate on her desk and chairs with disgust. If only, Amara thought, her colleagues knew the truth about her own life. Maybe a sixteen-year-old wasn't ready for a child, but who is? Amara wasn't.

This epiphany struck Amara with a force that propelled her to call out sick for the rest of the day and phone her mother. Denise wanted Amara to come home, but Amara urged Denise to come downtown because she did not want to be anywhere near Harlem since the news had broken about Asali's charge. She feared that there would be a riot or, worse, she would be attacked.

Denise arrived in the late afternoon with a bag of Crown Fried Chicken and said, "Hey, baby, I brought your favorite."

Amara, who was now dressed in a pink robe, her curly hair tangled and matted, hugged her mother and brought her into the apartment, where they sat and ate in the kitchen.

"Girl, what is going on with that head?" Denise joked as she slathered butter over her buttermilk biscuit.

"I just needed to take a quick nap. Ain't feeling too good today."

"Is it because of Asali?"

Amara was about to bite into her chicken wing but closed her mouth and placed the meat back on her plate.

"Uh-huh. I thought so."

"Do you think I went too far, Ma?"

Denise sighed. "What's done is done. What good would it be if I gave you my opinion now?"

"It would help to keep me in check."

Denise took a beat. "Fine. I do think that it was too harsh. Way too harsh. You know she might land in Rikers, and she won't last three years, that frail thing."

"But, Mom, I'm a prosecutor. That case was horrific."

"You're a Black woman before you're a prosecutor. And you're from Harlem too."

"I can't use that in court, Mom. That's beside the point."

"Is it? If it is, then where's your guilt coming from?"

Amara rubbed her hands together, and her eyes escaped to some other spot in the room. "I don't know."

"You're lying."

"What?"

"You're lying because you didn't look me in the eye when you said it."

Amara looked her mother in the eyes and laughed to dilute the awkwardness from being put on the spot. "Mom, I am trying my best, okay?"

"I told you years ago, back when you were at Columbia, that you would come to me when you're ready, and I know that whatever that was is still messing with you now. And that mess is gonna turn you inside out if you don't let it out, Mar. I'm telling you. You let things stew in your body like that and you'll go crazy."

"Let's change the subject, okay? How's Aunt Laila? She doin' okay?"

"Same ol', same ol'. She has days where she's quiet and just stares off into space and then some days she has her fits, where she screams and yells so much that I hear ringing in my ears. But lately she's been doing something different that I can't quite put my finger on."

"What's going on?"

"She'll be having these conversations with herself in her bedroom. Like . . . full-on conversations. But when she's talking, she's going back and forth."

"What is she saying?"

"All sorts of things. Talkin' about the child she's carrying, how she was turned away by the Melancons, the money. And I just let her keep going, but she's been saying Landon's name over and over and I don't know why."

"Landon?"

Denise nodded.

"How long has this been happening?"

"Only for the past few weeks. I tried to get Landon on the phone, since I thought she wanted to speak to him, but she'll spaz out into a fit if I even bring him up. I don't get it."

"Landon," Amara said. "Huh."

The door opened and a male voice yelled, "It's just me!" Denise closed her eyes and quietly groaned, and Amara hurriedly hushed her mother before Ethan entered the kitchen. Her long-term partner was one of those Connecticut blue bloods: He was educated at the elite Hotchkiss School, and his family had a summer home in Narragansett. Always dressed in either Hugo Boss or Ralph Lauren, Ethan was a John Kennedy Jr. look-alike who'd met Amara in a Legal Writing course back at Yale Law. Paired together for an assignment, Amara learned that Ethan had been accepted by the skin of his teeth, after a phone call and blank check to the office of admissions from his father, another Yale Law alumnus. Unlike Amara, Ethan was a mediocre student, but there was something about her ambition and beauty that lit a fire underneath him: he aced the assignment and got his priorities together in order to woo her. Ethan's parents, who voted for Barack Obama twice, welcomed Amara with open arms, whereas Denise shook Ethan's hand with one of hers while the other was kept clenched by her side.

Ethan entered into the kitchen and grimaced at the fried chicken, buttermilk biscuits, and mashed potatoes all across their marble table from Williams-Sonoma. He contorted his face and shook his head as he went to the refrigerator to mete out a portion of niçoise salad and a bottle of vitamin water.

"There a problem, Ethan?" Denise placed an arm on the back of her chair and twisted the upper half of her body to face him. Amara shielded her face with her hand and turned her body in the opposite direction facing the living room.

"You two shouldn't be eating all that junk. It's heavy in calories and saturated fats, and it can mess with your cholesterol."

"Thank you for the public service announcement," Denise said sarcastically.

"Mom," Amara whined.

"I'm just trying to look out for you both. You're more prone to having high cholesterol and heart disease because—"

"Because we're Black, Ethan, is that it?"

"Mom!" Amara said.

"Well"—he swallowed an olive and continued—"yes."

"I don't think one meal is going to kill us, sweetheart," Amara said.

"You call that one meal? That's enough to feed a whole village."

"Village?" Denise said. "You know what? I think it's time for me to go." Denise walked over to the other side of the table and pressed her lips to Amara's forehead. She rubbed the back of her daughter's head before releasing with a loud kiss smack and said dryly to Ethan, "Have a good day." He stood to his feet, and she held up a hand. "I'll see myself out, thanks."

After Denise left, Ethan grabbed his food and drink and sat across from Amara.

"What's going on with her?"

"Nothing. She just—nothing."

"What?" Ethan asked in between bites of his salad.

"You have a bit of egg on your mouth."

"Where?" He licked the left and right multiple times as Amara laughed at his failing. She then got up from the table and used her finger to flick it away at the same time that Ethan tipped his head down to kiss her wrist. He moved his hands underneath her robe and slapped her ass before he laid her down on the table, pushing the rest of the Crown Fried Chicken off to the far side.

This is how their dynamic always worked: a fight or disagreement served as the best kind of foreplay. But this time, however, Amara did not come. He finished without her and kissed her on the lips before heading into their bedroom to grab his gym clothes. This is also how their routine was: they slept together, he worked out in the gym within the apartment building, he'd come up to shower, and if he wasn't working on a brief himself either in the living room or at his office in Midtown, he would lie in bed with her. Once Ethan was out the door, she threw all of the Crown Fried Chicken in the trash and splashed cold water from the kitchen sink faucet on her face and neck.

From there, Amara walked past her living room to her bedroom, where she opened the first drawer of her nightstand on her side of the bed. Tucked toward the middle pages of the Book of Common Prayer was the royal-blue-and-crystal-bead *eleke* that she'd kept safe ever since Hallow's birth. She made the sign of the cross over her body then held the *eleke* to her abdomen, took three large breaths, and a torrent of tears gave out until she couldn't see directly in front of her.

All Amara needed was five minutes. Five minutes to feel the grief and move on. Every part of her life was systematized, from the arguments and make-up sex with Ethan to the cathartic cries whenever a case filled her with remorse. She would hold the *eleke* with her fingers around the beads like a rosary and remember the greatest sacrifice she made to achieve her dreams. She would re-member the crisp October sky when her water broke and the com-ets that shot across the darkness as she bore down to usher her child into the world. Afterward, she'd return the *eleke* to the inside of the Book of Common Prayer and pull out the bottom drawer of the same nightstand, where pink, blue, green, and yellow sticky notes marked the many pages of a thick, black notebook. Amara held that notebook to her chest, carried it into the living room, and opened the pages beside her laptop, where she scoured the dark web and other corners of the internet for the other remembrance of the sacrifices she made that filed into one sharp purpose: to take down the Melancons.

She had been studying independently for years. There existed a thriving network of people who spoke of caulbearing women through coded language on the blogs and private message boards for which she developed multiple aliases and avatars to gain access. On some nights, she would call a driver to take her by the Melancon brownstone, where she would sketch the exterior before she expanded into sketching the entire block. There was no stoop or doorknob on West 145th and Frederick Douglass whose features she didn't know. On weekends, she would travel to the New York Public Library near Bryant Park to descend into the large columns and rows of books full of folklore and occultism, searching for anything she could find about cauls, caul selling, and birthing. From there she pored over how to translate these practices into illegality. None of her colleagues knew about her research, and she didn't confide in Ethan about it either. She did not want anyone stifling the passion that preceded her becoming an assistant DA, and she especially did not need anyone interrupting her course when she believed that she was on the precipice of quenching her thirst for revenge.

Once the frequency at which the news outlets were reporting on Asali Givens began to taper off (though not by much), Amara ordered another driver to take her uptown to the 32nd Precinct, where she had not visited since she was in her early twenties. She forewent makeup and other accoutrements because she wanted to make sure Officer Robinson could recognize her. Unlike in the past, when she entered the precinct and everyone was running to and from the main area to file papers or discuss ongoing investigations, when Amara entered, all the conversations gradually slowed down, and everyone lifted their head to see what she would say or do. Amara was immediately drawn to a few officers whose uniform shirts were stained pink and whose red faces were dotted with seeds.

"What happened here?" Amara asked.

"Protestors," one officer responded while removing chunks of tomatoes from his scalp and groaning as he tossed them into a nearby garbage can.

Rapidly changing the subject, Amara asked, "I'm looking for an Officer Robinson. Is she here?"

"Yvonne Robinson?" someone else asked.

"I don't remember her first name."

"Kinda heavyset, short curly hair, nice smile?" another asked.

"Yes, that's her!"

"She retired a few years back, but that man back there was close friends with her if you're looking for more details."

Amara saw a large office with glass windows toward the back of the main area. A Black man with a thick moustache of gray and black hairs was whirling around while sitting in his chair, moving between his desk and the coffee machine. She promptly knocked on the door then entered before the officer had a chance to tell her to come in. She said hello then reached in her pocket to show her ID, but the man smiled and said, "I know who you are. Everyone in every precinct knows who you are. Have a seat."

Amara lowered herself into the chair in front of the officer's desk and said, "I'm seeking information about Yvonne Robinson. She used to work here, but I hear she retired?"

"Yeah, five years ago. One of my favorite colleagues. Is there something I can help you with as a proxy?"

Amara looked at his tag that indicated his name was Evans and replied, "I'm not sure. Me and Officer Robinson connected on the fact that she was born and raised in Harlem, and it helped with her understanding a particular issue."

"I was born and raised in Harlem too. What is the issue?"

A white man walked past the windows, and Amara waited until

he was gone before she continued, "You familiar with the Melancon women?"

He burst into laughter. "Of course I am. Why?"

"I'm seeking more updates on them. Any . . . suspicious activity that you've seen, since you are close by?"

"Nothing too much out of the ordinary. Not enough for an arrest warrant, if that's what you're implying, so don't think about just showing up, because that's already been done."

"Been done? By who?"

Officer Evans leaned over his desk and perched his fingers on the surface. "By me."

Amara blinked and crossed one leg over the other. "I'm listening."

"Both me and Officer Robinson had issues with those women. Quite a few do, but—"

"You need more muscle to really take this on, I know. Robinson told me this years ago."

"Yeah, like a pro—"

"A prosecutor. I know." Amara nodded. "That's why I'm here."

Officer Evans raised his right eyebrow and folded his hands on top of his desk. "So what is your plan of action, then? What charges are you going to go for, because what they do technically exists in a gray area."

"No, it doesn't."

Intrigued, Officer Evans raised his eyebrows. "I'm listening."

"Organ trafficking. There's your charge. And if the caul is traveling across state lines, that could be federal racketeering."

"But the caul isn't an organ. It's not like kidney selling."

"Is skin not an organ?"

"Heh. Well, I'll be damned. Is it?"

"If the caul has tissues and it performs a task, then it is an organ. Trust me, I've been studying this for a very long time."

Officer Evans said, "And so have we. Do you know how long we've been trying to nab them? Many false starts. Probably before you were even alive."

"Yes, but I have the power."

"Not yet, you don't. If you want the manpower and the resources, then you, Miss Assistant DA, aren't powerful enough."

"I know that, which is why I'm going to run for DA."

"Hmph." His eyes drifted to the corner.

"What?"

"You got a plan for that?"

"Like a campaign?"

"No, no, a plan. I hope you don't think you can just take the podium and say that you plan to go after these women."

"No, of course not."

"Good. Don't tell anyone. Don't let your right hand know what your left is doing. You just keep doing your job downtown and work on getting that money for your campaign. I'll be watching. And if it picks up steam, we'll find each other. Deal?"

"Deal."

14

Months after Hallow held her meeting with the other caulbearers, Maman's health had weakened and she needed more assistance. In the mornings, Josephine would tiptoe down the stairs with a bar of soap, towel, and washcloth inside of a plastic basin. Though on this day, Maman was not lying flat on her back in bed as she always did while Josephine bathed her but was instead sitting on the window seat facing the street. The sunlight that permeated through the window emphasized the sharpness of the bones in her body and the innumerable wrinkles on her face and neck. Her mahogany cane rested at her feet, and the wraps of her turban were folded across her small lap. From where Josephine stood at the foot of the staircase, her mother's hair looked prickly as a porcupine's but much more sparse and uneven, and the skin sagged so deeply that not even the sash around her waist could keep her body from looking as if it would droop onto the floor at any moment. She didn't immediately call out for Maman but watched her by leaning against the bannister with a chest that ached for her mother.

This kind of reserve had been uncharacteristic for Maman only a few years prior, but now, she always looked out the front-facing window every afternoon or evening to watch passersby.

Oftentimes, she would cry into the inserts of her bra or bite down on her knuckles with the heartbreaking realization that West 145th and Frederick Douglass might as well have been East 66th and Madison because of all the white people moving in. All of the women save Abigail—Patricia, Sister McCleary, and Claudia—had moved out to the Bronx, or to places in New Jersey like Elizabeth and New Brunswick. Starbucks outbid the bodega that the Melancons leased when it was time to renew, and Maman couldn't bear to walk down that street any longer, because upon signing on the dotted line for that lease handover, Maman discovered that it wasn't just about the money. She wanted to maintain a stake in Harlem, but she was disillusioned at the possibility that she was being uprooted.

"Maman?" Josephine drew closer to her mother.

"Hmm?" Maman turned her face toward Josephine. She could see from the redness extending beyond the gray rings around her mother's eyes and the puffiness in her cheeks that she had been crying, a reaction that worried Josephine due to its increasing frequency.

"It's time for your bath."

Maman took a deep breath in and coughed from the exhale. She tried to lean over to grab her cane but wheezed and held on to Josephine instead.

When Josephine opened the door to Maman's bedroom, she caught a coughing fit herself when a rancid smell ambushed her nostrils. She was reluctant to lay Maman down on the bed because the claws that had announced themselves in the years past were now transformed into talons that stretched farther across the walls, appearing as if they were propping up Maman's bed with their own might. But Maman grabbed on to her chair, then the edge of her desk, before reaching the bed and nonchalantly beginning to remove her clothes.

"Ma—" Josephine coughed. "How can you stay in there? Let me go get some air freshener."

"Tried that. Ain't no Lysol, Pine-Sol, Febreze, or Glade that can overcome the smell, so I've just gotten used to it. It's not so bad."

"Ugh." Josephine filled up the basin with warm, soapy water in the kitchen and gathered as much air in her lungs as she could before returning to Maman's bedroom. As Josephine placed her washcloth in the basin then rubbed over Maman's bare arms and legs, she tried her best not look at her mother, who was sighing and sniffling, looking somewhere off into the distance with her arms folded over her chest.

"Still feeling upset, huh?" Josephine asked.

"Couldn't shake it if I wanted to."

"Is there anything I can do to make you feel better?"

Maman touched the side of Josephine's face and smiled. "This is enough, child. This is enough." Despite Josephine lamenting over Maman's decline, she couldn't help but appreciate that the weaker her mother got, the nicer she became. There were no more smacks across the face and no more verbal jabs.

When Josephine bent down to dampen the washcloth again, from the corner of her eye, she saw Maman caressing the last piece of caul on her body, right in the middle of her chest. She was thumbing around its edges with her almond-shaped fingernail, and Josephine gently grabbed ahold of that hand. "Maman, stop. Don't do that. You know how uncomfortable that makes me feel."

"I can't help it, Jo. I'm in a bad way, baby. A really really bad way. One thing my people never warned me about is that the longer you stick around, the more you see everything else surrounding you die."

"There's still this brownstone, though. We still have it."

"Yeah, that is true. I better call Landon soon so we can discuss potential clients. Hallow needs to get her head back in the game and focus on what's happening here and not on other women's messes out there."

"I think it's too late for that."

"I'm sorry?"

"She's planning on going to some town hall meeting this afternoon."

"Town hall meeting? For what?"

"For that Asali girl, I think."

"Aw, shit. Hurry and dry me off. Hurry, hurry." Josephine obeyed and styled Maman in another dress and turban.

"Hallow!" Maman called out, violently coughing each time she yelled her granddaughter's name while hobbling out of the bedroom. Josephine ran to grab Maman's cane from the bottom of the window seat and placed it underneath Maman's right hand.

"Yes, Maman?" Hallow leaned over the bannister.

"What's this I hear about you going to some town hall meeting?"

Hallow cut her eyes at Josephine.

"Well, young lady? I'm talking to you."

"Yes, I'm going. It's right at St. Philip's, just a little over ten blocks away, no big deal."

"Get down here while I'm talking to you."

Hallow sighed and trudged down the steps.

"I don't want you going there. It's not safe," Maman said.

"It's not safe to be around our own people? Do you hear yourself?"

"They are not our people, Hallow. How many times do we have to say it? We're not like them and they're not like us."

"Whatever. I'm still going. I need to know what's going on in this community, and I've about had it with being cooped up in here all my life. You're not gonna have me like her." Hallow pointed her chin at Josephine and crossed her arms across her chest.

"How dare you talk to me like that?" Josephine said. "After all I've done for you?"

"I am going, y'all, and your cane or your words are not gonna stop me."

Maman swung at Hallow's face with the intent to strike her but missed completely and fell onto the floor. Josephine was in a stupor after what just happened. She recalled the memory of Hallow as a baby in her arms, where, just a few feet away, she was tempted to leave out the front door and never come back, only to be slapped onto the same floor where Maman now scrambled to get to her feet. She oscillated between being proud and envious over Hallow forging the independence that had eluded her for her entire life. When Josephine returned to the present, she realized that Maman had been calling her name over and over again to help her to her feet.

Hallow walked toward the front door and pivoted on her right heel to watch the two women regain balance by leaning on the adjacent wall.

"I have a question: What happened to the spearheads outside?"

"What are you talkin' 'bout, girl?" Maman said.

"The spearheads. There are red marks all over them if you chip away. Why is that?"

"What?" Josephine asked.

"Forget it. I'll be back later. Call me on my cell if you need me."

The frigid wind almost knocked Hallow over from the moment she stepped out onto the front porch. She pulled the drawstring of her hoodie and breathed into her palms, surveying the area to see if

anyone was walking down the block, but it was far too cold for anyone to be taking a leisurely stroll. She pivoted again on her right heel
to see if either Josephine or Maman would snatch her back inside,
but when no one came for her, she felt foolish for not having walked
out the door sooner. The last time she remembered leaving the Melancon brownstone by herself was four years ago when she had to
bring Josephine something from their home to the bodega. There
was still an hour and a half left before the town hall meeting would
begin, and since the new Starbucks was on the way, she decided to
sit there and read in the meantime.

What Hallow did not expect while she traversed one block after another was disorientation. It had been five years since she'd
really seen Harlem beyond her block, but she knew that her neighborhood had changed when she noticed many shops that hadn't
been there before: a Japanese crepe shop and nail salon side by side,
an artisanal cheese store, and a bagel store with exclamatory announcements about matcha lattes and golden turmeric tea painted
on the windows. At the Starbucks, where she took a small round
table near the window for herself, she watched the many people
who came in and out—white joggers, white parents with small children, white students decked out in Columbia University apparel.
The entire Starbucks staff save one girl was Black, and the music
playing overhead was Frank Ocean. Hallow also reasoned that a
good portion of the people who stuck around to drink their bever-
ages and eat their egg, ham, and cheese sandwiches were not from
the area either, just from the fragments of conversation that she
picked up:

"... my street corner is too loud on the weekends ..."
"... people congregate outside of my building at all hours of
the night ..."

". . . I wonder if they will build more cafés around here . . ."

". . . I love living in SoHa . . ."

Hallow's eyes almost rolled out of her head when she heard that distasteful portmanteau. Thankfully, upon checking the time on her cell, she figured she could start walking toward St. Philip's. Once she passed the train station at West 135th and Malcolm X, she saw that there were many police cars on the corner of West 134th and Adam Clayton Powell Jr. Boulevard. At first, she assumed there'd been a terrible accident because the police car lights were flashing. But there were no other passersby watching to see what was going on. Some of the police officers leaned against their cars bantering with colleagues or eating breakfast food. When she looked in her pocket for her phone to verify St. Philip's location, this was the intersection where she had to make a right. She swallowed a wad of spit and turned right only to find the police officers patting down a line of Black women who were shifting their balance from left to right and blowing in their hands as they waited to enter the church. Though Hallow didn't have much experience with the police to pull from, she remembered Abyssinian Baptist Church for Sister Evans's funeral, and didn't recall any of the cops there patting her or her family down.

She took her place at the back of the line behind a young woman who was rubbing her hands together then cupping them over her cheeks. She had black-and-cerulean ombré braids and a septum piercing, and when she made eye contact with Hallow and smiled, Hallow seized the opportunity to strike up a conversation.

"Cold day, right?"

"Heh. Hell yeah. It's brick out here."

Hallow didn't quite understand the phrase, but she nodded all the same. "What are all these police officers doing here?"

"Being pigs, that's what. They can't deal with Black women coming together for anything, so they harass us, patting us down like
this. Why the hell would we bring weapons into a church anyway?
We aren't loner white boys."

"I see . . ."

The young woman looked Hallow up and down and said,
"Where you from?"

"Oh, I'm from here. I just don't get out much."

"I see."

When it was Hallow's turn to be patted down, she was shocked
at how roughly the Black female officer grabbed her breasts and
crotch, turned her around, dug deep into her pockets—even put
her fingers through her hair. Fortunately, the officer did not com-
mand Hallow to remove her coat and reach underneath her baggy
sweater, because she worried that her caul might draw a spectacle. After the inspection was over, she was greeted by two other
Black women who stood at the entrance to the sanctuary to give
pamphlets and a meeting agenda to all the attendees. The room was
packed. All the chatter was made more uproarious by the acoustics from the dramatic high ceilings and the stained-glass windows.
Hallow sat toward the back and flipped through the pamphlet,
where she saw advertisements for all kinds of events and organizations: volunteer shifts at homeless shelters, food and school supply drives, coupons for local hair salons, campaigns for city council
members. Within that pew, amongst all the women, Hallow felt
like she was a part of something larger, and she could not have been
more excited.

The town hall meeting began thirty minutes late, and the emcee made a joke about Colored People Time, or CPT, to defuse the
antsiness that many felt. After the emcee, who went by the name of

Abeni, asked everyone how they were doing, the crowd fractured into different kinds of reactions: some shouted out that they were good, others excessively sucked their teeth, and a few stated their concerns about the excessive police presence outside. To bring the group back together, Abeni apologized for the cops and led a ten-minute meditation so that everyone could refocus their energies on discussing Asali Givens. The town hall format was that if someone had something to say, they would be given two minutes to speak—no exceptions. At first, there were women who spoke of efforts to donate to Asali Givens's lawyer and family household expenses and others who sought to organize a call-in where they would not only call up their representatives but also send letters to Asali as she sat in jail awaiting trial. But when the topic got onto Amara Danville, the women disregarded the format and jumped at once to get a word in.

One woman with a reddish brown bob stood to her feet and said, "Mm-hmm, girl. She's a piece of work."

"Do y'all think she's gonna run for district attorney?" Abeni asked in the microphone at the altar.

"Of course! That's why her name is in all the papers. The press wants us to remember it. Tuh." The older woman, who was encouraged by others with a "Go 'head, Auntie," continued, "If she think she's getting my vote, she can forget it. I'm not voting for that house nigga."

The crowd whooped and hollered. Hallow blushed at her bold statement.

"But wait just a minute now." A woman with a salt-and-pepper wig adjusted her pointy red glasses and sat upright. "Is Asali someone we should really be fighting for?"

The crowd began to groan.

"Hold on now, hold on now. Hear me out, 'cause y'all young folk like to always jump the gun without listening to what elders like me are tryna say. Is she someone we should really be rallying behind? Whether or not she killed that baby, she had to have known the consequences. Why aren't we fighting for the Black boys getting gunned down in the streets by police and trigger-happy white folk? Why aren't we fighting for people stuck in Rikers waiting for trial for just having a half gram of weed on 'em?" Another elder beside her nodded her head.

"Let me ask you something, Miss—" Abeni asked.

"Witherspoon," she said.

"Witherspoon. Do you believe that Asali deserves to be charged as an adult?"

"Well, I don't know! If she murdered that child—"

"What if she didn't?" Abeni pressed.

"Still. She should still be punished."

"Do you agree that Black people get more severe punishment by our current criminal justice system compared to white people?"

"Of course!"

"And assuming you are aware of the Raise the Age law, how could you think that Asali being charged as an adult has nothing to do with her being a Black girl?"

"I never said that, now."

"So then if you believe our system is unjust toward Black people and if you agree that her sentencing may be influenced by her race and gender, then would you say the sentencing is appropriate?"

Miss Witherspoon remained silent.

Another woman stood to her feet. "Bottom line is that Asali shouldn't have been charged as an adult in the first place. It's prosecutorial brutality. It's too harsh of a sentence and we all know why. I know Asali. I taught her at PS 149. That girl was afraid of her own shadow. She wouldn't hurt nobody. This is the problem. She doesn't need jail; she needs help."

The ladies in the audience agreed in unison.

"I still don't get why she did it, knowing the consequences," Witherspoon added.

"Because she's a child," Abeni said. "And her immaturity should be taken into consideration in the eyes of the law."

"Mm-hmm," the crowd said.

"So what do we do now?" a young voice called out.

"We're gonna need more mobilizing—more prayer, meditation, money—and even then, there may not be much else to do. We just have to keep up the fight—protesting, donating, educating, whatever we have to do," Abeni said.

"What about the Melancons?"

Every woman in the sanctuary turned around toward the back, where Hallow stood to her feet and fidgeted with her fingers.

"What about 'em?" Abeni asked.

"Well, you've all heard the story about them, right?"

"Speak up or come up to the mic," Abeni said.

Hallow loudly repeated herself and added, "They may have some money and they've been in Harlem for a long time. Maybe they can help donate." The women's jeers caused her armpits to be drenched with sweat, and she held on to the back of the pew in front of her to keep balance.

"Tsk. Please. Like they'd donate anything. They won't even help us with that caul they got. Fuck those women." A Black woman in the front-left corner looked up to the ceiling, apologized to God, and made the sign of the cross over her chest. Though Hallow was offended, she was relieved that no one could recognize who she was, much less her relation to the Melancon family. Maybe her rarely leaving the brownstone while growing up due to Maman's strict orders was her saving grace now. She walked up to Abeni for the mic and said, "I got a cousin who hoped the caul would help with her diabetes. They didn't help her."

"They turned me down when I asked for help with my sickle cell!"

"Me for lupus!" two disembodied voices called out.

Then the crowd broke out into more chatter that Abeni was unable to control, even with the microphone back in her hands. Hallow couldn't recall ever hearing Landon or anyone else in the family speak about someone needing help with their diabetes, or sickle cell, or lupus and wondered if no one brought it to her attention or she was too young to remember. Nevertheless, she was paralyzed with guilt and disbelief over those who had been affected by her family. When Abeni assessed how slowly Hallow sat back down in her seat and pulled the drawstring of her hoodie farther out, she said, "It's okay, sweetheart. It's just—we know this neighborhood well, and you look young, so maybe you don't remember, but those women don't have a good reputation. They're money grabbers. They ain't sticking out their necks for no one. All skinfolk, what?"

"Ain't kinfolk!" the other women yelled in a call-and-response.

For the next few hours, Hallow sat in the back of the church in a daze. She wanted to dash out of St. Philip's from the moment those voices spoke out about her family's rejection of them, but she knew that would've been inappropriate and suspicious. So she endured the entire meeting teetering on the verge of tears and unable to gather a coherent thought in spite of her pain. If, Hallow thought, she were to confide in one of them that she was a Melancon, it might do her and her family more harm than good.

Once the town hall meeting concluded, Hallow did not hesitate to leave the church, crossing streets without so much as a cautionary glance toward the pedestrian signals. The cold sapped the moisture from her face, and she wasn't sure if she was crying because of the bitterness of the afternoon or the embarrassment for having brought up the Melancon name to those women. She could not wait to return home and bury herself under a mountain of covers to sulk in peace, but the brownstone was not the same as it had been when she left. Construction workers were knocking the spearheads clean off their necks before throwing them into the back of their truck. New spearheads of the same design were removed from small plastic bags and welded onto the gate. She'd never called someone to come repair them, and before she could ask who exactly reached out to them, she saw Maman sitting by the left front-facing window with a proud and surly look on her face.

15

Hallow knew that Maman was trying to throw her off course, but why? Unless there was something that she was not supposed to know, something beyond just the dirtiness of the spearheads that Iris neglected to mention. She couldn't confide in anyone. Josephine would always defer to Maman, and Hallow was too impatient to talk to Iris and endure her circumlocution. Only one option remained.

Helena had not exactly left her room spotless when she moved out two years ago, and their communications with each other had been few and far between since then. There were loose sheets of paper wrinkled or crumpled into balls strewn across the wood floor. A few jackets still hung in the closet, and a large chest was underneath the bed. Hallow rummaged through them all, searching for some kind of clue as to where her cousin might be. Helena spoke of different neighborhoods when she last visited the Melancon home, but there were too many to take a good guess at one in particular, and her social media profile just listed New York, NY, as her location. She did have Helena's number, though. At least the number Helena wrote down out of pressure from Maman. It was the only thing Maman asked for since she agreed to cosign on Helena's lease in order to keep tabs on her in some kind of way. The number could've changed, but Hallow had no time to rack her brain over every and any hypothetical situation. Hallow dialed the number and took a deep breath.

"Hello?" Helena responded.

"Helena? It's Hallow."

"Oh, hey. Hey, what's up?"

"I'm good. Look, I was wondering if it was possible for us to see each other."

"Everything okay?"

"I'd rather us talk in person . . . if that's okay."

"All right. Hmm. Meet me at Harlem Nights—on the corner of 138th and Adam Clayton Powell? Not too far from Abyssinian if you remember from years ago? It's a wooden-looking building. Go there at four p.m. sharp—as soon as they open—and sit all the way in the back. I'll meet you there."

Harlem Nights was a rustic, juke-joint-like establishment wedged between Strivers' Row and Abyssinian Baptist Church that had just opened its doors when Hallow approached it. Hallow took a seat toward the back of the venue near the kitchen and bathroom and folded her hands across the table. When a waitress came over, Hallow asked for grapefruit juice and artichoke dip and saw a silhouette of another person growing larger and larger the farther it moved toward the back. Before Hallow could get a look at the face, she was in awe of this person's silvery white hair and smooth hands that defied what Hallow presumed to be old age. The woman pushed back her hair and revealed herself to be Helena, who had become the mirror image of her mother. Her hair was unkempt yet shiny and full of volume. Her eyes were all-consuming and unfocused. Her smile was both inviting and mocking all at once. She was beautifully unrestrained, confidently full of herself, and Hallow wanted to shrink underneath the weight of Helena's heels or hide within one of the pockets of her leather jacket.

"Hey, did you find the place all right?" Helena asked.

"Y-yeah," Hallow stuttered. "Where are you coming from?"

"Just the Upper West Side. I got a cramped studio down there. Very small, but it's right near Central Park, and I like running, so it balances out. So what's up?"

The waitress returned with Hallow's artichoke dip and grapefruit juice. When Helena declined ordering anything else to drink besides water and the waitress walked back to the front of the place, Hallow started to tell Helena about what happened at the town hall meeting at St. Philip's and said, "I don't know what to do, Helena. I don't know what to do."

"How is Maman treating you?"

"She's just—the worst!" The waitress came with Helena's water, and Hallow smiled at her until she walked away. "Let me ask you something: Do you know anything about the spearheads on the gate?"

"No, what about 'em?"

"Yeah. Iris told me to check them, and then when I did, I saw these red marks there, and they—they almost looked like blood. But then Maman had them replaced after I asked them about it. Do you know anything about it? Because I don't remember anything."

"Spearheads. Hmm." Helena stroked her chin and took a sip of her water. "If you don't remember, then it might've been before your time."

"And since you're older than me, I thought I'd ask—"

"Yeah, but not by much . . . and I blocked out a lot during that time. A lot of memories from that time are a bit"—Helena held her hand horizontal in the air and made a downward swooping motion—"shaky."

"Why is that?"

Helena soothed the back of her neck and winced. "I really don't want to get into that right now. It makes me uncomfortable."

"Oh. Sorry."

"It's whatever. But no, I don't know anything about spearheads. Is that all you wanted to talk about?"

"No." Hallow laced her fingers and said, "I can't take it anymore, Helena. I really can't. I want to be more a part of Harlem. I want to help more people who look like us. That Asali Givens case just shed light on a lot, and we act like we are our own island, like nothing we do affects where we live, and today made it all too clear that it does."

"I want to tell you a story. Back when I was getting my master's in social work at Hunter College?"

"Mm-hmm." Hallow nodded.

"I met a white woman in that program with a huge guilt/savior complex. Those kinds of programs are full of them. Rowan was her name. Somehow we kept getting paired up together for group work, but I didn't mind because she had her shit together. But I always thought something was strange about her, more than that complex I told you about. She was also just fucking reckless—falling out of chairs, getting kicked out of bars, ending up in people's beds who she didn't know, just . . . a lot, and she told me all about it. One day, we had to volunteer at a juvenile detention center, and one of the teens in there had a shiv. Stabbed her right in the neck and twisted. Rowan screamed and yelled, but I knew something was off. She didn't pass out or anything, and she wasn't shocked when the doctor came back to tell her that she would be okay. 'A weaker person would've died,' he said. But she wasn't extraordinary. She ate terribly, drank a ton, and hardly worked out. She was given two weeks to recuperate, and I thought it would be okay to visit her and bring some flowers or soup. You should've seen her. She was up and walking, doing yoga poses in the living room. Not the slightest bit dizzy or in pain. When I made a comment on the miracle of her being alive, she opened the locket of the necklace she always wore and waved a piece of caul in front of my face and, God, Hallow, I wish I could have lunged at her neck and committed to not missing that time."

Hallow said a long drawn-out "Shiiiiit" and leaned back in her seat.

Helena's eyes widened, and she laughed. "You see that guilt? You're old enough to feel it too. Do you ever stay up at night like I do, thinking about all the white people who have parts of our bodies hanging around their necks for protection?"

"Sometimes."

"That's one thing I didn't account for when I left—something like that happening: actually seeing another person with the caul. I know that New York is big, but not that big, and maybe that's part of the reason why Maman kept us sheltered, so we'd never have to reckon with what we've done. Who knows how many people have parts of me with them . . ." Her voice tapered off as she looked off to the side and scratched at her chest. "It was like the universe meant for me to see it, and I've been trying to do good since. Hell, before then—that's why I went into the program. I wanted to help people since I can't—you know." She began caressing her bare right arm.

"Right. Do you still keep in touch with your mom?"

"Who, Iris?" Helena soothed the nape of her neck again and said, "Sometimes. You know she and I never had the best relationship."

"I know."

"Has she mentioned me at all?"

Hallow shook her head.

"Figures."

"But you know she's mostly downstairs. She doesn't do that much talking to anyone. You should stop by and see her for yourself."

"When I'm ready. I haven't seen her since I graduated, and even then, I was moving my shit out. I'll figure it out. In the meantime, if you want to help more women in the community, I'll pool my resources together, but you have to stop testing Maman and Josephine. You know they crave money, so do whatever you have to do to keep the cash flow coming in while you do this work on the side. Then they won't be up your ass the way that they are. Comply. Grit your teeth and just get it done, got it?"

"Got it."

"Gimme two weeks or so. I'll be in touch."

16

Josephine lay awake in bed waiting for Landon to bring her news. He had been hinting to her for weeks that there was someone who was interested in the caul, though not in the way that any of them would expect. When Josephine pressed him for more details, he told her that in due time, they would come, but for the moment, she should think of the life that she wanted to live. She was excited by the possibility of finally leaving the brownstone once and for all. Her own daughter was an inspiration and proved that there could not have been a more suitable time to leave. Iris would be preoccupied in the basement as usual, Helena was gone, Hallow was the successor and still regenerative, and, best of all, Maman didn't possess the physical strength to stop her. It was perfect. In the two weeks since Hallow met with Helena, Josephine was surprised that Hallow returned home with a new, pliant attitude. She stayed up late alongside Josephine to go over the expenditures and stayed still when Josephine cut her caul to give to white customers who came in and out. All the while, Josephine wondered when the day would come that Landon would tell her that it's time. She had bought all kinds of *Architectural Digest* and *Elle Decor* issues to imagine her dream home. At night, if Landon were to visit her, they'd exchange ideas of the kitchen interiors and patios. The dream of having a single-family home with no neighbors in close proximity excited her.

Another two weeks rolled by and finally Landon called and asked all the women to dress in their Sunday best because an important someone would be visiting. Maman wore a long plaid skirt and tights, with a Swarovski gold-plated brooch. Josephine styled herself in a bold women's cobalt-blue suit jacket with matching trouser pants, and Hallow wore a houndstooth tweed minidress in black, with a hint of rouge lipstick for a pop of color. Iris remained in the basement.

Per tradition for any guest, Josephine put tea on the stove and prepared a charcuterie board with the Dexter-Russell knife placed to the side of the cheese and prosciutto. Hallow carried the ceramic pot, cups, and coasters to the living room table and played some music on their vinyl record player near the fireplace. Then she struck a match and waved the smoke around the room to cut through and remove the stale air.

The doorbell rang and Josephine grabbed Hallow's and Maman's hands so they could stand in formation in the hallway while she answered the door. A tall, gray-haired white man with a prominent jaw and a self-satisfied grin stood next to Landon. He took off his hat and placed it in front of his chest.

"Good afternoon." He extended his right hand.

"Good afternoon." Josephine shook his hand once and attempted to pull away, but to no avail. The man lowered his lips to her hand and kissed it, exaggeratedly breathing in her scent. Landon's eyes bulged, and Josephine glared at the gesture until Landon cut in, "Let's go inside, shall we?"

This visitor was beside himself upon looking at Hallow and

Maman. He clasped his hands together and smiled. Then he whispered to Landon, "I thought that there was one more."

"Yes, yes, but don't you worry about that. These are the ones you want to meet."

"Wonderful. I'm Robert Epelbaum." He extended his hand and just before Hallow was about to shake it, Josephine gently stepped in front of her and said, "Please, let's go into the living room. We have a few things prepared for you."

"Where are you coming from?" Maman asked as they took their seats—she in her chair, Landon and Robert on the living room sofa, and Josephine and Hallow in chairs on the opposite side of the sofa.

"Just from the Upper East Side," Robert replied. "I must say that it is an honor to be in your presence. I've heard a lot about you."

"Oh yeah? What have you heard?" Maman asked.

"I've heard that you've been given a gift, and I want to make that gift worth your while."

"Mr. Epelbaum here is a multihyphenate. He's a laboratory scientist as well as a philanthropist."

"Tea?" Hallow asked.

"Yes, please." Hallow poured Mr. Epelbaum a cup and watched as he sniffed the raspberry notes before sipping slowly. "Really good." He lifted his face and looked around the room. "Beautiful home you have here."

"Thank you," Maman said.

"Looks a little old, though. Those cracks over there in that corner look pretty serious, and I caught a whiff of something when I came in here. How long have you had this place?"

"Close to eighty years."

"Eighty years? Wow. And you never thought of selling—"

Maman leaned forward with her mouth wide open to comment,

but Josephine nervously laughed and interjected. "We love living here. It's our home."

"Hmm. Too bad." Mr. Epelbaum placed his cup on a coaster and said, "Look, I don't want to waste all of your time, so I'll cut to the chase. I'm here to make you all an offer—"

"Us an offer?" Hallow asked.

"That's correct. Landon has already told me how powerful this caul allegedly is, as well as the business you have set up here. But I think I have a way for you to expand further than you ever thought possible—with a science patent."

"I don't think I'm following."

"The process is very simple: we take some of the caul from you, study it in our lab, duplicate and patent it, then sell it on the market. Imagine the killing you would make."

"That depends on if you can even successfully sell it," Maman said.

"I'm very well connected, Ms. Melancon. I know everyone from Wall Street traders like Landon to Virgil Clarence over at the DA's office to scientists at Weill Cornell Medicine and the Icahn Lab at Princeton University. Trust me, I wouldn't lie to you."

"The DA's office, you said?" Hallow asked.

"Yes."

"And what about the customers? Could we decide who gets it?" Hallow asked.

"It's a free market. That's capitalism for you. The way of the world—a cornerstone of the American Dream." He sipped more of his tea and ate some of the prosciutto.

"Can we have some time to think?"

Josephine darted her eyes at Hallow.

"Certainly. Better yet, how about you all come to a party of mine that I'll be holding at the end of the month? You can meet my social circle so you can get a better sense of my world and how I can help, so that the decision can be made easier for you."

Hallow opened her mouth to speak, but Josephine interrupted again, "That sounds perfect."

"Very well. I'll have Landon send over details soon. Good day." He tipped his head and Landon saw him out the door but stayed behind so he and the Melancon women could debrief.

Before Josephine could give Hallow a tongue-lashing for dragging her feet in giving Mr. Epelbaum an answer, Helena was making her way to everyone from the foyer with a set of keys dangling in one hand and a black leather wallet in the other. Maman was at a loss for words. She alternated between looking to the other side of the room where the stairs led to the basement and the top of Helena's crown.

"What?" Helena asked.

Maman curled a finger around one of Helena's strands and said, "Your hair. When did it turn all silvery like this?"

Helena shrugged her shoulders. "I had a few gray hairs here and there, and then one day, my entire scalp turned."

Maman grabbed ahold of Helena's shoulders and pulled her close to her face. "You're not . . . seeing things, are you?"

"No. I'm fine."

Maman sighed. "Good. You don't need any more disabilities."

"Disabilities?" Helena raised her eyebrows. When Maman did nothing but deliver a sympathetic stare, Helena lowered her face and returned to eye level with a smirk. "Nice to see you too, Marceline," she said, and walked past Maman to the living room.

Hallow stood to her feet in shock. "Helena. H-H-Hi," she stammered. "What are you doing here?"

"Figured it was better to stop by than to call. Wanna go upstairs or something to talk?"

"No, no, uh-uh." Josephine wagged her finger. "We all need to talk as a family about Mr. Epelbaum."

"Who is Mr. Epelbaum?" Helena asked Hallow.

"Somebody who's about to change all of our lives, that's who," Josephine said. "A scientist wanted a piece of our caul to turn it around, sell it on the market, and distribute it to a wider audience."

"What?" Helena faced Landon. "He's legit?"

Landon nodded. "As legit as they come."

"I guess we don't need to speak in private, then."

"Speak in private about what?" Maman asked.

Helena shot a glance at Hallow before fishing in her tote bag for a folded pamphlet. She unfolded it and placed it on the coffee table.

Hallow leaned over and read the big bold font in the center of the front page. "Blessed Waters Doulas?"

"Mm-hmm." Helena nodded. With pride, she crossed her arms over her chest.

"I don't get it," Hallow said.

"You told me that you want to be more a part of Harlem and you want to help more people who look like us, right?"

"Right."

"This is the place to do it. I used to take classes here. Got certified and everything. Even saw a few clients as a doula myself till I burned out. But I still wanted to be involved, so I did a bit of grant writing for them a little over a year ago. The practice was started by this older woman—she's a saint. Getting you in should be no trouble because with all these conversations surrounding Black motherhood both online and off, they are probably gonna need some more help."

"Getting Hallow in to do what?" Maman asked.

"To moonlight as a doula apprentice. It's in East Harlem. Not too far from Central Park. I know, given your special circumstances, that's a voyage. And if that Epelbaum guy is legit as y'all say he is, then it's the best of both worlds. You give him the caul, you make a lot of money, and then you can also do some community work. Everybody wins." Helena clapped her hands together once. "Boom."

A pronounced creaking sound from outside the living room interrupted the conversation. Iris entered with one staggered stride after another. Her wide, unblinking eyes rocked the three ladies, who stared back at her with not a clue as to what to do or say. Iris looked at Helena, and tears pooled in her eyes.

"I didn't want to call your name because I didn't want to hear nothing and be wrong."

"It's me. I'm here."

Iris touched the top of Helena's head and cupped a cheek in her hand. "You look beautiful. You look like—"

"You. I know. Maman already said that. The apple doesn't fall far from the tree."

She crouched down beside Helena and softened her tone. "How is life outside of here? Are you having fun? Are you making friends?"

Helena guffawed at such juvenile questions but quickly understood that her mother was trying to make casual conversation, as it had been years since they had last seen each other in person. And besides, what else was Iris going to ask her? The last time Helena could recall Iris being outside was when the accident happened, or maybe she herself had forgotten because her small mind could not process her mother leaving somewhere, someplace without her. And now she, as her daughter, her carbon copy, was off somewhere, someplace that Iris didn't know, which left Iris to remain suspended in time, a fixture in this home like the others, both sentient and non. Everyone was waiting for Helena to respond, and when she did, she too had tears rising in the corners of her eyes. "It's fine, Mom." There was so much Helena could have said—places she could've named, men she entertained, incidents she was thankful to have survived, but it was not the time or place. Though the two women were alike in looks, they resided in different times, their frayed bond unable to be sutured with the casual conversation of "catching up." Helena didn't expect to see her mother. She thought that Iris would stay downstairs and Helena could speak to Hallow without their ever crossing paths. Now that Helena had seen her, she expected to have some residual rage left in her spirit or at the very least more warmth toward Josephine, who mothered her more than Iris ever did, but she didn't. She was calm and centered, feeling strong enough to be standing between her two mothers, not as a hurt little girl but as an empowered woman.

Unbeknownst to everyone else in the brownstone, Iris kept to herself in the basement not only to avoid scaring and inconveniencing anyone with her conversations but also because she could not stand to suffer the secondhand embarrassment of how Josephine's life was playing out. She hadn't wanted Helena to grow up to be as sycophantic as her sister. Once Helena was of no use to the family business, she became as bitter and unruly as Iris hoped. Whenever Helena had an outburst as a child, Iris grinned with pride. Whenever Helena back talked, Iris encouraged it so that Helena realized early on that nothing she could do would ruffle Iris's feathers. The freedom that Iris gave Helena to roam and rant and the flimsy and irregular admonitions that Josephine handed out triggered within Helena a surging desire to destroy, until finally, the fire petered out. She grew older and found herself by living away from the brownstone and seldom came to visit. Iris dabbed at the corners of her eyes as she imagined Helena blooming unbridled with all of her humanity somewhere along some avenue in the city. Reuniting was unnecessary. Iris knew that she was alive, so there was no need to cry.

Helena reluctantly gave her mother a hug, and Iris hugged her back. Josephine and Landon had already gone upstairs to their bedroom and Maman to hers, but Hallow quietly observed the heartwarming scene. She watched the two silvery-haired women sway from side to side, with Iris kissing Helena's scalp and Helena gently patting her mother's back. Hallow shrank into a nook in the corner and thought of her birth mother again, wondering where she might be and if she too thought of her at any time.

17

Amara wasted no time in putting the word out amongst her innermost circle that she intended on running for district attorney, and the feedback she received was unanimously in her favor. She never expected that getting the support would be the easiest part, but she knew that soon, journalists would dig into her history, which is why her office's public relations got involved. Their constant interrogations about her time in college, romantic affairs, and family background were increasingly laborious. Is there anything that we should know about that might hurt your campaign? Are there any pictures and/or videos of you floating around—maybe from undergrad or law school—in compromising situations? Have you joined or attended any meetings of organizations that could potentially be controversial? Have you been vocal about Palestine? Are there any family members who are "radicals"? Anything at all? Amara's answer was no. The answer was always no. She gave a list of all of her activities throughout her education, yearbook pictures, and the contact information of all her closest friends. There was nothing about Hallow. Both she and Landon had made sure of that. But no matter how much Amara had hidden, neither she nor any doctor could forget her body's history.

To be safe, Amara booked a routine checkup with her gynecologist, and as he was lubricating the speculum, she said, "Doc? Can I ask a question?"

"What's that? Deep breath in."

Amara complied and gritted her teeth once the speculum was inserted. "Can you tell things by looking at a . . . cervix?"

"Polyps. Cysts. Discoloration—"

"I didn't mean that. I meant . . ." She lowered her voice. "You can tell that I've . . . had a baby before, right?"

"Oh, of course! You can always tell by looking at the cervix. Plus it's in your file."

"And that file is strictly confidential, yes?"

"Strictly confidential."

"Are you sure?"

"Yes, ma'am."

"But these things can get out. Can I see your notes?"

"Ms. Danville, you always get a summary for each of your visits within twenty-four hours, provided we don't have to conduct any sort of tests. You can sit up now."

Amara sat upright and said, "You sure it's strictly confidential?"

The doctor laughed while discarding his latex gloves. "I don't have my malpractice insurance for nothing."

Amara dropped her shoulders and remained on the examination table with one hand resting in the palm of the other on her lap. She knew exactly what was happening—her nerves were getting the best of her.

"If I may—"

"Yes?" Amara responded.

"I know what's going on. I read the report this morning while coming into the office. It's exciting."

"Report? What report?"

The doctor pulled out his phone from his pocket and showed her a *Daily Beast* headline with her image as the header. It was a good photo of her. She was either speaking at the annual conference for the National Black Prosecutors Association in Chicago or giving another fruitless speech about diversity and inclusion at some East Coast law school. They all tended to blend into one another. Her hands were held out in front of her and she was midsentence, her mouth open and eyebrows arched. Her nails had been filed to fine, round shapes, and from the angle that the photograph was taken, the light hid the gnawed skin around her cuticles, a nervous tic she tried to suppress by applying thick tape around her fingers so she wouldn't bite them. When her eyes finally scaled the headline, she gasped: *Is Amara Danville Running for Manhattan District Attorney? Sources Say Yes.*

Amara hopped down from the table and hurriedly redressed before the doctor had time to exit the room. Before she had a chance to call the office to explain that she would be away for most of the morning, her boss suggested that she work from home for the rest of the day in order to avoid the media circus. In the meantime, he and the interns would field press calls and respond with "No comment" until further notice. *Good*, she thought. She had to make a few calls of her own. One of them would be to Landon, whom she had not seen for a while. If she tried to estimate how long it had been since Hallow was born, the sadness and shame would set in, and she would stop trying to remember. She and Landon had exchanged niceties over the years—brief calls and text messages, updates about the family, church announcements—but that was all. As a matter of fact, while showering for the second time before noon, she thought about the last significant time they'd shared together and realized that it was on All Hallows' Eve. He was the only one she wanted to talk to now, and luckily for her, he agreed to meet her on her terms: at her apartment and with two chopped cheeses—one for him and one for her.

When the doorbell rang, she looked through the peephole and saw a man with fine, silvery hairs in his beard that shone in the light.

"Landon?"

"Yes. Girl, you better open up this door." He faced the lens, and his smile filled her with shame again.

She invited him in then quickly fastened every bolt on the door. Afterward, she wrapped her arms around his neck and leaned her weight onto his chest.

"Whoa, whoa, girl. Jeez, how long has it been since we met up last? Five? Ten years?" He gently grabbed her to stand her upright. "I want to get a good look at you. Wow. Look at you." He then looked over her shoulder at her spacious living room with floor-to-ceiling windows and an exposed brick wall and said, "You definitely made something of yourself."

Amara recoiled. "I'm doing okay," she said. "Please." She directed him to the island in her kitchen, where there were two seats available and two glasses already filled with water.

"Thank you." He took his glass and guzzled the water in one sitting.

"I can get you some more."

"That would be fine."

When she turned her back, Landon leaned over to her glass, sniffed it, and his face contorted. By the time she turned back around, he was already digging into his chopped cheese.

"God, I miss these." Amara held her sandwich in her hands and took in the greasy smell with her eyes closed.

"Harlem is only a train ride away, you know. It's not like you're on the other side of the world like East New York or Staten Island."

"I know, but . . . I haven't had much of an interest in going there, you know."

Landon nodded. "You're going to have to if you are actually running. I saw the headline."

"Everybody and their mama saw that headline, and it's still early in the day."

"So let me ask you a question: Does that news drop have anything to do with why you called me down here?"

"It has everything to do with it."

Landon wiped the corners of his mouth and made an L shape with his right pointer finger and thumb against the side of his face. "I'm listening."

"Are you sure that no one knows about—" She cut herself off and took a deep breath. "No one knows about . . . her? At least no one who can harm me?"

"No one. I've made sure of it. Is that all?"

"No. I want to know what happened to her. What did you do with it? Her, I mean."

"I gave her to another family—you know that."

"Yes, but can I at least know their names?"

"It's not important."

"Landon, yes, it is. This is my career. Somebody could pay them off to talk about me!"

"They don't know you. I never gave your name."

"And how do I know for sure?"

"Have I ever steered you wrong before?"

"No, but—"

"Everything is fine, Mar. You are fine." Though Landon rubbed her shoulder for reassurance, she could not have been any more incredulous.

"I just feel like you're being cryptic for no reason."

He retracted the hand that rubbed her shoulder. "I'm not being cryptic."

"Yes, you are. If you aren't, then why can't I know who they are?"

"Because have you thought that maybe they have a career and reputation to protect just like you do?"

Amara sighed. "Point taken."

"Look, I get it. You interrogate people for a living, and you're about to hit the big leagues at your job. You're nervous, understandably so. But you have got to calm down." He took another bite of his chopped cheese.

Her eyes never left him. She was leaning over the island from the other side, and her right hand was clenched into a fist on the surface. He was afraid to move. Afraid to say a word lest she cut him off or maybe even put hands on him.

"What?" he asked.

She blinked twice. "Nothing."

"No, say it."

"I just find it pretty weird how you got so offended so quickly. All I did was ask a question, and now you're acting strange."

"I think you're projecting."

"I'm not projecting!"

"Look, I answered your question already. You're fine. The bases are covered. Anything else?"

"Actually, there is something else."

"Go 'head."

"Mom told me about Laila. Said she's been bringing you up but won't talk to you on the phone. What's that about? Y'all used to be close."

"What do you mean, 'What's that about?' The poor woman lost

her mind after she lost her child. How should I know what's going on with her? And what does this have to do with Hallow?"

"I just find it strange that Laila has started to say your name in connection with her lost child. We already know your connection to mine. The common denominator is you."

"Your child wasn't lost; you abandoned her."

Amara ran her fingers through her hair and turned her back on Landon.

"Look . . ." He walked over to her side, and she turned her back on him again while dabbing at the corners of her eyes. "You made a decision, and there are no loose ends. Hallow is with a good family now. She's fine. It's done. Leave it alone."

"She's fine?"

"Yes."

"So you've seen her again after that night I gave birth?"

"Yes, I've seen her. And what of it?"

"Why would you need to see her again if it was just a onetime deal?"

"I think we should table this." He finished his chopped cheese and left the wrapping on the kitchen island.

As he started toward the door, Amara called after him and blocked his exiting by standing right in front of him. "Landon, I want to know what happened to my daughter."

"Your daughter? Your daughter? You didn't want a daughter, remember? You wanted to get rid of her, and I helped you do that so you could graduate from college and go on to law school. Everything worked out. Why are you purposely trying to throw a wrench in your own plans?"

"I . . . I just want to know."

"Wrong. You care about your career. That's what you care about.

Leave motherhood to the women who wanted it in the first place. This . . ." His finger circled above their heads. "This is your life now, and it's a damn good one. Don't fuck it up now and be a cautionary tale."

Amara relaxed her body, and Landon was able to reach for the doorknob to leave, scooting her out of the way in the process. She sank to the ground and hugged her knees to her chest. A few moments passed before she realized that her entire body was shivering. Now she felt more tethered to her own flesh and bone, more rooted in the earth, and less in her head about all the professional commitments that now whittled away like dust into insignificance. Hallow had still come from her body, and she was out there somewhere. The blood coursing through her veins and pumping her heart became electrified as her yearslong denial was now over. But she had no idea what to do, what to say. So she returned to the past through memory, scanning over incomplete conversations, images, and people's faces from when she was pregnant. She had her mother. St. Philip's was still there. There was Landon and his family.

How had he already had a family on standby—no questions asked? Why did he never tell her about this family while she was pregnant? But that's what she'd wanted—for everything to be quick, secretive, and easy. But if Landon had seen Hallow after giving her to this family, then he had to have some idea where she was—maybe even a connection to these people. It would explain his not telling her their names . . . because he had some kind of conflict of interest. Landon was right: Harlem was only a train ride away, and she had to go back to investigate for herself whatever had happened to Hallow so that she could make sure that her daughter didn't jeopardize her campaign—and to see what the hell kind of connection Landon had with Laila and the Melancons.

18

Seeing Helena and Iris together after all these years left Maman feeling less warmhearted and more sorrowful over her relationship with her other daughter, Josephine. Maman wondered if their family was indeed entering into a new season, one that she wasn't sure she was equipped to handle. What if Iris and Helena left the home together? Iris wasn't the most lucrative asset to the family, but she still had a bit of caul left on her. She could easily walk out like she had done with Helena as a child. And Hallow—Hallow was planning to spend a considerable amount of time outside of the brownstone too. Who's to say that she would simply not return home one evening? Everything on the inside of the brownstone was changing, just like the landscape of the block and neighborhood altogether, and Maman despised it.

She woke up the next morning with Scuff greeting her to the right side and the photo of Alexandre—or "Alex"—standing in a square frame on the desk to her left. She moved closer to the photo until her body was at the edge of the bed and studied his emotionless face, from the evenness of his hairline to his generous lips and the sharp incline of his cheekbones, before falling down to the hooked shape of his Adam's apple. There were many times when she could've hidden his photo away in some drawer, cut it up into little pieces, incinerated it, then danced around its ashes, but she couldn't. There was too much heat still contained in that eight-by-eight-inch photograph. The promise in those dark brown eyes would make any woman willingly lose herself inside of them if given the chance. Some days she missed him and wondered about the family he'd left her for. She wondered what it was about the other woman, whose novelty furnished his soul more than the longevity of their relationship ever could. She wondered why he never fought for her or the children when she put him out. She wondered why he never came back. And it was there in her bed, between Scuff and that photograph, where Maman asked herself in her head, *Was it me all along?*

Maman was not one for painful emotions. She either redirected her attention to the upkeep of the home or pulled from a blunt to numb the edges of her most difficult memories. But lately in her old age, she couldn't control her own mental faculties as much as she wanted. At least when Hallow was a child, Maman could invest all of her energy into properly grooming her. Now that Hallow was older and everyone could move and think for themselves, Maman wallowed without a particular project to occupy her time, so she folded into what she always loved: the home. There had to be a way to add beauty to the home, and gardening seemed like the safest option. She kept a notebook where she sketched a design of how her plot would look in the space surrounding the front of the brownstone and she'd monitor the amount of rainfall and sunlight Harlem would experience over the course of several weeks by the street-facing window seat. Today was the day that her bare-root roses, which had been pre-soaked and readied for planting, were set to arrive. Maman pulled out a pair of dusty overalls that she hadn't worn in decades to wear for the occasion. The denim slid off her small frame, but it was nothing that a silk taffeta sash couldn't fix. Then she brought out a large wide-brimmed hat and stuck a pair of gloves into the right pocket of her overalls.

When Maman grabbed her cane and stepped out of her bedroom, she saw Landon coming out from the living room. They halted when they saw each other. Maman looked toward the front-facing windows, and the sun was shining brightly. Landon was still in their home after sunrise, which was highly unusual, especially since he hadn't informed Maman that he would be coming early to discuss business affairs. Maman leaned over his shoulder, saw Josephine beaming while she smeared her croissant with butter and jam, and walked into the dining room.

"All right. What's going on here?"

Josephine looked up. "Oh. Morning, Maman."

"Don't 'Morning, Maman' me. I know you're not grinnin' like an ol' Cheshire Cat over some breakfast."

"Maman . . ." Landon walked into the dining room and pulled out a chair. "Have a seat. We'd like to talk to you about something."

"No, I'd rather stand, thank you."

Landon sighed.

"Landon." Josephine nodded and smiled.

"Very well."

"What the hell is going on here? Your wife finally filed for divorce?" Maman asked. "That would explain why you're still here in the morning like this. Hallow ain't down here, and you didn't call me, so what is the meaning of this?"

Landon strode over to the other side of the table and sat down beside Josephine. He placed his arm on the back of her chair while Josephine kept her head down, though her smile was still visible. He said, "Maman, Josephine and I are making plans to leave."

"Leave where?" Maman asked.

"Leave here. Once this agreement with the Epelbaums goes through, we're going to move away from here."

"And how do you know it'll go through?"

"It will. All Hallow has to do is say yes. We've agreed that since she's your heir apparent, she has final say. And since we can't think of a reason why she'd say no, it's as good as done. And your family is set to profit in the millions. Enough to not have to sell caul to anyone again. Enough for all of us to do whatever we want."

"What if this *is* what I want? I've been doing this business longer than you've been alive."

"Yes, but you're older. Much much older, if you don't mind me saying. Don't you want to not worry about money anymore?"

"And what about your daughter, Hallow? You're just gonna up and leave her? Have you even told her?"

"We figured it's best to tell her after the deal is done. Besides, she's grown. She can get her own place like Helena, live her own life, and we can check on her from time to time."

Maman could feel the rage welling up in her spirit—so much so that she could hardly see straight for several seconds. When her vision cleared, she saw Josephine still grinning like an ol' Cheshire Cat and saying nothing at all. She hated how much Josephine receded next to Landon, almost like she could lose herself in his dark brown eyes, like she was in Alexandre's.

"Well, young lady," Maman said. "What do you have to say for yourself? You're gonna let him do all the talkin' or what?"

Josephine gripped Landon's hand before speaking: "He said everything that I—we both—wanted to say."

"Oh, don't be such a goddamn doormat, Jo. Look me in my eye and tell me that you're leaving. I wanna hear you say it."

Josephine removed her grin and regarded her mother with a severity that stopped Maman's heart. "We're leaving," she declared.

"I'm not giving you a dime," Maman snapped.

"If you want to withhold money from Josephine, which will be hard since it'll be coming through our daughter, fine. I still take my cut from the deal to begin with, and that'll be enough for us to move on with our lives."

"She's not going anywhere."

"What are you gonna do? Gonna stop me with your cane?" Josephine asked.

The doorbell rang, and Maman hesitated to get up because she needed her cane to do so. It was the first time that Maman was pushed to the brink of tears, and she could not give Josephine or Landon the satisfaction of seeing her break down. She puffed out her chest and swallowed her pride before using the cane to start toward the front door. Her roses had arrived. Perfect. She had had enough of the nonsense, and this was her best distraction to get through the day at the very least. On her way to the door she took in all of the brownstone, and her stomach suddenly twisted in knots. From one angle, the brownstone looked lopsided. From another angle, it appeared to be sliding into the earth. And then from another angle, the brownstone seemed fine. Maman blinked multiple times and tilted her head in all sorts of directions to confirm which perception was correct, but all she gathered from the experiment was nothing more than a migraine.

Outside, she crouched down to her knees and started pulling out the weeds and shrubs to make room for the roses. Just before she was about to place one into the ground, she heard someone giggling behind her back. A white woman in a sports bra and spandex tights slightly jumped when Maman snapped her neck to glare at her.

"Sorry."

"What do you want?" Maman asked.

"I'm sorry, I—I'm one of your neighbors."

She walked toward the gate and was about to touch it when Maman yelled, "Back up."

"Oh." The woman took a step backward with both hands up. "Okay, sorry. Boundaries, I understand."

"You still ain't tell me what you want, girl."

"You shouldn't put your roses in that kind of soil."

"Excuse me? What are you talkin' 'bout? I've been living here for eighty years, I know my own dirt."

"With all due respect, ma'am, that soil is dead."

"Wh—" Maman sputtered her words like a car engine. "What do you mean dead? This soil ain't dead!"

"May I come in?"

"No, no! Just stay right where you are and point."

"Well, for starters, look at it. It's all gray in some spots and light brown in the others. That means it's dead. Take a bit of it in your hands and smell it."

Maman cupped her hand down into the soil and then held it to her nose.

"Does it have a slight metallic smell?"

"No."

"Does it smell like wood debris or does it have a forest floor smell?"

"No."

"Does it smell like rain on a fresh spring day?"

"I said no, girl! No, no, no. Why do you keep asking me these questions?"

"Because your soil is dead. By looks and smell, the soil is dead. But you can repair it."

"Repair it?"

"Yeah, just buy some nutrients or get some compost. That's how you start repairing it."

"But what if it keeps getting damaged?" Maman asked while digging again into the dirt and tossing it over her shoulder before digging and digging some more like a gopher. Though the white woman was beginning to slowly back away at this point, Maman kept asking.

"What if it keeps becoming damaged, hmm?" Maman asked. "What if you keep repairing and repairing and repairing and something keeps going wrong? Then you gotta repair again and again and again and nothing works and—" Maman noticed that the entire front of her overalls was dirtied. A small tear cascaded down the round mound of her dirt-stained cheek. Then another. And another. Until her vision blurred again. She wiped her eyes with her gloved hands and the white woman was nowhere to be found. Maman grabbed her cane and started back toward the brownstone.

Back inside, she heard the sound of ecstatic lovemaking coming from upstairs and voiced her disgust downstairs, where no one else was present. She inspected the ceiling as well as the nooks and crannies, and the number of cracks and holes that greeted her with every turn frayed her nerves. How much more repairing could one family do? Maman asked herself. When did one give up? What if the brownstone was just dead and there was nothing else to put inside of it to make it better? What if it was dead and anyone who wanted a chance at a real life had to leave to make it happen?

When Maman returned to her bedroom, something in the air did not feel quite right. It didn't take long for her to find the aberrations. The photo of Alexandre had been turned facedown, and her blunt and lighter were lying too close to the corner of the sheet that hung over the bed. Her mind wasn't as sharp as it used to be, but she was almost certain that she had not moved the photograph or placed her blunt and lighter that close to her sheet. The blunt was not ignited, but that did nothing to mitigate Maman's distrust of herself and her own space.

After staring at the photo, blunt, and lighter for a while, Maman looked beyond those items to find that there were shadows on the walls, shadows much larger than her body or any piece of furniture in the room. When Maman followed their amorphous shapes, all leaned toward Scuff, whose claws were so large now that she dropped her cane at the sight of them. She couldn't repair that. The hands were too deep. The damage too wicked.

As she leaned against the hinge of the door, Maman sniffled and wiped the last tears from her eyes. Then she said, "All right now, Scuff. You win."

19

Amara's conversation with Landon about Hallow's whereabouts weighed heavily on her spirit, and she found it hard to concentrate on her responsibilities. With permission from Virgil, she was able to work from home again, where she took frequent breaks to lounge about in bed or on the sofa in the living room. When she wasn't distracted by thoughts of her daughter and the stress of her work life, she could not stop sleeping. Sometimes she'd go to bed before dusk and wake up in the middle of the night to gorge on snacks from the kitchen. Ethan was concerned with her behavior and made a commitment to be more present so that she would not fail.

One morning, Amara awakened to the sounds of Ethan moving around in the kitchen. She dragged herself from the bedroom and saw him placing avocado slices with a sunny-side-up egg on wheat toast. The rest of the plate was full of olive-oil-drizzled arugula with a few cranberries and almonds sprinkled on top. His sleeves were rolled up above his elbows, and two buttons loosened from his shirt. Amara leaned against the threshold of the kitchen, flattered by his meticulousness. When Ethan saw that he was being watched, he winked at Amara and said, "Mornin'. Hope you're hungry."

"I am."

"Come sit down."

Ethan placed the plate of avocado toast and greens in front of her, along with a yellow drink in a stemless wineglass.

"Bon appétit," Ethan said.

"Thank you." Amara sipped from her glass and scrunched up her face. "Oh man. What is that?"

"A lemon turmeric flush drink," he said proudly. "It's got ginger, cayenne, and cinnamon. I added a teaspoon of honey in there so it wouldn't be too strong of a kick."

"Oof. I don't know why I thought it was pineapple juice or something."

"Too much acidity, especially in the morning. Studies show that turmeric can help with anxiety, and I know you've been feeling on edge for a while." She hated how clinical Ethan was with everything. Some days, she missed a bit of the loose attitude that he had when they were in law school. Still, she had to admit that he knew her more than she'd like to admit, and he was just trying to help.

"I have been. I wish I would've had more time with this campaign preparation, no thanks to that *Daily Beast* leak."

"Hey, it worked out, didn't it? You've become a media darling, and besides, I thought the writers did a good job."

His comment left an uncomfortable feeling in Amara's chest. It was the second time that a man had irked her nerves in her own damn kitchen. She would've asked him to leave had she not worked up an appetite in her sleep. And if she was being honest, she loved his cooking for her in spite of his pettiness, that no matter how upset he was with her, he always made sure he nourished her body. Whether out of love or habit, she wouldn't stand in the way of his generosity.

"Why do you think they did a good job? I thought it was a bit premature. I wish I had gotten a tip that it was going to be published and jumped ahead of the story."

"Well, it got people talking, and it drummed up buzz. You should be excited, not worried. Dan did a good job editing it."

"How did you know who edited the piece?"

Ethan smiled. "He's the politics editor on the masthead. Process of elimination. Plus I know a couple of people over there. You're liked. It's fine."

"Huh."

"And I might have made a phone call."

Amara slammed her fork on the table and said, "Ethan!"

"What? The story was written in a way that spoke highly of you."

"That's not the point. Why would you go behind my back and do something like that?"

"I didn't go behind your back; that would imply betrayal. I did this for you. You needed that extra kick in the ass. This is all good news, Mar."

"I don't need you deciding what's best for me. Just like I didn't need you deciding what kind of drink I need for my 'anxiety' or how fried chicken will mess up my cholesterol."

"What?" His mouth contorted with confusion, and Amara realized that he hadn't remembered the snide remarks he made to her and her mother about their eating habits. She was surprised that she could recall the months-old exchange, but it confirmed what her mother warned her about: safekeeping painful secrets would turn her inside out.

"Look," Ethan continued. "I know you're under a lot of stress, so I'm going to let this outburst slide."

Amara scoffed at the nerve of him.

"Don't forget we have that party at the Plaza this evening."

"Oh, shit. That's tonight?"

"Yes, tonight. You still have the whole day to prepare. Cocktail hour isn't until seven p.m., and it's not even ten a.m. yet. You can decompress for the day but not too long. You've got people to ingratiate yourself with. Remember, it's black-tie, so we have to dress accordingly."

"How could I not? It's the usual Upper East Side soiree."

"Ah, but it's not." He blended a protein drink and raised the glass to her. "You, my dear, are the guest of honor. Unofficially, but still. Everybody will be talking about you, and you should make an impression."

"Who's all gonna be there?"

"The usual. No one's gonna be there who you don't know. I made sure of it. Had a look at the guest list. You know how to socialize. And I'll be right there with you." She leaned in for a kiss, and he kissed her forehead.

"You have morning breath. Now eat."

Ethan walked past her humming an upbeat jingle, and she expected to hear her front doorknob twist, but he ran her shower instead. The thought of joining him vanished as soon as it came to her. Him telling her she had morning breath had turned her off from trying to have a quickie. Now that he was out of the way, she could finish her egg and get her mind right for tonight.

She had it down to a science, how much time one should spend mingling with one person before moving on to another conversation. The most precarious topic to discuss amongst wealthy people was money—how much someone needed for their philanthropic organization, how much a ticket costs to attend a charity ball, how much someone makes. At the same time, to occupy this particular milieu was to taciturnly commit to a veil of secrecy about how money was made, circulated, and maintained, so that if they achieved anything great, they could purposely attribute it to hard work and discipline, a foolish and undying loyalty to the meritocracy myth.

But Amara needed money for her campaign. There was not enough goodwill she could accrue from Manhattanites that could surpass the weight of the green. She made enough money to take care of herself but not enough to shift anything in her favor, and she didn't trust a single one of those people. No matter how much they smiled in her face or placed a hand on the small of her back, she was still their shining example of the meritocratic myth, and if she thought about it too long, she'd lose focus. Though she didn't want to admit it, the *Daily Beast* article knocked her off her game, making her feel as though she had already lost control of a moving train.

She wore a Badgley Mischka gown that she borrowed from Rent the Runway, and Ethan dressed in a Giorgio Armani suit. While Ethan scrolled through his phone in the car on the way there, Amara stared out the window. Then she absentmindedly grabbed Ethan's hand, and he took it out of habit without looking up from his phone, leaving her more and more dissatisfied.

No matter how many times she'd traveled this route for work or play, she was also fascinated at how quickly the exteriors of apartment buildings changed, signaling a different world into which one was about to enter. Once one headed into the street intersections between Madison Avenue and East Sixtieth Street, everything looked so polished that Amara would joke to herself that you could be fined for looking too hard at any building. The border between the Upper East Side and Midtown was where everyone wanted to be, though their reputations were quite stodgy. This was the New York most shown in television and movies, the New York where most transplants wanted to live and shop. She could not care less about it. Manhattan as a whole kept changing the longer she stayed, and she thought it best not to get attached to one neighborhood. But with that intention came a sense of loss, then melancholy that without one place to call home, she would always be swept away by some current. And then she did think of her former home. And of Laila again. But she could not think for long because the doorman opened her car door and held out his hand for her.

The party took place in the Oak Room. Its grape-laden chandelier, high ceilings, and Flemish oak walls were a nod to European castles. The grandeur of the centerpieces and the ice buckets full of Krug Champagne made Amara feel grateful to be in such high company. But as soon as she saw the host and hostess—Robert and Jillian Epelbaum—standing at a high-top cocktail table near the center of the room, she snapped out of her trance and straightened her back. This was the point in the night when Ethan was usually the most affectionate, his arm draped around Amara's waist as he planted a kiss near her left earlobe before they entered the foyer. Once they crossed into that area, such tenderness would be socially unacceptable. The couple nodded and mouthed *Hello* to a who's who of people—lobbyists, politicians, and political donors—and they passed by quickly, which was to Amara's relief because she had forgotten half of their names and how she knew them. Once Amara and Ethan were approaching the hosts' cocktail table, Robert and Jillian skillfully ended their conversation with a pair of other guests and shifted their bodies away from them to indicate that their attention was elsewhere.

"Ah! Amara." Robert shook Amara's right hand and kissed her on both cheeks before shaking Ethan's hand. Jill switched sides with Robert, cocked her head to the side, and smiled. "Amara," she said in her disarming voice that always reminded Amara of jam, the way it could spread all over anyone who heard the sound, making them feel both full and sweetened. When Jill leaned in for her usual half hug, consisting of a hand on the shoulder to pull the person in but not all the way, Amara felt a wetness to the touch that piqued her curiosity. The room temperature was mild, and the space was adequately ventilated.

"Amara, I was just telling Ethan here that the thought of you being the Manhattan District Attorney—well, that would be such progress! You don't see many Black female district attorneys here or across the country. You'd be a maverick. But I do have to ask . . ." Robert leaned in and smirked. "Is it really true? Every paper in town is speculating but none can confirm."

"Merlot? Chardonnay?" A waitress interjected. Robert and Jill shook their heads.

"Merlot," Amara said. She took a large sip and said to Robert, "I am courting the idea."

"Well, we do hope that this courting turns into something serious, Amara. You have many people in your corner, like us," Jill added, to which Amara smiled then looked down to the handkerchief that Jill was fiercely grasping with her right fist.

"We're going to need all the support we can get," Ethan said. "Up in Harlem, everyone is seriously overreacting. I was shocked to see the way those people reacted to the case when the girl's crime was so terrible."

"Those people?" Amara asked.

"I mean, it was an impressive feat that you stood your ground, even though I bet you knew that there would be backlash." Jill practically talked over Amara's question to Ethan. "Throwing away a child in a garbage can." She placed a hand over her chest. "It's—it's unforgivable, I'd say. No child would ever do something like that, and you were so right to have her tried as an adult."

Amara took another large sip of her wine and nodded at the waiter to bring another glass. "It's not a decision that I'm particularly proud of."

Ethan stamped her foot underneath the table then laughed. "What she means is that it was a very stressful time for her. She's not so far removed from her cases that she doesn't have feelings."

"Feelings, yes, of course, but you still got the job done," Jillian said. "Murderers shouldn't be allowed to have children."

"Asali Givens won't be around any more children." Amara emphasized Asali's full name and took a large sip.

If there was one topic that could torpedo an otherwise fine night, this was it. She did not want to discuss Asali Givens, whose name Jill had either forgotten or didn't care to say. Discussing this kind of work at an evening party was rare, especially when it involved the prison system. If the context were different, Amara would explain that like any case, any story, the details were much more complicated than what Jill chose to summarize to fit her own judgment. But with wealthy people like Jill and Robert, the details would destroy their long-held view that the criminal justice system was actually just. The explanation would anger more than bore them. But at the base level, Amara did not want to bring a young Black girl into focus in a conversation where she was outnumbered. If Amara told Jill that she still received letters and emails from Black women across the country asking her to retroactively put the girl into the juvenile system and that she had been seriously considering it, her courting the idea of being district attorney would collapse into an afterthought.

"It was tough, for sure." Amara nodded. "But given all the information that the office received, we had to act accordingly and make our decision."

"You did a damn good job, Amara," Robert said. "I hate that. You know, it really bothers me because that child could have had a good life with someone else, someone who wanted to be a mother. The point is, the baby deserved a chance at a life." Though Amara knew that Robert was referring to Asali, her chest became sore with the guilt that overwhelmed her body.

Jill violently coughed into her handkerchief and caught the eyes of other guests who were standing on opposite sides of the room. The overhead music had gotten louder the longer she coughed. When she finished, the volume gradually descended, and she balled the handkerchief back into her fist as Amara noticed that there were dots of red speckled within the creases. Robert placed his hand over the hand that Jill used to grasp the handkerchief and that gesture signaled to Amara that they were both hiding something.

"Forgive me," Jill said while soothing her chest. "I've been a little under the weather, but don't worry. It's not contagious. You are both fine."

"We didn't worry at all," Ethan said.

Robert, who was facing the door like any good host would, raised his head, and his eyes got wider. "Would you all excuse me just a moment?" Robert proceeded toward the door with his arms outstretched toward a group of incoming guests.

Why would Robert need to help any guest get situated? Why couldn't those guests approach the cocktail table just like she and Ethan had done? Did these guests procure some kind of favor with Robert, and if so, who were these people? She was on to her second glass of wine. She took another large sip and the slight numbness provided some relief. *Ethan was right*, Amara thought. She was nervous. She turned around to see two Black women standing in the doorway, but Robert's body was blocking Amara from getting a good look at either of them. Yet when they turned the corner, she saw the side profile of the younger one and suddenly felt queasy at how inexplicably connected she felt to that woman. Maybe it was how both shared the same nose and stride. Amara blinked her eyes several times to verify that she really saw what she saw, but when she finally stared straight ahead again, Robert and the two women were gone.

There was a deafening ringing in both of Amara's ears as she whipped her body around to face Jill and Ethan. Jill's face transformed. Every aspect of her profile transformed into a delirious excitement. The smile that hung in the middle of her face was not normal. It alluded to another secret. Then Jill turned toward other guests, as she had done when Amara and Ethan approached, letting them know that their time interacting was over for now. Ethan grabbed Amara's elbow and pulled her off to the side.

"What the hell was that? Where did you go?"

"What do you mean? I was standing right there."

"That's not what I mean. You just completely lost focus back there. What's going on?"

"Nothing, just stop being overbearing."

"Are you drunk?" He tried to look into Amara's eyes, but she kept dodging his line of sight. "You need to pull it together; this is important."

"How many times are you gonna say that? You're not my father."

"Then stop acting like a child."

"Fuck you, Ethan."

Ethan held his finger up in Amara's face and said, "I'm gonna go mingle with the other guests. Get your shit together and don't make us look bad."

Amara stumbled after Ethan walked away, yet she still had enough sense to move away from the main area down a small hallway. It was there, in that hallway, with its gold barocco wallpaper and green carpets, that she heard a glass shatter and a pair of feet running, followed by Jill's laughter. There was a cracked door with a beam of light that drew Amara closer and closer. From the sliver of space between the door, Amara could see a white hand holding a lighter with an ignited flame and hear some whimpering coming from another place in the room. Her mind swarmed with the possibility of what the hell was going on in there.

She returned to the main area, found the nearest waitress, and took one glass of merlot in one hand and a glass of chardonnay in the other. She knocked them both back quickly. The liquid courage she now felt coursing through her body was enough for her to entertain conversations with other gentlemen in the room as they spoke about their time at Princeton and Yale, respectively, the latest *New York Times* headlines, or how and when their social calendars would coincide again. Soon she was lounging on a sofa laughing at some white man's jokes before she chimed in with her own, then made an extemporaneous speech on her imminent run for district attorney, to which she received tons of applause, handshakes, and negotiable donations to her campaign. Everyone was smiling at her and she back at them. She was able to nod and back herself into the same corner where she and Ethan had their argument so that she could run down that same hallway to the bathroom at the end.

After Amara emptied all the contents from her stomach in the nearest stall, she opened the door to find another woman standing at the sink in front of the bathroom mirror. Her face was just as flushed as Amara's, cheeks reddened and tear-soaked. Amara squinted and thought she was seeing double: her reflection in the mirror and a doppelgänger standing to the side of her. The girl was wearing a simple black dress with pearls, and her curly hair was half pulled up in a bun while the rest of her hair fell down the sides of her face. She was beautiful, but Amara was not sure if this woman was real or the merlot and chardonnay had produced a hallucinogenic effect that she had never experienced before. They didn't say a word to each other, but the woman stared back at her in disbelief, her jaw suspended in the air. She looked a bit younger and a little shorter, but not by too much. And Amara recognized the caul that was visible on her wrist and parts of her neck. The room started to spin, and Amara hobbled around while grabbing her stomach.

The woman faced Amara to get another good look at her and then dashed out of the bathroom. Amara stood still and felt the breeze from the departure. She could not have conjured that breeze. She could not have conjured the water beads still sliding from the sink that her likeness had just hovered over. She touched them to make sure. But before Amara could follow after her, everything disappeared into darkness again and she lost consciousness. When a restaurant staff member found her minutes later, she attributed Amara's state to food poisoning and moved quickly to nurse her by placing a cold compress to Amara's forehead until she came to, and then by giving her glasses of ginger ale.

20

I can't believe you," Josephine said to Hallow on their ride home. She leaned against the window and shook her head. "I cannot believe that you did that."

Hallow did not expect to snap in the way that she did, and now there was nothing she could say. When she received an invitation to the Epelbaums' party at the Plaza, Josephine harangued her with the rules of dinner etiquette as well as the importance of sealing this deal to maintain their brownstone and family business. She memorized what she would say from notes on index cards, had her clothes dry-cleaned, and shined her best patent leather heels. Because Maman wasn't feeling up for socializing, she allowed Hallow and Josephine to go, but they could not have been less in sync with each other. A few short hours before a driver was scheduled to pick them up from their home, Hallow spied on Josephine excitedly stuffing many dresses and blouses into a large, vintage trunk suitcase while humming a little melody. On the ride to the Oak Room, Josephine could hardly sit still in her seat and was smiling so hard that Hallow thought her face would get stuck like that. She was confused as to why Josephine was assuring her that this deal needed to happen for their home's sake when she looked like she was in the process of leaving. Josephine's ulterior motive was only a harbinger of things to come that evening.

Hallow expected that when she and Josephine entered the Oak Room, they would be allowed to talk with the other guests, as Robert mentioned, to convince them that he was a good business partner—not immediately whisked away to a room down a narrow hallway off to the side, where no one could see them. She also didn't expect that as soon as they entered that room she would be offered a glass of absinthe even after she told Robert and Jillian that she was only twenty.

"Pfft," Robert said and shrugged his shoulders. "We won't tell if you won't. Loosen up."

Josephine had already helped herself to the bottle of cabernet sauvignon in the bucket next to the green velvet sofa where they sat opposite the Epelbaums. The three sets of eyes on Hallow made her begrudgingly swallow the entire glass of that bitter alcohol, and Jillian promptly poured her another serving. She coughed again into a handkerchief while taking her seat on the sofa opposite the Melancon women, and Robert patted her on the back.

"You'll have to excuse my wife; she's very sick."

"Oh, I'm sorry to hear that," Josephine said. "Are you all right, Mrs. Epelbaum?"

"No, I'm afraid I'm not," she replied, and dabbed at the sides of her mouth. "I have rapidly advancing stage-four lung cancer. Chemotherapy is a mess, and I hate it."

"I'm sorry," Josephine said.

"So am I. But not for long."

Hallow leaned forward and soothed her forehead, but Josephine snapped, "Sit upright, dear." Hallow did as she was told despite her having a splitting headache.

"What—" Hallow cleared her throat. "What do you mean, 'not for long'?"

Robert and Jillian smiled at each other and Hallow shot a glance at her glass. She hated the taste but appreciated how loose her body felt, so she drank a little bit more.

"Ms. Melancon, do you know why we wanted you here, hmm?"

"To socialize with other guests and get to know your circle so that we could negotiate this deal?" Hallow asked.

"Yes, well, my wife is a part of that circle, and like she said, chemotherapy is a mess. Wouldn't wish it on my worst enemy. Now, the offer still stands for the deal, but I want to know that I'm getting what I'm paying for."

"You want to give a piece of caul to your wife? That's fine."

"Ah." Robert raised his finger and clicked his tongue. "That's not it either. I want to see if this caul can really heal as you all and Landon purport it to do."

Josephine slapped Hallow on the arm.

"Ow!" Hallow yelled. "What are you doing?"

Josephine tugged Hallow's arm toward the Epelbaums and pointed. "You see how quickly the redness clears?"

"No, that's too easy. That could be because of youth and elasticity. Trust me, we've thought long and hard about this, and we wondered, what could really—and I mean really—damage the skin? A slap? No. A punch? Mm-mm. Maybe a cut or a stab—a little bit too messy. We don't want to bloody your beautiful dresses. But then we thought . . ." Robert reached deep into his pocket and pulled out a lighter. He ignited it and continued, "It'll be very simple. We just want to see."

Before Hallow knew it, she'd screamed and knocked over a glass vase as she ran to the nearest corner. Crouching down in the fetal position, she whimpered then hyperventilated. Josephine was still sitting on the sofa with her upper half facing Hallow, and she was mouthing for her daughter to get up through clenched teeth and bulging eyes. Jillian was affectionately rubbing Robert's back, and he sat upright watching the flame flicker. Hallow closed her eyes, and her splitting headache splintered her thoughts into incoherent shards until they coalesced into her most visceral memory about fire: she was back in Harlem in the basement of that Presbyterian church on her block, and Maman held her finger under the fire until it became charred and unrecognizable. From that moment on, Hallow promised herself that she would never be put on display again, but it was only now as a young woman that she realized her life's work as a caulbearer was no different from that of an exhibitionist; she would always be a spectacle. There was no reconciliation. All the caul that was cut and sold from her body, all the initial conversations with vendors—there was no pocket of space to preserve her body and name it rightfully hers.

There in that corner, Josephine helped Hallow to her feet as she stumbled (an aftereffect of the absinthe) and said, "She needs a moment. Hallow, why don't you go to the bathroom and freshen up, hmm?"

Hallow stared blankly, and Jillian chimed in, "Of course. Right at the end of the hall—you can't miss it."

In the bathroom, Hallow was able to get herself together not through her own strength but by her disgust at the violent retching coming from the occupied toilet. She thought of asking the woman if she needed help, but the sound was so loud that she wasn't sure if the woman would hear her anyway.

When the bathroom stall door opened and Amara snapped her head back to move her hair away from her face, Hallow was surprised by how much they resembled each other. The woman didn't seem real. If only she could've touched her, Hallow thought, and pressed her finger into the woman's flesh to see if a dent would remain once she pulled away. If only, Hallow thought, she could've said something to the woman to hear what she sounded like. Regret swarmed in her head on the Melancon women's ride back home. Both she and Josephine were silent and either distracted with their own thoughts or asleep. Hallow leaned against the car window. She saw the reflection of her face and that of Amara. She figured it was better not to tell anyone about what she saw since she was drunk anyway, and even if she did say something they would tell her to think nothing of it. But she could not escape this feeling. It was a wonderful one that defied logic, because when she saw how much she resembled that other woman, she felt like she was home for the very first time.

"Do you hear me talking to you?" Josephine interrupted her thoughts.

"What?" Hallow asked.

"Don't 'What?' me. What happened back there? Why did you freak out like that?"

"Are you seriously asking me this question?"

Josephine just stared and Hallow scoffed.

"Some days I don't know if we're on the same side here. I mean, when I was a kid you perfectly understood how I felt about fire, and now it's like, do you want to protect me or throw me to the wolves?"

"How can you say that? I have been protecting you! Would you rather have me be like Iris and—" Josephine bit down on her lower lip.

"What?" Hallow asked.

"Nothing."

"What are you saying?"

"Nothing. It's nothing."

"Just spit it out, Jo!"

"Since when do you call me Jo?"

"Tsk," Hallow said and leaned the side of her face against the window again.

"You better not have pissed them off. I hope to God the deal is still on the table."

"Why, so you can run off with Dad? You're living in a fantasy world."

Josephine grabbed Hallow's chin and pulled it close to her face. But when she looked deep into Hallow's unyielding eyes and saw how blatantly unfazed she was by Josephine's grip, she pushed her chin away and buried her face in her hands.

"Why would you speak to me like that? It's like I don't even recognize you nowadays."

"I can say the same about you."

When the two women returned to the brownstone, Hallow walked up the stairs behind Josephine and each disappeared into her own bedroom without saying another word to the other. Neither woman could sleep in her bed that night. They twisted and turned and ached with the inability to reconcile their hearts' truest desires, and their obligation to the home made them feel imprisoned. Josephine hated that her destiny hinged upon Hallow, who was now the one who made executive decisions as the successor of the caulbearing business. She hated that she could have found the strength to leave the brownstone sooner. She hated how the room smelled of a hint of decay, beyond simply being "lived in," how the cracks on the ceilings were more familiar than the outside environment, and how maybe she should give up on living, for there had been too many false starts to believe that things would ever be different.

As for Hallow, she was already confident in her decision but could not get a decent night's rest out of fear of what everyone's reaction would be. Before sunrise, Hallow phoned the Epelbaums, hoping that the call would go straight to voicemail. She didn't want to lead them on. Robert picked up, and his voice was clear and firm. She cut him off before he could ask how she was doing and declined his offer. He did not attempt to convince her to reconsider. He merely laughed. This outburst left Hallow speechless, and Robert gathered himself and said, "You have no idea who you're dealing with." Before Hallow could respond, he added, "You just made a huge mistake."

Hallow could only hear her heavy breathing on the line.

"I've been following your family since before you were even born. You have no idea what you are doing, little girl. But all right, you've made your decision, and I'll have to be going now." Then he hung up.

Panicked, Hallow phoned Helena multiple times until she finally picked up with a raspy-voiced greeting. She urged Helena to come home as soon as she could because it was an emergency, and Helena told her to give her ninety minutes to get uptown. When she arrived, Hallow pulled her into the kitchen.

"What's going on?" Helena asked while stretching and rubbing her eyes.

"I told him no."

Helena blinked. "What?"

"I couldn't do it, Helena. It just didn't sit right with me. He tried to burn me, and I'm tired of these white folks. I don't want no part of them, and I don't want them having a part of me."

"You know what this does, though, right?"

"What *what* does?" Helena and Hallow peeped their heads out into the dining room, where Maman was entering with her cane.

The sisters looked at each other before Maman repeated herself in a volume that they had not heard since they were children.

"Tell her, Hallow," Helena said lowly.

Hallow looked down at the ground and said, "I told Mr. Epelbaum no. We're not going to do that."

"Oh." Maman leaned against the nearest wall and rubbed the caul on her chest. "On one hand, this may not be a bad thing."

"Huh?" Hallow and Helena said in unison.

"Yes, you can all remain here and work to get more clients. Since you've made up your mind, I assume you have a plan B, so let's hear it."

"I don't have a plan B. I need time to think it over."

"Think it over? You didn't think it over before you said no?"

"No?" Hallow said quietly and flinched.

Maman waved the free arm she had out in front of her and shook her head. "I give up. Don't nobody give a damn about this home but me, and all of y'all conspiring to do it and me in. I give up." She walked out into the hallway, where she sat in the window seat to sulk again.

"Damn," Helena said.

"What?"

"Didn't think she would have that reaction."

"Neither did I."

"I guess it'll make it that much easier for you to get out more and into the community from time to time, but I don't know, girl. Maman may have another trick up her sleeve, knowing her. Why exactly did you say no anyway?" she asked as they walked back into the kitchen.

Hallow recounted everything, from the moment she and Josephine walked to the door into the Oak Room down to when Josephine thought it was best to leave after Hallow's meltdown from the fire.

"And so Josephine still thinks you're gonna go through with it?"

Hallow shrugged her shoulders. "Maybe. We haven't spoken since last night."

"Girl. Shit."

Hallow did a double take at Helena and asked, "Can I ask you something?"

"Go 'head."

"Last night, I told her that I don't know if she really wants to protect me as her kid, and she compared herself to Iris. Now, I know you and Iris don't have the best relationship, but do you know what she meant by that?"

"No. Why did you ask?"

"Never mind."

"No, tell me."

"It's not important."

"Obviously it is, since you brought it up!"

"Did Iris have something to do with your accident and the reason why you stayed away from home for so long?"

Helena began to slowly back up toward the wall. "Hallow . . ." She rubbed the back of her neck and looked at the tile floor.

"Is that why you two never had that good of a relationship when we were growing up?"

"No. I just—I lost her and I fell and—no. No, she didn't do that. No."

"But after the accident happened, was she there with you or was she—"

"Dammit, Hallow!" Helena yelled. While caressing her wrists, Helena continued, "You don't know what I've been through. You don't know what it's like to look everywhere and see all these kids with their moms and you can't find your own and you scream and cry out for her and before you know it you have teeth in your back and you think you're gonna die because there's no one else around to make it stop."

Hallow took a step closer, but Helena shook her head. "I'm trying to move forward. I've been trying to move forward for damn near twenty years now. I been trying to heal on my own, so why are you bringing up the past to stop me from that healing?"

"I'm sorry. I am."

Helena sniffled. "Just change the subject. Please. I didn't come over here for that."

"Well, there is one more thing." Hallow lowered her voice. "I saw someone at the party who . . . I . . ." Hallow raised her hands to the sides of her head. "I can't explain it. She—she looked just like me. I mean, I know I was drunk. I know. But I wasn't completely out of my mind. She was real. And she looked like me but an older version of me, and I feel like she could be my—"

"Hallow." Helena scoffed. "You didn't see anyone. Absinthe can do that to you from time to time, trust me."

"You're lying."

"No, I'm not. One of the ingredients in absinthe—wormwood? That shit will make you hallucinate."

"It will?" Hallow frowned.

"Yeah. Maman used to keep absinthe in her nightstand. That with the weed would have her all kinds of fucked up. I don't think you saw what you think you saw." Helena touched Hallow's shoulder and gently shook her. Discouraged from believing she'd found a real family member, it was now Hallow who crumbled under the weight of Helena's touch. She was offended by how quickly Helena discounted what her cousin saw when she wasn't at the party.

But what else could she do? Hallow thought. Absinthe was her first drink, and because she had no other point of reference and Helena was of age, she said nothing else.

Helena kissed Hallow's forehead and said her goodbye with a smile on her face that disappeared once she walked out. She lied about wormwood being strong enough to cause hallucinations. She only told Hallow that because she carried an anger that she could not place. Returning to the family business in some kind of assistant role was not what Helena wanted. She loved being free, but Hallow bringing up Iris and the accident angered her to where she wanted to take the wind out of her sails too. Back on the subway downtown to her apartment, she couldn't help but wonder if what Hallow said was true, that she had seen a woman who looked like her, and if she had, could that woman have been Hallow's mother?

When Helena left, Hallow started to feel remorseful over the Epelbaums. They were a lifeline, and she shouldn't have said no without having a backup plan. There she was, jumping the gun before having all matters in place so that she could forge her independence and do whatever she wanted to do outside of the home, in the belly of Harlem. Maybe, Hallow thought, she should've gotten close to the Epelbaums to have a greater chance of being in another space where she could possibly see that woman again—if she were real.

Hallow wanted guidance on how to make amends with the Epelbaums and knocked on Maman's bedroom door, which was left unlocked, so she pushed it open. She expected to see Maman reading yesterday's paper or some fashion magazine, or scribbling away at her desk, but she was uncharacteristically sprawled out in her bed, facing the wall. The clawlike cracks on those walls stretched farther toward the center, and they appeared like they were cradling Maman in their hands. Hallow took one step back, and a bead of water dropped on her forehead. She tried to ignore it until another bead fell, and then another. There were tentacles stretching from corner to corner. The vertices of the walls were discolored and blotchy. The longer Hallow stayed at the threshold, the further a faint mildew smell crept out from the corners. And there Maman lay, her body rising and falling, inhaling the fumes and breathing out into Scuff, which seemed to pulsate, enlarge, and recoil in synchronicity with her breathing.

If Hallow were not overcome with shock, she would have asked Maman how long it had been. When did she first notice the scuffs? Why didn't she say anything? She had briefly forgotten why she wanted to speak to Maman in the first place and instead proceeded to do an inspection around the entire first floor, pulling back chairs, rugs, and other furnishings. Every single corner featured a crack, some webbed, others lightning bolts, many spirals. As much as Maman got on her nerves, she could not allow her to live in this condition and brainstormed on how best to save her family.

A few days later, a messenger rang the doorbell to the Melancon brownstone and didn't seem to want to leave until Hallow opened the envelope in front of him. When she thanked the messenger for the notice, he cast a surly look and tipped his hat at her. After going back inside, Hallow reread the message, which consisted of a single line: *We regret to inform you that Jillian Epelbaum has passed away.* The Courier font was in black ink. There were no details as to what had happened, no requests for prayer, no charities listed on where to send money instead of buying flowers, no funeral contact information. Nothing. This wasn't some courtesy; it was condemnation. Robert wanted her to know what she had done. Hallow's intuition churned in the pit of her stomach like a windmill whirling in the thick of a storm. She peered out the front window and saw a police car, whose red and blue lights were flashing, parked along-side the sidewalk closest to their home.

She squinted because she knew the man in the car but failed to place him in a particular memory, until she recognized him as Officer Evans. He looked the same except for the increasing patches of gray in his beard and scalp. He tipped his cap at her and grinned, and she moved away from the door. But not before another bead of water dropped onto her head—this time in a new place—and she sensed it wasn't just the brownstone that was on the verge of caving in. She was too.

21

Once Josephine heard the news from Maman that the Epelbaums would not be getting the caul, she was so enraged that she did not confront Hallow about her decision. Like Maman, she didn't know if anything she could say or do would change Hallow's mind. Rather than resign herself to living the rest of her life in the brownstone, since the science patent was off the table, Josephine dug in her heels. She occupied herself inside her bedroom, where she cut out images of home decor and interior design and pasted them onto a vision board, then scanned her entire wardrobe to see which outfits she'd like to keep for when she and Landon would finally leave Harlem. The longer she fantasized, the more she lost track of time, until one day, she realized that a month had passed. Landon hadn't called or visited. There was not a single time during their decades-long relationship when he had gone more than a week without touching base. Josephine was reluctant to reach out first because she felt like she was the aggrieved party. He had inspired her dreams about a new life and was now MIA. But she was restless.

Josephine's fantasies collapsed, and she paced around the room wondering when Landon would call. Then she felt embarrassed that their relationship had regressed so much. Flouncing downstairs to Maman to vent about her problems with Landon was now an outmoded habit of hers, because Maman was either too busy with crying on the window seat in the hallway or staring mindlessly at the four walls of her bedroom. Ultimately, Josephine put aside her pride and called. The redirection of the phone call to voicemail after only two rings was the final straw. She wound up yelling at him for avoiding her before she could take a breath.

In the middle of the night, the doorbell rang. Josephine awakened and sat upright in bed, confused at who could be coming at this hour. She was about to pull the blankets back over her head until the doorbell rang again, and then she tiptoed down the steps to check the peephole of the front door. She quickly unbolted all the locks and pulled Landon in by the collar. He was dressed in all black, and a hat too large for his head obscured the majority of his face. When he entered the foyer, he neither hugged nor kissed Josephine, despite her falling over to spoil him with affection. When Landon didn't move to relieve himself of his coat or seductively follow her up the stairs as they had always done in the past, Josephine took her arms away from his neck and crouched down to search his eyes underneath the hat, only to find a large shadow.

"What's going on? You've been gone all this time, and you can't say hello."

"Look, I can't stay long."

"You just got here, and you're already talking about leaving." Josephine pulled him closer to her body and wrapped her right leg around his waist. "Come on," she purred in his ear. "Let's go upstairs."

He pushed her hands away and said, "Jo, stop. None of that tonight."

Josephine turned to Landon's left and right to check behind his body. "No suitcase. A part of me hoped you'd finally be coming so we can leave."

"I've thought about leaving, but I don't know if we can do that together."

Josephine backed up and sat down on the penultimate step of the staircase. "I don't understand what you're saying."

"Have you gotten any calls lately from Robert Epelbaum?"

"No. Why would I?"

He walked up to her and said, "I have tried to reach him since the day after you and Hallow went to the party, and he won't return any of my calls. I kept calling and calling, but he won't answer."

"Beats me. I don't know."

"And you haven't gotten any suspicious calls, right?"

"No. Why are you asking this?"

"Cars have been parked outside of my home. They'd be parked along the side of the street where I live, and their lights would be turned off. I couldn't see who was in there, but they're there all night. Sometimes by morning they're gone, but Valerie told me that there will be times during the day where she'll go get groceries and she'll feel like a car was following her, then it leaves as soon as she turns down our block. Have you seen anything?"

Josephine shook her head. "I don't know, I—I haven't been outside."

"What about Maman? You know how she likes to hang near the windows."

"She hardly is talking nowadays. Even when I give her a bath in the morning, she only says a few words."

"What?"

"'I give up.'"

"Man."

"What do you think is happening?"

"I don't know, Jo. All I know is I'm being watched, and all of a sudden I have not been able to find any new clients. I got nothing in the pipeline. Nothing. Now, your family has rejected people in the past, but I think Hallow made a mistake."

Josephine sprang to her feet and walked up to Landon. "Which is exactly why we should leave now. If she wants to do her own thing, let her. There's no need for us here anymore. Don't you see?" She smiled and turned his face toward her. "This is finally our time. It's time to go, right?"

"Jo—"

"Right?" she said more sternly.

Landon sighed and said, "Right."

"Good. Now, that's more like it." She closed her eyes and kissed Landon's lips and he kissed hers with his eyes open. He was unable to meet her in the space of her dreams when he was quietly panicking over being seen with her because of how much he was being surveilled.

22

Cars were in fact parked outside the Melancon brownstone, and it was Helena who brought this up when she finally came to visit. They convened in the dining room, where Hallow was making beef stew for dinner, and Helena asked, "How long those cars been out there?"

"Huh?" Hallow asked as she poured stew from a wooden ladle into two bowls for both her and her sister.

"Those black cars? How long they been out there?"

"What black cars?"

"Girl." Helena sucked her teeth and shook her head. "If you're going to be running things around here, you gotta know what's going on."

"I haven't been out in a while. I was waiting for you to come and get me so we can go to Blessed Waters."

"You still wanna go after all that with the Epelbaums?"

"What's one gotta do with the other?"

Helena looked over her shoulder for Maman, but realized that she would not be coming down the hallway to eavesdrop on their conversation.

"Hmm," she said. "Where's Jo?"

"Upstairs as usual. It's nothing."

"All right, well, let's hurry up and eat, then, hmm?"

"We're gonna go?" Hallow asked, thrilled, leaving her mouth wide open after the question.

"Yeah. But let's go out the back door, okay? I don't feel comfortable going out the front, and I got some things to relay to you before we actually get there."

Hallow's alias would be Bianca Anderson, and she was getting her bachelor's in women's and gender studies at Hunter College. She and Helena met while Helena was doing volunteer work at a homeless shelter on the Lower East Side, and from then on, they had become friends. If anyone asked for more specifics, Helena would take over from there.

"Why Bianca? Why can't I just go by Hallow?" she asked as they stood on the platform.

"Because—" Helena chuckled. "A lot of those women don't like Melancons. They're not just doulas and pregnant women. Some of them work in the community."

"Yeah but I went to a town hall meeting months ago and no one recognized me."

"And you didn't tell anyone your name?"

Hallow shook her head.

"Good. But we can't take any chances. We get in through the alias, and once you have some trust, then it'll be easier to tell them who you are, later, got it?"

Hallow nodded. "Okay. Do you have an alias too?"

"Just my last name. If anyone asks, it's Helena Jenkins. That's about as common of a Black last name as you can get."

"Why not your first too? You don't think they can trace you back to our family?"

"No because unlike you, I don't live there anymore and—" Helena pulled up her sleeves to show her scars. "I don't have the caul. At least not anywhere they can see. Now come on."

While on the train, Hallow sat so close to Helena that the seams of their jeans pressed together. Every time the doors automatically opened and more passengers boarded, Hallow leaned into her cousin, afraid that someone might grab ahold of her and rip her caul. But after the third stop, she realized that no one gave a damn about her, or anyone else on the train, for that matter. Everyone was preoccupied with a phone, a book, or the tunnels that they could watch through the windows. Everyone carved their own private space and ignored whatever did not directly affect them. After all the years of her being posited as something special, Hallow didn't feel special at all. She disappeared into the crowd. As much as she yearned for years to be amongst everyone, now that that desire had been realized, she felt lost, unsure of who she was, which made her ease into her alias with less reluctance than before she headed to the station.

Blessed Waters Doulas was located directly above a botanica where herbs and folk medicine were sold, which was wedged between a Taco Bell and a Crown Fried Chicken in Spanish Harlem near East 103rd and Lexington Avenue. Loads of trash littered the sidewalk, and the streetlight was rapidly blinking its way into being totally inoperable. Groups of men were congregating along the intersection and outside the corner stores, and a few women were escorting their children or elderly relatives into their apartment buildings. As soon as Helena pressed the buzzer, she looked at Hallow's stiff stance and said, "You okay?"

"Just a little nervous."

"You'll be fine, trust me. They're the warmest people you'll ever meet."

As they waited outside for someone to respond, Hallow peered up and wasn't sure if they were going to a place of business or someone's bedroom, because all she could see were blue curtains fluttering and a warm light glowing from somewhere inside.

As soon as the two women stepped into a large room, a eucalyptus scent entered Hallow's nose and she could feel her entire body open up. Women's magazines and an oil diffuser that gently exhaled warm, thick clouds in the air were placed on a table. There was a visibly pregnant woman lounging on a green velvet sofa with her feet hanging over its arm. A dark-skinned woman in a blue-and-white floor-length dress and whose hair was wrapped in a carnelian turban with matching lipstick came over to the seating area. Much to Hallow's surprise, this woman did not tell the pregnant woman to get her feet down but rather fluffed the pillow behind her head and asked if she preferred her water sparkling or still and her tea iced or hot.

Once this dark-skinned woman caught sight of Helena, she did not hesitate to hug her, then cup her cheeks with her hands. Through their giddy reunion, Hallow picked up that the woman's name was Odessa. Despite her youthful face, her commanding presence made Hallow think she carried herself as a woman twice her age. Then again, if she were not maternal, maybe she would not be working here.

"We've missed you already here, girl!" Odessa said to Helena. "Everybody misses your light and warmth." Odessa's chestnut eyes caught Hallow in her line of sight and she asked, "Is this Bianca?" Helena stood side by side with Odessa, and with her eyes stern and unyielding toward Hallow, she said, "Yes, this is she. She's a little bit shy." Hallow half smiled and stuck out her hand. "Oh, you don't do hugs?"

"Hmm?" Hallow asked. "Oh. I'd love a hug."

Odessa took Hallow's hand and pulled her into her body. With her right hand, she rubbed Hallow's back and greeted her with a honey-toned "Welcome." It was the first time that Hallow had ever been hugged by someone other than Josephine. Entranced, Hallow forgot her reservations and struggled to pull away even when Odessa grabbed both of her arms to get a good look at her head-on.

"Let's go over by the window, actually. Maya here is due in about three weeks, and she's not feeling too good about heading down those stairs you came up. Let's give her some space, hmm?" Odessa directed them toward the window and asked if either of them would like something to drink. Helena said she was fine without, but Hallow asked for tea because the odds of Odessa bringing the whole pot were high, and if she did, Hallow knew she could pour and pour if she didn't have anything to say.

While Helena and Odessa caught up with each other for a few more minutes, Hallow looked over every corner of the place. Near the front door, there was a bulletin board cluttered with notices for rent-raising parties, school supply and food drives, marches and protests, city council and block association meetings, missing children. Only blue curtains divided one room from the next, and there were places to sit everywhere: small chairs, stools, ottomans.

"So, Bianca, what's got you interested in becoming a doula?"

Anxious about Hallow's response, Helena closed her eyes.

"I want to help women like us," Hallow said. "There's always work to be done, and I thought I could lend a helping hand. After a while, you have to step outside the classroom and throw yourself into real-world experiences, right?"

Helena smiled.

"And . . ." Hallow held her breath in and exhaled upon looking at the Angela Davis mural on the wall closest to her. "Asali Givens's story, and the fact that I went to a town hall meeting not too long ago where she was brought up, amongst other things."

"Was it the one at St. Philip's?" Odessa asked.

"Yeah. Yeah, it was."

"I helped organize that one! It was good, wasn't it? Have you been to any others?"

"No."

"Sometimes we hold some meetings here. It's a really safe space, or at least we try to make it one. It's been a bit crazy around here lately."

"What's going on?" Helena asked.

"Well, you remember all those police that day at St. Philip's? They haven't stopped coming around. They're just trying to intimidate us, that's all. Nothing our ancestors ain't been through."

Helena thought of the unmarked cars parked outside of the Melancon home, and her hands trembled.

"Anyway—" Odessa said. "Those are all good reasons. I've been working here for five years, and I love every bit of it. We usually have you shadow someone more experienced and then once you pass your certifications, you can start seeing clients. The other doulas aren't in tonight, but if you come on the first Saturday of the month, you'll meet them. Though you will meet the founder and CEO tonight. She's just in the back meditating. She had to do a breech birth this morning, and it took a whole lot out of her."

"Ooh," Helena hissed. "How are the mother and baby doing?"

"Safe. Alive. Tired but alive."

"Thank God," Helena said.

"You know, Bianca, you're really lucky to have Helena as a doula to bring you in here."

Her eyes widening with curiosity, Hallow turned to Helena, who was now blushing from being put on the spot. "Really? Why is that?"

"Because she's a gift. You wouldn't believe how many women

come in here thinking they want to do this, but when it gets tough, whether with their clients' anxieties or doctors' negligence, they bow out. But I knew from the moment Helena told me her reason for being here that she was different."

"What reason was that?"

"We really don't need to get into that," Helena said as she waved her hand.

"No, no, don't be embarrassed. It was quite sad but moving, actually. She wanted to give new mothers the tenderness that she never got from her own and give babies the best possible introduction into the world."

Hallow briefly thought of how Helena's disposition had changed from cruel to kindhearted when they were children. Moved, she looked over at Helena, who could not stop nervously rubbing her thighs.

"Beautiful, huh?" Odessa asked.

"Beautiful indeed. Though you're right. It is sad. May I ask a question?"

"Of course. Ask away!"

"Why all the blue?"

"Oh." Odessa smiled. "You're not familiar with the Yoruba religion."

Hallow shook her head.

"Well, you should be. It's a part of your heritage, hon. All of our heritage, actually. You see, Yemaya, or Yemoja, is an orisha. A great spirit. A water deity. She is a protector of women, especially those in childbirth. So, we adorn this place with royal blue to invite her into this place and protect all of our expectant mothers."

"Does it work?"

Helena coughed. "Ha—Bianca—"

"No, it's okay. Well, since I've been here, we've lost no mothers and no children. That's an impressive feat given what we know about Black motherhood, don't you think?"

Hallow nodded.

Odessa excused herself and went toward the back room. When she reappeared, she motioned for Hallow and Helena to follow her past the royal-blue curtains that partitioned a quaint kitchen to the left and a small room to the right. When Odessa saw that Hallow was crouching behind Helena as they walked, she asked for them to switch places.

Odessa opened the door to that small room to reveal an elderly woman sitting cross-legged on top of a large pillow. The royal blue of her dress made an optical illusion where she looked as if she were floating. There were innumerable wrinkles on her sagging face, and the lines in her neck splintered off and multiplied into more lines. She too wore a head wrap, but her dark curly hair peeked out in front. Shells adorned her arms, wrists, and ankles, and she smelled of rose, lemon, and orange flower. Her eyes were slightly clouded and unfocused, but she smiled when she realized that she had visitors.

"Bianca?" She held out her hands. "Come sit down in front of me."

Hallow did as she was told, then the woman took Hallow's hands into hers. She thumbed around the lines in her palms and the veins in her wrist. Then her smile weakened.

"Give us privacy," she said sternly to both Odessa and Helena, who scurried out of the room.

She smiled again and said, "What is your name?"

"Bianca."

She gripped her hands tighter. "Are you sure?"

Hallow could feel the sweat beads rolling from her armpits and down her arms. Her mouth dried up, and her breathing quickened. "Yes, ma'am. My name is Bianca."

The woman rolled Hallow's sleeves to her elbows and inched

her fingers up her right arm. Hallow wanted to snatch her hand away but did not want to risk being rude and ruining her cover. She hoped that the thickness of the woman's hands would compromise their acuity for feeling out anything unusual about her body. Hearing her rough coughing, Odessa and Helena ran back into the room and Hallow hurriedly rolled down her sleeves.

Odessa patted the woman on the back until the coughing subsided. The woman said, "I'm fine. I'm fine. We're finished here."

"Can she go through the process?" Odessa asked.

"Yes. She's meant to be here." The woman nodded at Odessa, and Odessa helped Hallow to her feet to escort her out the room.

When Helena pulled back the curtain to exit, the woman said, "Melinda."

Hallow turned around. "What?"

"Melinda, honey. Remember that name. I already know yours."

23

Amara was inundated with donations following the Epelbaums' party. The couple didn't hesitate to send over their first check the weekend following the event, and Amara meant to get back in touch in order to thank them, but life was moving quickly. She and Ethan decided that it was in their best interest to give one *New York Times* journalist the scoop that she was officially announcing her run. By the month's end, she had taken calls from Vox, *The Nation*, the *Washington Post*, *New York* magazine, and a few other prestigious publications. She could hardly remember every journalist's name, but all that mattered was that they remember hers. She had been sugared with far too many compliments. She was a double Ivy League alumna. She was young, thin, and beautiful. She was smart. She was a shoo-in.

When Amara was finally able to catch her breath one evening, she noticed that Landon had left her a frenzied voicemail asking if she knew anything about the cops or detectives or someone spying on him because his answers as to Hallow's whereabouts were not good enough for her. The time stamp of this voicemail was from two weeks prior to her listening to it. She had no idea what he was accusing her of doing, but nevertheless the message reminded her that she had been meaning to go to Harlem to tie up some loose ends, and she might as well go now or else she wouldn't have the time in the near future.

During the Uber ride uptown, Amara thought of Hallow and then of the young woman in the bathroom. Amara had been blackout drunk before—especially during law school—but she had never hallucinated at all before. But there was no evidence that she existed. Amara never got her name. She didn't know with whom or with which organization she was affiliated. If she were to play investigator to her own memory, the only anchor she could hold on to was that this woman looked like her. Amara was overwhelmed from remembering that woman's face and how concerned her expression was. A dull pain sprouted from her abdomen to her groin.

Dressed in all black with large sunglasses and a bold red lip, Amara stepped out of the car when it pulled up to her childhood home, and she was taken aback by the foreignness of the block. She couldn't recognize anyone jogging or carrying groceries to and fro. There were more cafés, more signs to promote new high-rise luxury condominiums.

Denise stood bug-eyed when she opened her front door.

"What?" Amara asked.

"I . . . I know you said you were coming, but I didn't think you were really going to show up."

"Why can't you take me at my word?" Amara smiled.

"Well, it's because you made it a point years ago that you didn't want to spend too much time 'round here. Come on inside. Hurry up." Denise placed her hand on Amara's shoulder and moved her into the foyer.

"I wish you would've given me a heads-up of a specific date and time for when you were coming, because then I would've put something on the stove."

"Don't bother. I'm not that hungry. My stomach hurts, actually."

"Have you eaten anything today?"

"No."

"That might be why. Let me go the store. Wanna come with me?"

"No, I'll stay here, that's fine."

"Oh. Well, okay. I'll be right back, then."

Denise's errand run was perfect timing. Amara didn't have the heart to break it to her mother that her visit had nothing to do with her and all to do with Laila. The apartment seemed quiet. Today must have been one of those days when she was at peace. Amara placed a hand on the bannister but delayed in going up the steps when she recognized just how afraid she was of her aunt. There was a reason Denise never talked about Laila or put Laila on the phone with Amara to speak to her. She was as protective as she was embarrassed of her sister. Sometimes when Amara would call her mother, she would hear thrashing or wailing in the background. Maybe Laila was totally medicated or still asleep. Amara said a silent prayer and went up the stairs. Everything was uncomfortably still and cold, and the light breaking through the ceiling windows was the only evidence of any kind of vitality.

"Aunt Laila?" Amara stammered as she stood outside her aunt's bedroom door.

"Yes?" Laila called out, her voice strong and direct.

"It's Amara. Your niece?"

Silence.

A door opened, and there was Laila in a wrinkled sweater and jeans that were many sizes too large and sliding off her body. Her collarbones and ribs protruded, and her skin was pallid. She asked, "Amara? Is that really you?" Amara ran over to Laila and took her in her arms and was immediately repulsed by how many bones she could feel in Laila's back, and how the strength of her embrace was enough to lift Laila off the ground. She was troubled by how Laila sank in her arms, becoming like dead weight from the touch. When Amara let her go and stared at Laila's face, there was still some beauty left. The light hadn't completely dimmed from her eyes, and her cheeks were round and blessed with a soft pink blush. Anyone who looked at her now could have guessed that she had once been resplendent. But if anyone knew of her story, they, like Amara, would behold Laila's beauty with mournfulness.

"I wish I would've known you were coming. I have company right now, but you might as well join us."

Join? Amara thought. She hadn't heard anyone shuffling inside of Laila's bedroom or sensed another presence anywhere upstairs, for that matter. But when Laila pushed her bedroom door open, Amara saw a bed, stripped of its sheets and linens, pushed all the way to the side opposite her closet. A group of life-sized dolls encircled a sheet and pillow on the ground.

"Er, on second thought, Aunt Laila, why don't we go downstairs? Let's sit in the kitchen like we used to do."

"You sure? My guests don't mind. They're very cordial."

Amara nodded fervently. "I'm sure."

"Hmm." Laila shrugged her shoulders and held a finger up to her closed lips at the dolls, and bade them goodbye. Laila grabbed ahold of Amara's hand and the bannister to make her way down the stairs. When she reached the ground floor, her body wobbled to re-acclimate itself to a lack of an incline. She waited a few moments to steady herself then proceeded toward the kitchen, where they sat opposite each other. With the abundance of natural light coming from the window behind Laila, Amara could accurately see just how much loss her aunt had experienced. Decades ago, despite her miscarriages, she'd still looked fresh, vibrant, and expectant. Now she was gray and discolored in some areas around her body, and her chest barely rose and fell with her breaths. It looked like the womb that once imperiled her child now endangered her, turning her life inside out, into one of false reality and unquenchable sadness.

"Aunt Laila, I—"

"I know it's been a long time. I know. I haven't been able to keep up with the years as much as I'd like, but I know. I mean, look at you. You don't walk up in here a grown woman without some time passing. I know you're making both me and your mother proud."

"Yes, a lot of time has passed. I went to—"

"Yale, I know. Graduated at the top of your class, I know. My memory isn't entirely gone. I could never forget about you, sweet."

Tears clouded Amara's vision, and she wiped them with the back of the sleeves of her blouse.

"Aww." Laila leaned forward and massaged Amara's hands. "So, what's got you up here?"

"Well, you, actually."

"Me? What about me?"

"I need to ask you some questions. About something that happened years ago."

"I can try and answer. I'll try my best."

"Do you remember the Melancon family?"

Laila blinked spasmodically and clasped her mouth with her right hand. Her body tensed, and she tapped her foot to pull herself together.

She exhaled deeply and replied, "What about them?"

"Do you remember how you went to their home to confront them and you cried and screamed but they wouldn't face you? How did you connect with them? I mean— How did the first conversation between you and that family happen? Did you just go to their place unannounced?"

"No."

"Then who connected you? I mean— They went to St. Philip's, right? Did you talk to them there?"

"No," Laila said.

"Then maybe you have a mutual friend? Starting from the church . . ." Amara began to rattle off names of other parishioners until she finally landed upon Landon.

"Landon! What about Landon? Landon! Landon?" Laila stood up and kept repeating his name while pacing across the kitchen. Then her yelling quieted to mutters, with her teeth piercing her knuckles.

"Mom told me that you've been mentioning him. Aunt Laila?"

"What did Landon say to you? Anything? Anything?"

"Well—"

Laila lost her balance from pacing and dropped to the ground. She lay on the floor catatonically and Amara rushed to her side.

"Aunt Lay?" Amara nudged her. "Lay?"

Laila wheezed and looked up at her niece. "You know, you have some nerve waltzing in here with your fancy degrees to question me about my choices and whether or not I'm hiding something. You would think that as someone who's also lost a child, you'd be more sympathetic."

Amara leaned back against the island kitchen with her knees up to her chest. "What?"

"I knew you were expecting because you couldn't stop stuffing your face. And you smelled. I could smell you, and you had the nerve to not tell me. Me! Your aunt Laila. But I stayed quiet, thinking you'd probably confide in me. And then I felt bad because it was your first loss. Hopefully it'll be your last."

Amara dropped her jaw. Laila smiled, impressed with the reaction she'd received, and said, "Aha. A hit dog will holler."

The door opened. Denise was humming a jingle as she carried her groceries into the home. But when she came into the kitchen and saw Amara and Laila glaring at each other, she asked, "What's going on here?"

"Nothing, Mom."

"Aht, aht, it looks like a whole lot of something. Here, Lay, sweetie, let me help you get up." Denise placed the bags on the kitchen table and guided Laila toward the corridor. "Okay, easy now."

"No, no!" Laila snatched away and stomped back into the kitchen. "We're not finished with our discussion. Is there anything else Miss Amara wants to talk about?"

"Was it Landon? That's all I want to know. Was it Landon who connected you to the Melancons?"

"Landon who?" Denise yelled. "Landon? Not our Landon! Laila?"

"Ask Amara about her pregnancy!"

"What?" Denise yelled. "Now I know you're off. Come on up the stairs. Let's go get you some rest. I don't want to hear anything about no pregnancy or no Landon."

"Landon. Lan-don. Landon." Laila cried as she repeated his name all the way back to her room. Downstairs, Amara was putting the pieces together: her aunt had never told anyone who'd brokered the deal for her to receive the caul from the Melancons. In that moment years ago, she thought she was protecting him, since the agreement was hush-hush and maybe he didn't want the church or the entire community as a whole to know what he did on the side. But that protection left her empty-handed, with no baby and subsequently no man.

When Denise came back down, she asked, "Mar, what the hell is going on?"

"I'll be back."

Amara grabbed her coat and dashed out the front door before Denise could stop her.

24

Once Amara stepped outside, she saw a police car parked directly in front of her mother's apartment building. Whoever was in the car flashed the lights at the same time that her feet hit the welcome mat. She hailed a cab that was fortuitously coming down the block and gave the driver another address in Harlem. As the driver approached the new address, Amara saw a woman in a purple muumuu slouched in a wicker chair, her legs spread wide, on her front porch. She had a sharp, gray streak on each side of her plaited brown hair and a thick crucifix around her neck. The intensity in her gaze made Amara realize that this woman wasn't a stranger but Valerie, the mistress of the home herself, looking worn-down and dejected. Behind her, the paint was peeling off the sides of the brownstone, her hydrangeas were wilting, and her windows were covered in a thick film. The Valerie she'd known would never be sitting on her porch dressed in a muumuu. The Valerie Amara remembered would not have had so much as a single stitch out of place from her clothes or a strand left unstyled. While her presentation had always looked like it required a lot of work, she'd made it seem effortless, creating an understated yet undeniable elegance about her. But it seemed this version of Valerie had given up.

When Amara removed her sunglasses and smoothed down the back of her head, Valerie eyed her up and down and said, "Yes?"

"Valerie? It's me, Amara."

"Yes, I know it's you, Amara. I asked, 'Yes?' because I want to know what it is that you want."

Taken aback by her surliness, Amara straightened her posture and lowered her voice. "Can we talk inside? We have things to discuss."

"Why must it be done inside? I got nothing to hide." She stretched out her legs toward Amara and moved her knees in and out. "Do you?"

"Fine. Where's Landon? I need to speak with him."

"He's not here."

"Do you know when he'll be back?"

Valerie's eyes ricocheted to the police car parked along the sidewalk close to her home and said, "You ain't have to get backup, you know. Thought we were family."

"I didn't call them."

"Pft. A DA not having any connection to the police is like the Archangel Michael saying he don't know Jesus. Come on inside, girl."

Once the women were in the foyer, Valerie said, "Now, what is it you want to know about Landon?"

"I want to know when he'll be coming back—it's important."

"I don't think he's coming back."

"What?"

"Yeah. Ain't that a blip? Oh," Valerie scoffed. "I forgot. You haven't been up in here in a while, so you wouldn't know. And since you're a grown woman now, let me just give it to you straight—Landon ain't been faithful to me. I allowed it because my home—

this . . ." She stamped her foot, and the ceiling creaked, causing Amara to look up with great concern. "This home was maintained. But now he done had enough and left. He actually left!"

"How long has he been gone?"

"A little over a week. I tried calling him and everything. I can't get ahold of him."

"Do you know where he could've gone?"

"Don't you think if I knew that it would be because I actually spoke to him?"

"Point taken. I can't believe he just up and left."

"Wherever he is, he's probably with his mistress now. They probably rode off into the sunset, as they say."

"Mistress?"

Valerie squinted. "How old are you, girl?"

"Forty."

"Exactly!" Valerie interrupted. "You full grown. If a woman told you her husband left, what you think he done did? Vanished into thin air? Come on, now. You were legally an adult when you laid up in here for months; you ain't stupid. I know you saw or heard him creep down the steps several times a week."

"Oh," Amara said. Valerie was right. Amara immediately recalled the times when Landon would leave at night and wouldn't return till morning, a detail that she'd thought nothing of when she'd stayed with them, but now his affair became clear.

"Do you understand where I'm coming from?" Valerie asked.

"I do."

"Now, is there anything else you need to ask me? Because please believe the boys in blue out there already tried."

"No. That's it."

Amara left Valerie's home and saw Officer Evans leaning against the side of his cop car. She approached him and said, "So it was you who's been here this whole time. I couldn't hardly see you. What are you doing here?"

"Come take a ride with me. I'll explain."

Amara and Officer Evans took seats at the table in the farthest corner on the second floor of Amy Ruth's. At Sylvia's, they would have drawn more attention to themselves, and anywhere on or around West 125th and Lenox they would have as well. The waiter brought out two glasses of water with lemon wedges and corn bread with butter to start. As Amara combed through the menu of plates named after Black celebrities, she sensed Officer Evans's eyes on her. To break the awkward silence, she looked up and asked, "You know what you want?"

"The Nate Robinson with a side of potato salad and collard greens," Officer Evans said. "The usual. I come here a lot."

"Enough small talk. You said you wanted to talk business while on the ride here but wouldn't say a word. So what is it?"

"I know you've heard about Robert Epelbaum's wife, haven't you?"

"Yeah. Tragic, huh?"

"Yeah, very tragic. Well, no sooner after his wife died did I get a tip from my colleagues about the Melancons again and their activity, and apparently said tip came from Robert. Now, how would he know anything about them like that?"

Amara took a moment to think and finally said, "They rejected him."

"Boom. He talked about the interior of the brownstone, what they served him when he went there, Landon—"

"Landon?" Amara and Officer Evans stared at each other before she said a long-drawn-out "Fuck." She placed her face in her hands and said, "I don't believe this. That's just incredible."

"Believe it."

"So that's why you were outside Landon's place?"

"Yeah, and seeing as how he skipped town, that makes him look even more guilty. Amara, we got 'em. This is what we've been waiting for."

Amara took a bite of her corn bread and dabbed at the sides of her mouth with her napkin.

"So what do we do?"

"Keep watching them. Following them. We know how they move and where they are."

"They don't move much, though. They don't have the bodega anymore."

"Ah, but there is one place."

"Where?"

Officer Evans grinned and leaned forward. "Blessed Waters Doulas."

"Blessed Waters Doulas?"

"Mm-hmm. Some of the Melancon women have been seen there. It's very connected to the community. Very leftist-heavy, pro-Black women."

"And you do realize those are the same people who can't stand me right now, right?"

"But money talks. You have your donations, yes?"

"Yes, but . . ." Amara stopped herself. An idea came to her like a flash of lightning. She didn't have to say a word. Her mouth opened in awe at the clarity of what Officer Evans was insinuating, and she rubbed her hands together with excitement over how the plan was coming together.

25

After Hallow felt the water beads on her forehead on the ground floor, she waited for someone, anyone, to complain about how badly the brownstone was deteriorating. She stared out her bedroom window to see if a repairman would come walking through the gates, waiting to see if Maman had appointed one to fix another thing like she used to do. But no one came besides the neighbors, who walked past and scaled the brownstone with their eyes. Not too long after Hallow saw the leaks, the smell began to disturb her nose and stomach. The faint mildew smell amplified into a deeply entrenched funk, and there was no diffuser or spray that could get rid of it.

So Hallow took matters into her own hands and found the names of some construction companies in one of the kitchen drawers. Once she was able to get one on the line, she urged them to come as soon as they could. For long stretches of days, they replaced parts of the ceilings and inspected the roof for any flimsiness before they removed their glasses and told her that that was the best that they could do. She didn't feel the beads upon her brow anymore, but there were noticeable bubbles in the ceiling that were a shade darker than other areas that she assumed to be dry. To see if the changes were amenable overall, Hallow knocked on both Josephine's and Maman's doors, but no one would open. Josephine cried for her to go away, and Maman croaked that she didn't want to be bothered.

And then one day, Hallow heard a firm knock on the front door and opened it to see a white man in a navy-blue uniform.

"Can I help you?"

"Are you the owner?"

"No."

"May we speak to the owner then?" The man leaned to the side, took a big whiff, and contorted his face in disgust.

"She's not well."

"How long has that smell been there?"

"I don't know. Who are you again?"

"Gary Davidson, and I'm with the Department of Buildings of the New York City government."

"Okay?"

"We've been receiving noise complaints from all the construction and repairs you're having done on your home. Would it be all right if I came in to assess what's going on?"

"No." Hallow blocked his path as soon as she saw him stepping forward.

"Then I will come back with a warrant."

"You do that. Have a good day."

Hallow shut the door in Gary's face and jumped when she saw Iris standing in the middle of the hallway in regular clothes with a hint of gloss on her lips. Her hair was still bedraggled, and the linings of her jean pockets were turned out.

"Damn, Iris!" Hallow said as she rubbed her chest. "You scared me."

"There's nothing that you can do to stop them coming for this brownstone, you know."

"Who, the neighbors? They've tried many times before. They're not getting it."

"I'm not talking about them."

Iris cracked her neck and looked up toward the ceiling. "I'm talking about *them*."

Hallow followed her eyes to the large, dark pockets in the ceiling, which looked heavier and deeper than when she last saw them just a few minutes ago. She rubbed her chest harder as it tightened over how spooked she was.

"Them? Who's 'them'?"

"The spirits, of course. The spirits of all those we chose not to save. Every crack you've seen, every bad scent you smelled—did you think that that was just because the place was . . . old? They're coming. They're all coming, and we're all on our own now."

Hallow tried to pay Iris no mind by continuing on with her rest of the day studying and preparing to go to Blessed Waters later that night. She frequented the facility four times a week, where she either took classes or helped to clean and maintain the space, and she loved every second of it. There was nothing else in life that excited her more than the messy complexities of a woman's body: the perineum, the Bartholin's glands, the Pitocin, the oxytocin. Nothing else she'd learned required such keen repetition. Even when Hallow memorized the terms and functions of each organ and groove of the reproductive system, she was reminded in practice that every woman was different, which meant that she would have to recalibrate with each and every client. This kind of training was foreign because of its different foundation. When Hallow sold caul, she did not need to be bogged down with all the intricate details of the recipient's body and the sickness that plagued it. A cut here and there, a sophisticated packaging, an invoice, and that was that. Hallow found during the first several weeks of being at Blessed Waters that she made simple mistakes: her eyes giving a perfunctory glance over terminology and her mouth too fast to interject when her mentors were trying to educate. Learning to be silent and subordinate was what she'd never known she needed, an oasis amidst the chaos.

By nightfall, she had her tote bag filled to the brim with books and writing utensils, and as she was about to head out, her intuition told her to check the front-facing windows first. There was yet another police car parked outside the brownstone. It was accompanied by a second one stationed right behind it. To avoid the hoopla, Hallow left out the back door like she had done with Helena in the past and circled around from the small yard in the back to the street. Once she saw that the red and blue lights were becoming dimmer, she breathed easy, believing that the police were not following her. By the time she went underground, she didn't spare a thought for them. If her family could be careless or willingly neglectful about what went on inside the home, then she would be the same with what happened on the outside. Back on ground level, Hallow saw another police car parked right outside the exit where she emerged, but she inserted herself in the crowd of people before walking as fast as she could to Blessed Waters, where she arrived unexpectedly in the middle of what appeared to be an intense meeting.

Odessa was standing at the podium in front of the Angela Davis wall mural and was raising and lowering her arms multiple times to quiet the women. Hallow sat in the back, cross-legged, and watched.

"Look, I know it doesn't look good optics-wise, but this is a big damn donation from the prosecutor's office, and this can help us out a lot around here," Odessa said. "All we have to do is hear them out."

"Hear them out?" said a woman, whose large, round belly made it impossible for her to stand to her feet. "This money is from the feds. Look at how the NYPD have been intimidating us. They park outside here, and they make these little smart-ass comments when we don't even do nuffin'."

The rest of the woman vocally agreed.

"All money ain't good money. They're just trying to get in our good graces because Amara Danville is running for DA. I'm not voting for nobody. It's nothing but pandering, and she can't be trusted," the same woman said and caressed the top of her belly.

"So do you want me to throw the check away? You want to rip it up for me? Come on, y'all. We need this. Y'all know how much rent costs nowadays. With this money we can support doulas like myself and continue to do this work and bring more people into the fold. Bianca, help me out here."

Everyone turned to face Hallow, whose cheeks were flushed with redness and skin pallid from the embarrassment. "Well—" Hallow said. "If Amara wants to come, then she should agree to our terms. Put her on the spot. Get her to agree to certain things if she wins and ask her the hard questions. She's yielding to us, not us to her."

"But what about all the harm she's done? How can she be for us when she's a part of the carceral state?" another woman asked Hallow.

"Are any of us beyond redemption, though? What if . . ." Hallow took a deep breath. "What if she's sorry and she's trying to make amends now? Is that too far of a reach?"

The women who huddled on the sofas and beanbags or sat on the sofa pondered the idea in silence.

Odessa nodded. "Accountability is important. It is."

Everyone left Blessed Waters with more uncertainty than when they'd first walked in. A significant swath of women said that they would stay home if Amara Danville showed up, and others supported Odessa's decision, even staying behind to help her figure out how to allocate the donation to what needed the most attention. As for Hallow, she did not return to the brownstone that night. She phoned Helena to see if she might be able to crash with her for a few days to clear her head, and much to her surprise, Helena agreed.

During that time, Amara was in conversation with Odessa over the course of multiple phone calls during which they exchanged information on how her appearance at Blessed Waters would proceed. Odessa requested a detailed breakdown of when Amara was coming and if she'd be accompanied, whether the meeting would be on or off the record, and the granularities of the speech to appeal to potential voters that she prepared. Afterward, Amara phoned Officer Evans to give him the logistics of when the event would take place and how long she would be there to collect intel.

When the day arrived for her to be in Spanish Harlem, she was unsettled by how many police cars were on both sides of the block where Blessed Waters was located. An officer rolled down his window, perturbed, but straightened up once he realized who was staring back at him.

"Excuse me. What is the purpose for all of this?"

The officers in the vehicle looked at each other, then at Amara.

"Hello?" Amara said. "I asked you a question. What is going on here?"

"You gave us the order."

"Excuse me?"

"We're supposed to be out here to ask the occupants of that

building about their knowledge of the Melancons. Officer Evans conveyed the information to us."

"But all of these cars? You aren't busting some drug cartel here."

"We can't be too safe."

"At least turn your fucking lights off, damn."

The officers begrudgingly contacted Officer Evans through their walkie-talkies and did as commanded. She was beside herself that the officers would get clearance to leave from someone who was beneath her, but she didn't have the time to argue. When Amara went into that building and up the stairs, Odessa greeted her with a handshake as the women, some twenty to thirty of them, abruptly halted their conversations and watched her. Amara nodded her head and smiled before Odessa walked Amara into the kitchen for a debriefing.

"Thank you again," Odessa said.

"I'm sorry?"

"Thank you for coming, and for the donation. I know it came from the DA's office, but I know that it must've come from you, since you're the only one here and you have a campaign on your hands."

"Oh. Well, you're welcome. How long have the police been out there? Just today or . . ." Amara asked.

"They've been out there for a while."

"Odessa, before we start, let me ask you a question."

"Sure."

"Do you know of the Melancons?"

"Psh. Yes, I'm familiar."

"Have any of them been in here, by any chance?"

Odessa shook her head. "Not at all. They would have no reason to be. Besides, we're not exactly big fans of them over here."

"I see."

Odessa leaned forward and whispered, "I know, you know."

"Excuse me?"

"I know what those women did to your aunt years ago. My mother told me. She was one of the people in the crowd that day, and I'm sorry."

Amara touched the side of her coat pockets that held her index cards scribbled with notes about her speech, in which she planned to cover her time at both Ivies and her current job, but now she found them useless. It was there within those walls, blue like primordial waters, that she suddenly felt protective of everyone in Blessed Waters—maternal, even. Pain revisited her pelvic area, and she cupped her hands over the most afflicted spots. When Odessa suggested tea or a heating pad, Amara calmly declined and stood to her feet. Side by side, the women returned to the main area, where the women shushed each other to a deafening silence. Amara walked up to the podium that had been set up for her at the front of the room near the fireplace. But when she approached that podium, she moved it to the side before grabbing a soft cushion and sitting on the floor with the rest of the attendees. She noted the different degrees of apprehension tinged with exhaustion and rage engraved on these women's faces, how their bodies leaned slightly from her the farther she moved into the circle. And she deserved it. She closed her eyes and drew back into herself. When she opened her eyes and mouth, again she leaned into the audience.

"I apologize to each and every one of you. I am sorry for the harm that my colleagues have caused you. I am sorry for making you feel as if your concerns as mothers and as Black women have been ignored. I am sorry." She didn't want to cry so soon after her apology because she didn't want anyone to suspect that she was pandering in any way. She lowered her head, and the pain from her pelvic area pierced through her. Was it all worth it? The yearslong thirst for revenge?

The crowd shushed themselves. Amara lifted her head and saw an elderly woman draped in various shades of undulating blue. Her stomach pain intensified, and she yearned for some kind of alcohol to calm her nerves. Amara knew this woman but was paralyzed with disbelief that they would ever meet again. Everyone was mesmerized by what was unfolding. Before Amara could say anything, Melinda knelt down beside her and placed a crystalline bead bracelet around her wrist. She kissed Amara's palm three times and then asked, "What is your name?"

"Melinda." Odessa laughed. "You know her name."

"No, no. I want to hear her say it. I want to hear her say her name. What is your name?"

"Amara." Her voice cracked.

"No. That is not your whole name. Let yourself be whole, child. What is your name?"

"Amara Danville."

"Do you remember all of your names? The ones given and the ones you gave?"

Amara contemplated all the confused faces in the room, and her throat dried up. All the muscles in her body locked into place, and she didn't know what to say or do, so she remained still.

"Come on, now. You know."

"Ms. Danville, I'm sorry. Sometimes Melinda gets carried away and—" Odessa added.

Melinda beamed at Amara and said, "You know. You remember, don't you?"

"Yes," Amara finally said. "I do."

The front door of the center swung open, and Helena and Hallow casually entered. Hallow lifted her head above the large circle of attendees and saw the woman from the Epelbaums' party. That woman's eyes riveted her. Hallow shushed Helena, who was in the middle of whispering something to her, and started moving toward the inner circle. Helena pulled her arm to avoid drawing attention to them, but Hallow snatched the arm away. The women parted ways to allow Hallow to get a closer look. There she beheld the drunken apparition, who she could now see was human and as beautiful as everyone else in this room. The woman looked at Hallow, and they were spellbound with each other. Murmurs rippled across the room. Odessa touched her heart in disbelief. Amara slowly removed her wrist from Melinda's hold and faced Hallow, whose resemblance to her could not be denied. There were too many witnesses for it to be a case of collective delusion.

"What's going on?" Odessa said.

"So you are real," Hallow said.

Melinda said, "There you are, baby. There you are."

"What on earth is going on?" Odessa asked again.

"I delivered this child years ago. She was meant to be here. And this here lady is her mother."

A "What?" multiplied across the room.

Melinda gently pulled up Hallow's sleeve and revealed the caul, to which everyone gasped.

"You're a Melancon?" Odessa yelled. Helena inched farther back toward the door and kept her hand on the knob.

Hallow shut her eyes and nodded. "Yes." Her voice cracked. The women started to get loud. "I didn't want to say anything because I knew you wouldn't accept me."

"You damn right, we don't accept you!" someone called out.

"Ladies—" Amara interjected.

"Is that why you asked me about them in the kitchen?" Odessa asked Amara. "Is that why you wanted to come here? Are you doing some kind of investigating? And this is your own daughter?"

"I told you she was a cop! She's not for us!" another voice called out.

"Ladies, please." Amara saw the red and blue lights flashing from the adjacent window and started to get more nervous as more of the women began to yell and voice their concerns. "Please calm down, please!"

"Don't tell us to calm down! You're a disgrace! You fucking hypocrite!"

The women began to push to the front to get in Amara and Hallow's faces, and before either of the two women could stick their arms out in front to keep them at a distance, they were engulfed by the crowd until there was a loud boom from the door getting kicked in. A thick cloud of smoke filled the room, and everyone unleashed several rounds of bloodcurdling screams.

26

This was not a part of the plan. It was never a part of the plan. When the NYPD burst through the doors with their tear-gas canisters, Amara was seized with terror. Without thinking, she grabbed Hallow's hand before the gas blurred everyone's vision. Before a large hissing sound was released. Before smog covered the entire room. The scene unraveled both quickly and slowly simultaneously—the sounds of bodies trampling over each other, the pleas for the officers to stop, the screams, the cries, glass breaking, feet racing, fabric ripping, and blood drizzling down indiscernible faces. The crowd that had formed outside Blessed Waters hollered and cursed out the cops. Some attempted to break through to help the women who were falling down the steps and out the building because they were desperate for fresh air. But another round of police officers detained them and brandished their guns in case anyone dared to move forward. Ambulance trucks sped down the intersecting streets, and personnel were hurrying to get the visibly pregnant women strapped to gurneys, but they were so overwhelmed with the pain that they clawed at their cheeks or doubled over holding their stomachs.

Eyes red with blood leaking from her widow's peak, Hallow called out for Amara until the fog's density began to lighten and she could see her birth mother passed out on the ground beside her. Helena was nowhere to be found, and neither were Melinda and Odessa. The main area of Blessed Waters had been all but ruined, with tables and chairs toppled over, pages torn from magazines, scratch marks all over the walls and furniture, and foam ripped from the sofa cushions. Everyone had cleared out except them, and the people on the streets clamored around the police.

"Amara?" Hallow nudged her mother, but she lay limp. She placed her hand over Amara's nose and confirmed she was breathing, but barely. With both arms held underneath Amara's arms, Hallow dragged her to the entrance and heaved to pull Amara up to her feet. The descent down to street level was laborious, and Hallow worried that the sweat from her hands would make her slip, but they made it to the bottom safely. On the four intersecting streets, she could hear police sirens and people yelling and she did not know where to go, but miraculously, a taxi was about to turn a corner a block down from the mayhem when she hailed it down.

"Where do you wanna go?" the driver asked.

"Outside the city—anywhere."

The driver hopped on the George Washington Bridge, then he dropped them off at a Marriott in Weehawken, New Jersey. A bellboy was walking back and forth across the entrance mat when the women arrived, and when he opened the car door on Amara's side, he caught her fall before she smacked her forehead on the concrete. Hallow begged for any spare room they had no matter the size, and the bellboy guided them to a side entrance to avoid a scene. He suggested they call an ambulance, but Hallow refused. In an otherwise unattended corridor near the courtyard, Hallow propped Amara against the wall and heard her groaning by the time the bellboy returned with a key and directions for sending payment once they checked into their hotel room.

There in the deluxe suite, Hallow placed pillows underneath Amara's head and feet, then fetched ice from the machine in the hallway. She was about to start toward the bathroom to wet a washcloth for Amara's forehead when the view of the New York City skyline captivated her. The lapping waves of the Hudson River glimmered from the Midtown skyscrapers towering above them, and the George Washington Bridge lights were pearls against the backdrop of the obsidian sky. Hallow sat on her knees on top of the chair near the window, and her heart quickened with the revelation that she'd escaped the Melancon brownstone.

Amara breathed heavily and curled into the fetal position on the bed. To avoid waking her, Hallow moved to the sofa and traced every feature of her mother's face with her eyes. From the top of her mother's widow's peak down to her dimpled chin, she wanted to know what was burrowed in her cheeks, what resided behind her eyes, and what other secrets were nestled in her mouth. She wanted to know everything. But most of all, Hallow wanted to know if Amara could be home and replace the one she'd fled. Hallow moved farther down to inspect Amara's neck and then her arms and hands before she drifted to sleep.

The following morning, she awakened with a large blanket over her body and a pillow behind her head. The TV had been turned on to MSNBC programming, and Amara was sipping a cup of coffee at the edge of her bed. The chyron read: MAYHEM ENSUES IN HARLEM OVER RISING DA AND ABANDONED CHILD—followed by a professional photo of Amara Danville sitting next to the American flag and a candid photo of Hallow somewhere out on the street. One of the MSNBC national correspondents, a Black woman with a pixie cut, moderated a roundtable discussion with other Black women about police violence. According to the correspondent, the police officers used excessive force against pregnant Black women, and sources said that several miscarried en route to Mount Sinai Hospital. The conversation cut to a local organizer, who was standing in front of the Melancon brownstone with a crowd of protestors whose posters said LEAVE HARLEM and ALL SKINFOLK AIN'T KINFOLK, and who yelled into the interviewer's mic about how much the Melancons had damaged the bonds between Harlemite Black women with their unwillingness to help others. Someone jumped in front of the camera and blurted out how the Melancon family hadn't helped an auntie of hers: "Danville and the Melancons are family. It's been exposed. They the feds. They don't help nobody 'round here. A stain on the community," she said and spat on the ground.

"I think I gotta go home," Hallow said.

"No, Hallow." Amara shook her head and turned to face Hallow. "You can't go back there. It's not safe. Those people are angry, and they're out for blood."

"Well, thank God I got something extra to protect me." Hallow waved her arm in the air and stood to her feet.

Amara watched as Hallow dusted off the sleeves of her shirt, bewildered. "You want to go back to them after what they done to you?"

"What they done to me?"

"Yes! Hallow, they cut your body and sold it to people. They abused you, and you wanna go back to that?"

Amara placed her hands on Hallow's shoulders, and Hallow swatted them away. "They did not abuse me! They were my family."

"You call that a family? Hallow, think what other kind of life you could've had away from them."

"What, with you? If you didn't have the chance to give me up, would you have thrown me in the garbage too?"

"That's not fair."

"Isn't it? Maman and Josephine helped you, didn't they? They took me in and you got this fancy, important job, didn't you? From the looks of it, life turned out great for you." Hallow flicked her hand at her mother, pursed her lips, and crossed her arms over her chest.

"No, it didn't."

"Oh, give me a break."

"No, Hallow. Listen." Amara moved her head toward Hallow's face to force her daughter to look her in the eye but was met with resistance. "I wasn't ready. I—"

"But who is ever ready for a baby?"

"Let me finish. As soon as I felt you leave my body, I closed my eyes, afraid that if I got a good look at you, I would've held on to you. And I couldn't have given you the life that I would've wanted to give any child. You would've been raised with resentment for what kind of parent I could've been had I had you at a later time. What I'm saying is . . . mothers are made just like children are, and I wasn't enough. I wasn't enough."

Hallow looked her birth mother in the eye and loosened her arms. Together, they sat down on the bed. "Is that why you went to Blessed Waters? Were you looking for me?"

"I was looking for the Melancons so I could prosecute them."

"So you wanted to hurt me?"

"No, sweetheart, listen to me." Amara closed her eyes and took in a deep breath. She opened them and started: "I knew about the Melancon women long before you were born. You see, I'm from Harlem too, and my aunt was like some of those women at Blessed: expectant and full of worries. She lost many children before they even took their first breath, and she sought the help of the

Melancons, but they turned her away. She went to confront them about what they did after she lost her last child, and it was terrible, Hallow. She screamed, she cried, she pulled at the gates to try to get to them. Her mind hasn't been the same since."

Iris's question about the spearheads, the sounds of the construction worker knocking them down, and the images of Maman watching from the window finally coalesced into a clarifying sense of their shared history. Hallow said, "They didn't want me to know about her."

"Now you see why the people are upset? The anger fueled my entire career. I can't let you go back there. I won't let you go back there."

"Where else can I go? I don't know where my sister is, and I don't know where Landon is either."

Amara held Hallow's hands and folded them in the shape of a heart. "You will come with me."

27

Like her mother, Josephine was unable to move from her bedside for a number of days. Her body faced her window and the wall where the cracks extended in infinite directions. The side of her face sank into her pillow, and her body ached from the immobility. She got lost in her thoughts as to which crack would be the first to burst, crumble the entire wall, and cause her to fall out onto the concrete below and bust her head wide open like a melon. She idealized that end if it was possible. That would be the perfect conclusion to her story: Josephine Melancon dead in the home that imprisoned her. A dark fairy tale of sorts. How she'd nurtured the dream of finally escaping with her Prince Charming for so many years seemed embarrassingly laughable, even in the midst of her private moments.

Landon had promised her that they would leave together, but he never came back. He never came back. She should've known that all of the meticulous planning of upholstered chairs, new paint jobs, and granite tabletops in the kitchen, where she would hear neither a creak in the floor nor smell a whiff of mildew slithering from the corners, would never be a part of her story. For all she knew, he could've gone back to Valerie or fled to Tangiers. Tangiers.

He could've been anywhere in the world and he thought of her as too much baggage to accompany him along the way. Worst of all, Hallow was gone too. She hadn't heard her footsteps or voice for days, and assumed that she too had escaped and would never look back, lest she turn into a pillar of salt. Without Landon or Hallow or the persistent bullying from Maman whom she hadn't heard downstairs either—she didn't feel like a caulbearer or an ordinary. She felt incorporeal, and perhaps this dissolution was the ultimate sacrifice to this brownstone.

She wasn't sure if her room was beginning to decay or whatever was left of herself was starting to smell from not bathing. She could not separate herself from the architecture, as much as she had tried throughout her adult life. Now that Josephine was alone without her child, she felt purposeless. She figured she'd failed as a mother because she could not encourage Hallow to stay put like she did. It was a loss that gave way to her remembering Laila and her loss. On that one fateful afternoon, when she saw that bloodied and frenzied woman sneering at her from out in the street with the crowd and police surrounding her, how Josephine wished she could have just brought Laila inside and disobeyed Maman's orders. Josephine had analyzed this scene many times over, but only this time, in her depthless quiet, did she consider a different angle: that woman was both accompanied and alone. Where was the father of her child? Where was the man who could've comforted her in her grief? Maybe she too had been abandoned. She wasn't sure why she thought of this woman in her solitude, why the interconnectedness of their stories haunted her again.

Then she thought about Harlem. She could hear the sounds of the protestors outside the brownstone right from her bed. Harlem's mouth was full of bellowing cries and obscenities from neighbors, passersby, and interlopers alike who hurled sharp insults as though they were rocks and pellets toward the windows. They pinged from many angles of the brownstone, and if this brownstone could breathe, she would be asphyxiated. Her body was already wounded beyond salvation.

Josephine writhed in her bed and imagined what would happen if the bravest person in the crowd lost their patience and became the first person to break through the doors and destroy everything. She would do nothing. She wanted them to push themselves into her bedroom and do whatever they wanted with her. In fact, she might invite them to draw and quarter her body so that she could be divided to heal the entire neighborhood. After all, that was her life's purpose as a Melancon woman. If she had the strength, she would open all the doors and windows and wave everyone in to expedite the festivities. She'd boil hot water for tea and cook food for the revelry, where the climax of the night would be her offering. She was starting to become impatient. Hasn't all the tension led to this moment? She couldn't wait for the day or the hour. The brownstone had become unbearably quiet. Not even Iris emerged from the basement. She couldn't take the ringing in her ears, the stale bedroom smell, and the creaking due to a boisterous wind or sudden rainfall. She was eager for the ruin.

"Josephine? Josephine?" Helena, who had entered the home through the back door, softly rocked her body from side to side. "Jo?"

Josephine raised her eyes to the ceiling, where her decorations were not stained with dampness, and shook her head. "What?" She recognized Helena's voice, but she refused to believe that she was so preoccupied that she could not hear the front door being opened or—hopefully—that same door being knocked down. She refused to believe that she hadn't heard footsteps climbing up the steps and into her bedroom. Helena had not been by her side since she was a child, and now that she was free, there was no cause for her to return.

"Jo, it's me, Helena. I'm here. We have to get you up."

"No, leave me alone. You have better things to do. What about that whole doula thing? Go there. Go to them. Leave me here. I'm best to stay here."

Helena shook her head. "I can't go back, Jo. I can't. Come on, we don't have a lot of time."

"What are you talking about?"

With her hand on Josephine's shoulder and the other on the small space between her aunt's back and the sheets, Helena took a beat and said, "They found out about Hallow first. She found her mother, Josephine. You won't believe who it is. Amara Danville."

Josephine laughed then broke down into tears. "Now I really have no one."

"You have me. You can't stay here, Jo. You have to leave with me. We gotta go, like, now."

"And why the hell do I have to do anything?"

"Because the people outside are gonna tear this place up soon. Do you finally want to be free of here or not?"

Helena looked out the window and saw that the sky was already a mélange of colors—orange, pink, brown, yellow, and blue. The lights from nearby homes and the headlights of cars were already on. Her heart galloped. She swallowed and reluctantly went down two flights of stairs into the basement with that last glimmer of hope that she could save at least one member of her family. As she crept to the lower level, she heard Ella Fitzgerald crooning in the background. The smell of the air transformed from its usual staleness to that of fresh eucalyptus and lavender. Helena didn't hear Iris's usual mutterings, although she did hear the sound of latches being disengaged and feet moving back and forth. The door to her mother's bedroom was left wide open. Her bed was stripped of its sheets and linen, and all the drawers were pulled out. The stacks of books and vinyl records were gone; only nicks on the walls were the vestiges of them having ever been there.

When Helena turned the corner, she found Iris, whose silvery hair was pulled back into a slick bun and her nails manicured. She was leaning on her love seat and languorously smoking a long pipe, relishing the curlicues her exhales produced in the air and watching with satisfaction as they disappeared. She was dressed in a wine-red double-breasted wool trench coat and matching hat, fishnet stockings, and black leather pumps. Helena had never seen Iris look this sharp. Two large suitcases were near her feet, and a large tote bag sat beside her. She turned her head to the side and said, "You want to join me?" She extended the cigarette to her. Helena sat next to her mother and had a drag, quivering in her body from its fill.

"Good, isn't it? I haven't taken it out in a long time. I only use it for special occasions."

"Special occasion?"

Iris blew and rested her elbow on the opposite knee. "I've heard the news. Hallow finally found her mother, and things came full circle. I was wondering when anyone was going to say anything, but since they haven't, I thought I might as well make arrangements anyway."

"So you're not going to stay."

"I thought about it. I did. But I never was like Maman and Josephine. I was marked from the moment Maman neglected to make that caul tea for me. I know that no matter where I'll be, I'll never be alone. And since the business 'bout to be gone and no one's summoning me to be cut, well . . ." Iris blew again. "I can move on. Do like you did. Move away, take on an alias. Don't you see, my sweet Helena?" She cupped Helena's check in her palm and said, "You're my dream."

Helena touched her mother's hand and tilted her face farther into her palm. "Mom, but how will you make a living?"

"I hadn't thought that far."

They laughed in unison.

"Did you ask yourself how you would make a living?" Iris asked.

"No."

"No, right? You just did it. Well . . . same difference. Sometimes you gotta just go. And I've been here long enough already."

"Are you already packed?"

"Not quite. I still have a little more to go. You wanna help me?"

"Yes, because we don't have much time. The crowd outside is getting crazy. Where do you want me to help?"

"In the bedroom. In the drawers. I might have missed some things, and we may have to double-check."

"On it." Helena sprang to her feet and went into the bedroom. She began to sift through the many miscellaneous papers in the drawers, but none seemed quite as important as the rose-gold wrapping paper in the bottom drawer. Its ridges were neither ruffled nor torn. Helena was not sure how long this wrapping paper had been there, but she inferred that there had to be something valuable enveloped within. She touched the wrapping paper and got nervous. She glanced at the bedroom door, which she'd left open, and realized that Iris had left her alone to search. She peeled one corner of the paper back and stopped breathing. Slowly, Helena removed the entire paper and saw a photo of herself at the Bronx Zoo that was taken from a distance. Beholding this photo transported Helena back to the quest for Iris somewhere around the Bronx. Her body recalled every bite, every rip, and every scratch. When she opened her eyes, Iris was standing at the threshold of the room with her hands clasped in front of her head. She was beaming with pride.

"Don't you see, Helena? You are my dream. I did that for you. For you to be free and not live here and become like Josephine, like the rest. And you've grown bigger and better than I have imagined."

"Iris, you wanted to kill me."

"Never." Iris took one step forward, and Helena took one back. "The plan was never to kill you. The plan was that you would never be useful in that way to our family ever again."

"Do you know how much pain I went through that day?" Helena screamed through her tears.

"Does it outweigh what you would've gone through here as a prisoner?"

"That should've been my decision to make—not yours!"

"But aren't you happier?"

"That's not the point!"

"But it is," Iris said sweetly, her tone more resembling honey-dew than its usual cold intensity. She continued with conviction, "A mother will do whatever she has to, to ensure her child's happiness, even if it has to hurt. You always wanted to be free, Helena. I sensed it in you even as a baby, when you would scream for hours and no one knew what to do. Or how you always squirmed in anyone's arms. How the only time I got you to calm down was if I nursed you near the window, and I always had to draw up the curtains. You were always looking beyond this place. I didn't make the decision impulsively, but when I knew, I didn't second-guess it."

"You are sick."

"I'm a mother."

Helena brushed past Iris's shoulder to go back upstairs while

Iris repeatedly called out to her. Iris followed her daughter upstairs to the second-floor corridor, where there was an uproar coming from outside and fires aglow near the front-facing windows. Josephine was in front of Maman's door, calling out her name and twisting the doorknob until she knocked it clean off its spindle. When the door wouldn't budge, she kicked it down and rushed to Maman's bedside. Maman was facing the wall where the cracks now resembled large tree branches that stretched border to border.

"Maman? Maman? Come on, we gotta go. Maman?"

Josephine pushed Maman's left shoulder down to get a good look at her and Maman was mindlessly smiling at the ceiling.

"Ma?" Josephine shook her head.

"Don't you understand?" Maman curled a pointy fingernail underneath the last bit of caul on her chest.

"Mom—"

"I told you that I'm gonna live and die here, didn't I?"

"Don't!" Josephine cried.

Maman tore the caul away with one sharp yank, and her breath began to get shorter and labored just as a Molotov cocktail flew through one of the front-facing windows. The curtains were in flames within a matter of seconds. Helena ran into the room and struggled to pull a resistant Josephine away from Maman.

The three women ran out the back door, kicked down the balusters of the fence, and started on foot. Before they could decide which corner to turn down next, Josephine fell on her ankle but urged them to keep going and that she'd try to catch up with them later. Helena and Iris ran until they couldn't hear their breaths in the wind or the cheering of the large crowd back at the brownstone that had been set ablaze. Ran until they couldn't feel their feet or the heat scorching the nape of their necks. Ran until their knees wobbled and their feet gave out. Ran until a person opening the door to a multistoried building gave them a means to enter and hide there. Ran several flights of steps to the rooftop, where the fire from the brownstone illuminated the night. There were puddles of water beneath their feet here, and they finally saw their reflections—damp, sooty, and sweaty faces—and perhaps that camouflage was how they were able to get as far as they did. The cheers from the crowd stretched higher than the ambulance sirens once the roof caved in and sparks became shooting stars in the evening sky. The scene was elegiac and glorious.

Iris and Helena stood huddled next to each other in the bitter cold, getting the last bit of their coughs out and nursing the wounds they gathered while running.

"Why didn't you just leave me there, Helena? You could've left me there." Iris resumed crying.

"Didn't you want to be free too?"

Iris abruptly stopped crying. She wanted to wrap her arms around her daughter but refrained. Instead, the two women continued watching the fire as if it was the starkest of endings. Now they were both free—no home, no origin. The possibilities were grand, but for that moment, they quietly mourned for their family and the uncertainty of their lives now that they had nothing else but each other.

28

People were shocked that the brownstone took less than thirty minutes to burn down and that the fire did not spread to other homes, though the neighbors had fled nevertheless. They found Maman's body in her bed. She looked mummified yet not burned beyond recognition, which provided the community with gossip fodder for days. When her body was brought to the morgue, the coroner noticed that her right hand was closed into a fist. He opened it to find that there was a piece of caul in her palm.

The people of Harlem could smell the smoke and ash in the air for days. There was less chatter and activity on the streets. Whatever needed to be said would be said within soul-food restaurants, the church pews, or at home. They didn't know what to think about the Melancon women anymore now that the matriarch was gone. Though no one wanted to admit it, the burning of the Melancon brownstone was worthy of documentation in the Studio Museum or the Schomburg. It was a powerful beacon in the neighborhood, and many imagined what life would've been like if there was something—anything—that could have been recovered for history's sake. A mighty era was over. No matter one's opinion on the Melancon women and the brownstone in which they lived, no one could deny their influence. They were peerless, an empire in and of themselves. They were embodiments of both old and new Harlem now returned to dust, as everyone else would in due time.

A few days after the brownstone burned, Amara and Hallow returned to Manhattan. Amara arranged for her daughter to stay in a hotel right beside her apartment building while she handled a few things. To her surprise, Ethan was sitting on her couch with his feet on her coffee table and his hand on the remote, flicking through channels. There was a plate of food scraps beside his feet on one side and an open bottle of Heineken on the other. "Goddammit, Amara." Ethan shut off the TV and slammed the remote down on the coffee table. He lowered his voice and said, "Do you know how much you put me through? Do you?"

"What I put you through?" Amara emphatically laughed then scoffed. "Is that all you think about, yourself?"

"I've been here trying to maintain your home for you. I've been trying to ward off the press. I even talked to your boss about letting you keep your job. But you don't text. You don't call. I thought we were partners."

"Do you not understand the situation I was in the other night? I was afraid to talk to anyone."

Ethan approached Amara and kissed the top of her head. "Where is she?"

"Who?"

"Hallow. Your daughter. Where is she?"

"She's in a hotel."

"Why didn't you bring her here?"

Amara smiled. "You want to meet her?"

"Of course. We have to prep her to respond to journalists, and we don't have much time."

"For what?" Amara asked.

"Your boss is holding a press conference tomorrow at ten and they are expecting you there. Someone at the hotel where you were staying tipped off the office and if you refused to go, they would've come for you anyway. So it's good your daughter is here now. You're going to need all the sympathy you can get."

Amara backed up from Ethan's embrace and said, "No."

"I'm sorry?"

"I'm not letting you do that."

"You don't have a choice."

"I do have a choice! That's your problem: You're too damn controlling. Too busy trying to micromanage me to make yourself feel like you're my equal when you're not."

"You'll be lucky if you have a career by tomorrow."

"Are you done?"

"Good luck," Ethan said as he exited and shook his head.

As soon as he left, Amara sank to her knees and pleaded with her hands to stop shaking. They were disobedient—stopping and trembling, shaking and stopping. Amara rushed to put a phone in one of her hands to preoccupy the muscles before they became unruly again and dialed her mother. But when Denise picked up the phone on the other end, her mother announced her presence with a heavy, long-drawn-out sigh.

"Mom, I—"

"No, Amara. No. Let me go first. Please. I've been waiting for you to call me and I've been trying to figure out if I should call you. You know, Amara, I've always supported you. Always. I thought I could give you the best love that I was able to give, which is why this is especially hard for me . . ." Her voice cracked. "To hear that this thing—my grandbaby—was something that you felt too ashamed to tell me. Me!" Amara could hear her mother slap some hard surface as an emphatic punch to her words. "I'm your mother. I'm your mother, and I feel like I failed to see."

Denise took a beat. "Well? Now you can talk."

"I don't know what to say or where to start other than I'm sorry."

"That's a good place to start. And I'm sorry too."

"About what?"

"Like I said, for failing to see. Maybe parents never really know their children, and this was my lesson. God, Amara. Both me and Laila were worried sick about you these past few nights. Give me a moment." There was some shuffling in the background and an opening and closing of doors. "Okay," she spoke in a hushed voice. "I don't know what's happened to her, but a miracle came the night when the Melancon's home burned. That crowd came for us, you know. They were going to carry Laila back to the Melancon brownstone and have her right in the front while they protested. But she refused to go. She said she knew what was going to happen because she seen it in her dreams. I thought she was having another one of her episodes. But sure enough, her dream happened. They burned that motherfucka down, Mar. Burned it all the way down to the white meat of a wood chip and then some. And the next morning, I went up to check on Laila and all her dolls were gone. She put sheets on the bed, she showered. She asked to make me breakfast! I haven't seen her have this much clarity in so long. She was of sound mind, Amara. I almost cried. She was just like old times."

"Jesus," Amara said.

"Now, when do I get to meet that baby?"

"She's here. I have her in a hotel near me. Listen, Mom. I have a press conference tomorrow. Could you and Laila be there? I can give you the address if you can swing it."

"We will be there. On the dot."

• • •

Amara got Hallow from the hotel and brought her back to her place, where they ordered Popeye's from Postmates and watched movies until Hallow fell asleep. Amara, on the other hand, was on edge. Her tremors kept her awake, and she spent the early hours of the morning scribbling on index cards with notes for her speech and subsequently discarding them all. Before she could request an Uber, the front desk called and said that there was already a car waiting for her that the District Attorney's Office had booked—perhaps to make sure that she couldn't flee this time. As Amara was readying herself in her bathroom mirror and Hallow was watching her, she said, "I have to speak at a press conference today on Centre Street. If you don't want to come, you don't have to. It's pretty boring stuff. But if you do, that's where I'll be."

The paparazzi were swarming the front entrance, snapping photos of her on the sidewalk outside of her apartment and calling out to her to look this way or over here, and she always fell for the summoning because of the fast-paced nature of the pandemonium itself. The building personnel surrounded Amara and held out their hands to block the paparazzi and reporters from getting too close to her as she slid into the luxury sedan to go down to Centre Street. Before her passenger door fully closed, a disembodied voice asked her about Hallow's whereabouts and Amara coarsely told the driver to hurry so she wouldn't be pictured in tears. She dabbed the sides of her eyes with her fingers and napkins; she didn't know if Hallow would be coming to support her. If Hallow didn't come, Amara understood. She didn't believe that she deserved that kind of grace.

"Are you ready?" the driver asked.

Amara nodded.

A team of police officers assisted in getting Amara inside the courthouse where there were reporters hanging about with cups of coffee and donuts in hand. They hurriedly grabbed their record-ers, pencils, and papers when they saw her walking through the en-trance. Some ran up to her and unleashed a series of questions that were spoken too quickly for Amara to know where one inquiry ended and another began. The police officers guided her to a small, frigid room by herself, with nothing but a small paper cup of water on a long, wooden table. The clock on the corner of the wall ticked with each second, and the sounds of people shuffling past her room were incessant.

The district attorney kept his hand on the doorknob and half his body on the other side of the threshold. He took one look at Amara, who was hunched over and shaking in her seat, and sighed. "Danville. We're ready for you now." She nodded and got to her feet. The walk from that small, frigid room down the corridor and into the press conference room disrupted both time and distance. She knew these steps from memory and how easy it was to get from one end of the hall to the other. On this morning, however, every-thing stretched like a long rubber band that pulled further back, dis-torting all the decorative features until finally snapping back to the immediacy of the moment. Everyone in the Polaris Room quieted when Amara entered. She kept her head down until she reached the podium and found both Denise and Laila seated in the front row. Her mother squirmed in her seat to ensure that she could sit as tall as possible, with her neck extending and her nose tipped toward the ceiling. With her shoulders slightly raised, Denise was prepared to carry pride for the whole of her family. And Laila had reinvented herself. No one would have guessed the severity of her history be-cause the lines in her face had vanished and her hair was trimmed and polished, although there resided a hint of sadness that pooled around the corners of her eyes and an unsure smile.

Amara didn't pay attention to her boss's opening remarks, the applause, or the silence before it was time for her to speak. She looked at her family, gripped the sides of the podium, and said, "I haven't prepared that much of a speech for you all today because I honestly didn't see a point. I apologize to the public for crafting an image that I was this young, single, childless person. Only the first two are true."

There was sparse laughter in the audience.

"Twenty years ago, I made a decision to give up my child because I thought that being a mother was incompatible with what I wanted to achieve. I wanted to be a prosecutor, and I was inspired to be that because my beloved aunt was taken advantage of by a family who sold parts of themselves for profit. She believed in the power of the caul. I will not tell her story for her because she's here with us this morning, but what I will say is that my anger fueled my ambition. I wanted to punish that family within the confines of the judicial system."

There were reporters huddled around the entrance of the press conference room who began to part ways. Amara lifted her head to see what caused the commotion and spotted Hallow in the back of the room. Everyone turned around to get a good look at the disturbance and then did a double take at Amara. Hallow bowed her head as she made her way through the crowd, and once she got to the front, Laila grabbed her hand and said, "You sit right next to me, baby."

With tears in her eyes, Amara continued her speech of self-abnegation, apologizing to her team and to the public and talking about her oversight in how her ambition outpaced strategy. Laila locked arms with Hallow and rubbed her hand to assure her that everything would be fine. She could feel the caul shielding Hallow's skin and wiggled in her seat from the delight and irony of their stories.

Hallow inconspicuously passed Laila a small bit of wax paper, which Laila opened. There was a small piece of caul inside, and she teared up at the gift. She held it in both of her palms and remembered all of her children. Remembered the conversation with Landon in the pews of St. Philip's. Remembered the birth. Remembered the fury. Remembered the screams. Remembered the blood. And when she finally returned to the present moment, she admitted to herself that she had nothing left and pushed the caul back into Hallow's hand. She kissed Hallow on the forehead and said, "You are my blood. You are my family. You came back, and you are home."

29

Amara departed from Centre Street after making the dual announcement that she was dropping out of the race and resigning from her position as the assistant district attorney. Everyone had figured that was the inevitable result of the matter. To lick her wounds and pull herself together in private, Amara sought refuge at her mother's home and saw that her childhood bed had been cleaned and prepared with fresh linens and blankets. Per Amara's suggestion, Hallow took that room, and Amara created a makeshift bed on the living room couch, where she researched routes for what Hallow could do with her life. When the time came, they would discuss Hallow going to college—maybe SUNY or CUNY. Or she could go to vocational school. But first, Hallow wanted to get her proper GED and subsequently enroll in preparatory classes at the Manhattan Educational Opportunity Center right on 125th Street, near the Apollo Theater.

No one knew what happened to Landon. There was no trace of him anywhere. Some folks believed that they saw him roaming the streets at all hours of the night while others thought that he didn't have a distinct enough look for anyone to be sure that it was actually him. Valerie, who had been a housewife, remained job-less out of her own stubborn belief that he would come back to her. Rumor has it that when the police evicted her, she was kicking and screaming, and her bloody nail marks are etched onto the sides of the front door. No one knew what happened to Josephine. Hallow hoped that perhaps in their wandering, Landon and Josephine had found each other somewhere where they could finally be together in peace. Amara perused through the files of property owners in Pleasantville and couldn't find a Josephine or Landon listed either separately or together.

As for Helena and Iris, they cozied up to the bohemians of the East and West Villages, and never stayed in one place for long. They took thankless jobs and abandoned them without warning, entertained countless men and tossed them without remorse, and learned more about each other with a love that positioned the pain of the past as a stepping-stone rather than an impasse. After a few months of gallivanting and lollygagging, the duo moved to the Mari-gny neighborhood of New Orleans, where Iris set up another shop as a medium and Helena found a job at the National Birth Equity Collaborative to reduce maternal and infant mortality rates amongst Black women.

In the meantime, Hallow had to acclimate herself to a new home whose walls did not speak of foreboding doom and whose stairs did not invite more discord. Each time Hallow descended and as-cended the floors of Denise and Laila's home, her mind overlapped in memories until the new eclipsed the old. When someone called out her name, she didn't feel a twinge in her body signaling that she would have to give another part of herself away. Instead, she would be invited to run errands or eat dinner with the family. Laila always sat to Hallow's left and Amara to her right. The two women called Hallow "daughter." They never warred for Hallow's attention but collaborated to provide her with as much safety as she could stand at her adult age.

It was getting to be toward the end of October, and the weather was still nice enough for a light jacket. Because of this, the Danville women conspired to throw Hallow a twenty-first birthday party right at home. The planning easily went over Hallow's head because she thought that they would all be attending an All Hallows' Eve service at St. Philip's and, furthermore, she hadn't communicated any desire whatsoever to celebrate her birthday. The evening prior, as Hallow slept, Amara made a triple-layered confetti cake, and then the next morning, she took her for a manicure and pedicure and lunch while Laila and Denise baked the macaroni and cheese, cooked the greens, yams, and rice and beans, and fried the chicken wings and plantain.

By dusk, the children of the neighborhood were starting to go door to door, so by the time Amara and Hallow returned from their get-together, the food was already set up on the porch—along with candy for the trick-or-treaters—paper lanterns and streamers were hung on the trees, and music was playing. As Amara and Hallow approached the brownstone, Laila and Denise screamed, "Happy birthday!" and blew kazoos, a sight that made Hallow clutch her heart, overwhelmed from the love.

With her arm around Hallow, Amara rubbed her shoulder, pulled her close to her chest, and said, "You didn't think we forgot, did you?"

"I don't know," Hallow nervously replied.

"We hope you're hungry," Laila said. "Now, do you want to blow out your birthday candles first, or eat first?"

Hallow looked over her shoulder at some of the passersby stopping to see what was going on and kept her head down as she spoke: "Do we have to be outside? You didn't have to do all of this."

"We didn't have to, but we wanted to," Denise said. "You okay, sweetheart?"

Hallow peeked over her shoulder again. The passersby who had stopped to watch were beginning to form a crowd, and she could feel the sweat sliding down her arms. Despite Amara being by her side, she wasn't sure if the people were going to try to damage Denise's home, hurt her, or both. The truth was that Harlemites wanted to get a good look at her once and for all. Hallow was the reminder that the Melancon family existed, and seeing her out in the open with her other family enthralled them.

"They won't hurt you, Hallow. We promise," Amara said.

Hallow nodded. "Can I blow out my birthday candles first?"

"You got it," Denise said. She lit the candles and motioned for Hallow to sit in front of the cake facing the street and said, "On the count of three, one . . . two . . . three . . ." Unexpectedly, the crowd joined in with the Danville women to sing "Happy Birthday" to Hallow before segueing into the Stevie Wonder version.

Hallow blew out all her candles, and the resounding cheers made her blush.

"Wait, wait! You didn't want to make a wish?" Laila asked.

"I didn't need it." Hallow smiled. "Denise, I didn't realize how good of a voice you had."

"Oh God, here we go," Amara said with a groan.

"Don't get her started," Laila said and started making Hallow's plate.

"What?" Hallow asked.

"It's in my blood. Our blood, rather," Denise responded as she cut the cake. "My great-grandmother was a cabaret singer. In fact, it was said that her voice was what attracted our great-grandfather Alex, who, from what was passed down, was married at the time, but that's a story for another day. If it wasn't for them, none of us would be here. Okay, now eat up, baby."

Hallow grabbed the silverware and took one bite of the macaroni and cheese before shoveling as much as she could into her mouth. She poured herself a glass of lemonade from the pitcher then speedily pulled apart a fried chicken wing before hissing and waving her hands in the air because they were still steaming hot.

"Slow down, slow down." Amara laughed. "The food ain't going nowhere. Take your time."

"Sorry," Hallow said. She set her silverware down and lifted her head from her plate to see a mysterious figure standing away from the crowd underneath the streetlight. As the rest of the Danville women diverged into another conversation entirely, Hallow squinted, hoping to see this person, whom she presumed to be a woman, beyond her trench coat and cloche hat. The woman tipped her nose toward the streetlight, and its illumination highlighted enough of her face for Hallow to recognize her as Josephine. Hallow stopped breathing, unsure of whether to invite Josephine up to the porch or let her stay exactly where she was. So she stayed still and watched her mother, whose smile juxtaposed melancholic eyes.

After Maman's death, the authorities contacted Josephine to inform her of another account Maman had. The money was to be divided evenly amongst her descendants, but Josephine could not get in touch with Helena or Iris, so the money was left to her. The settlement wasn't enough to live lavishly, but it was enough for her to afford a tabby cat and an apartment in Sugar Hill where she could spend her days people-watching and dining at the nearby Ethiopian and West Indian restaurants. When she first moved there, often someone would recognize her and would have something slick to say. But when Josephine wouldn't verbally lash out, and no one heard of her trying to sell her caul to anyone—white or Black—the comments ceased, even if passersby would still give her a side-eye here and there.

She didn't have friends whom she could call on, but she had acquaintances with whom she'd engage in casual conversation as she got her morning coffee or retrieved a package. She never heard from Landon again, but she was too self-satisfied to miss him. At the end of the day, Josephine Melancon was free. But she did yearn for Hallow most nights, which is how she ended up strolling through Harlem on All Hallows' Eve, in hopes that she'd get just a glimpse of her daughter somewhere celebrating her birthday.

Now that Josephine saw Hallow from the crowd, she was afraid that the people would try to hurt her daughter. She had her right foot in front of the left with the intention of moving forward, but when she figured out how different this crowd was for the Danvilles and their home versus the Melancons and theirs, she stepped back.

"Hey." Amara placed a hand on Hallow's shoulder, and Hallow faced her. "You okay?"

Hallow checked the streetlight again, and Josephine was gone just as quickly as she'd appeared. She straightened up her back and said, "Yeah. Yeah, I am." The crowd started to disperse, and a group of trick-or-treaters reluctantly advanced toward the gate, holding their jack-o'-lantern buckets close to their chests and gawking at Hallow.

"You can come up. It's okay," Hallow said. She grabbed the bucket of assorted candy and held it out to the trio. They stood still. "It's okay." The tallest one looked at the caul's sheerness then placed his entire open hand in the bucket, at which Hallow laughed. Then the other two ran and did the same before sprinting to the next stop while yelling out their gratitude. Laila, Amara, and Denise watched Hallow straighten her back and breathe a deep sigh of relief into the night. She didn't get hurt. She didn't get hurt, and she was hesitant but willing to believe that she would be okay, one day at a time. This one holiday reconfigured her life as a Danville and a product of Harlem itself—a girl whose body forged the gap between myth and reality.

She could start anew. She would heal in places where the caul could not reach.

ACKNOWLEDGMENTS

Thank you to all of my family and friends, particularly Danny Vazquez, Jennifer Baker, Jade Jones, Maraiya Hakeem, Liz Cook, Sire Leo Lamar-Becker, Brigitte Malivert, and Brandon Zamudio, for all of your support.

Thank you to my editors, Emily Griffin and Amber Oliver, for their constant shepherding through all the nooks and crannies of this world and (fictitious) women who I hold dear to my heart.

Thank you to Monica Odom, my wonderful agent, as well as the rest of the HarperCollins team for always taking such good care of me.

Thank you to Dennis Norris II for being a beta reader in the midst of a global pandemic and international protests in honor of George Floyd and Breonna Taylor. This book would not have been completed on a pressing deadline without your critical eye and warm guidance.

Thank you to all of the doulas, healers, midwives, and doctors who care for Black mothers and their children.

Thank you to the Bennington Writing Seminars and particularly Alexander Chee, who insisted that this initial short story be made into a novel. Have you ever steered anyone wrong?

Thank you to Leipzig University and ZORA Magazine for giving me the space to write and rewrite this novel as I managed teaching and editing, respectively.

Thanks be to God for peace beyond all understanding as I grappled with very difficult topics.

Thank you to Harlem for all her history, sound, cuisine, and magic.

Thank you to RD for all of your love.

ABOUT THE AUTHOR

MORGAN JERKINS is a senior editor at Medium's ZORA magazine. Her work has been featured in *The New Yorker*, *Vogue*, the *New York Times*, *The Atlantic*, *Elle*, *Rolling Stone*, and BuzzFeed, among many other outlets. She lives in New York.

READ MORE BY
MORGAN JERKINS

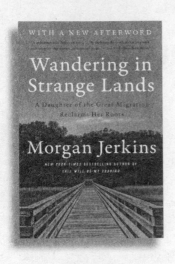

"A quintessentially American story. . . Jerkins makes plain that denying space for Black identities in history is itself a legacy as American as its original sins of racism and enslavement. By exploring the truth of that past with such integrity, this memoir enriches our future."

—*New York Times Book Review*

"A beautiful example of possibility, nuance and passion coexisting, even in our heightened political moment. . . . There is a brutal honesty Jerkins brings to the experiences of Black girls and women that is vital for us to understand as we strive toward equality, toward believing women's voices and experiences, and toward repairing the broken systems that have long defined our country."

—*Los Angeles Times*

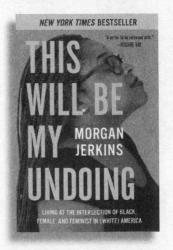

HarperCollinsPublishers   HARPER ● PERENNIAL

DISCOVER GREAT AUTHORS, EXCLUSIVE OFFERS, AND MORE AT HC.COM.